BETHAN'S CHOICE

Book Five of the Evans Family Saga

C.J. PETIT

1

C. J. PETIT

TABLE OF CONTENTS

BETHAN'S CHOICE 1

PROLOGUE..4

CHAPTER 1.. 12

CHAPTER 2..38

CHAPTER 3..109

CHAPTER 4..134

CHAPTER 5..158

CHAPTER 6..183

CHAPTER 7..239

CHAPTER 8..287

CHAPTER 9..353

CHAPTER 10..381

CHAPTER 11..422

EPILOGUE...512

PROLOGUE

Double EE Ranch
Mar 21, 1876

Kyle held Katie's hand tightly as her brother, Father Daniel Ryan, blessed the small gravesite. He knew that there wasn't anything he could say to ease her grief because he was fighting his own overwhelming need to punish someone or something for taking their young son. He knew that it wasn't possible because there was no evil badman to hang and only God to blame if one chose that level of desperation. But to lose Johnnie this way; to watch him dying and having no way to prevent it was heartbreaking.

He knew that they were fortunate that Bess, Colwyn and little Meri had all survived the horrific flu that struck Denver, but it didn't diminish their sense of loss. They hadn't even had time to fully mourn the loss of Johnny's namesake, John Wittemore or Meri's grandmother and the first Meredith Evans who had both succumbed to that killing disease just days earlier. The entire month was nothing less than a nightmare for the Evans family.

Kyle didn't hear his priest brother-in-law's voice as he prayed. Instead, he scanned the faces of his brothers, Dylan and Bryn. He never thought of them as his uncles any longer. Ever since he'd had his name changed to Evans, they'd accepted him as a brother, and he felt he'd earned the relationship because he felt as if he'd grown up with them.

Now Dylan was the true head of the Evans clan, although for all practical purposes, he'd been the patriarch since they all arrived in Denver. Gwen, the smallest of the adults, was still the rock for Dylan and the rest of the wives.

Lynn's wife, Addie, was nearby holding their bundled three-month-old daughter, Gwendolyn Ann, while Lynn slowly bounced their toddler, Dylan Lee, in his arms to keep him from making too much noise. He appreciated that everyone had attended the burial, despite the cold.

Alwen and Garth had come from their ranch in Bear Canyon to attend the funeral and burials of John and their grandmother, then stayed after little Johnnie had died.

He then looked at Bethan who was standing slightly off to the side with her younger siblings, Cari, Brian and Conway. Bethan was a handsome young lady with a formidable personality that she'd inherited from her parents. She was tall for a woman, already five feet and nine inches and may even grow taller.

Kyle then studied Bryn and Erin's family, which had miraculously been left untouched by the flu. They had their three boys, ranging from eleven-year-old Mason to eight-year-old Huw with nine-year-old Ethan in between, before they ended the Evans male baby curse and had Grace Lynn just a minute after Erin gave birth to her brother, Huw. Their youngest, Kyle Lynn, had celebrated his fifth birthday just four days before his grandmother had died.

Kyle's eyes lingered on his namesake for a few seconds, knowing that he had been christened with the name because of the actions he'd taken to prevent those two assassins from killing Bryn's entire family. The boy was staring at the small pile of dirt and, as sad as Kyle was for his own loss, he was grateful that all of the other Evans children had been spared Johnnie's fate.

Father Ryan ended his prayers and stepped away from the newest gravesite in the Evans family cemetery.

When Lynn had returned from Dakota with Addie's mother's remains to be buried, this had just been an empty small hill on the Double EE. Hers had been the first grave to be dug and it wasn't until Flat Jack Armstrong was buried there that it had a second grave. He didn't think that there was any irony in the fact that the first two grave markers in the Evans family cemetery didn't have 'Evans' carved into the granite markers. To him and the others, both Beatrice Price and Jack Armstrong were part of the family. Even the third grave wasn't an Evans as it held the remains of John Wittemore, yet was another adopted member of the Evans clan.

Now the cemetery had its first Evans; Meredith Anna Evans, wife of Lynn Colwyn Evans, the true patriarch of the family, and one of the youngest Evans, his and Katie's younger son, John Lynn Evans. He prayed that none of their other children would lay in the ground near Johnnie before one of the adult Evans left this earth. It was a horrible thing for a parent to lose a child and he knew that it would take some time for him and Katie to get past their loss. Yet they had to continue to care for their other children and maybe God would bless them with another baby to add joy to their home after taking their son.

Kyle then squeezed Katie's hand, and she turned to look at him. Her eyes were still red, and he knew that his most important job wasn't the prosecution of another killer. It was helping Katie to return to her normal, cheerful self. Having her brother, Dan, here would be a great help, even though he would be leaving soon. He was the only male member of her family that had shared Katie and Erin's good humor and honest character that they had inherited from their mother.

As the family began meandering down the hill toward the main house, Kyle took two-year-old Meredith Ann from Katie's arms and she took Bess and Colwyn's hands as Father Dan walked beside Bess.

———

At the head of the loose group, Dylan and Gwen walked with their hands clasped tightly.

"I hope that we don't have to make this walk again soon," Gwen said.

"I think the flu is abating now, but it left a lot of tragedy in its wake. Doctor Corbin said that it had taken over a hundred in Denver alone. At least mom knew that there was another Meredith Evans to carry on her legacy."

"I'm glad that Kyle and Katie thought of it, Dylan. I guess we all thought that mom would always be here."

"It does seem that way; doesn't it? We never expect death to take us, even when we're old and gray. Mom was only fifty-seven and in good health when the flu arrived. I still find it hard to believe that you're thirty-six already. I know that I'm even older, but you don't look any different to me now that when I first saw you on the foredeck of the *Providence* twenty-two years ago. You may not be wearing pigtails, my love, but you're just as pretty and I don't think you've put on a pound since then, except when you were having babies."

Gwen shook her head and replied, "Oh, I've put on a few pounds, Marshal. You're just too kind to say it."

"It's not a matter of being kind, Gwen. It's just how I see you and that's all that counts."

Gwen looked up at her tall husband and understood what he meant. She still saw him as the same man who had risked his life to save her and had given her the wonderful life that they shared with an incredible family.

"Are Garth and Al going to be leaving soon?"

"Not for a couple of days, and they'll be taking some more horses with them."

"I wish they started their ranch on the south end of the Double EE."

"They wanted to go off on their own, Gwen. They're doing fine and it's less than thirty miles away. You can ride there and back in a day."

"Maybe you can, husband, but I'm not about to try. I just miss having them nearby."

"They're growing up, Gwen. Pretty soon we'll lose Bethan, too."

"I don't believe that it will be because she'll be getting married. I swear that girl has broken more hearts in Denver than Bryn has horses on the Double EE."

"She's just very particular, sweetheart. One day, she'll meet a young man who she loves as much as you love me."

"I hope you're right. I just don't want her trying to find a boy who's her father's equal because that's not possible."

Dylan glanced down at his petite wife and said, "Sure it is, Gwendolyn. Bryn and Kyle are at least that and probably more. Even Lynn could fill my shoes, as he's already doing."

"They're all Evans men, Marshal Evans, and that probably makes it worse. Everywhere she looks, she sees honorable, strong men who can still enjoy themselves. I won't add that each of you is also a very handsome specimen of manhood. How can other men compete?"

"They can and will, Gwen. Give her time and everything will work out."

"As long as you don't make her a deputy marshal. I can't believe that she seriously asked you if she could wear the badge."

"She's frustrated because women aren't allowed to do many of the jobs that men can do. Or almost all of them, to be honest. She has so much going for her yet so little opportunity to use her talents and skills. Maybe I should have spent less time teaching her to shoot and ride."

"You didn't have much choice in the matter. If you hadn't shown her, she would have asked Bryn or Flat Jack. I couldn't force her to be anyone other than herself, Dylan. But it's not as if she's become a tomboy, despite those skills you've taught her. She's been a godsend in helping with our other children and now with Lynn and Addie's youngsters."

Dylan glanced back at Bethan who was walking with her brothers and sister, then returned his eyes to their approaching house as he replied, "Our daughter is one hell of a woman, Gwendolyn. She's inherited the best of us and probably has more potential than her brothers. It's almost a curse for her to be born female."

"I believe that Bethan will find a way to turn that curse to her advantage and then all we can do is hope that she finds happiness in whatever she does."

"It'll be her choice, Gwen, not ours."

Gwen squeezed her husband's hand as they neared the house. It was a somber day, despite the bright sun, and she hoped that none of them would have to make that long walk up the hill anytime soon.

But with her United States Marshal husband and now her oldest son working with him as a deputy marshal, she had lived in almost constant fear that she'd be making that trek to bury either of them before long. When Dylan had mentioned that Bethan had asked to join them, she'd been horrified. Even knowing that it wasn't possible, the fact that her daughter had even seriously broached the subject had created a new concern.

But it was Bethan's decision what to do with her life and Dylan had been right when he'd said that their children were growing up and had to go their own way. She only hoped that Bethan wouldn't pursue anything to cause her mother to add another brick to her worry wall.

CHAPTER 1

Double EE Ranch
Southwest of Denver
April 13, 1877

"Do you think I'm wrong, Addie?" Bethan asked as she sat with eighteen-month-old Gwen on her lap.

Addie was nursing six-week-old Nathan Lynn and shook her head before she replied, "No, Bethan, I don't believe that you're wrong, but I do think that you're giving up too soon. There's a true joy that's hard to describe when you're holding your baby to your breast and know that it was you and the man you love that gave him life."

Bethan smiled as she said, "I know, but you still have to wake up in the middle of the night and change diapers fifty times a day."

"You know it's not that many, and Lynn helps, too," Addie said with a laugh.

"It's not as if I'm against getting married and starting a family, Addie, it's just that I feel so frustrated. For as long as I can remember, I've learned all the same skills that Lynn was taught by our father. Now he's a deputy marshal and I can match him in shooting, riding, tracking and any other measure of what it takes to be a lawman. But even the name shuts me out from pursuing that life. I don't recall ever hearing of a lawwoman."

"Lynn tells me that you're actually a better shot than Bryn is, especially with your Winchester. Is it because you can't find a boy that measures up to your father, uncles or brothers?"

"Not really. I don't use them as a measuring stick. I'm just tired of boys treating me like some helpless little girl. I swear, the next one that calls me Bess or Bessie will find himself joining the girls' choir. I don't like Beth, either."

"You've got to be less demanding, Bethan. You do tend to put them under intense scrutiny right from the start."

"If they can't handle the glare, then they're not a real man."

Addie sighed before she lifted Nathan to her shoulder to burp him.

After the anticipated belch, which was luckily dry this time, she fixed her dress and settled her son into the crook of her arm.

"You'll be eighteen next month, Bethan. That's quite a big step, at least as far as the law is concerned. What are you going to do?"

"I'm not sure yet. I know that I'm more than just frustrated. I'm getting too anxious about just sitting around and need to prove that I can do what Lynn is doing, if only to myself."

"You do much more than sitting around. You help me with the children and help Katie with hers, too."

"Alba helps you more than I do, and Katie has the deputies' wives to help her. I'm just a fifth wagon wheel around here."

Addie sighed, then looked at her sister-in-law and said, "Have you talked to your mother about all this?"

"I've talked to just about every adult in the family, but you're the closest to my age and I thought that you'd understand better. When I talk to my parents and uncles and aunts, they all say pretty much the same thing; to wait until the right man comes along and then I'll know what my future is."

"I guess they say that because each of us has found that to be true. The moment my eyes met Lynn's I knew that he would change my life, even if I didn't know how extraordinarily happy that he would make me. I won't repeat that mantra because I'm only two years older than you are and it might sound a bit silly."

Bethan smiled, then said, "My brother is lucky to have found you, Addie."

"Oh, I think that I was pretty fortunate too, Bethan."

April 14, 1877

"Do you know where she went?" Dylan asked.

"I haven't seen her since Friday night, Dad," Cari replied.

Gwen looked at her husband as she said, "It's not like Bethan to miss a Sunday family gathering. I'm worried that something has happened to her."

Almost-ten-year-old Brian said, "I didn't see Nippy in the barn this morning, but I thought that she must have gone for a ride, so I didn't say anything."

"Have you been to her house yet, Gwen?"

"No, I've been too busy with the family."

"I'll go check and I'll be right back," Dylan said as he snatched his new, dark gray Stetson and headed for the door.

Bryn followed as Brian shouted, "I'm coming, too!", and scampered behind them.

Fifteen minutes later, Dylan, Bryn and Brian returned, and Dylan said, "I don't think that anything bad has happened to Bethan, Gwen. Some of her clothes are missing and so is her new Winchester and her gunbelt."

"Where could she have gone?" Gwen asked with a good deal of concern.

"I think I know," Addie said as all eyes turned towards her.

———

Western Fremont County, Colorado
April 17, 1877

United States Deputy Marshal Bryn Evans walked his tall dark gray gelding, Aesop, past the enormous granite outcrop as fellow Deputy Marshal Bert Hoskins trailed on his buckskin mare.

He wasn't expecting an ambush, not from this bunch, but that didn't mean he wasn't scanning the terrain for a waiting Winchester. The sun was already in his eyes, which made it ideal time for an ambush, so all he could hope was that the sun would give him some warning by flashing off of a Winchester's steel sights.

After clearing the gap, Bert Hoskins brought his mare beside Bryn's gelding and asked, "Why didn't they just take the train or at least just stick to the flatlands? Why in God's name did they take this mountain route? This is really getting to be a pain in my backside."

"I don't think they wanted to wait for the train. They made a pretty mad dash out of Canon City. I'm just surprised that they went northwest into the mountains. I guess they figured that we couldn't or wouldn't trail them if they made it difficult. There's not much out in this direction. I'd also like to know how they knew we were coming."

"Why do you think that they knew we were going to show up, Bryn?"

"Did you think that they'd leave that press behind if they were just planning on moving their operations to a new place? They got word that we were coming and skedaddled out of there in a hurry. They just grabbed their printing plates and all the real and phony money they had and lit out."

"Why the hell are we going after them in the first place? This is the Secret Service's problem."

"You know why, Bert. They're stretched thin over there and have more counterfeiting than you can shake a stick at. Since Dylan got rid of those paper deputies and replaced them with real ones, we're in good shape and these boys were closer to our office anyway."

Bert's eyes were roving as he scanned for potential ambush sites as he asked, "If they knew we were coming, don't you think they'll be waiting to take a shot at us?"

"Maybe, but usually counterfeiters aren't the shooting kind. These boys were even smart enough to print one-dollar banknotes because nobody expects them to be fake. Print anything bigger and most merchants and bankers take a second look."

"But they aren't gonna get rich with one-dollar bills."

"Sure, they can. After they print a few, they start exchanging them for real currency and only use the singles for their daily expenses. That way, they know that the fives and tens are genuine and keep them. They've been in operation for over a year now and I'll bet that they've got over five thousand genuine dollars with them by now."

"But you don't think they'll try to kill us for that much money?"

"It's possible, but I think they believe that once we found the press and that they were gone, we'd just head back to Denver and let them go."

"Why are we chasing them, Bryn? They'll probably be setting up in Utah or Arizona anyway."

"In case you've forgotten, Bert, we're United States Deputy Marshals, not Colorado deputy marshals. Besides, you could use some time away from home. You look plum tuckered out because little Aaron is keeping you awake these nights."

Bert grinned, then said, "I reckon I do, but I still feel kinda bad about all that. Do you think Al is still mad about me marrying her? I know he was sweet on her when he returned to Omaha and he even told me that he was going to court her."

"He wasn't happy when I told him. I'll grant you that. But he was more upset because the reason she told him that she couldn't marry him was because she wouldn't marry a lawman. It was one of the reasons that he decided not to join us in the first place. When I told him about your engagement, he threw up his hands and just left the room. I think he's okay with it now."

"Is that why he and Garth bought that ranch down in Bear Canyon?"

"Nope. They approached me long before you even thought about marrying her. I think that they just wanted to go their own way. They could have just combined the two quarter sections that they were going to get anyway, and I would have probably given them a whole section at the south end of the Double EE, but they wanted to start something new. So, after they found that ranch in Bear Canyon, I gave them a good start with a stallion and a dozen mares, then they added some mustangs. They got the place for a good price and with the money that Lynn had left them, they had plenty left over to fix it up.

"They're doing pretty well, and have branched into mules, courtesy of Chester and Acorn, Peanut's offspring. I swear I can see the smiles on those two donkeys' faces when they come back after visiting the mares. Al and Garth sell them to the miners and have two other ranch hands working with them now. They have six sections of land, good water and good pastures. So, for two young men, they're off to a fine start."

"But they don't have any women out there, do they?"

"Nope. They visit Morrison pretty often, but I don't think either of them is ready to invite any ladies to visit permanently."

Bert nodded and sometimes wished that he had followed Al and Garth's path. He was already beginning to feel trapped after their son was born and now Martha was pregnant again. The idea of having two babies in the house was almost terrifying. She'd been getting even more adamant about him giving up the badge since Anna was born and they'd had some serious arguments on the matter. There had been more than one argument about her friendship with fellow deputy Pete Towers, too.

His mood distracted him from the twisting climb up the mountain trail, but Bryn didn't notice. Bryn was too busy scanning for potential ambush sites.

———

Eight miles west, Clyde Fremantle was looking back to the east, still unconvinced that the lawmen had given up the chase. Since they had been notified that the U.S. Marshal was sending some deputies, he'd been expecting them to appear with guns blazing.

Tom Lilly looked over at him and laughed before saying, "They're not there, Clyde! Quit your worrying. We didn't kill anybody so they're not going to waste their time chasing us across this nasty country."

"You don't know those guys. I heard all the stories and I'm not going to rest until we get to Granite and get on that train."

"We'll get there by tomorrow or the day after at the latest, so even if they're back there, they won't catch up with us in time."

"I thought you said it would only take a day to get there!" Clyde exclaimed.

"That was before we ran into this rough country. It's not like we're riding the rails, Clyde."

Clyde harrumphed, then looked back again and found their backtrail empty.

Fifteen feet in front of them, Irv Thompson heard their conversation and suppressed a grin. Those two were always arguing about something, but usually it wasn't as important as whether or not the law was on their tail. He agreed with Clyde that there was a good chance that those U.S. marshals were behind them, but also believed that Tom was right in that they'd reach the train station in Granite before the marshals even got within twenty miles. The twisting path that they were following was on hard ground and would be difficult to follow. He assumed that they'd gotten a quick enough head start after receiving the warning from Fremont County Deputy Sheriff George Lynch. That alone was worth the bribes they'd been

21

paying him to keep quiet about their location after he'd discovered it four months earlier. It was some damned miner who had mentioned the place to the sheriff, and if it hadn't been for Lynch, they would have been caught red-handed.

With at least a full day's lead, he didn't think there was a snowball's chance in hell for those lawmen to catch up with them. By the time they trailed them to Granite, they'd be clear up in Boulder where they could set up operations in the bigger town.

————

What the counterfeiters hadn't counted on was that after arriving in Canon City, Bryn and Bert didn't waste the time to go to a hotel or board their horses. They had ridden directly to the location that had been reported by Fremont County Sheriff Bo Johnson. They hadn't even checked in at the sheriff's office because Bryn wanted to find the place first. It had turned out to be a fortuitous decision when they'd found the old ranch house recently deserted with the printing press and lots of their supplies still there.

It didn't take long to pick up their trail as they had four horses and either a pack horse or pack mule with them. By the time they'd begun to track the counterfeiters, they were just twenty miles behind.

Their biggest disadvantage was light, so after just four hours, they'd had to set up a cold camp.

They started out early the next morning, but only twenty minutes before the four lawbreakers had begun to move. Leading the pack horse did slow them down, but they weren't worried about being followed, except for the very twitchy Clyde Fremantle.

———

"Where do you think they're headed?" Bert asked.

"They don't have much of a choice. Once they exit the pass, they'll either have to head north to Granite or south all the way to Saguache."

"Why won't they just go to the closest train station? There must be four or five before they'd reach Granite."

"They might do that, but I just have a gut feeling that these boys aren't the usual hard men that we usually run across. They make phony money, so they're more like con men than bank robbers. They'll head for a big town so they can relax until they catch a train. Small towns don't have very good accommodations."

"Well, I suppose it doesn't matter. We're getting close now, aren't we?"

"Yup. I'd say we're only about two hours behind them now and they'll have to stop pretty soon."

"So, will we. Are we going to have another cold camp? It was pretty chilly last night. There's even snow on the ground up here."

"I'm not going to start a fire, Bert. You should have packed more winter clothes before we left Denver."

"I didn't think we'd be running around the country, Bryn."

"I didn't either, but it's always better to be prepared than freeze your butt off."

"I'll remember that," Bert grumbled as they continued walking their animals.

Bryn may have placed their prey into the non-violent category, but he still had that other, nagging feeling that they were going to run into a sticky problem when they did catch up with them.

He absent-mindedly rested his gloved right hand on the brass butt plate of his new Winchester model 1876. It was the rifle version with the longer barrel and used the new .45-77 center fire cartridge. He and Dylan had each ordered one and so had Lynn. Lynn had even ordered the musket version with its longer, thirty-six-inch barrel. They had gotten good results past two hundred yards with the new Winchesters, and now he was glad he had the range advantage. His nagging concern had been growing and he didn't know why. It was almost as if they were being followed; not the other way around.

———

Irv turned to Rowdy Joe Corrigan who was riding to his right and asked, "How much longer do you want to keep going, Joe? We're almost to the crest of this pass."

"I reckon we're better off on the other side. If those lawmen really are behind us, we'd pick them up a lot faster when they crossed over."

"If they're that close, then maybe it doesn't matter."

Joe laughed, then replied, "I suppose not. Let's get on the other side of the crest, then we'll wait until after the trail turns and we can camp there. That way one of us can keep watch on that pass until it gets dark."

"It should be Clyde. He's already nervous," Irv shouted.

As expected, Clyde yelled back, "I heard that, Irv. I'm not nervous. I'm just being cautious."

The others all laughed, but Clyde didn't care. He thought it was just plain stupid not to pay attention to their backtrail.

———

The sun was setting in glorious fashion as Bryn and Bert walked their horses toward the crest of the pass.

Bryn then motioned to Bert to stop, then after they'd pulled up, he dismounted and let Aesop's reins drop.

Bert stepped down and asked, "What's up, Bryn?"

Bryn had his left hand resting on his gelding's haunch as he replied, "I think they're close, Bert, and I don't want to let them see us when we get to the top of that pass. If they're there, then we'd be sitting ducks."

"Then what do you want to do? I don't see any place where we can set up camp."

"I know. I figure that I'll just take a quick look down the other side of the pass. I'll climb those rocks over there and then take a peek."

"Okay," Bert said as Bryn removed his hat and hung it on his saddle horn.

Bryn then handed Aesop's reins to Bert and thought about taking his Winchester with him, but when he glanced back at the rocks, he knew that the climb would be impossible to make if he carried the repeater.

He walked to the nearest boulder, stepped up and began his slow, winding climb up the side of the mountain, making every effort to keep his head down so it didn't let the counterfeiters know that he was there. That was assuming they were close enough and checking their backtrail.

———

The outlaws had already unsaddled their horses, and Tom had begun to strip the pack mule, but Clyde's mount was still wearing his saddle as Clyde stood a hundred feet away in the center of the trail and watched the pass.

There would be little moonlight tonight, so Clyde expected that in another twenty minutes or so, there would be no use in keeping an eye on the pass, but he wasn't as confident as the other three who didn't believe that they weren't being followed.

He was staring at the pass when he caught the tiniest bit of movement just to his left up in the rocks and immediately shifted his focus. He wasn't sure that he'd really seen anything, and if it was something, it was most likely a hawk or maybe even a mountain goat. It could be one of those marmots, too.

Whatever it was, Clyde didn't see it again as he stared at the spot. Then just as he was about to dismiss the movement, he saw it again and was still unsure of what it was. It looked enough like the top of a man's head for his worries to kick up a notch, so he sidestepped a few feet to his left and then crouched slightly behind a ragged rock outcrop.

He was still watching as the sun's last gasp shone on the pass and spotted a man's head slowly rising from behind an enormous boulder.

He ducked behind the outcrop and then slid away to return to the campsite.

———

Bryn had spotted the movement below but wasn't sure if he'd been seen. It put him into a dilemma and wished that he hadn't made the climb. They might not have known they were being followed, but now they could have seen him. But as long as he was there, he remained on the boulder for a few more minutes to get an idea of their location. From his high perch, he could see the trail through a gap about a thousand yards past where he'd seen the movement, so if they were leaving, he'd be able to spot them through that gap. He didn't have much light left, but if they were spooked, then he'd see them soon enough.

He waited until the sunset was almost done, then began his slide and downward climb to talk to Bert. He wished that he was with Dylan or Lynn rather than Bert, but it was too late now. Bert may have been an experienced lawman, but he wasn't in the same league.

When he reached the relatively flat ground of the trail, he walked over to Aesop, pulled off one of his two canteens and took a long drink before putting the cap back in place and returning it to his saddle.

As he pulled his hat back in place, Bert asked, "Well? What did you see, Bryn?"

"I think they're on the other side of the pass maybe three hundred yards or so setting up camp. The problem is that one of them might have spotted me."

"Why is that a problem? We know where they are so we can just pick them up in the morning."

"I'd agree with you except that in the morning, we'd have to cross that pass and we'd be even bigger targets when we were silhouetted with the morning sun at our backs. We'd have to wait for them to leave and hope that they didn't double back or set up for an ambush."

Bert scratched the right side of his jaw as he asked, "So, what do you want to do?"

Bryn glanced back at the crest of the pass less than a hundred yards away before he answered, "I don't like the idea of just waiting. If they do know we're here, then they could turn the tables on us and come back after it's dark. That would actually be to our advantage if there were only a couple of them, but if all four try to sneak back, it wouldn't be pretty."

"So, are we going to get them tonight?"

"Sort of. What I think we'll do is to wait until its dark, then set up on the other side of the pass. We'll leave our horses on this side because they'd make too much noise. If we each wait on opposite sides of the trail, then if they come back, we'd be in a good defensive position. The lack of light will be bad, but it would be worse for them."

"But what about the horses? I mean, we'd still have to come back and get them and that would be the whole silhouetting problem again."

"If nothing happens tonight, then tomorrow morning, we're already on that side of the pass and we'll trot down there on foot and see where they are. If they've already ridden off, then we'll come back and get the horses. We're only dealing with a few hundred yards, Bert."

"Okay. I just hope this works out."

"So, do I," Bryn said as he took Aesop's reins and led him off the trail to a secluded cove with enough grass and a tiny pond of melted snow to keep him and Bert's gelding happy.

———

"Are you sure?" Irv asked.

Clyde shrugged and replied, "I'm not positive, but I'm pretty sure. I reckon those two lawmen are on the other side of the pass right now."

"Did he see you?"

"I don't think so. I was hiding behind some rocks when I spotted his head."

"What do you want to do, Irv?" Rowdy Joe asked.

"I'm not sure. We could just mount up and head down that trail in case they figure on coming at us tonight."

"They might not even be there, Irv," Tom Lilly said, "And if they are, I don't want to be caught with my pants down when we're saddling the horses. Besides, they need to rest."

The others were staring at Irv as he faced a similar dilemma to Bryn's. The biggest difference was that he was unsure if the lawmen were even there or Clyde's imagination had created them after spotting some mama hawk feeding her chicks.

After almost a minute, Irv said, "There's not a lot of light with that sliver of a moon, but it's enough to find out if they're over there. If they are, then we work out what to do."

"You mean you want one of us to cross back over that pass in the middle of the night just to find them?" Tom asked in disbelief, "What if they're expecting us? Did you think of that?"

Irv opened his mouth to argue, but then snapped it shut. Tom had a valid point, and it only added to the problem.

It was Rowdy Joe Corrigan who came up with the answer, or at least his answer.

"Hell, if they're trailing us and they're this close, we won't make it as far as Granite anyway and I don't like the idea of having them behind us. We should wait a little while, then all of us walk back over that pass with our pistols ready. If they're waiting for us, one of us might get hit, but two of us could open up on his muzzle flare and then the other one would fire, and we'd pick him off."

Clyde then said, "They'd have to warn us first; wouldn't they? I mean; that's the law."

"Maybe," Irv replied as he began to evaluate Joe's plan.

Tom Lilly then said, "I think Joe's right, Irv. We get our pistols and after the light's all gone, we sneak over that rise and see if they're there. I won't sleep right until I know."

Irv exhaled, then nodded and said, "Alright. Let's get ready and talk this over some more. We can't be stupid and just go charging over the top of the pass."

––––––––

"Are we taking our Winchesters?" Bert asked.

"Nope. I think that we're going to be pretty close when we find them, but we need to have that sixth cylinder full when we leave. They could have decided to leave already."

Bert snickered then said, "You mighta been seeing things too, Bryn."

Bryn grinned at Bert but knew he hadn't seen anything but one of those counterfeiters. He still felt uneasy about this situation and couldn't remember the last time he'd felt this way. He always fell into his 'danger' zone when everything slowed down, but maybe it was because there were so many variables in this situation that made the difference. It wasn't a very strong argument, but it was the best he could manage.

They loaded their pistols with the sixth .44 giving them twelve shots between them. Neither really expected counterfeiters to give them a gunfight because it wasn't a hanging offense and they'd been told that this group had no other history of crime. It was bad information because two of the men on the other side of the pass were far from non-violent before they became counterfeiters.

As they waited for the deep darkness to overtake the night, Bryn and Bert chewed on jerky and kept silent as they listened to the sounds of the night and anything that didn't belong.

Twenty minutes later, Bryn nudged Bert who then popped his last piece of jerky into his mouth before pulling his Colt and cocking the hammer.

Bryn slid his Smith & Wesson free, thumbed the hammer back into the ready position, then the two deputy marshals stepped out onto the path and began their slow and stealthy climb up the pass.

———

Less than a hundred yards away, the four outlaws were already moving in a line with a gap between each pair. Irv and Tom were on the right and there was a four-foot gap between Tom and Rowdy Joe with Clyde on the far left. Each of them had his pistol drawn and cocked as they stepped toward the crest of the pass.

For almost two minutes, the four outlaws and the two lawmen closed the gap as they made their way to the top; the low light and the normal sounds of the night prevented them from seeing or hearing each other.

It was twitchy Clyde who first spotted Bert as his face reflected just enough of the weak moonlight.

As he aimed his pistol, he shouted, "Shoot 'em!"

Bert was momentarily stunned before he began to bring his pistol level, but by then, Clyde had pulled his trigger and his .44 raced through the fifty-seven feet of thin air and slammed into the left side of his throat. Bert dropped his pistol as he stumbled back and grabbed his neck with his hands to try and keep the blood from gushing from the wound, but then fell onto his back as he began to fade.

Bryn fired at Clyde's muzzle flash before he dropped to the ground, but his bullet remembered where it was pointed and exploded into Clyde's left shoulder, shattering the joint. He screamed as he spun to the ground, and before he sprawled onto the rocky soil, his partners all had fired at Bryn, but all three missed.

After hitting the ground, Bryn quickly rolled into a prone firing position and had his hammer cocked as he waited for the three shooters to come over the crest of the pass.

Tom, Irv and Rowdy Joe knew that one of the two lawmen was down and had seen the second drop after they'd fired, so after a brief hesitation, they quickly stepped to the top of the pass with their pistols cocked and ready.

Bryn knew he was in a bad position and couldn't take out all three of them but hoped that they'd run after his first shot yet couldn't wait around to be sure. He couldn't take his eyes off the narrow pass to check his surroundings but knew that the left side of the trail was a downslope of about twenty to thirty feet, so after he took his shot, he would have to roll that way to buy some time. It was his only chance. He wished he could check on Bert's condition, but right now, he needed to eliminate the danger.

The three counterfeiters reached the crest and just as Irv spotted Bert's inert form in the shadows, Rowdy Joe noticed Bryn on the ground on their right. The light wasn't good enough to make out anything more than a dark lump on the ground, but Joe turned his pistol toward Bryn to take a finishing shot to be sure.

Bryn had hoped that they'd be more exposed, but when he noticed one of them turning his pistol toward him, he squeezed his trigger.

The black night was illuminated with the foot-long flash of light from his Smith & Wesson's muzzle, then Joe felt the .44 slam into his chest, just to the right of his sternum. The bullet then drilled through the center of his chest and crushed the sixth thoracic vertebral body, cutting the spinal cord.

Before he screamed and crumpled to the ground, Irv and Tom had whipped their pistols to the sound of the shot and fired at Bryn's muzzle flare.

As soon as he'd fired, Bryn rolled quickly to his left, and soon felt the tug of gravity yank him down the slope. As he lost control of the descent, the rocks and small boulders slammed into his body and bounced him like a human pinball. Suddenly, he felt nothing at all.

Irv and Tom ran to the rocky slope and looked down at Bryn's unmoving body about thirty feet away.

"We've got to get out of here!" Tom exclaimed.

"Hold on," replied Irv as he leveled his pistol at Bryn and fired.

It wasn't an easy shot in that light, and his .44 ricocheted off a watermelon-sized rock just six inches in above Bryn's head. It was the same chunk of stone that had met his head on his way down.

Tom then fired and his shot buzzed past Bryn's right hip before blasting into the dirt another fifteen feet down the long slope.

"Hell, if he isn't dead, he's still not going anywhere," Irv snapped as he holstered his pistol.

"Do we take their guns and horses?" Tom asked.

"We have too many already and it'll make us noticeable when we get to Granite. We'll take Clyde and Joe's horses and the pack mule and start moving. It'll be slow, but I want to get away from here. That sheriff back in Canon City will probably be checking on them in a couple of days and I don't want to be anywhere near here by then."

"Okay, Irv," Tom replied after holstering his Colt.

Irv took one last look down at Bryn before they quickly turned and trotted back down the hill.

Ten minutes later, Irv and Tom were leading two saddled horses and their pack mule back down the trail in the darkness.

CHAPTER 2

"Can you hear me? Wake up!"

Bryn was freezing as his body felt every one of those rock hits as he lay in his awkward position in the dark and wasn't sure that he'd really heard a woman's voice. *How did Erin find him? Where was he?*

"Erin?" he asked quietly with his eyes still closed.

"No, it's Bethan, Uncle Bryn. Wake up!"

Bryn slowly spread his eyelids as he asked, "Bethan?"

"Your niece, if you remember. What happened?"

"Where am I?"

"You're about thirty feet down the side of a mountain. I didn't find any blood, but is anything broken?"

Bryn wasn't sure yet as he hurt in places that had never experienced pain before.

"Give me a minute. How did blue blazes did you get here? Why are you even here in the first place?"

As Bryn began moving his legs and arms, Bethan replied, "I've been trailing you and Bert for a day now. I've been about two miles back until the sun began to set and then I figured you'd be setting up camp, so I set up camp early and I was already asleep when I was awakened by the gunfire. Dad always said to sleep when you can just in case you had to move unexpectedly. I had to saddle Nippy, but I came as fast as I could."

"Bert?"

"He's dead and there are two other bodies up there."

"I screwed up, Bethan, and I got Bert killed."

Bethan didn't comment, but slid her canteen from her shoulder, unscrewed the cap and handed it to Bryn.

Bryn lifted his head, took a long drink of water, then handed it back to Bethan who screwed the cap in place and looped the strap over her head.

"Are they gone?"

"I haven't checked very far after seeing the other two bodies. I didn't hear anything, so I think that they probably left already."

"I'm bruised, but I don't think anything's broken. Can you help me up?"

"Okay," Bethan replied, then stood and took Bryn's hands.

Bryn was glad that Bethan was such a tall, strong young woman and even though she shouldn't have been there, he was enormously pleased that she was.

After she'd helped Bryn into a vertical posture, he scanned the dark ground, spotted his hat, then said, "Could you pick up my hat, Bethan?"

"Can you stand by yourself?"

"I think so. I'll lean on this boulder."

Bethan released him, then took two steps, picked up his hat and handed it to him.

Bryn gingerly pulled his hat onto his head then said, "I can't find my pistol."

Bethan slipped his Smith & Wesson from the back of her waist and gave it to him as she said, "I found this on the way down."

"Thank you, ma'am," he replied as he slid the revolver into his holster and hooked the hammer loop into place.

Bethan then picked up the rope that stretched along the slope from the trail, looped it once around her before she wrapped it around Bryn's waist and knotted the end.

Bryn looked at his niece's calm demeanor and wasn't surprised at all.

"Are you ready?" she asked.

"If we go slowly," he replied.

Bethan nodded, then looked up the dark slope and shouted, "Walk, Nippy!"

The rope suddenly snaked to their left then snapped taut before Bethan yelled, "Stop!"

With the tight rope already tugging them upwards, Bethan then shouted, "Slow!"

Bryn felt the rope's measured force pull him and Bethan up the slope and he was able to lean back and move his feet to keep his balance.

Bethan acted as crutch giving him added support with her arm around his waist above the rope.

The climb took almost two minutes, but soon they were back on the trail and Bethan shouted, "Stop!", and her young mare froze.

Bryn bent over at the waist as Bethan undid the knot and let the rope drop. After she released their rope belts, Bethan helped Bryn to the ground where he sat staring at Bert's body just fifteen feet away.

After a minute or so, he asked, "Are our horses still there?"

"Yes, and your Winchesters are still in the scabbards. I was kind of surprised about that. How are you doing?"

"I'm okay, I guess. I need to take care of Bert's body, then decide what I need to do."

"It's what we need to do, Uncle Bryn. I'm not leaving you."

Bryn finally pulled his eyes from Bert, looked up at his niece and asked, "What made you decide to follow us, Bethan? Does your father know about it?"

"Nobody did. I knew that you were going to be going to Canon City to arrest some counterfeiters, so I took the train before you did. I waited for you to show up, but when you didn't, I figured you and Bert had gone out to their place, so I left town and picked up your trail."

"You didn't answer my question. Why did you do it?"

Bethan sighed, then answered, "I'm frustrated with being pushed into a tidy little box where my future is mapped out for me. I'm just as good as Lynn but I'm not allowed to wear a badge. I guess I just wanted to prove it to everyone, including myself."

"You know that you're better than Lynn is and he's very good. I can understand why you're frustrated, Bethan, but even if you prove yourself, you can't be sworn in as a lawman."

"I know. I'll come up with somethin, even if I have to become a bounty hunter."

Bryn shook his head before he said, "We can talk on the way, but you really need to talk to your father and listen this time."

"I have listened. I've listened to everyone and I still need to do what I feel is necessary. Now, you stay there, and I'll go bring your horses around."

"Alright."

Bethan began wrapping her rope around her elbow and hand as she walked back to her mare, hung the coiled rope over her saddle hook then mounted, turned then walked back Nippy down the trail to their two horses.

As she strode in the dark, Bethan wondered if there really was any point in what she had decided to do when she'd left the Double EE. It had seemed so obvious when she'd boarded the train, but she hadn't expected to be in the situation that she now found herself. She'd expected that she'd simply follow and then watch their takedown of the counterfeiters. Despite all of her instruction in shooting and other lawman skills, she'd never been permitted to go with her father, uncle or brother when they'd gone on a mission. Now she would not only watch; she would have to help Bryn. She just didn't know if he'd allow her to help chase down the escaping outlaws.

She led the two horses back to where Bryn still sat, then after tying their reins to Nippy, she removed Bert's slicker from behind his saddle and spread it on the ground next to his body.

She undid his gunbelt, slid it free, then rolled him onto the slicker and covered his body with the rubberized canvas.

Bryn felt helpless as he watched Bethan, but when he had tried to stand to offer his assistance, he almost fell.

Bethan may have been tall and strong for a young woman, but she was still a woman and she estimated that Bert probably weighed over a hundred and seventy pounds. She'd need her uncle's help to get the body on the saddle before rigor mortis set in or they'd have to wait until the rigor lessened and that would be a long wait. It might not be a bad idea to wait, though. She wasn't tired because she'd had some sleep, but she thought it might be better if Bryn slept and recovered from his injuries.

She then turned and asked, "How can we get Bert's body onto his saddle? Do we wait until morning?"

"What time is it? Do you know?"

"I'd guess that it's only about six hours past sunset, so we have another four or five hours before the predawn."

"I don't want to wait that long, Bethan. Can you help me up, so I can walk around and get my muscles working again?"

44

"Are you dizzy? You were knocked out, Uncle Bryn."

"I'm not dizzy at all and that surprises me. I should be throwing up, but I'm just really sore."

"Okay," she replied, then walked to where he sat, took his hands and leaned back, pulling him slowly to his feet.

Once he was upright, Bryn said, "Alright. You can let go now. I'm going to try to move on my own."

Bethan stepped back but stayed close as Bryn took his first careful step, then his second.

Bryn stretched his back and flexed his arms as he began to walk with more confidence, but Bethan still stepped closely beside him.

"What happened, Uncle Bryn?" she asked as he hobbled along.

Bryn replied, "We found their place empty and took off after them. Somebody must have tipped them off. I knew we were getting close at sunset...."

For five minutes Bryn explained what had happened as he continued to warm and use his damaged muscles. When he finished, Bryn stopped and turned to Bethan.

"I think we can get Bert's body onto his horse now before rigor sets in. Then we'll start down the trail after those other two. Where is his pistol?"

45

"I have it in my saddlebag. I picked it up when I was searching for you. The other two don't have their pistols. I guess the survivors picked them up before they left."

Getting Bert's body over the saddle wasn't as hard as she'd expected as Bryn still did most of the lifting.

After they finished, Bethan asked, "What about the other two bodies?"

"Leave them."

Bethan nodded before taking down her canteen as Bryn removed his from Aesop.

After satisfying their immediate thirst, Bryn stepped into his saddle and Bethan mounted Nippy. Bryn was trailing Bert's horse in case they ran across the survivors. In that event, he wanted Bethan to run but hadn't told her yet.

Once in the saddle, Bryn asked, "How long ago did you hear the shooting?"

"I'd guess around seven hours by now."

"If they did leave right away, then they'll be a good ten to twelve miles away. I don't think they expect me to follow, so they won't set up an ambush."

Bethan didn't reply before Bryn started Aesop back up the trail and she nudged Nippy into step on his left as Bert's horse trailed behind.

They soon crossed the crest and passed Clyde and Rowdy Joe's bodies without comment.

Once they were walking their horses down the barely visible trail, Bethan asked, "Where are we going, Uncle Bryn?"

Bryn glanced at his niece and realized that he really didn't have an answer yet. If Lynn had arrived and found him, then there would be no question about where they would be going. They'd chase after those last two killers and either arrest them both or take them down. But despite his conviction that Bethan had good skills in the tasks that were needed to do the job, he didn't want to risk Dylan and Gwen's first daughter in such a risky venture.

"We'll stay on the trail until we have enough light and then pick up their tracks. I originally thought that they'd ride to Granite to catch the train, but now they might head to a smaller town or even head south once they reached level ground. We'll have to see where they go."

"Alright," she replied, then said, "I don't think you screwed up, Uncle Bryn. It was just one of those things. If you'd set up camp back where I was, they'd have found you and you'd have been in worse shape. It was just bad luck."

"No, Bethan. It was a mistake. I should have held back and given them more space. I should have waited for daylight."

"And then what? Crossed that pass with the sun at your back? You and Bert would have been easy pickings. No matter when you decided to cross that pass, you risked being shot. It was just a freak of coincidence that you both met at the crest. Sometimes, it really is bad luck, like having your horse step on a sleeping rattlesnake. You shouldn't blame yourself, Uncle Bryn."

Bryn looked across at her shadow and replied, "Maybe you're right, Bethan. And don't call me uncle anymore. I think you've earned the right to call me Bryn."

"Okay."

Bryn was still uneasy having Bethan with him, but he'd been surprised by how quickly she'd understood the tactical problems that he had encountered when they were close to the summit. He supposed that he really shouldn't have been surprised at all. Ever since she'd taken to the saddle and spent time with him and Dylan as they trained the boys, it seemed that she was always a step ahead of Lynn, Alwen and Garth. She could outshoot and outride them all and had a sharp, logical mind that would have put her at the top of the law profession if she'd been born male.

———

Irv and Tom were about five miles ahead of Bryn and Bethan as the crow flies, but probably closer to nine or ten as they followed the twisting trail to the flatlands. Neither expected the lawman to be following but believed that both deputy marshals were dead, so their only concern now was to reach Granite and get on the train. Yet they still maintained the same pace as Bryn and Bethan because of the poor visibility and the danger of a fatal misstep

Both pairs of riders made their way down the long sloping trail in the dark; each unaware of the other's location, but the pair in the lead didn't even know that the second duo even existed.

———

Bethan and Bryn didn't talk as their horses stepped along the rocky surface. The metal horseshoes striking the stony ground already made enough noise, but neither of them really believed that they were close enough for it to matter. The big reason for the silent descent was that each of them was thinking about what would happen when they found the last two counterfeiters.

Bryn hadn't told Bethan that he wanted to go in alone after he located the outlaws. If it was in a town, then he'd drop off Bert's body at the mortician before he confronted the two, hopefully with the assistance of the local law. He'd have Bethan wait outside of town or go to a hotel and get some sleep while he dealt with the killers. He may have been knocked unconscious, but he was still sleepy, and sleepy and sore wasn't a good condition to be in when going into a gunfight. Bryn was counting on his shift into his 'danger zone' of heightened awareness when he caught up with the two men.

Bethan was thinking of a totally different approach if they found them. She wasn't naïve enough to believe that her uncle would want her with him when he confronted the two men, but at the same time, she knew that she had an enormous advantage. She was a girl, and most men never viewed females of any age as a threat, which was an enormous mistake, especially in her case.

She'd never shot anyone, of course, but had steeled herself for that possibility. Years of listening to her father and uncles and now Lynn, had given her a solid foundation of what to expect. So, as she walked Nippy beside her uncle's tall gelding, she was already formulating a plan that would provide him with support, even if he didn't want it.

She was still concerned about the damage that he'd sustained when he'd tumbled down that rocky slope and if it came to exchanging gunfire with two men who knew they'd hang, she wasn't sure that his hurt muscles would respond as well as he thought. She probably wasn't nearly as tired as he was, either. She'd gotten a couple of hours of sleep and she wasn't even eighteen years old. He should have taken time to get a few hours' sleep before starting out but wasn't surprised that he hadn't. If there was one thing that she'd learned living in a household and family that was overwhelmingly male was that men often seemed to feel the need to prove to themselves that they were men, even if it meant putting themselves at a greater risk.

———

The predawn was arriving when Irv and Tom finally reached level ground and could pick up the pace. Within forty minutes, they'd spotted the tracks and headed north and after bypassing Riverside, they knew they were just twelve miles from Granite.

Tom glanced behind them, then asked, "What time does the train leave?"

"I have no idea, but when we get into town, we'll take the horses and the pack mule to the station and drop them off then see if we can get a deal on those two that we don't need."

"What about the packs? We're not going to leave that money and the plates on the mule; are we?"

"Sure. It'll look odd if we don't. We check the time for the train, drop off our horses and the mule, then take the others to the livery. Then, if we have time, we can check into the hotel and get cleaned up before the train."

Tom wasn't sure, but didn't have a better plan, so he nodded then said, "Alright. I just hope that train leaves soon."

"Relax, Tom. We'll be in Boulder before they even go looking for those two dead lawmen."

"I wish we'd been sure about that one we left down in that gully. He might have climbed out of there."

"Even if he was alive, he'd be so sore and probably even have some broken bones. He's gone, Tom. Take it easy."

Tom blew out his breath and tried to relax, but the recent gunfight was still too fresh in his mind.

––––––

With the added light of the predawn, Bryn and Bethan could pick up their pace.

"We've got another three hours or so on the trail, Bethan," Bryn said, then asked, "How are you doing?"

"I'm good, and probably better than you. How do you feel?"

"I'm tired and sore, but I'll be all right."

After another minute of silent riding, Bryn figured he may as well try to convince Bethan that this would be a one-man job and was ready for the argument.

"Bethan, once I figure out where they are, I'm going to give you instructions that I want you follow without question. Do you understand?"

Bethan looked across the gap and replied, "Yes, sir. Do you have any idea of what they'll be yet?"

"If I find that they've gone into a town, I want you to let me go in alone. I'll drop off Bert's body at the mortician before I try to locate them."

"You want me to stay sitting on Nippy outside of town?"

"No. I want us to separate and you can go to the hotel and get a room. Wait there while I do my search. I'll be getting help from the local law first. If they go to Granite, then that will be Lake County Sheriff John Schuler. He's a good man."

Bethan replied, "Okay. I'll head for the hotel if they're in a town. What do they look like? I don't want to run into them and not know."

Bryn was surprised by her quick and unexpected acceptance and glanced over at her. This wasn't like Bethan at all, and he was suspicious of the reason for her sudden submissiveness. He was going to question her further about it but decided that it would serve no purpose. He had another few hours to figure out what she was really thinking. He did think it was a good idea to know what they looked like, even though he only had their descriptions from their wanted posters.

"The two that are still alive are named Irving Thompson and Tom Lilly. Irv is the taller of the two, just about two inches taller than you with black hair and brown eyes. He has a full beard and his eyebrows are really bushy. Tom Lilly is a couple of inches shorter, tends to fat, and has lighter brown hair and brown eyes. He's usually clean shaven, but probably has a good growth of stubble by now. Irv is the boss."

"Okay. What kinds of horses were they riding?"

"I don't know. They'll be trailing two saddled horses and a pack horse or mule, so that would be noticeable. If they're heading for Granite to take the train, my guess is that they'll be leaving them at the stock corral at the station."

"Do you think they'll still go that way, or will they curl south to the flat lands? With a pack horse of supplies, they could just curve around and head back to Canon City."

"They could, but I don't think they'll head back that way because they know that Sheriff Johnson knows they're in the area."

"You said that they were tipped off. Do you know who it was?"

"It had to be either the telegrapher or someone in the sheriff's office. I'm leaning toward one of his deputies, but that's for another day."

Bethan nodded then looked at the spreading vista to her left as Nippy stepped along the long downslope. It was still cold, and she was glad she'd brought her heavy, long coat with her. It had the added advantage of hiding the Smith & Wesson at her hip and the Webley Bulldog in its shoulder holster. She even had a ,41 caliber Remington derringer in her coat pocket. Bethan had more firepower than her Uncle Bryn carried, and was proficient in the use of each of them.

———

The sun's morning rays finally topped the mountains and Irv and Tom were bathed in light as they entered Granite and headed for the first livery that they spotted on the south side of town.

"Let's get something to eat first, Irv," Tom said as they neared a diner.

"I guess that wouldn't hurt. The liveryman probably isn't even awake yet."

Tom grinned as they turned to the front of the eatery and stepped down. His stomach was already growling when he smelled the aroma of cooking bacon.

———

As Irv and Tom were shoveling their breakfast into their mouths, Bryn and Bethan were still on the trail.

"Are you going to send a telegram when we get to Granite?" Bethan asked.

"If they aren't there, then I'll send the telegram after dropping Bert's body at the mortician. If they are, then I'll drop off the body, get the sheriff and then handle those two. When it's all done, then I'll send the message to Dylan. He'll have Benji tell Martha about Bert. I don't know how she'll take the news. She'll probably hate me and anyone else named Evans."

Bethan turned to look at her uncle and said, "I'm not so sure, Bryn. I think that her marriage to Bert was on rocky ground. After Al told me that she'd broken off their romance because he was thinking of becoming a lawman. When I talked to Martha about that, she said that she realized her mistake, but was too proud to tell Al and she actually asked me to talk to him about it. I told her that she had to be the one to do it, but she never did. When she married Bert, I thought it was as if she was trying to prove that it didn't matter.

"Now she has a baby and is already pregnant again. I don't know how Al is going to react, but I don't believe that Martha will be that upset. I just hope that Al doesn't feel guilty about it and then marry her out of some sort of misguided sense of nobility."

Bryn stared at Bethan as he replied, "I hope you're right that she won't hate me, but I don't understand why you would think that Al would be making a mistake to marry her. He and Garth have a stable, productive operation at their ranch and I'm sure that a woman's presence out there would be an improvement."

"I agree with you that having a woman there would be beneficial, but not if she was Martha. She isn't right for Al. She wants a husband who dotes on her and I don't think that Al would tolerate it."

Bryn smiled, then said, "And you don't, Bethan? Don't you want a man who worships you and answers to your every whim?"

"Hell, no!" Bethan exclaimed, "I want a husband who challenges me and makes me feel alive. I don't want some dewy-eyed sycophant who doesn't understand me. I want someone who can tell me when I'm wrong and doesn't sulk when I do the same to him."

"So, it doesn't matter what he looks like, Bethan?"

"Of course, it matters. I'm not going to marry some weasel and bear children that look like rats. I'm just saying that what matters more is that he treats me as his equal and not as nothing more than his housekeeper and bedmate."

Bryn laughed, sending large clouds of steam into the cold air, then replied, "Well, good luck finding any man that can be your equal, Miss Evans."

"I've met a few, Mister Evans. Unfortunately, they've all been related. I'll find him one of these days; I just hope I'm not old and gray when I do. Until then, I'll do what I'm good at."

———

After eating their big breakfast, Irv and Tom took their extra mounts to the livery and spent twenty minutes bargaining with the liveryman over a price but left the place with another hundred and sixty real dollars added to their stash. They were surprised that he had that much cash in his big barn but didn't even think about trying to relieve him of the rest he may have had. They needed to get on that train.

They walked their horses and the pack mule down Granite's main street and passed the jail without paying too much attention. They soon reached the train depot, stepped down and tied off their tired horses.

When they reached the ticket window, they found it closed, but a posted schedule gave them the bad news. The southbound train had passed through the night before and the northbound train wasn't due until 5:10 that afternoon.

As he stared at the poster, Tom asked, "What do you want to do, Irv? Do we keep riding or take the train when it comes in?"

Irv almost didn't hear Tom's question as he peered at the schedule. It would be more than eight hours before that train arrived, but he was already tired after the long time in the saddle and he didn't think there would be any problems if they had to wait. They could catch up on their sleep, too.

He finally turned to Tom and said, "Let's get the horses and mule taken care of and then we'll get a room at the hotel to get some shuteye."

"That sounds good, Irv."

Irv nodded, then they returned to their horses, and led them to the nearby livery used by the railroad rather than take them to the first one.

Less than an hour later, both men were sound asleep in their room at the Taylor House hotel after telling the clerk to knock on their doors at four o'clock.

———

"It looks like they're still heading to Granite, Bethan," Bryn said as he glanced down at their trail, "Let's pick up the pace a bit."

"How far is it to Granite?"

"About two hours or so. When we're within sight of the town, I'll slow down and you can ride ahead, but I want you to swing around to the east and just ride in on your own."

"Okay," she replied as Bryn glanced at her, still wondering why she was so compliant. It seemed very much out of character.

———

It was ninety minutes later when the roofs of Granite's southernmost building crept above the horizon and Bryn brought Aesop to a stop.

"Go ahead, Bethan. I'll stay put for ten minutes, then start at a slow walk. I should be there in forty minutes or so."

"Alright," she replied, then nudged Nippy into a fast trot.

Bryn watched his niece ride away, then yawned and rolled his shoulders. He wished that he'd gotten more sleep other than the unplanned period of unconsciousness that didn't seem to help at all. He was still sore but knew that if he did take a short nap, it would be worse when he started to move again. He was counting on his oft-used 'danger' sense to give him the advantage that he needed; that and the presence of Lake County Sheriff Joe Schuler or a deputy.

Bethan rode with a purpose as she headed for Granite. She'd follow Bryn's instructions but would do all she could to back him up. He may be depending on the sheriff, but she wasn't sure if he was up to it. She did know her own abilities and had confidence in herself.

It only took Nippy fifteen minutes to reach Granite, and after she rode past the town along its eastern edge, she walked her across the tracks and stopped at the depot.

She dismounted, tied off Nippy, then stepped onto the platform after taking a glance at the empty stock corral. Either the train had already gone, they had already ridden out of town, or their horses were in a livery. Everything depended on the train schedule, so she stepped up to the ticket window, read the schedule, then let out a sharp breath. That eliminated their departure on the train. Either they were still in town or had ridden off already.

She stepped down from the platform, then untied Nippy, and led her to the closest livery stable.

Once inside, she spotted the liveryman who was shoeing a horse near the back of the big barn.

"Good morning," she said loudly as she walked inside.

"Howdy, miss," the liveryman replied as he let the horse's hoof down, "What brings you by? I don't reckon havin' seen you before."

"No, sir. I just rode in. I'm waiting for my uncle. He's coming in a little while after he stops at the mortician. We had an accident on the way and his friend was thrown from his horse and died."

"Well, that's downright sad, ma'am. What can I do for ya?"

"I need to have my horse boarded for a little while and have her shoes checked. I think we'll be taking the train now after the accident."

"I'll take a look at her as soon as I can. I already finished one of them horses and I'm almost done with the second one. You've got a mighty pretty lady there. Takes after her owner, I reckon."

Bethan smiled, not worried that the old man was trying to become too familiar, then handed him Nippy's reins. She noticed that in addition to the horse he was shoeing, there was another horse and a mule in the barn with two full sets of tack, a pack saddle and several panniers all stacked in the corner. She had no doubt as to their owners.

"Thank you, sir. I'll be heading over to the hotel to wait for my uncle."

The liveryman smiled as he took the reins, then watched Bethan leave the barn. He then turned to her mare and noticed that the girl's horse was carrying a new Winchester and a shotgun, which surprised him.

Bethan stepped out onto the main street, then stopped to get a lay of the town. There was some street traffic, but not too much. The jail was on her left about four blocks down, but she didn't see the mortuary. She spotted the nearby Taylor House and assumed that the two men were either there or in a diner having their breakfast. She gave more weight to the likelihood that they were sleeping rather than eating. They'd been in town for a few hours already because one of their horses was already sporting new shoes and the second one would be soon.

She stepped along the boardwalk with her heavy coat effectively masking her personal armory. Even her masculine attire wasn't that noticeable under the long coat and if she hadn't been wearing the Stetson, she'd look no different than any other young woman in town.

Bethan stepped into the hotel, didn't see anyone in the lobby, then walked to the front desk as she removed her hat.

"May I help you, ma'am?" the clerk behind the counter asked with a big smile.

"I'll need a room to get some sleep before the train arrives, but I have to wait for my uncle to get here. Do you mind if I just wait in the lobby for him?"

"No, not at all."

"Thank you," Bethan replied before she turned and stepped to the far end of the lobby and took a seat where she could see both the stairs to the second floor and the hallway entrance.

As Bethan sat and Irv and Tom slept, Bryn was approaching the southern edge of Granite. He'd been to the town twice before and as he studied the foot traffic, he didn't see anyone that matched the wanted posters' descriptions of the two men. He wanted to go and check the train schedule but headed for the jail first. Sheriff Schuler would be able to tell him what time the train left and might have noticed the two strangers ride into his town.

He pulled Aesop to a stop before the sheriff's office, dismounted, and tied him off before stepping onto the boardwalk and entering the jail.

As he opened the door, Bryn was surprised to find the front office empty, but the heat stove was hot and there was a coffeepot sitting on top.

"Joe?" he shouted as he closed the door.

He didn't hear a reply but did pick up the sheriff's footsteps as he exited his personal office down the short hallway and then as Sheriff Schuler spotted Bryn, he broke into a big smile.

"Bryn! What brings you our way? I don't suppose it's anything good."

"No, sir. It's all bad."

Joe's smile disappeared as he approached Bryn and asked, "What's the problem?"

"I was tracking four counterfeiters from Canon City and we both decided to go looking for each other just after sunset. We exchanged gunfire, and Bert Hoskins took a .44 in the throat, killing him. I got one of them with my first shot, then hit the dirt when they opened fire. I took out a second one, but then rolled to my left down the side of the trail. I must have smacked my melon into a rock because that's all I remember. My niece, Dylan's girl, Bethan, had been trailing us and found me. Don't ask why, Joe. She's Dylan's daughter and that should give you an idea.

"Anyway, she helped me back up to the trail and we led Bert's horse with his body as we followed their tracks. They're here now, unless they were able to board the train. When do the trains come through?"

Joe quickly replied, "The southbound comes through in the wee hours, waking us all up in the process. The northbound train leaves here around five-thirty."

"So, they're either still in town or have already ridden off. Have you seen them? They would have ridden in trailing two empty saddled horses and a pack horse or mule."

"I haven't seen them, but let's go to Ted Elliott's livery. It's on the south end of town and they'd stop there first."

"Okay, but I need to drop Bert's body off with the mortician so he can prepare it for return to Denver. Where's your deputy?"

"I'm on my own at the moment. My one deputy left two months ago to take a job in Arizona Territory, and I haven't replaced him yet. I'll tell you what, you drop off the body at Franklin's Mortuary and I'll go check with Ted about those horses. The mortuary is two blocks south and one block east."

"Okay, Joe. You might want to keep that badge under your coat. These boys will be nervous and they're likely to shoot first. I don't think they know that I'm here, though. They didn't exactly race away when they reached flat ground."

Sheriff Schuler nodded as he walked to the wall where his coat and hat hung from pegs, pulled his coat off and slipped his arms through the sleeves. He didn't button the front before snatching his hat and pulling it on.

The two lawmen exited the jail, then after scanning the traffic and boardwalks, Bryn untied Aesop, then led the gelding south, walking alongside the sheriff.

Bryn soon turned east, and Sheriff Shuster continued to walk toward the livery.

———

Bryn arranged for Bert's body to be prepared for return to Denver and paid the fee, then left the mortuary just fifteen minutes later. He didn't know where the sheriff was, but assumed he was already back in his office, so he turned north after reaching the main street.

When he entered the jail, he found the sheriff sitting behind the front desk, pulled off his hat and asked, "Well?"

Joe replied, "They're here. Ted said that they'd dickered for selling the two horses this morning and then led the pack mule away. They had breakfast at Sally's Diner, but after that, I'm not sure where they went. They're either at the Granite Hotel or the Taylor House. How do you want to do this?"

"Well, they're not going anywhere until that train leaves, and I don't want to have bullets flying around in a hotel. I could use some sleep myself. Do you mind if I sack out in back?"

"I think that's a good idea, Bryn. You look pretty worn out."

"Worn out and pretty beat up. I feel like I've gone a couple of rounds with a mule."

"Go ahead to the back room and I'll take your horses down to Ted's and have him take care of them. I'll do my usual rounds and act as if I don't know they're here. When do you want me to wake you up?"

"Give me until around four o'clock. If you see them, just let them go. We'll get them at the train depot where it's less likely to have many people around. They'll have to get there early to leave their horses."

"Okay, Bryn."

Bryn took a deep breath, then headed down the hallway to the back room. Ten minutes later, he was stretched out on the narrow bunk and in deep sleep.

———

Bethan had been waiting in the lobby for more than two hours now and began to wonder if the two outlaws were in the hotel at all. She was hungry and just sitting quietly was making her drowsy. She'd spent the time thinking about how to confront the two men when they did appear, but now she thought that they might have chosen the other hotel at the other end of town. Even the clerk had left his post, probably to get some lunch.

Because she hadn't removed her coat, she was getting overly warm, which enhanced her need for sleep. She finally stood, leaving her hat on the chair and walked to the front of the hotel. She looked out the window and scanned the traffic as she debated about leaving, getting some late lunch and checking the other hotel.

She turned to retrieve her hat when she heard voices from the hallway as the clerk returned to his desk. Her lethargy vanished as she calmly walked back to her chair and glanced at the end of the hall as two men exited into the lobby. She had no doubt that she was looking at the two killers.

They spotted her and the taller one smiled as she reached her chair but didn't take her seat.

Irv and Tom both gave Bethan a onceover, but neither said anything as they slowly passed and headed for the front door.

Bethan forced herself to remain calm as she listened to them pass and once they were a good ten feet away, she slid her right hand into her unbuttoned coat then slipped her Smith & Wesson from its holster.

As Irv was reaching for the doorknob, Bethan brought her pistol level, then after she cocked the hammer to let them know it was there, she shouted, "Stop where you are and put your hands in the air!"

Irv and Tom were more than stunned but neither put their hands up as they both turned to look at the pretty girl.

Bethan's eyes were steady and her pistol's muzzle unwavering as the two men turned. She hadn't expected them to do as she ordered because she was a young woman and understood that they'd probably dismiss her warning, even after they saw her revolver.

"What the hell do you think you're doing, girl?" shouted Tom.

"It's kind of obvious, isn't it? I want each of you to remove your pistol with two fingers on your left hand. If you do anything else, I'll send a .44 right between your eyes."

Irv didn't laugh or even smile as he stared at the determined young woman, but she was still just a girl and he didn't believe she even knew how to use that six-shooter. But how she knew that they were wanted or why she had the pistol did bother him.

"What are you talking about? We're just waiting for the train. We got in on the one last night."

"That's kind of stupid, don't you think? Why would you take the southbound train that showed up in the night just to turn right back around? Did you come all this way just to have your horses' shoes changed?"

Irv was becoming more concerned about what the girl knew than the pistol she was still holding steadily. *How did she know they were here?*

"It doesn't matter, does it? Who are you, anyway? You live here?"

"No. I live up near Denver and my name doesn't matter. You two are wanted men and I'm going to get you two to jail and collect the rewards on your heads."

Tom stared at Bethan with big eyes and arched eyebrows as he exclaimed, *"You're a bounty hunter? A girl?* That's crazy!"

"I'm pretty new at it, but when I saw you two walking down the street, I was pretty sure who you were."

Irv calmly asked, "You ever kill a man, missy?"

"Not yet. The first two came quiet, but the third one I had to shoot to make him come along. I wasn't in any real danger, so I only shot him on the outside of his left calf. It was still pretty messy, though. A .44 does a lot of damage."

Irv was evaluating the girl and wasn't sure if she was telling the truth or just trying to impress them. Regardless, they couldn't afford to let this go on much longer.

"We would have heard about some girl bounty hunter, so I think you're just bluffing."

Bethan had her sights already set to the left of Tom's right ear as Irv talked. She needed to alert Bryn and the sheriff and couldn't keep her pistol level much longer.

She squeezed the trigger and her pistol barked, sending the .44 buzzing past Tom's left ear, under his hat and through the hotel's front door.

As the two men jerked and the echo rebounded from the walls, Bethan cocked the hammer.

"That was just to let you know that my bullet goes where I intend it to go, mister. Now, I want those pistols on the floor just as I told you!"

The bullet's passing so close to him unnerved Tom, but Irv had already come up with another plan.

"Alright, miss. You made your point. How much is the reward on us?"

"Not much. You're worth a hundred and fifty dollars, and your pal is worth a hundred. Where are the other two?"

"They didn't come with us. So, you're only going to get two hundred and fifty dollars. I can double that if you'll let us go."

Bethan laughed and replied, "Not if it's in those counterfeit bills that you've been passing."

"No. I'll pay you in tens. We only print singles."

Bethan paused, then replied, "Make it seven and we've got a deal."

Irv smiled, then said, "Okay. We've got the money in the livery near the railroad station. We'll have to go there to get it."

"I'll be right behind you."

"Not with that pistol out like that. Folks would notice."

"I'll have the barrel in my coat pocket. Nobody will care," she replied, hoping her warning shot had given Bryn enough time to get here.

Irv stared at Bethan for a few seconds as he tried to modify his original plan for subduing her after they got into the barn. At least she was acting the part and maybe she really would take seven hundred dollars and let them go.

———

Sheriff Schuler was at the other end of town when Bethan fired, then turned and raced back to his office, believing that the outlaws had run afoul of a nosy citizen. It had happened before.

He blasted into the jail leaving the door open and shouted, "Bryn! We got problems!"

Bryn was groggy as he lifted his head then slowly sat on the bunk.

"What?" he yelled back as he stood and stretched his aching muscles.

Joe trotted to the back room and said, "I heard a gunshot from down the street, but it was muffled, so it had to be from inside a building."

Bryn was instantly awake as he grabbed his hat but left his coat on the bed.

"Let's go!"

They stopped in the front office where each of them grabbed a Winchester from the rack, then headed for the open doorway.

———

Irv stared at the hole in the door as he opened it and wished that he wasn't wearing a coat. It gave that girl a big advantage. He and Tom then stepped out onto the boardwalk followed by a Bethan. Bounty hunter or not, it was just damned embarrassing to be caught by a girl.

Bethan walked behind them and even though one of them might suddenly make a move, she glanced to her right toward the jail, hoping to see either Bryn or the sheriff, but all she spotted was normal street traffic. At least normal in that none of them had guns drawn. There were a few sets of eyes looking at the hotel, but no one was approaching them. She thought it was strange but as her eyes began to shift back to the two outlaws, she glimpsed the sheriff and Bryn as they bolted from the jail. She didn't keep her eyes focused down the street but turned her attention back to the two men. She figured that the two lawmen would find her soon enough.

———

"That's Bethan!" Bryn said loudly as he stared down the main street, "And she's got the two of them in front of her!"

73

"What's she doing?" asked Joe as they trotted along the boardwalk.

"What we should be doing."

———

Irv and Tom crossed the road diagonally with Bethan walking eight feet behind them. Tom was just as nervous as he'd been when they were riding because it was his nature. They were halfway across the street when he looked to his right and saw the sheriff and Bryn on the boardwalk with Winchesters.

"It's the law!" he shouted as he threw open his coat and reached for his pistol.

Irv whipped his head to the right and spotted the two lawmen with their repeaters just as they stopped and were bringing their Winchesters level. He instantly mimicked Tom's action and threw back his coat to get to his Colt. Neither of them even gave a thought to Bethan.

Bethan knew that a gunfight was imminent, but had already expected it, so as soon as Tom had shouted and made his move, she slid her revolver from her pocket. As Irv was preparing to pull his pistol, she aimed and fired.

The .44 spiraled down the six and a half inches of barrel and crossed the eighty-seven inches of space before ripping through Tom's right bootheel, ricocheting off the hard

Colorado dirt, then lifting his boot from the ground as it punched through his leather sole. He screamed and collapsed to the ground, grabbing for his mangled foot.

Irv heard the nearby pistol report, suddenly remembering that Bethan was there, and even as his partner screamed, forgot about his pistol and threw his hands into the air. Clyde was the one who'd killed that deputy marshal, not him. All they had on him was counterfeiting.

Bryn and Sheriff Schuler trotted up to the two men and Bryn let the sheriff use his handcuffs on Irv Thompson while he pulled the pistol from Irv's holster before picking up Tom Lilly's pistol from the ground near his head.

Bethan then slid her pistol home and waited as Bryn wrestled Tom to his good foot.

"Come with us, Bethan," Bryn said once Tom was upright.

"I have to go and get my hat first. Are you taking him to the doctor?"

Bryn looked at Sheriff Schuler who said, "Let's take them both to the jail. I'll send someone to get the doc."

The sheriff then looked at the crowd and said, "Ed, go and tell Doc Waters to come to my office."

"Yes, sir!" Ed exclaimed and trotted away.

Bryn then turned to Bethan and said, "Meet us there after you get your hat."

"Yes, sir," she replied, then turned to go back to the hotel.

She wasn't sure how Bryn would react to what she had done, but it really didn't matter to her. She'd accomplished what she had hoped to do when she'd left the Double EE. She'd been uncertain of how she would deal with the danger of facing hard men but hadn't really expected to have to do it on her own. She thought that she'd be watching Bryn and Bert as they made an arrest and maybe talking them into letting her help. This was a much bigger test that she had successfully passed.

What it meant for her future was still debatable. She knew that they'd never let her wear a badge, but when she'd told Bryn that she'd become a bounty hunter, she wasn't joking. It was also what had inspired her to use the ploy when dealing with the two outlaws.

She entered the hotel under the staring eyes of about a dozen residents, then strode across the lobby and snatched her Stetson from the chair and pulled it on.

———

As they escorted Irv and Tom along the boardwalk, Joe Schuler said, "Did she miss that bad, Bryn?"

"No. She never misses. It was the perfect place to put that bullet, Joe. It did as little damage as possible but had enough of an impact to keep more bullets from flying around."

"What do we do with this pair now?" he asked as they reached the jail and he pulled Irv through the door.

Bryn didn't reply until he'd helped a limping Tom Lilly inside, but then answered, "I'll take them back to Denver where they'll be tried for the murder of a Federal officer and attempted murder of another."

Irv whipped his head around and exclaimed, "I didn't murder anyone! That was Clyde who shot that deputy!"

Bryn didn't say anything until the sheriff had Irv in the cell and then he'd set a bleeding Tom Lilly on the bunk.

Once the cell door was slammed shut, Bryn stared at Irv and said, "You really should study the law. You were there and I watched you take a few shots, so you'll hang just like your wounded pal there."

"That's crazy!" Tom shouted, then asked, "How'd you find us so quick? You should have been at least a whole day behind us."

Bryn smiled and replied, "That's a mystery. Isn't it? Let's just say we didn't bother going to visit your workplace after stopping by the sheriff's office."

Tom snapped, "That bastard Lynch! He got religion!"

Bryn glanced at Sheriff Schuler, then he and the sheriff walked to the desk where the sheriff took a seat and Bryn sat in one of the two straight-backed chairs.

After they sat, the sheriff opened his right-hand drawer and pulled out a stack of wanted posters.

"What was his name?"

"Irv Thompson, but I think that might be an alias. The other one is Tom Lilly, and I'm not sure that it's the one he was born with either."

The sheriff grunted, then began flipping through the wanted posters and quickly found the four counterfeiters. After setting them aside, he continued more slowly, looking for wanted men that met the general descriptions of the two in his cell.

As he scanned them, the doctor entered the jail and asked, "What do you have, Joe?"

Joe Schuler looked up, then replied, "One of the boys in the cell took a bullet in the foot. It doesn't look too bad."

Bryn rose and escorted the doctor to the cell, then took down the ring of keys, opened the door and followed him inside.

The doctor set down his black bag, opened the jaws and removed a pair of heavy scissors.

Tom Lilly's eyes went wide, believing that he was preparing to cut off his foot, but felt almost as bad when the doctor began to cut into the boot's leather.

Once the boot was mostly split, he quickly yanked the footwear free and Tom screamed in pain, but no one, not even Irv, felt any sympathy.

Bethan entered the jail as the doctor was examining the wound and the sheriff looked up from his wanted poster review.

"You did a mighty good job, young lady," he said.

"Thank you, Sheriff. I was just surprised to see them walking past me and I suppose I should have just let them go, but I was worried that they might spot you or my uncle and try and shoot you in the back."

"Well, I'm glad you stopped them."

Bethan's eyes shifted to her uncle, wondering if he believed her excuse for acting alone, and was certain that he hadn't.

Bryn had listened to her and knew that her story was for the sheriff's benefit but would be spending enough time with her on the train ride back to Denver to get the full story. He also knew that his own report would be much more difficult when he returned to the office. Bert's death only added to the sorry results for what had started out as such a routine mission.

Bethan remained standing as she said, "Sheriff, I did make a hole in the hotel's door. I'll pay for the damage, but it was the only way I could let you know what was happening."

"Don't worry about it. Either the county can pay for it or they'll handle it and brag about it."

She nodded as the doctor finished his examination.

"He's pretty lucky. That bullet just exploded his bootheel, then when it ricocheted, it hit his third metatarsal and it broke before the bullet lost its energy. I'll stitch up the gash on the bottom of his foot and he'll be done."

Bryn nodded as the doctor removed his suture kit from his black bag.

Tom Lilly whined as the doctor began to sew his wound closed, and Bryn stared at Irv, trying to match him to one of the other wanted posters. He was almost certain that he'd seen that face somewhere before but only as a sketch. It had been their actions on the pass that had given him the notion that he wasn't just a counterfeiter. They rarely resorted to gunfights because it wasn't in their nature and they usually weren't very proficient.

He was still trying to match the face when Sheriff Schuler said, "Maybe he's Roddy Plunkett. He matches the description, but he's not wearing a beard in this picture. His known associates included another one who looks kind of like that bootless whiner in the cell. This guy's name was Jimmy Rose."

Bryn nodded as he said, "I think you've found their little secret, Joe. Now that you mention the beard, I can see it."

"Those two boys were wanted in Kansas for murder and robbery. I guess they found it was easier to just print your own money."

"I remember that case. The local law and some angry citizens down in Abilene weren't happy with Mister Plunkett's band and took out three of them before losing the other two. That was a couple of years ago."

"Well, they're going to hang now for what they did to your partner. I guess Kansas won't be needing them back."

Irv or Roddy didn't react at all to what they said after hearing the deputy marshal say that they were going back to Denver to be tried for murdering a Federal officer. It really didn't matter what name they carved in his grave's marker.

Tom or Jimmy was concentrating on the pain from his foot as the doctor stuck his needle and thread into the sole to repair the hole put there by that girl who was standing in the office just watching.

Sheriff Schuler left the six wanted posters on his desk and dropped the rest of the stack back into the drawer before standing and walking around the desk.

"You can sit down, Miss Evans."

"Do you need me to write a statement or anything?" she asked before sitting down.

"Nope. I reckon your uncle will handle it from here. All they did in my jurisdiction was to show up."

She nodded and then just silently waited for Bryn.

―――――

Twenty minutes later, Bryn and Bethan were having lunch at the diner. Neither had spoken since leaving the jail.

"What do we do now?" Bethan finally asked as she cut into her overcooked steak.

"We'll get our horses and pick up their animals and gear from the livery, then drop them off at the station after I get our tickets. We'll come back to the jail and escort our prisoners to the train station thirty minutes before the train leaves and then spend the next four hours on the train to Denver."

She swallowed her dry cut of meat, then asked, "Are you going to send your telegram first?"

"The telegraph office is next to the train depot, so I'll do that after we get our tickets."

"What will you say?"

"I'll let your father know that Bert was killed and that you're with me and safe. I won't go into details. We'll explain the rest after we arrive."

"Do you think that he and mom will be mad?"

"I'd be surprised if they weren't. You didn't even leave a note, did you?"

"No. I couldn't because if I did, then dad would tell you that I had gone ahead and ask to have you send me back. I'll suffer the consequences for what I did, but I'm not ashamed for doing it, either."

Bryn set his fork down, looked at his niece and said, "I really do understand, Bethan. When I was just about your age and arrived in Omaha with your grandmother, I had no idea what I would do with my life, only that I wanted to make a difference. I was lucky that I was able to find my way, almost as if God had illuminated a path for me. You'll find your own way, Bethan, but I'll tell you one thing; you've already proven yourself to be a very special person."

"Thank you, Bryn. I just wish I wasn't so limited in my choices."

Bryn smiled as he replied, "We're all limited in one fashion or another. Some of us are too slow to learn or too fast to react. Even men like your father, me or your Uncle Kyle have limitations."

"Like what?"

"We can't have babies, Bethan. I know that sounds almost silly to you, but it's a genuine miracle that men never get to experience. I watched Erin after she had each of our five children, and every time, she had the same look of unrestricted joy on her face as she held her newborn child. It's a look that I know that I can never wear or a joy that I can ever experience. The best I can do is to share it with her."

"I may never have a baby, Bryn. I just don't know."

"That'll be one of your choices, Bethan. It's up to you."

Bethan nodded as she cut another piece of steak, unsure of whether it was worth eating.

———

The sun was setting as the evening train pulled out of Granite. Bryn and Bethan each sat on a bench and their prisoners were handcuffed to the seats in front of them.

Bryn had sent his telegram an hour earlier and expected to have a large reception committee at the large depot in Denver when they arrived. Bert's body was in its shipping coffin in one of the train's boxcars and he knew that Dylan would arrange for Smithton's Funeral Home to pick it up when they arrived. Despite what Bethan had told him, he wasn't sure how Martha would react to Bert's death. He wouldn't be all that surprised if she tried to shoot him when he stepped off the train.

———

Dylan and Lynn had been the last ones in the office and were preparing to leave for the Double EE when Bryn's telegram arrived.

The messenger was still standing before him as Dylan anxiously unfolded the sheet, hoping that it was from Bryn and had information about Bethan. Gwen had been on knife's edge since they'd discovered that Bethan had gone, and Addie had suggested that she was with Bryn and Bert.

Lynn tipped the messenger as Dylan read:

US MARSHAL DYLAN EVANS DENVER COLO

COUNTEFEITERS RAN AND WE TRAILED
GUNFIGHT IN MOUNTAIN PASS
BERT KILLED
BRINGING BODY AND TWO PRISONERS
LEAVING ON NIGHT TRAIN
UNHARMED BETHAN WITH ME

BRYN EVANS GRANITE COLO

Dylan handed the telegram to Lynn who quickly scanned its contents.

"We need to get moving, Lynn," he said, "That train will be here in four hours."

"Yes, sir. What do you want me to do?"

"I'll ride back to the Double EE to tell the family, and I'll let Addie know that you'll be late, so she won't worry. I'll tell Kyle when I get back to town. I want you to tell Benji what happened and have him tell Martha. Then go to Smithton's and have Jerry arrange to pick up Bert's body at the station. When you're done with that, roust Pete Towers and have him come with you to the station to meet the train. We'll have two prisoners to bring to the county jail."

"Okay, boss," Lynn said as he handed the telegram back to his father, then turned, took his hat from the peg, pulled it on and grabbed his coat before leaving the office.

Dylan looked at the sheet in his hand, let out a breath, then slid it into his pocket before walking back to his office to get his hat and coat. He was glad that Bethan was safe but wasn't sure how Martha or Benji would react to Bert's death. He'd have to send someone out to the A-G Connected to tell Alwen and Garth and wondered what Al would do when he realized that Martha was now a widow.

———

Bryn and Bethan hadn't spoken much for the first twenty minutes of their train's circuitous journey to Denver in the dark of night because their attention had been focused on their two prisoners. But after their charges had both fallen asleep, Bryn stepped over to Bethan's bench seat and sat down beside her.

Bethan looked at her uncle as he asked, "What will you do when you return to the ranch, Bethan?"

"A lot will depend on how my parents react. I don't have any real plans anyway, but I hope they don't treat me like a child. I'll be eighteen in another month and I'll be free to do what I choose, but I'd rather do it with their blessing."

"I suspect that after their initial angry reaction for leaving without telling them, pretty much the way your older brother did when he went off with Ryan a couple of years ago, they'll listen. I know my brother better than anyone and I'm pretty sure that he'll give you more freedom than you might expect. It's your mother that you'll have to convince."

Bethan nodded, then said, "I'll convince her. She's not very different from my father, you know. She may be small and cute, but she's every bit as strong as my marshal father."

"That she is. It seems that each of us Evans men have found strong, confident wives that keep us under control without being overbearing or smug about it. It's a gift, I guess, and one of the reasons that we love them so much."

"I don't think Cari is that way, though. She's fourteen now and I think she's more of a lady than I am. Your Grace is more like me, Bryn, so you'd better watch out for her when she reaches her teenage years."

Bryn laughed, then said, "Don't remind me. She's already a handful and she's just ten. Mason's on the cusp of the dreaded teenager life and is beginning to be harder to understand."

"Are you disappointed that you only have one daughter?"

"Not at all. We're just extremely pleased that all of our children are still healthy and growing. When Kyle and Katie lost little John last year, it really drove home just how fortunate all of us have been. Do you know how unusual it is for a family as large as ours to have all the mothers survive childbirth with their children? Not only that, until we lost John, none of the children have been lost to disease or accident. That just doesn't happen, Bethan."

"Dad and mom have talked about it, too. Maybe it's being saved for some big disaster."

"I doubt it," Bryn replied, then asked, "Is that one of the reasons that you've decided to go a different direction with your life?"

"What do you mean?"

"Are you worried that having a baby might cost you your life?"

Bethan shook her head and answered, "No, I'm not worried about it at all. My only real reason is the frustration of not being given many choices of what to do with my life. I can get married and be a housewife or become a schoolmarm or a nurse. Even those jobs require that the woman doesn't marry. Then there's always the world's oldest profession where you don't get married but get bedded three or four times a day."

Bryn glanced at Bethan and noticed she was smiling as she expected him to react in shock, but nothing she ever said would surprise him.

"You can't have it all, Bethan."

"Maybe not, but I can try to get as much as I can."

———

"Thank God that she's all right!" Gwen exclaimed as she handed the telegram back to her husband.

"You know how good she is, Gwen. She was better prepared than Lynn was when we let him go to Fort Benton, and she had Bryn and Bert with her, too."

"She was alone all that time before she caught up with them and Bert is dead."

"You didn't object to letting Lynn go when he was younger, and it was much further away."

"That's different," she snapped, "he's our son and we expected him to leave eventually."

Dylan smiled, kissed his small wife on the forehead, then said, "We'll discuss this later, Mrs. Evans. We've got to get to the train station. While you get changed, I'll ride over to tell Erin, then you can send Cari to let Addie know that Lynn will be late. I'll saddle Duchess when I get back from telling Erin."

"Okay. Cari probably already heard you. Just because we told her that we needed to talk privately doesn't mean that she took it to heart."

Dylan kissed her again, then turned and left the house as Gwen walked down the hallway to tell Cari in case she hadn't been spying on them.

———

Lynn had stopped at the mortuary first, swung by and told Kyle and Katie the news and then notified his fellow deputy, Pete Towers, that he was needed. He had avoided stopping by the Green residence because Martha may be with her parents while Bert was gone, but he knew he had to be the one to break the tragic news. They hadn't lost a deputy marshal in the Denver office in five years, and this was supposed to be a routine job. He'd even offered to go with Bryn, but his father/boss didn't usually let them go on jobs together in case they both were lost in a gunfight. It was one of the few times that Gwen had made a request about how he did his job.

He stepped onto the porch of their house just two blocks from their office, knocked on the door, then stood with a stoic face as he waited for it to open.

Thirty seconds later, the door swung wide and Benji quickly asked, "What's wrong, Lynn?"

"Is Martha here?"

Lynn's question and his somber demeanor answered Benji's question before he replied, "Yes. She's with Alice in the parlor," then stepped onto the porch and closed the door.

"What happened?"

"We got a telegram from Bryn about an hour ago. Bert's dead, Benji. I don't have the details yet, but he's arriving on the train in three hours with his body. He has two prisoners, too."

Benji exhaled sharply, then said, "Okay. Let's go inside and tell Martha, then we'll go and meet the train."

Lynn really wished that he didn't have to go through that door but removed his hat and followed Benji inside and soon stepped into the parlor.

Alice Green was holding her baby granddaughter as she talked to her pregnant daughter-in-law when they entered.

Martha smiled at him and said, "Hello, Lynn."

"Hello, Martha," Lynn replied, then glanced at Benji, expecting him to deliver the news, but Benji apparently was waiting for him to be the bad guy.

Lynn looked back at Martha's smiling face and said, "I have bad news, Martha. We just received a telegram from Bryn. Bert was killed in a shootout with those counterfeiters. Bryn's bringing his body back on tonight's train. I'm sorry."

Martha's smiling face was instantly replaced with a tight-lipped, angry visage as she stared back at him and Lynn braced for the attack.

"That bastard!" she exclaimed in a low, harsh voice as she glared at Lynn.

Lynn quickly said, "I'm sorry, Martha. I really am. I'm sure that it wasn't Bryn's fault."

Martha then turned her eyes to her father-in-law and sharply asked, "I told him to find another job; but did he listen to me? No, of course not! He had to wear that badge so he could be important. Who's going to take care of me now? I told him to quit, but he's dead now, and I'm pregnant!"

Lynn was startled. Bert had never said a word about quitting and he doubted if Dylan knew about it, either. He shifted his eyes to Alice and immediately realized that she knew.

Benji stepped close to his daughter, placed his hand gently on her shoulder and said, "We'll take care of you until things are better, Martha."

Martha looked up at her father, then dropped her eyes, covered her face with her hands and began to sob.

Benji looked at his wife, who nodded before she said, "You go with Lynn. I'll stay with Martha."

"Thank you, dear," Benji said.

He motioned to Lynn, then the two deputy marshals left the parlor. They stopped in the foyer where Benji pulled his coat from the brass hook and after slipping it on, grabbed his hat and gunbelt, then he and Lynn left the house.

Once they were back on the porch, Lynn asked, "Why didn't Bert tell anyone in the office that Martha wanted him to quit?"

They stepped down from the porch and were walking on the sidewalk before Benji replied, "It was a family thing. She started asking him to quit when she was about six months pregnant with Anna, but Bert wasn't about to give in. It kept building even after she gave birth. I guess Bert put her demands to her emotional state created by her pregnancy and figured she'd forget about it when she had to care for their new baby. After she had Anna, things were quieter for a while, then it all exploded when she discovered she was pregnant again."

"What do you think was going to happen?"

"I have no idea. Alice thought that she was going to give Bert an ultimatum, but I'm not sure that Bert would have quit even then. As horrible as this may sound, in a way, this might be the best solution. I don't know what she'll do now."

"She's still a pretty young woman, Benji. I'm sure that she'll find another husband soon."

"It'll be hard to find one as good as Bert. You know who she probably will want to call on her now, don't you?"

"I know, but I don't think Al will make the offer. He'll probably just stop by and offer his condolences then he and Garth will return to their ranch and their horses."

"Alice tells me that just a few months after she married Bert, she already regretted spurning Alwen; especially after he

92

decided to become a rancher and not a lawman. But I don't think she's expecting Al. I'm guessing that she'll be seeing Pete."

Lynn looked at Benji and asked, "Pete? How did I miss that?"

"I reckon that was just another wedge that was pushing her and Bert apart. If it amounts to anything, we might lose Pete, too."

"Well, I guess we'll just have to see how that works out, but I'm glad that I don't have to live in your house."

"I wish that I didn't either," Benji said as they continued toward the train station along the shadowed street.

———

Dylan, Gwen and Erin trotted their horses along the road to Denver after leaving the Double EE. Erin was nervous as Bryn hadn't mentioned anything about his own condition in the telegram. She had been surprised that Bethan was with him but suspected that she had somehow arrived at the site of the gunfight and helped her husband. She just wished that Bryn had added a single word to that telegram to let her know that he was also unhurt. She would remind him of his error when she met him on the platform; after she embraced and kissed him, of course.

Gwen was still in a disjointed mood about Bethan's unannounced departure that had put her into a state of perpetual worry for three days. She was angry, yet still proud of her older daughter. She decided to delay any chastising until she and Dylan were alone with her back on the ranch.

Dylan wasn't conflicted at all. When Addie had suggested that Bethan had gone to Canon City to follow Bryn and Bert, he hadn't been surprised at all. She'd told him more than a few times that she was frustrated in her inability to wear the badge, and the more she learned, the greater was her frustration. She'd asked him if she could accompany him or Bryn on a mission, but he'd always denied her the opportunity.

It wasn't as if she was rebelling against her parents, because that wasn't in her nature. She was trying to prove to him, and maybe to herself, that she was just as good as any man. Dylan knew that she was, and now she'd shown it. He didn't doubt that somehow, Bethan had played a significant part in what had happened in southern Colorado and he really wanted to get the details. What she did after that was the real question.

———

By the time the train rolled into the Denver station, the two shackled prisoners were awake, and Tom Lilly/Jimmy Rose was grousing about his damaged foot.

Bethan ignored them as she looked out the window at the depot and tried to spot their welcoming committee on the platform as it slid into view. There wasn't much light on the open area, but she soon spotted Lynn standing beside her father. She didn't doubt that her mother was on her father's other side but was hidden behind Benji Green and Pete Towers.

She turned to her uncle and said, "Are you going to take the prisoners, Bryn?"

"I think that would be a wise thing to do, Bethan. You go first and Pete will help me with these two."

"Okay."

———

Gwen wished she was taller as she peeked between Benji and Pete Towers to get a look at the lone passenger car's front platform.

She soon had a clearer view when Pete walked to the slowing car to help with the two outlaws and soon spotted Bethan as she stepped down but stayed where she was to let her husband do his job as the United States Marshal.

Bethan finally spotted her mother, quickly read her mood, then switched her eyes to her father who was already walking towards her.

When they met, he simply asked, "How are you, Bethan?"

"I'm fine, Dad. I'm sorry about Bert."

"You and Bryn can tell us about it when we get back to the ranch. Let's get those prisoners to their new home in the county jail."

Bethan smiled, then replied, "Okay, Marshal."

She then stepped to her mother, wrapped her arms around her and then kissed her on the forehead.

Gwen looked into her daughter's eyes as she said, "It's good to have you home safely, Bethan."

"I'm glad to be home, Mom, but I'm not ashamed for having gone."

Gwen sighed, then replied, "I know. We'll talk when we get back to the ranch."

Bethan released her mother, then turned to see Pete and Bryn escorting the two prisoners across the big platform.

Bryn then handed Irv Thompson/Roddy Plunkett over to Lynn and stepped over to Dylan, prepared to explain what had happened.

Dylan held up his palm and said, "Hold off on your report, Bryn. Let's get Bert's body to the mortuary and then we need to take care of the evidence. I'm assuming that you have their horses with you."

"Two horses and a pack mule. I checked the mule's panniers and there was a lot of phony and real cash inside and I found their printing plates as well."

"Okay. Let's get the valuable stuff into our safe and their critters in our corral. Then we'll head back to the Double EE where we'll talk."

He slipped some folded sheets of paper from his jacket pocket and said, "Alright, but I did write my report on the train. Do you want me to give it to Benji?"

"There's no need. He's coming with us to the ranch to listen to what happened before he returns to the house to tell Martha."

Bryn nodded, then slipped the report back into his pocket, then turned to embrace and kiss Erin.

"Are you all right?" she asked after kissing him.

"Just bruised, battered and tired."

"I won't press you for any details, mister. That will come later."

"Yes, ma'am," Bryn replied with a smile.

Erin then hooked her arm through his before they walked across the platform to the stock corral to get the horses.

Bethan and her parents walked behind them so she could retrieve Nippy. She still wasn't sure how her mother would react when they reached the ranch house or even if she'd still be allowed to live by herself any longer. She'd grown accustomed to having the small house mostly to herself after Al and Garth had moved out to start their horse ranch and would hate to return to the big house with the rest of the family.

Cari came to visit fairly often, and she spent a lot of time with Addie during the day, but still cherished her privacy and independence. She hoped that she wouldn't lose her privileged housing situation.

———

Forty minutes later, the group of riders rode out of Denver then turned south.

Bethan rode between her parents and almost felt like a prisoner but knew that they were probably just being protective more than restrictive.

No one spoke during the thirty-minute ride which seemed almost eerie as the only sounds were the steady hoofbeats and the occasional coyote howl.

As she rode, Bethan continued to formulate her arguments that she'd started to build before she had even boarded the train, and almost all of them were for her mother.

Bryn rode behind them with Erin on one side and Benji on the other. He was finding it difficult to stay awake as the rhythmic sounds and rocking motion lured him toward dreamland. He hadn't gotten a good read from Benji or Lynn about how Martha had taken the news and wondered if Bethan was right in her evaluation of Bert and Martha's marriage. He'd find out soon.

Lynn brought up the back of the group, still thinking about Martha's reaction. It had been such a shock to hear her almost blame Bert for his own death. The following conversation with her father about her demand that Bert quit was almost as surprising, as was his stunning revelation about Pete Towers. Now he just wondered what Al would do about it. At least he understood his brother's attitude better than he could fathom Martha's. He doubted if Al would want to marry her because he was content out at the A-G Connected, but there was always the possibility that his old flame would be rekindled. Only time would tell.

———

By the time the family assembled in the big parlor in Dylan and Gwen's house, even Addie had arrived with her two-year-old twins and infant son.

They had to move some kitchen chairs into the large room, even though the youngsters were all in bed.

Bryn was the only one still standing as he finally narrated the events of the past three days.

"The simple part was the ride down to Canon City on the train, then when we arrived, Bert and I went straight to where they were supposed to have their printing operation. When we arrived, we found the place mostly empty. I found out from one of the two prisoners that they'd been alerted by Fremont

County Deputy Sheriff George Lynch. We picked up their trail easily and I estimated they were just a few hours ahead of us.

"We were surprised that they took the mountain trail rather than the flatlands, but I guessed that they wanted to avoid being tracked. It was nearing sunset when we reached the top of the pass…"

Bryn stopped when he reached the point where he lost consciousness and looked at Bethan.

Without further prompting, Bethan picked up the narration, saying, "I had taken the earlier train to Canon City and knew that Uncle Bryn and Bert would be arriving the next day. When they didn't show up at the sheriff's office two hours after the train arrived, I guessed that they had gone straight to the counterfeiter's location. I picked up their trail and continued to follow them up the mountain. I had already set up camp and fallen asleep when I was awakened by gunfire. I had to saddle Nippy and make the dark ride up the trail, then spotted their horses off to the side, dismounted and pulled my pistol. Then I found Bert's body and the other two but couldn't find Uncle Bryn. I finally spotted him down the slope and had to use a rope to help him out."

She then let Bryn take over again, knowing that she'd have to explain what happened in the hotel.

The report continued for another twenty minutes, then as soon as Bryn finished, Benji left to return to Denver.

After some rudimentary lawman questions, Dylan said, "It's getting late. We'll talk more in the morning after we all get some sleep."

Most of the family was grateful for his decision, but Bethan expected that she would need to stay, so she just watched as the others began to leave.

After Cari stood, smiled at Bethan, then left to go upstairs to her bedroom, leaving her alone with her parents, Dylan took a seat on the couch next to Gwen.

He tilted his head slightly and asked, "Aren't you leaving, Bethan?"

"I don't think I'll be able to sleep until we've talked."

"I think that's a good idea," Gwen replied, "and you can start by giving me a good reason for sneaking off like that without giving me a hint of what you were doing."

"I do apologize for that, Mom, but it would you have let me go if I had asked?"

"No, I wouldn't, and you can understand why. You shouldn't be riding across this wild country unescorted."

"Mom, you and dad let Lynn go all the way to Fort Benton on his own and he was younger than I am. And that was after he'd run off with Ryan without telling you. He was even living in the same house where I live now."

"That was different," Gwen replied, knowing that it was eerily similar.

"No, it wasn't. The only difference is that I'm a female and Lynn is male. You know that I'm better than he is in almost everything, too. And that's now when he's a deputy marshal. When he left to go to Fort Benton, he wasn't even close. I can understand why you're upset because I didn't tell you, but not why I was out there on my own."

"You're not your father, uncles or brother, Bethan. You're my daughter."

"No, Mom, I'm not dad, but I am his daughter and I've learned a lot from him. I am also your daughter, and I'm not much different than you were when you were young. Ever since I can recall, I've heard the stories about you and dad. I was thrilled when I listened how you left a place of safety even though you were unarmed to help dad when you thought that he was about to be killed. I can even remember that the Crow called you Ia Aaptaatbishe because of your courage.

"I won't pretend to be a proper young lady like Cari, but please accept me for who I am. I know that I'm still young and prone to make mistakes, but I need to learn and do it on my own. You know how frustrating it has been for me to learn so much, then to honestly appraise my skill level and know that I'm better than most men who wear a badge."

Dylan glanced at Gwen, knowing this conversation was strictly between her and Bethan. He had made up his mind as soon as he'd received the telegram from Bryn.

Gwen sighed, then said, "I know it's been difficult for you, Bethan. Believe it or not, I felt the same way when I was put on the *Providence* wearing pigtails that I hated. I was being forced into a life that I didn't want, and I hated the world. Then I met your father and I was actually more frustrated because it wasn't long before I understood what I would be missing after we arrived at Fort Benton."

"I understand that, Mom. I don't know what is waiting for me, but I have to find it my way. I need to be myself."

Gwen then turned to look at her husband and asked, "What do you think, Dylan?"

He smiled at her, then turned his eyes back to their daughter and said, "Bethan, on the 25th of May, you'll turn eighteen and legally, you will be an adult and free to make your own decisions. We have a lot of things that need to be cleaned up from the last few days. There will be a trial for the two men that you captured, and you'll have to be here for that."

Bethan quickly asked, "Is Uncle Kyle going to prosecute?"

"No. This will be held in the Federal court. He'll help with your preparations. Bryn will be a witness, too. Because you were the one to capture them, you're entitled to the reward, too, but I don't know how much it is right now. You'll also get their two horses, mule and all their tack. That'll take a week or so, which will push us into May."

"I don't care about the reward. Can't you just give it to Martha? What will happen to their money?"

"We'll turn it over to the Secret Service. We were just helping them with the case because they were so understaffed. Don't worry about the reward yet. We'll have time to talk about it."

"Alright. What do I do after the trial?"

Dylan smiled, then replied, "What I am going to do, Miss Evans, is to deputize you as a temporary United States Deputy Marshal."

Bethan's mouth dropped and her eyebrows shot upward to compensate before they both returned to their normal positions and she said, "Can you do that? I mean, I thought I couldn't be a lawman...or lawwoman."

"You can't. If I tried to deputize you and sent the paperwork to the head office, they'd have my head instead. I can deputize temporary, unpaid deputy marshals as I see fit without them being any the wiser because you won't be paid."

"Then why do it?"

"To make whatever you do legal and to give you some measure of authority. Bethan, you may be a strong young lady, but you're still a very handsome filly. When you pulled your pistol on those two men in the hotel lobby, did you see fear in their eyes?"

"No. They almost laughed at me."

"What do you think their reaction would be if I was the one holding your pistol?"

"I understand, Dad, but I've always expected it, which is why I shot through the door. It served two purposes. It let them know that I was serious and to let the sheriff and Uncle Bryn know where they were."

"Then you understand the reason for the badge, although I'll admit that being a pretty young woman does give you a big advantage in certain situations. If I had been in that lobby and they spotted me, then they'd already be suspicious, no matter how innocent I try to appear. You, on the other hand, they dismissed at first glance."

"Then I'll keep the badge with me?"

"Yes, ma'am. By the way, Bryn and I are both extraordinarily proud of the way you handled yourself in Granite. Shooting at the man's heel was brilliant. It must have been something to see when his foot exploded off the ground."

Bethan grinned, then replied, "It was pretty impressive."

Gwen then said, "If you two are finished telling war stories, I'd like to get to bed. What are we going to do tomorrow?"

"Bethan will ride into Denver with me and Bryn to do the paperwork and find out when the trial will be held. Then, after the trial, Bryn and Bethan will be returning to Canon City."

"Why?" Bethan asked.

"Bryn needs to arrest a deputy sheriff and I'll want you to go along to see how he does it."

"The one who put him and Bert into that mess by warning the counterfeiters?"

"Yes, ma'am."

"Don't you think that he might run once he learns that two of them are in jail up here?"

Dylan blinked then turned to Gwen, shook his head, then replied, "I'll send Pete Towers to Canon City tomorrow."

Bethan yawned, then stood and stepped over to the couch, bent over and kissed her mother on the forehead and kissed her father on the cheek.

"I'll see everyone in the morning."

"Goodnight, Bethan," Gwen said.

"Goodnight, Deputy Marshal Evans," Dylan said with a smile.

Bethan smiled at her parents before pulling on her coat, then yanking her Stetson onto her head and leaving the house.

After she'd gone, Gwen looked at Dylan and asked, "Do you think that giving her a badge is a smart thing?"

"She had mentioned that she'd become a bounty hunter, so deputizing her is the safest thing to do."

"Is she ever going to settle down?"

"It depends on what you mean by 'settle down'. She's been settled in her own mind since she was just a little girl and would ride Peanut around in the barn back in Omaha."

Gwen smiled, then said, "I can still remember how shocked we were when she didn't fall a single time. Even when she began riding horses, she's never fallen. Bethan really is special. Isn't she?"

"She takes after her mother," Dylan said before he stood, took her small hand and walked with her to their bedroom, blowing out lamps as they made their way.

———

A few hundred yards away, Erin was already in her nightdress sitting on their bed as Bryn stood facing away from her without a stitch of clothing as she examined his bruises.

Her gentle fingers slid across the mass of black and blue patches on his back that spread down his legs.

"What would have happened if Bethan hadn't followed you and Bert?" she asked softly.

"At the least, I suspect that those two would have made their escape. After that, I'm not sure."

"Would you have been able to get back to the trail with these injuries?"

"Eventually, but probably not until daylight."

"Then you would have dropped Bert's body off in Granite and still chased after them, wouldn't you?"

Bryn let out his breath, then turned and replied, "Probably, but it didn't come to that. I just hope that Bethan isn't getting an earful for what she did. After watching how she handled herself, I'd trust her more than most of the other deputies in that office."

"I don't think she'll be in facing any serious trouble from Dylan or Gwen. I just wonder what she'll do now."

Bryn smiled at Erin, then said, "If I wasn't so sore, I know what I'd like to do now."

Erin laughed before she replied, "Just get your nightshirt on and let's get to bed. You'll probably fall asleep in two minutes anyway."

————

Martha sat across from Benji after he'd explained what had happened to Bert and felt an odd combination of grief, shame and relief. She wasn't sure if Bryn had made a bad decision to chase after them in the dark but was ashamed of herself for not behaving like the grieving widow. She had almost been expecting this day since she'd married Bert and he'd refused her recurring demands that he'd find another line of work. Now that it had arrived, she felt empty; almost as if her grief had already been spent.

But now she had a baby to care for and another on the way. She knew that she could stay with her family again, but she'd become accustomed to having her own home and now she was back to the life of a daughter and not a wife.

"What should I do, Papa?" she asked quietly.

"I'll have Sam and Ben move your things into your old bedroom tomorrow, or would you rather stay in your house?"

"The rent is due at the end of the month anyway, so it's probably better if I move back here."

"Okay. After the burial, we'll sit down and talk about what to do in the long term. I'm really sorry, Martha. It's a hard life sometimes."

Martha just nodded before she looked at her mother and said, "Mama, can you watch Anna for me until I feel better?"

"Of course, I can. You know how much I love my granddaughter."

"Thank you, Mama. I'm going to go to bed now. I'm tired."

"Goodnight, Martha," Alice said as she watched her sad daughter stand, then slowly leave the room.

After she'd gone, she shifted little Anna to her shoulder, then said, "It's going to be hard for her to find a new husband, so I'll do all I can to take care of Anna."

"It's too soon to worry about that, Alice," Benji said.

Alice rose, then replied, "It's never too early. She's not showing yet, but in a few months, she'll have a much more difficult time."

Benji stood, blew out the first lamp, then walked with Alice to their bedroom, hoping that Martha would be all right. He did wonder why Alice hadn't mentioned the likelihood that Pete Towers would be visiting after an appropriate grieving period.

———

Bethan reached her small, dark house and didn't bother lighting a lamp. She left her coat and hat on the hook near the front door, then walked to her bedroom. After changing into her nightdress, she slipped beneath the cold blankets and quilts, feeling her legs erupt in goosepimples at the chill.

She then pulled the covers to her chin and closed her eyes. She was very tired, but still amazed by her father's offer. Even though it wasn't a real deputy position, it was much more than she could ever have hoped.

Her performance from the time she'd awakened on the dark trail from Canon City until they'd marched the prisoners onto the train had reinforced her confidence. Bethan had no doubt that she could do the job but wasn't convinced that it was destined to be her life. She still had a choice.

CHAPTER 3

It was early the next morning when Bethan, Lynn, Bryn and Dylan entered the U.S. Marshal's office.

Bethan had already written her statement on the train and Bryn had left it with his report in Dylan's office, so she sat and waited as the other four non-Evans lawmen assigned to the office began arriving.

When Benji arrived, all of them were present and most had heard the basics of what had happened in Fremont County.

They were gathered in the big front office when Dylan said, "As all of you know by now, we lost Bert a couple of days ago. We'll be joining Benji and his family at the funeral and burial service this afternoon at two o'clock at the Emmanuel Baptist Church. Pete, I'll need you to head down to Canon City on the late train. Come to my office when I'm finished speaking.

"After Pete was killed and two of the counterfeiters were dead, Bethan arrived in the night because she'd been trailing Bryn and Bert. She was the one who caught the last two and you're all free to read her statement and Bryn's report for the details.

"Because she's determined to continue to track bad men, I'm going to swear her in as a temporary deputy marshal to keep her on the right side of the law. I know it's a real stretch of my authority, but I believe it's the best solution. I'm not about to let her run around the state and territories like a bounty hunter. So, let's get that done."

He then called Bethan to the center of the room, swore her in as a temporary United States Deputy Marshal and handed her the badge. There was no applause from the others, and only the three men named Evans and Benji were smiling. Dylan assumed that none of them believed that Bethan was their equal and by giving her a badge, he was demeaning its importance. He hoped that their attitude would change once they read Bryn's report.

Within an hour, Dylan had briefed and dispatched Pete Towers to Canon City to handle the arrest of Fremont County Deputy Sheriff George Lynch. He'd debated about sending two men, but with knew that Pete would have the support of a very angry Sheriff Bo Johnson.

After a visit by two Secret Service officers to pick up the packs of counterfeit money and the printing plates, Dylan, Bryn and Bethan left the office, then crossed the busy street to the county courthouse. Even though it was a Federal case to be tried by Federal judge Morris Evers, the paperwork would be handled by the county prosecutor's office and the trial itself would be held in the county courthouse.

They walked into the prosecutor's office, stepped past the clerks and entered Kyle's office. Everyone in the front office knew the story, so none of them said a word.

Kyle looked up from the papers on his desk as the door opened and smiled at his brothers and niece, although technically, they were his uncles and Bethan was his cousin.

He asked, "How did Martha take the news?"

Each of them took a seat as Bryn replied, "Benji said that her first reaction was that she almost seemed to be angry at Bert for being killed. This morning, he said she seemed calmer and sad rather than angry."

"Do Al or Garth know what happened yet?"

"Not yet. Bryn sent Mason out to the A-G this morning so they could get here in time for the funeral."

Kyle nodded, then said, "It looks like the trial will be set for Tuesday, the twenty-fourth, but I don't have a time yet. They're both being charged with the murder of a Federal officer and attempted murder of a Federal officer. The boys over at the Secret Service are going to hold off charging them until after the trial in case they get off. When are they picking up the phony money and plates?"

"They already have. The real money is still in the safe until Judge Evers decides what to do with it."

Kyle nodded, then said, "They're sending a Federal prosecutor from Kansas City named John Locklear. I've never met the man, but he has a good reputation. Who did you send down to Canon City to arrest that crooked deputy sheriff?"

"Pete Towers is leaving right after the funeral. That'll be at two o'clock at the Emmanuel Baptist."

"You're sending him alone?" Kyle asked with raised eyebrows.

"I thought about sending someone with him, but Bo Johnson will most likely want to hang the man, so he should be okay."

Kyle smiled, then said, "Maybe you should send Bethan with him."

Dylan replied, "I need to have her stay here for a few days, but other than that, I could because I made her a temporary deputy marshal a little while ago to make sure that she stayed legal."

"Why am I not surprised?" Kyle asked, then said, "I read the two reports and I'll admit that I was impressed. What really caught my eye was the shot to the bootheel. I can't imagine anyone else thinking about doing that. If it had been someone else, like me for instance, that shot would have been a miss, but I'm sure that Bethan put that .44 exactly where she wanted it to go. That must have been something to see, too, with his foot popping back into the air like a big frog dropped onto a hot rock."

Bryn said, "Sheriff Joe Schuler and I were almost ready to fire when she took that shot. You're right about the impact it had. I don't think it was the bullet as much as the exploding dirt that shoved his foot about a foot into the air."

"I don't really need to prep you or Bethan for the trial. When John Locklear arrives on Saturday, I'll invite him to the family get together on Sunday afternoon to meet you both."

"Thanks, Kyle," Dylan said, then as he rose, he asked, "Are you going to show him your bat on Sunday?"

Kyle turned and grasped his heavy maple staff that he kept standing in the corner, then set it on his desktop.

"I still practice with it in our house barn, but not as often as I used to. I guess it's becoming more of a baseball bat now."

"The ball goes a country mile if you hit it with the tail end of that .44," Bryn said with a grin.

"Only if you hit it, Bryn. You're a better fielder than a hitter."

"Neither of us is as good as Bethan, either."

Bethan smiled at her uncles as she said, "I'm just younger; that's all."

––––––

When they left the courthouse, they stopped on the sidewalk and Dylan asked, "Bethan, are you going to head back to the ranch?"

"I think so. Do you need me to do anything else before I leave or after I get there?"

"Just help get everyone ready who's coming to the funeral."

"Who will that be?"

"The rest of our family and all of Bryn's. I don't think Addie will want to come because of the babies. Alba will stay with her."

Bethan nodded before they stepped into the street and crossed the cobblestones to the office. She watched as her father and uncle entered, then untied and mounted Nippy to return to the ranch.

––––––

"You're kidding!" Al exclaimed with big eyes.

"I wish I was, Al," Mason said as he sat on his chocolate brown gelding, Muddy.

Garth asked, "Did she get in trouble for chasing after your dad and Bert?"

"I don't think so. She rode off this morning with them to get sworn in as a temporary deputy marshal."

Alwen laughed, then after not hearing any replying laughter from his younger cousin, stopped and snapped, "You're serious!"

Mason nodded, then said, "I'll tell you both the rest after you pack up and we can make the ride back to the ranch and then to Denver."

"How did Martha take the news?" Al asked.

"Her father said she seemed to be mad at Bert for dying, but that sounded pretty odd to me. What are you going to do now that she's a widow?"

Al paused before replying, "It doesn't change anything, Mace. Let's get back to the house so we can get changed before we head out."

"Okay, Al," Mason said before they turned their horses back toward the ranch house.

As they rode, Al wasn't sure that it was a good idea for him to be at the funeral, but his father had asked him to attend and the question was rendered moot.

It was still a raw spot in his heart after Martha had refused him because of his desire to be a lawman, then even after he and Garth had bought and set up the ranch, she accepted Bert Hoskins. He liked Bert, so it could have been worse, but he wasn't about to go down that road again.

––––––

At 1:45 that afternoon, all of the Evans who were going to attend the funeral filled the first four pews on the left while the Greens and the remaining deputies and friends took the front three pews on the right.

Reverend Allison's eulogy was overflowing with words of praise for his honorable yet tragically short life despite his lack of regular attendance at Sunday worship.

As the minister droned on, Al glanced over at the Green family and found Martha with her four-month-old daughter in her arms. She was staring straight ahead at Bert's casket and Al was only able to see her profile, so he wasn't able to read her mood, at least not now.

She'd looked at him briefly when he had entered the church with Garth, and that momentary contact had been disconcerting. It was almost as if she was blaming him for putting her in her current situation and expected him to extricate her from it.

From the time that Mason had told him about Bert's death until they'd walked into the church, he'd had the impression that everyone expected him to marry her. She wasn't even twenty years old yet and still a handsome young woman, but Al knew that he wasn't about to go down that path. He had barely talked to her since his father had told him that she was being courted by Bert. He attended their wedding out of courtesy but avoided her as much as possible that day and ever since.

As soon as the burial ceremony was done, he'd mount Copper and get back to the Double EE. He and Garth would stay the weekend in Bethan's house before returning to their ranch on Monday, although they might stick around for the trial on Tuesday just to support Bethan.

He turned his eyes back to his sister who was already looking at him and each of them smiled. He and Bethan had always been close, or as close as brothers and sisters could be. For as long as he could remember, she always seemed to be in competition with him or Lynn. She had a drive that sometimes astonished him. When he'd been told what she'd done, he hadn't been surprised at all. It was his parents' reaction that surprised him and wondered what she was planning on doing with her new badge. He'd have plenty of time to talk to her before the trial.

Bethan had seen Al look over at Martha and hoped that he wasn't going to make the mistake of marrying her out of sympathy or some misplaced sense of nobility. She didn't believe he would, but a young man would get pretty lonely living with his brother and a couple of ranch hands. Visits into town every month wasn't nearly enough to chase away the need for female company. Martha had been a bit on the slim side before she married Bert, but after having her baby, she'd swollen in the areas that men seemed to admire, and that made the potential for a marital mistake more likely.

Al and Garth would be staying with her in what used to be the house they shared with Lynn, so she'd have some time to talk to him and hopefully convince him that marrying Martha wasn't a good idea.

What she also noticed when she looked at the Green family was that Pete Towers wasn't sitting with the other deputies. He was sitting in the same pew with the Benji's family, and she wondered if anyone else had noticed.

———

The burial ceremony was shorter and by early evening, the Evans family had broken up as Kyle's segment of the clan returned to their house in Denver and the others headed south for the Double EE.

Bethan rode with Garth on her right and Alwen on her left as they headed back to the ranch. She had been somewhat surprised that Martha hadn't even talked to her about what had happened and hadn't talked to Bryn much either. It was as if she'd accepted Bert's death and now it was time to move on already. Bethan knew that if her father, uncles or Lynn had died in a similar fashion, their wives would be in a much different state from simple acceptance. Each of them would be hell unleashed to discover what had happened, and woe betide the man who'd screwed up and created their widowhood.

She looked over at Al and asked, "Are you and Garth leaving on Monday or are you going to wait until after the trial?"

Al turned and replied, "I think I'll watch you on the witness stand, little sister. That should be quite a show."

"I don't think it's going to be that impressive because those men have worse records than just counterfeiting and were using aliases. I'd be surprised if it lasted longer than two hours, including the jury's deliberation."

"Well, I'll still be there to watch you and Uncle Bryn."

"Okay, but it'll be boring."

———

After a family dinner, Bethan, Garth and Al headed back to the small house.

Garth built a fire while Bethan started a smaller one in the cookstove and Al filled the coffeepot with water.

Forty minutes later, they were sitting in the front room with mugs of hot coffee in front of the snapping flames.

Bethan held her cup in her hands as she asked, "You aren't going to visit Martha now, are you, Al?"

Al set his cup on the center table and replied, "You don't beat around the bush, Bethan."

"You know that I never have, big brother. In this case, I think that beating around the bush is a waste of time, and you, sir, didn't answer my question."

"That's because you already know my answer. After the trial, Garth and I will happily return to our ranch. We have plenty of mares and fillies to keep us entertained."

Bethan laughed, then said, "Maybe for some purposes, Al, but you need to find a real woman one of these days."

"Good grief, Bethan! I only turned twenty on Sunday when you were out gallivanting around in the mountains. I have plenty of time to worry about it. I notice that you aren't exactly prowling for a mate, so you're hardly one to lecture me."

"I wasn't gallivanting, Mister Evans. I was proving something to myself. I only mentioned the whole marriage thing because I was worried that you might succumb to some sense of obligation to Martha."

"Well, I won't. I want to get our ranch in better shape. We're doing pretty well right now, but there's plenty of time."

Bethan nodded, then turned to her other brother in the room and said, "You make sure he keeps his word, Garth."

Garth laughed, then replied, "He'll be okay, Bethan. He's kinda fond of this one filly anyway."

Bethan's eyebrows rose slightly as she asked, "And what's her name?"

"We haven't named her yet. She only foaled last year."

Bethan stared at Garth for a heartbeat before she began to laugh. It was good having her brothers back, even if it was only for a few days.

———

After Dylan, Bryn and Lynn rode off to work Saturday morning, Bethan left the small house with Al and Garth and rode southwest across the big ranch to visit Addie. Her brothers hadn't had time to visit their newest sister-in-law yesterday and hadn't talked with her for almost a month now.

As they trotted along, Al asked, "How is Alba doing? She seems to be slowing down ever since Flat Jack died."

"She's okay, but you're right about the impact it had on her. She seems to be just waiting rather than living."

"How old is Alba? Is she sixty yet?"

"No, Mister Evans. You should know that by now. She'll be fifty-three in September."

"You didn't seem to remember my birthday, Bethan," Al replied loudly.

"I remembered it. I just didn't care that much."

Al looked across at his sister, then when she turned her sparkling brown eyes towards him, he laughed and shook his head.

Then he said, "You didn't buy me a present either."

119

"I didn't have to buy you one. According to our marshal father, I'll be given those killers horses, mule, tack and other stuff if they're convicted. They had four Winchester '73s, three Colts and one Remington, too. All of the pistols use cartridges, but one of the Colts is chambered for .45 caliber. The mule has a pack saddle and the other two have nice Western saddles."

"And you don't want them?"

"I don't want all of them. I'm debating about taking one of the horses or the mule, then I'll take two of the Winchesters, one of the Colts and the Remington. We'll negotiate for the rest."

Al grinned as he replied, "They're yours, so you just take what you want, and I'll be grateful for the rest."

Garth protested when he loudly asked, "What about me?"

Bethan swiveled in her saddle and answered, "It's not your birthday until February. So, if I catch some other miscreant by then, you can have his stuff."

Garth shook his head as he laughed, then said, "You're really going to go out there on your own. Aren't you?"

"I'm still thinking about it, but I was just joking about your birthday present. I'm sure that our generous older brother will be happy to share his unexpected gift."

Garth leaned forward to be able to see Alwen on the other side but didn't have to ask if he was going to share.

Al then asked, "Did you look at the horses and the mule?"

"Yes, sir," Bethan replied, "One of them is a tall dark brown gelding that I'd guess to be about eight years old with four white stockings and a white slash on his face. The other is a fairly young light gray mare. If I'd hazard a guess, you'd want the mare for your ranch."

"If you don't mind. Would you want the mare or the mule?"

Bethan had already made up her mind before she'd even made the offer and said, "I'd prefer the gelding. I think you'd be able to sell the mule faster."

"We would, and you're right about the mare, too."

"Well, that's all settled. Let's go talk to Addie."

"Little Dylan was talking the last time we stopped by. Has Gwendolyn said any words?"

"She said 'mama' just a few days before I left, and I don't think Lynn minded being left out."

Garth said, "I hope that Nathan says 'papa' first."

Bethan laughed, then said, "Nathan's only six weeks old, Garth. You'll probably be married and have your own baby by the time he says anything."

Garth was going to argue, but they were approaching Lynn and Addie's home, so he just said, "I don't need to get married first, Bethan."

Al ended the conversation by saying, "I hope you haven't left any in Morrison, Garth. I don't want to be surprised when some angry father shows up with a shotgun."

Bethan laughed as Garth turned red, but hoped the taunt wasn't a prediction.

_____

In Denver, Bryn and Kyle stood on the expansive depot platform as they waited for the arrival of Federal prosecutor John Locklear. Denver had only recently reached a population large enough to warrant having a Federal judge assigned to the city yet hadn't appointed a Federal prosecutor.

"Have you ever met him?" Bryn asked.

"Nope. I've read some of his cases, and he's very good. I don't think he'll have a problem with these two."

_____

It wasn't long after the train pulled into the station that they quickly recognized John Locklear just by his commanding presence.

He stepped onto the platform carrying a leather valise and a travel bag yet wore a Stetson and appeared to be more of a ranch owner than an attorney. If Kyle had paid attention, he would have seen an older image of himself in Mister Locklear.

John Locklear was just under six feet tall and wore his weight well. His hair and full beard were dark brown with gray highlights, and his deep blue eyes marked him as a man with a purpose in life.

He quickly identified Bryn and Kyle, even though Bryn's badge was pinned to his vest under his jacket, and strode toward them.

Bryn extended his hand and as Mister Locklear took it, he said, "Welcome to Denver, Mister Locklear. I'm Deputy U.S. Marshal Bryn Evans and this is my brother, Denver County Deputy Prosecutor, Kyle."

John then shook Kyle's hand as he smiled and said, "I'm pleased to meet you both. I was intrigued by what little information I received in the telegrams, so I'm anxious to hear what happened. Where will I be staying?"

Kyle replied, "I've booked a room for you at the Metropolitan. Would you like to go there now so you can rest after your long train ride?"

"I'd rather go to your office and read the reports, if you don't mind."

"That's fine," Kyle said, "Let's head that way. It's only a few blocks."

"I need to stretch my legs anyway," the Federal prosecutor said as they began walking, then looked at Bryn and asked, "Were you the Evans who chased after those four?"

"I was, but I'm sure that your interest was piqued by the name of the Evans who actually made the capture."

"I'll admit that I had to do a double take when I saw the name on the first telegram because I thought it was a woman's name. Then, when I read in the second one that she was the marshal's daughter, I knew that I couldn't send one of my deputy prosecutors. Is she here?"

"No. She's at the family ranch southwest of town. You'll meet her tomorrow when we have our weekly family gathering."

"I'll be looking forward to meeting her. She sounds like an extraordinary young lady."

"She saved my bacon and if she hadn't followed those two out of the hotel, I imagine that your presence here wouldn't be necessary because they'd both be dead."

"I don't reckon that they'll be alive much longer, and that's just from reading the preliminary information. With their history, we could send them to two other jurisdictions to be hanged, too."

"We didn't figure that out until we ran them down," Bryn said as they hurriedly crossed the cobblestone street.

"Your niece has quite a healthy reward headed her way. I checked before I left and it's six-hundred-and-fifty dollars for the pair. What about the other two? There's two hundred and fifty on them."

"I think we should just give it to Deputy Marshal Hoskins' widow. I know that we don't get rewards, but in this case, I think we should be able to work it out."

"It won't be a problem. I'll take care of it, but let's wait until after the trial."

"Thank you, Mister Locklear," Bryn said as they turned west on the sidewalk.

"If I'm going to a family gathering, you should call me John."

"I appreciate that, John. I'm Bryn and I'm sure that my brother won't mind if you call him Kyle."

"I'll do that. Is your famous brother going to join us in your office, Kyle?"

"I'll swing by our office and let him know," Bryn replied, then waved and re-crossed the street.

When he entered the office, he found Dylan pulling on his hat.

Dylan looked his way and said, "I was just going to look for you. I got a telegram from Pete a few minutes ago. Deputy Lynch must have heard about the arrest of the last two and skedaddled. I told him to just come back. Sheriff Johnson said he'd find his crooked deputy."

"I guess that's no surprise. You may has well keep your hat on. Mister Locklear wants to talk to us in Kyle's office."

Dylan nodded, then they quickly passed through the open doorway to cross the busy roadway again.

———

Five minutes later, Dylan and Bryn entered Kyle's office where John was already reviewing the statements and reports. In addition to Bryn and Bethan's written description of the events, Bryn had also included Sheriff Joe Schuler's affidavit about the takedown in his main street. Kyle looked up as they entered but didn't say anything while John continued to read.

Dylan and Bryn sat down in chairs that were placed near the window and sat with their hats on their laps waiting for the Federal prosecutor to complete his review.

Bryn almost snickered when he watched John's eyebrows pop up. He'd obviously just read about Bethan's bootheel shot.

It was another two minutes before he flipped over the last page, looked at Bryn and asked, "Did she really try to hit his heel, or did you just write it that way?"

"If you ask her to do some target practice tomorrow, you wouldn't bother asking. I was just as impressed with her decision to pretend to accept their offer for a bribe, so they'd walk out of the lobby in front of her. Then there was her decision to fire the warning shot through the door to let them know she was serious and to alert us to their presence. Altogether, they were a remarkable sequence of timely and well-reasoned actions."

"Too bad she's a girl. She sounds like she'd make a good lawman."

Dylan then smiled and said, "Well, it so happens that I did swear her in as a temporary deputy marshal yesterday. She said she was going to be a bounty hunter because she was so frustrated by her inability to wear a badge, and I didn't want her to go off without some measure of legality. She's not going to be on the payroll, so the main office won't even know about it."

"Until she arrests someone, and they get the report."

"I'll worry about that when it happens," Dylan said.

"Well, it's not going to come from my office, Marshal. Before we talk about this case, I need to ask you something else. Lynn Evans is your son and a deputy marshal as well. Is that right?"

Dylan suspected that Bethan's appointment may have tipped some nepotism scale that he didn't know about, but replied, "He is."

"Is he here?"

"He's in the office right now, but he'll be leaving in a couple of hours."

"I suppose this can wait until tomorrow, assuming that he'll be at your family get together."

"He will be. What's the problem with Lynn?"

"It's not a problem. He may be able to help us out with a case."

"Which case is that? I'd be surprised if he knows something about a case that I don't."

"Do you remember a bulletin we sent out about six months ago concerning the Gentry gang?"

"Sure. Four men who gave themselves royalty titles and then proceeded to try to establish their domain over western Kansas."

"That's them. Anyway, about a month ago, they tried to take over a small town called Atherton in southwestern Kansas. The town only had a couple of hundred residents and didn't have any lawmen, so they figured it was easy pickings. They soon discovered their error in judgement when they rode into town to take down the bank and before they knew it, they were outgunned by the local townsfolk.

"One of them, the one they called 'Earl' Kennedy, was killed and the others escaped. They were tracked by the locals into the Indian Nations before the posse turned back. I think they left Kansas and are now somewhere in southern Colorado. They wouldn't go into Texas because the Rangers aren't happy with them and those three know the Texas boys' reputation for quick justice."

"I didn't hear about that. Didn't anyone send out a warning?"

"That's not my call, Dylan. If you didn't get any notice, then maybe the county sheriff didn't do his job right."

"How did you find this out and why do you need to talk to Lynn?"

"The leader of the Gentry Gang is called 'King' George. The others are 'Prince' Edwards and 'Baron' Smith. The King's real name is Avery and he used to be a deputy sheriff in Yankton. Lynn was involved in some scuffle with him that drove him out of Yankton. He returned to his home in Iowa where his father was the sheriff and he expected to become a deputy, but his father didn't want him, so he left and formed his gang."

"Do you think he's got a grudge against Lynn?"

"I doubt it. I just want to talk to him to get a good description."

"Couldn't you get it from his father?"

"I could if the King and his new friends hadn't returned a month later and killed him. Nobody else, including his mother, will dare say a word about him in case he returns. The descriptions we've gotten from witnesses to their crime spree have been haphazard at best and I'm sure that we can get a better one from Lynn."

"Alright. Then we'll issue a notice from this office about their possible location. You might want to talk to Lynn's wife, Addie, too. She probably can tell you more than Lynn can because she saw him more often."

"Will I see her tomorrow?"

"Probably. She just had a baby a few weeks ago, but she was at the last two."

"Good. Now, let's do a quick review of your case, Kyle."

Kyle nodded, then took out his notes and outlined the preparation as John listened.

As Kyle talked, Dylan glanced at Bryn and tilted his head, wondering what was going on with the Gentry gang. He remembered the bulletin from Kansas City, but couldn't understand why it had come to the attention of the Federal prosecutor's office. The outlaws had committed a string of crimes, but none were outrageously violent. He wasn't even sure if any had been violations of Federal law.

When Kyle finished, Dylan asked, "John, why is your office so interested in the Gentry gang? That bunch isn't so much different from other small gangs and is probably less trouble than some of the others. They haven't even broken any Federal laws that I know of."

John leaned back in his chair and exhaled sharply before answering, "They have stolen some U.S. mail, but that's not unusual. My interest is strictly personal. My wife's brother was in the bank they tried to rob in Carlisle. He was the only casualty when King George must have thought he was going for a pistol when he sneezed. That sneeze cost him his life. His wife and two children are living with us now."

Dylan just nodded before John said, "Okay. I guess I'll head over to my hotel now. Kyle, will you be coming to get me tomorrow?"

"Yes, sir. I'll stop by your room around ten o'clock. It's less than an hour ride and I'll bring a horse and saddle."

"That sounds good," John said as he rose.

After they'd exited the courthouse, Kyle escorted the Federal prosecutor to the Metropolitan Hotel and Bryn and Dylan headed for their office.

As they dodged traffic, Bryn asked, "How do you want to handle the Gentry gang?"

"Let's get the wanted posters, but I'm not going to send out the notice to other law agencies until we talk to Lynn and Addie about Avery George. I'm not about to start calling any turncoat bastard like him King. The man wore a badge and now he's on the other side."

They stepped onto the opposite sidewalk, then turned to walk the one block to their office as Bryn replied, "There are quite a few men wearing badges that aren't exactly lily white, Dylan."

"I know that, but when one gets to the level of killing innocents, it makes my blood boil."

———

One hundred and eighty-four miles southeast of Denver, three men were filling their canteens in an unnamed creek that probably wouldn't be there in late summer.

After filling his canteen, Homer 'Prince' Edwards dipped his cupped hand into the water, slurped it, then spit it onto the ground.

"This ain't water! It tastes like beer that's been run through some drunk cowhand."

Avery had already drunk some of the bitter water and replied, "It'll keep us alive, Homer. We'll get better water when we get closer to the railroad."

"How far away is that?" asked Ted 'Baron' Smith.

"I'm not sure, but it can't be more than fifty miles or so. This is all farm country just like Kansas. I think we might want to stop at some farm and get some of their water from their pump."

"Just water?" asked Homer.

"Hardly," Avery replied as he stood, "We need to replenish our supplies and rest for a few days."

"You got that right," Ted said as he hung his alkali water-filled canteen on his saddle.

They mounted their tired horses then set them off at a walk heading west.

————

"That bastard is in Colorado?" asked Addie with furrowed brows.

"That's what the Federal prosecutor thinks," Lynn replied as he hung his coat.

"What does Dylan think?"

"He agrees that the gang is probably down in southeastern Colorado by now. They couldn't stay very long in the Indian Nations, and the prosecutor said that they wouldn't dare stick their noses back in Texas. That leaves Colorado. But it's a big state and that's a couple of hundred miles away."

Alba looked at Lynn and asked, "Do you think that he'd come here?"

"I doubt it. There are too many lawmen here and the last thing he'd want to do is run afoul of men who knew how to shoot. He lost one of his gang to a bunch of locals who must have filled the air with lead.

"Mister Locklear will be at the family shindig tomorrow to talk to us about Avery George. Dad said that they didn't have a good description of him, so we'll provide him with that. Can you recall anything else about him that might be useful?"

Addie was quiet as she recalled those days in the Yankton jail and staring at that deputy who was covering for the man who had killed her mother. At least the shooter felt enough guilt to kill himself, but the deputy felt no remorse whatsoever, then had chosen the coward's way out and run.

She finally said in a voice barely above a whisper, "I know what kind of man he is, and I hope someone catches him and they hang him. A bullet is too good for his kind."

Alba looked at Addie and could understand why she felt that way. She had heard the story of how her mother had died but had seemed to put that tragic event behind her. Now the memory was refreshed by Lynn's news.

"You can talk to Mister Locklear tomorrow, Addie," Lynn said as he hung his gunbelt on its peg.

"I'll tell him as much as I can if it helps to catch that bastard," Addie replied.

———

Garth looked at Bethan and said, "I can't believe that the deputy got away."

"Why not? Sheriff Shuster in Granite probably sent a telegram to his boss letting him know what happened, so he'd have time to pack up and get out of town long before Pete even got there."

"Why didn't dad just send a telegram telling the sheriff to arrest his deputy?" asked Al.

"Because it was just as likely that the deputy would get the telegram anyway."

"Well, I suppose it doesn't matter. What do you think about that other deputy resurfacing; the one who was involved with Lynn and Addie up in Yankton?"

"I imagine that Addie wants to see him drawn and quartered, but I doubt if we'll ever see him or his boys. If they're smart, they'll lay low for a while then maybe head over to Arizona or Utah."

Garth said, "I'll just be glad to head back to the ranch."

Bethan smiled and said, "With your new horse and mule."

Al grinned at his sister and added, "And our two new Winchesters and Colts."

Bethan returned his grin but was already thinking about that deputy who had given those killing bastards a warning so they could make their escape. That warning had cost Bert his life and almost killed Bryn. The obvious question was where he had gone. Wherever it was, she was determined to find him. As soon as the trial was over, she'd take the train to Canon City and begin tracking him.

CHAPTER 4

The Sunday afternoon family gathering was well underway when John Locklear and Kyle rode down the Double EE access road. Katie was at home with their newborn son, Collins, and eight-year-old Bess was watching her younger siblings, Colwyn and Meredith.

He had his bat sticking out of his bedroll behind his saddle and had already explained its significance to John on the ride to the ranch.

After having their horses led into the barn by Garth and Al, John was introduced to the rest of the Evans clan, which took a while.

He took care of his personal business first when he met in a group with Lynn and Addie to ask for the description of Avery George. Dylan, Bryn, Kyle and Bethan were also present.

John had his notebook and pencil ready when he asked, "Can you tell me about him?"

Addie said, "I can still see him as if it was yesterday. There was nothing really distinguishable about him. He was taller than average, but not by much. I'd guess around five feet and nine inches. He had an average build with light brown hair and brown eyes. He was right-handed and had attached earlobes. He did have a fairly large nose, but not excessively so."

John nodded, then glanced at Lynn, who said, "Addie's description is perfect, and I guess that's why he's hard to pin down."

Addie then said, "There was something odd about his horse, assuming he's still riding the same one."

"What was that?" John asked.

"It was a dark brown horse and I couldn't tell you if it was a mare or a gelding, but I noticed that it had an unusual marker on its face. You know how most horses, if they have any marks on their face, it'll be either a slash or maybe a star? Well, his horse had what looked like eyebrows."

"Eyebrows?"

Addie nodded, then said, "It almost made me miss seeing him. They weren't all the way above the eyes, but they started out that way and there were two of them."

Lynn smiled, then said, "I didn't see them because Addie was the one who noticed him, so I just looked at the rider. But do you know if he still has his badge?"

John blinked, then looked at Addie and asked, "Did he leave it with the sheriff in Yankton?"

"No."

"Then he probably still has it. I'll make sure we put that in the description."

John turned to Dylan and asked, "Can you put out that notice now with that information, including the possibility that he has a badge?"

"I'll do that tomorrow. How accurate are the other descriptions?"

"They're probably just as vague as the others, but at least now we have one good one."

"A good one that describes an almost invisible man," Kyle said.

Dylan said, "An invisible man that rides with two other invisible men on a brown horse with eyebrows."

Bryn laughed before saying, "I wonder if they go up when the horse is curious."

John then turned to Bryn and said, "Bryn, could I talk to you and Miss Evans about the case now?"

"Sure. It's about time to attack the food now anyway."

John grinned before headed for one of the picnic tables escorted by Bryn and Bethan. He had been almost shocked when he met Bethan and found her to be a very handsome young woman when he'd been expecting to find a somewhat masculine, or at the very least, plain-looking female.

As they walked, he asked, "Miss Evans, I read your statement, but, in all honesty, I wanted to meet the young woman who had taken those incredible actions that resulted in the trial."

"They weren't so incredible, Mister Locklear. I learned from my father and uncles, so it was really just routine."

"I find that hard to believe. Do you honestly believe that those two outlaws would have let your father or Bryn get behind them with a pistol?"

Bethan smiled, then replied, "No, sir. I'll admit that it wouldn't have been likely."

John Locklear then asked, "It didn't say in the report why you decided to follow them in the first place. May I ask why you did?"

"I just wanted to watch them arrest the counterfeiters. If that deputy hadn't warned the four men in that house, then I would have just watched the arrest, then turned around and left. No one would have even known that I'd been there."

"But you followed them after they started tracking the four outlaws. Why did you do that instead of going back to notify the sheriff?"

"It was another six miles back to Canon City and I thought I'd be more use following my uncle and Deputy Hoskins than wasting time trying to find the sheriff. Besides, he probably would have expected the two deputy marshals to catch up with them soon and wasn't necessary."

"You're probably right," John said as they reached the table and he took a plate from a stack.

Bethan took another plate and began adding food while John and Bryn did the same.

"Kyle told me that the deputy who alerted the counterfeiters ran off before the sheriff could arrest him."

"That's what I heard as well."

Bethan took a seat before John and Bryn joined her on the long bench seat that already supported various sizes of Evans.

John took a bite of a fried chicken drumstick, then after he swallowed, asked, "Can you flesh out your report for me?"

Bethan nodded, then set her plate down and repeated her statement, including details that she hadn't thought relevant to the prosecution.

As she talked, John continued to demolish his drumstick and started on a second. Even after reading her statement and Bryn's report, he thought he had a great case, but as he listened to her, he was now convinced that those two would hang. She would be an amazing witness.

He then asked for Bryn's detailed report and between the two, he had a firm grasp of the case and when he returned to the county prosecutor's office in the morning, he and Kyle would flesh out the path for conviction.

He had been impressed with the young lawyer and his whole extended family and wished his own family had been so cohesive.

———

After most of the food was gone, they played their second baseball game of the spring and Kyle let John use his maple .44 bat. John found it unwieldly after his first swing, so he switched to a normal bat.

The baseball game ended in late afternoon and the adults who were going to participate shifted to the target range south of the big barn. Today it would just be the adult Evans males and Bethan and the weapons would be both 1873 and 1876 model Winchesters and assorted pistols.

For almost an hour, the Double EE would be home to almost constant rifle and pistol reports as well as a large cloud of gunsmoke.

As Bethan picked up the first of the repeaters, she was torn about how she should shoot. She didn't want to appear to be showing off for the prosecutor, but she knew that if she did anything less than her best, her father would be disappointed, and that was unacceptable.

Her father wasn't disappointed, and neither was she when she put the rounds from both the .44 and .45 chambered Winchesters into the center at eighty yards. Hers were only marginally better than Bryn's and about the same as her father's marks. The results were as expected as they'd been that way for a few years.

When they switched to pistols and cut the range to forty yards, Bethan's steady hand put her hits all into the center ring except for one that was just outside. Again, only Dylan was able to match her results.

It wasn't until they switched to the shorter-barreled Webley Bulldog that she finally beat her father, if only barely.

When the last cartridge had been fired, they collected the guns and spent brass and walked back to the empty picnic table to clean and oil the still hot weapons.

As they walked, John looked at Kyle and said, "I wouldn't have believed it if I hadn't seen it."

"Gwen, Erin and even Katie can shoot, but not as well as Bethan. Addie is still learning. I've never beaten Bethan, even when she first started shooting. Granted, I can't beat any of the others either, but she really is impressive with her weapons."

"And with her mind as well. After talking to her, I'm surprised that your brother didn't make her a real deputy marshal and tell the boys back at the head office to come and try to take the badge away from her."

Kyle laughed and shook his head as the approached the picnic table, wondering how close Dylan had been to doing just that.

———

After John and Kyle had departed for Denver and the rest of the family had dispersed to their homes, Bethan walked to the barn that housed Nippy. She rubbed her mare down and gave her a leftover apple before turning and looking at Peanut and his family.

"Your boys were busy out at Al and Garth's ranch, Peanut. You should be proud of them. I imagine they've sired over a dozen mules already. I wonder if you've created any?"

Peanut stared back at Bethan and then looked at Hazel as if to answer her question.

Bethan laughed, then said, "I guess you're a monogamous donkey after all."

She then walked to the wide shelves that held their tack and checked her saddle and straps. She knew they were in good condition but made it a habit to inspect the leather often. Having a cinch snap at a crucial moment was a preventable problem.

Once she was satisfied with her gear, she closed her eyes and pictured the counterfeiters' horse and saddle. She hadn't spent much time looking at them because she hadn't expected to be getting them. But with her new plans already forming in her mind, she was trying to design a way to use the riding saddle as a makeshift pack saddle rather than use a real pack saddle.

She wouldn't need a lot of storage but liked the idea of having a second horse in case Nippy was tired or hurt. If the second horse had a pack saddle, then she'd have to switch saddles. But if it wore a riding saddle that already had its stirrups adjusted for her height, she'd be able to swap mounts quickly. She just needed to create a way to hang some extra supplies on the second horse.

She finally opened her eyes, then rubbed Peanut and Hazel's heads before leaving the barn and heading for her house to talk to Garth and Al. Maybe they could help with her design problem.

————

"Why don't you just use a pack saddle?" Garth asked.

"I told you already. I want to be able to switch horses quickly."

"Why?"

Bethan glanced at Al, then replied, "Because right after the trial, I plan on going down to Canon City and finding that deputy sheriff that caused all of the problem with those counterfeiters."

Al had expected something along those lines, so he just shrugged and asked, "Isn't the sheriff chasing him down?"

"No. They don't know where he went, and I don't want him to get away with it."

"Are you going to tell mom and dad that you're leaving this time?" Garth asked.

"Of course, I am. Even though I felt bad for not telling them last time, I knew that they wouldn't let me go if I had asked. This time, it's different."

"I'll say it's different," Al said, "This time you're not going to just watch. This time, you're leaving to act like a lawman."

"I am a temporary United States Deputy Marshal, Al. I'm not acting like anything else."

"What do you think dad will say?"

"He'll ask me if I want to have Lynn or another deputy to come with me."

"And your answer will be?" asked Al with arched eyebrows.

"I'll have to read their mood, but I'd rather go alone."

"Good luck with that," Garth said, "You might be able to convince dad, but mom will put her foot down."

Bethan smiled and replied, "My foot is a lot bigger than hers, Garth."

———

Monday, April 23, 1877

Ted 'Baron' Smith slid out of his bedroll, then quickly yanked on his cold boots, stood and shivered as he pulled on his hat.

"Lordy, it's cold!" he exclaimed before trotting to the nearby creek to answer nature's call.

Homer 'Prince' Edwards was the next to exit his bedroll and followed Smith's boot and hat donning process before silently heading for the stream.

Avery 'King' George opened his eyes and stared at the gray sky overhead and knew that a chilly rain was about to make them even more uncomfortable.

Forty minutes later, they were huddled around their campfire with tin cups of hot coffee in their hands.

"We need to find someplace soon," Avery said, "That rain is going to make riding miserable."

"I would have thought we'd come across a farmhouse already," replied Ted.

"We're not exactly on a road," Avery said, "We'll continue west until we pick up a road or spot some smoke. Farmers get up early and the wife starts cooking right off."

Homer then said, "Let's get those horses saddled and get moving. At least the horse will put some heat into my butt."

————

They'd been riding for almost two hours when Homer spotted the smoke to their northwest and they angled to the right.

"It's about time," he said, "I don't think that rain's gonna hold off much longer."

Avery glanced up at the sky and replied, "You never know about weather out here on the plains. One minute it's all nice and sunny and the next, you're looking at a tornado."

"I don't want to see a tornado or even some rain," Ted said, "I want to see the inside of a nice, warm farmhouse."

———

Just about two miles northwest of the three outlaws, Archie McDonald and his sixteen-year-old son, Mike, and his twenty-year-old son-in law, Jim Foster, were plowing the south field for planting. The ox that was pulling the plow that broke up the hard ground was giving Mike and Jim a hard time this morning and had already come to a sudden halt a half a dozen times. Each time he had stopped, it seemed as if it took longer to get him moving again.

They'd just convinced him to get his hooves working again when Archie shouted, "I swear I'm going to replace him with a nice, steady mule one of these days!"

Jim laughed as he turned around to look at his father and said, "You don't like the mules either, Pa. At least old Otto here can pull that plow a lot easier."

Mike just grinned as he grasped Otto's left horn and guided him along last year's furrow. It may have been plowed for the last four years, but that ground seemed just as hard as it had been when it was just unbroken prairie.

They reached the end of the field, then Mike and Jim began to work Otto into wide turn as the plow bucked in protest. If the sun had been out, they might not have spotted the three riders in the distance, but when they were halfway through the turn, Jim noticed them.

"We have some riders coming in from the southeast," Jim said loudly.

Mike and Archie both turned and spotted the three riders who were about a thousand yards out.

"I don't like the looks of this," Archie said, as he held Otto's reins, "they're probably coming from the Indian Territories."

"What do we do?" Mike asked.

"There's nothing we can do," Archie replied, "They're closer to us than we are to the house and they're mounted."

Jim wanted to run, but his father and brother-in-law hadn't moved, so he stayed put. He knew that his father was right and that if they were outlaws on the run, there was nothing they could do. At least they were far enough from the house, so maybe his mother and sister would see what was happening and hide. Hopefully, nothing bad would happen at all. Maybe they just wanted some food or to get out of the pending rain.

———

"What if they run?" Homer asked.

"Then we cut them off before they reach the house. They're not armed, so I don't see a problem. The only thing that could give us trouble is if there's another one in the house with a shotgun or a rifle," Avery replied.

Ted looked across at Avery and asked, "Do you want me to swing around to the house?"

"Wait until we're a bit closer. If they break for the house, you head that way and go through the front door. Until they run, act as if we're just passing through."

"Okay, King," Ted replied.

———

Archie stared at the riders, now just five hundred yards away, and said, "I don't care that they don't have those rifles in their hands, I don't like the look of them."

"Do you still want us all to stay here, Pa?" asked Jim as he continued to study the three riders.

Archie was reevaluating the situation and although he knew that it was unlikely that they'd reach the house before the riders, it wasn't a good idea to be a cluster of sitting targets either.

"Alright, let's split up and start walking back to the house. Don't run. Act as if we're just heading back for water or something. Just spread out a bit as we walk, but not enough to make them suspicious."

"Okay," Mike replied before he took his first long stride toward the house.

Jim then began walking before Archie took one more look at the riders, then followed.

———

"There they go!" exclaimed Homer as he stood in his stirrups.

Avery wasn't sure that they were running yet and knew that they had a distinct advantage, so he replied, "Keep up this pace until we're closer. If they're still walking, we'll cut them off when they're still a couple of hundred yards from the house. If they run, then we go."

"Alright," Ted replied as he released his Colt's hammer loop.

———

As much as they tried to appear casual, Archie, Jim and Mike couldn't resist glancing back at the three riders. When they were still four hundred yards from the house, it was Mike who panicked and began to run.

As soon as Mike stretched his legs and began pumping his arms, Avery and Homer slid their Winchesters from their scabbards, then set their horses to a gallop. Ted was going into the house, so he left his repeater in place as he peeled away and raced for the front of the house.

Archie and Jim watched Mike for five seconds, then heard the pounding hooves and began to run themselves.

Mike was already twenty yards ahead of them when he began to shout, "Molly! Get the shotgun!"

Archie wished that Mike hadn't run, but it was too late now and added his own loud warning and yelled, "Gertie, grab the rifle!"

Inside the house, Molly and Gertrude were doing the laundry and talking as they worked the heavy canvas britches into the sudsy water. Molly was in her fourth month with their first baby and was already tired, so Gertrude was doing most of the hard work. Neither of them heard the shouted warnings.

But as he raced across the ground, Ted heard the warnings and expected to be greeted by two women with guns in their hands. He was much more concerned about the shotgun than the rifle.

Just as he reached the front of the farmhouse and leapt from his saddle, he heard the first report as either Avery or Homer took the shot.

Both Molly and Gertrude did hear the Winchester's sharp bark, and quickly stood, but both turned toward the window and paused.

When they heard a second shot just a few seconds later, Gertrude said, "Get the shotgun, Molly. I'll take the rifle."

Molly didn't hesitate but trotted down the hallway to get the shotgun that hung over the fireplace while Gertrude quickly stepped across the kitchen to take the Henry that leaned in the corner. Both weapons were kept loaded, but the Henry didn't have a cartridge in its chamber.

Molly was near panic as she reached the main room, then crossed the floor to get to the fireplace and the shotgun.

She'd just lifted it from its pegs when the door flew open and slammed against the wall.

She turned with the shotgun in her hands and before she could even think about cocking the hammer, Ted fired his Colt twice, sending two .45 caliber bullets into and through her chest from just ten feet away.

Gertrude had already heard more gunfire from outside before she picked up the Henry, then levered in a round when she heard Ted's loud entrance followed by the two shots from the front room.

She took a quick breath, then began to carefully approach the hallway with the Henry's muzzle pointed at the hall entrance.

Ted knew that she must be in the kitchen and assumed that she had a rifle, so he quietly entered the hallway with his Colt ready to fire at any movement.

If Gertrude had been thinking straight, she would have pressed her back against a wall and waited for the man who had probably just killed Molly to enter, but she was thinking about Archie and her son more than her own safety. So, she stepped slowly across the kitchen and soon reached the hallway.

She only had enough life remaining to see the flash from Ted's Colt and feel the hammer-like blow from the bullet as it slammed into her chest. She dropped the unfired Henry to the floor and collapsed; her life's blood oozed onto the pine floor as Gertrude shuddered and took her last breath.

Ted holstered his smoking pistol, then walked to the kitchen door and swung it open. He saw Avery and Homer walking their horses with their Winchesters still in their hands and three bodies scattered across the ground.

Avery and Homer reached the back of the house and dismounted before Avery asked, "Anyone alive in there?"

"Nope. There were two women, but I got them both before they got a shot off."

"Alright. Let's get those bodies out of there before this rain starts coming down and then we can see what we have."

"Okay, King," Homer said as they tied off their horses.

———

Bethan hadn't broached the subject of her imminent departure yet because her father, Bryn and Lynn had already gone to work. So, after they'd gone, she spent most of the day preparing for the journey. She didn't expect it to be a quick job as the deputy had been gone for a few days already and the earliest she could get to Canon City was Wednesday, provided she could convince her mother to let her go.

———

Northwest of Canon City, ex-deputy sheriff George Lynch sat in the counterfeiters' abandoned farmhouse and sipped his cold coffee.

Once he learned that two of them had been captured and taken to Denver for trial, he knew that it wouldn't be long before they connected him to their escape.

Within an hour of hearing the news, he'd emptied his bank account, packed his saddlebags and left town. He had expected that his boss would soon track him out of town and there would be a shootout, but that hadn't happened.

For the first two days, George had been barely able to sleep as he watched the empty landscape through the front room's windows. He even avoided going to the privy and used a chamber pot so he wouldn't be spotted.

But now he was finally beginning to realize that the sheriff or those U.S. marshals weren't coming after all. He didn't want to stay in the house much longer because he knew that sooner or later, some other lawmen would come to pick up the printing press and the remaining supplies. Besides, there was only enough food for another three or four days.

The biggest question he had now was where would he go?

He believed that by now, no one really would care where he went, but still didn't want to tempt fate. He wasn't about to head toward Canon City or take the same treacherous route that the counterfeiters had used.

George gulped down the last of his cold, bitter coffee, then decided that he'd go east cross country and once he was out of Fremont County, he'd swing around past Pueblo. He knew that Cody Russell had gone back to his hometown just a month ago and Cody owed him. He knew that Cody didn't want to stay in that tiny burg himself, so after he found him, then they could figure out what to do next.

———

The trial preparation went well and by the time they were finished reviewing the case, neither he nor Kyle was expecting much trouble in the courtroom.

Their star witnesses, Bryn and Bethan, were rock solid as was the story itself. The sheriff's affidavit was just icing on the cake.

"What can you tell me about their defense attorney?" John asked as he leaned back in his chair.

Kyle grimaced slightly before he replied, "Bill Sanders is a bit of an oddity for these parts. He showed up from the east and we're really not sure what part of the east because he doesn't talk about it. He takes any case that can earn him a decent fee, although I don't know how he could get paid by these two.

"His courtroom antics are a bit unorthodox and earn him at least one or two threats of contempt at each trial I've had with him as the defense attorney. He tends to be theatrical and tries to joke his way out of a conviction by winning over at least one of the jurors by acting like a drinking buddy."

John nodded then replied, "I've run into those types before. How many times have you lost to him?"

"Me? I haven't lost any cases to him. Of course, that's only four and they were all pretty straightforward, much like this one."

"We haven't received a witness list yet, which isn't surprising given the location of their crimes. How do you think he'll work his defense?"

"If I'd have to guess, he'll hope that at least one man on that jury isn't fond of the Evans family, whether it's me, or one of my lawman brothers. He'll watch their faces during your opening statement and if he finds at least one who seems displeased, and he'll direct his show to him."

"Okay. I'll be ready for him," John said, before he asked, "Bethan isn't going to wear britches in the courtroom, is she?"

Kyle smiled, shook his head and replied, "No. She'll take the buggy here, although I'd love to see those jurors' faces if she took the stand wearing her britches, boots, Stetson and her gunbelt."

John laughed, then said, "I was pretty impressed myself. I imagine that Judge Evers wouldn't be happy, though."

"Probably not, but he should be happy that it won't be a long trial."

"I believe that you are correct, Mister Evans. Let's get out of here, Kyle."

Kyle nodded, then the two prosecutors stood and after grabbing their hats, headed out of Kyle's office.

———

The threatening clouds never did produce any rain, but the temperature dropped all day and by sunset, it was already close to freezing.

"When are you heading into town?" Garth asked.

"I'll be taking the buggy with dad and Bryn. I should be back a little after noon. Why?"

"We're thinking of coming along," answered Al.

"And then you can get your mare and the mule?" Bethan asked with a grin.

"And the guns you promised us," Garth replied with his own grin.

Al then asked, "Did you ask mom and dad about leaving yet?"

"I was going to head over there in a few minutes."

"I'd pay to watch that show," said Al.

"I'd pay to watch you tell Martha that you're not interested. Has she even said anything to you?"

"Nope. Of course, I'll admit that I've been avoiding her as much as possible. It's a lot easier being out here, though. Is she going to be at the trial?"

"I imagine so, although I doubt if she'd bring her baby with her. If she's there, she'll leave the baby with her mother."

Al nodded and was giving some thought to not going to the trial after all as Bethan rose, pulled on her coat and hat, then headed for the door.

"Good luck," Garth said.

"We'll see," she replied as she left the small house.

Bethan walked across the moonlit ground and was more curious about her parents' reaction than worried. If they were adamant about her not going, she wouldn't go. She would be eighteen soon and then she'd be able to go without asking, but she would prefer to have a personal stake in her first mission, and this was personal.

———

Twenty minutes later, Bethan entered the small house and found Garth and Al still sitting in the front room looking at her.

She hung her hat and was shrugging off her coat when Garth asked, "Well? What did they say?"

"It was odd, really. It was as if they both were expecting me and knew what I was going to ask."

"Really? That's odd," Al said.

Bethan hung her coat then stood before her brothers with her hands on her hips and said, "You told them. Didn't you?"

Al grinned and replied, "Maybe. What did they say?"

"All they said was to be careful. They didn't raise a single objection," she answered before taking her seat.

Garth glanced at Al before saying, "I thought mom might give you a hard time. After we told her, she wasn't happy at all. I guess that dad talked to her when he got home and convinced her that you'd go even if she tried to convince you not to leave."

"I think so. She was quieter than dad, but she still didn't try to change my mind."

"She didn't ask if you would bring Lynn or someone else along?"

"No. Not even that."

"When will you leave?" asked Garth.

"Right after the trial. You and Al can help me pick up those horses, the mule and the rest of the gear and then we'll come back here. I'm already set up for most of it, so it'll still be possible to catch the evening train if the trial is over quickly, which it should be."

Al asked, "When does the train leave?"

"A little after six o'clock and it gets into Pueblo just before ten o'clock. I'll stay there overnight and probably ride to Canon City. It's only about forty miles, but if the train out of Pueblo leaves in the morning, then I'll take it instead."

"Do you have enough money?"

Bethan nodded before replying, "Money isn't a problem, Garth. I never touched the four thousand that Lynn gave each of us from his adventure in Fort Benton and I have my own stash of more than two hundred dollars with me. I'll be fine."

Al then asked, "Are you sure you don't want someone to come with you, Bethan? I wouldn't mind coming along. Garth can handle the ranch with Joe and Hack for a week without a problem."

Bethan smiled at her older brother and replied, "Thank you for the offer, Al, but I don't want to have to worry about you."

"I'm just worried about you, Bethan."

Before Bethan could reply, Garth laughed, then said, "I think you have to worry more about Martha, Al."

"I don't think he really has to worry about her as much as you seem to believe, Garth. I think that Pete Towers already has a mind to take Bert's place after an appropriate time."

Garth and Al both quickly looked at her and Al asked, "What gave you that idea?"

"At the funeral services, didn't you notice that Pete wasn't sitting with the other deputies? He was sitting in the same pew with the Green family."

"So? What does that mean?" Garth asked.

Bethan shrugged, then as she rose, replied, "Maybe it doesn't mean anything. We'll see."

She then smiled at her brothers before leaving the main room to go to her bedroom. She had to finish her packing and set out her dress for tomorrow. It was going to be an interesting day.

———

Two hundred miles south, the three surviving members of the Gentry gang were sitting in the McDonald's farmhouse having coffee before the fire.

"How long do you reckon we can stay here?" asked Homer.

Avery replied, "I figure at least a week or so before we move on. It's a lot nicer than sleeping out in the cold. Where the hell is spring anyway? It's almost May and it feels like March."

"Are we gonna bury those bodies?" asked Ted.

"I don't feel like digging a big hole. They're going to get ripe in another day or two, so what we can do is drag them out into their own field where they already broke ground, and then just lay them out and cover them with dirt. If the critters come and get them, then so be it."

Ted nodded, then said, "They didn't have much money, but at least they had a lot of food."

"They were farmers, Ted," Homer said, "I'm surprised they had the sixteen dollars and forty-one cents."

Ted snickered, then took a sip of his hot coffee.

CHAPTER 5

The courtroom was already crowded as spectators arrived to witness the culmination of the story that they'd already heard or read. If it had been one of the Evans men who had captured the two killers, then there wouldn't have been that many visitors to the trial, but it had been Bethan Evans who had caught them and her testimony would be worth skipping out on a few hours of work. Besides, many of their bosses were there already.

Bethan sat beside Bryn when two Denver County deputy sheriffs led Irv Thompson/Roddy Plunkett and Tom Lilly/Jimmy Rose into the courtroom in shackles.

The deputies sat them in two chairs at the defendant's table with their attorney then sat on the bench behind them.

Bethan had watched Bill Sanders in two of Kyle's cases and didn't like him at all. He was almost a caricature of a shady lawyer with a short, sharply trimmed mustache and slicked down black hair. He didn't wear spectacles, but his dark, furtive eyes added to the effect. She wondered if he was really going to try to get her to break down on the stand. She'd seen him do it to a young woman who had accused a man of raping her and hoped that he tried it with her.

The bailiff called them to rise for Federal Judge Morris Evers, who entered the courtroom and took his seat behind the bench.

After the opening statements, John Locklear called Bryn and pretty much let him tell his story of the events that led to the arrest of the two accused.

After taking his seat, Bill Sanders mounted his flamboyant attack on Bryn's testimony that should have been a simple questioning of whether or not he had actually identified the two men.

Kyle could tell that the jury wasn't impressed and that Judge Evers was close to putting an end to his dramatic methods before Bill Sanders abruptly ended his questioning by looking at the jury and throwing up his hands in apparent disgust before returning to his seat at the defense table.

Bethan heard her name called, then stepped confidently to the witness stand, took her oath, then sat down.

Before he stood, John Locklear glanced at the jury and saw twenty-four male eyes focused on Bethan and held back a smile.

He walked across the floor until he was about six feet from the witness box and asked, "Miss Evans, would you tell us why you were following the deputy marshals?"

Bethan gave him the same answer that she'd given to him on Sunday, and then he asked her to tell the story of what had happened after she'd heard the gunshots.

It took Bethan almost fifteen minutes of uninterrupted testimony to narrate the story, and as she talked, John would glance at the jury and then at his opposing counsel. He wasn't surprised that, to a man, the jury was enthralled. He was curious that Bill Sanders hadn't raised a single objection to her long testimony and seemed to be almost enamored of the main witness against his clients.

Finally, Bethan concluded her story and John thanked her, then turned the questioning over to Bill Sanders, curious to which colorful approach he would take.

Bill Sanders rose, stepped closer to the witness stand and stopped for dramatic effect; at least that was his intention. He didn't ask a single question as he stared at Bethan in a vain attempt to make her look away.

After she continued to stare back at him without a single blink of her brown eyes, Bill Sanders finally asked, "Miss Evans, how old are you?"

"I'll be turning eighteen on the twenty-fifth of May."

"And you claim to have traveled to Canon City on you own a day before the two deputy marshals arrived and tracked them up a treacherous mountain pass. Then, after hearing gunshots, you rode in the dark up that narrow trail. If that wasn't so unbelievable, you then purport to have rescued your uncle, Deputy Marshal Bryn Evans, then ridden with him down the trail in the night to chase after two men who had supposedly ambushed him and Deputy Marshal Hoskins."

He then paused briefly, shook his head in apparent disbelief, then continued his long question.

"Once you supposedly arrived in Granite, you intentionally went to the hotel where you waited for the defendants, then held them at gunpoint, fired a shot through the door and then led them outside where they were captured by your uncle and the Lake County sheriff. Is that what you expect us to believe, Miss Evans?"

"Yes."

Bill Sanders threw his arms into the air, shook his head and exclaimed, "That is preposterous, young lady! You must think that we are all incredibly ignorant baboons to possibly believe that tall tale. What kind of parents would allow their teenaged daughter to even leave their watchful eye lest they engage in the expected behavior of young people when left alone? Nothing you have said contains even a shred of truth. If Deputy Marshal Evans had been smarter, he would have had one of your brothers fabricate this extraordinary fantasy to cover up his failure.

"I believe, Miss Evans, that you are nothing more than a distraction employed by your uncle to hide his disastrous mistake in murdering two innocent men on that pass that also resulted in the death of Deputy Marshal Hoskins. He then told some story to Sheriff Schuler in Granite before he arrested my clients to pin the blame on them for the murders. I don't believe you were even there."

Bethan knew she couldn't say anything because she hadn't been asked a question, so she just stared at the defense attorney, hoping he would ask her something.

Instead, Bill Sanders turned to the jury and said, "I have no more questions for this young woman pretending to be a witness."

Bethan stayed on the witness stand as the defense attorney returned to his seat and John Locklear rose.

"Do you wish to redirect, Mister Locklear?" Judge Evers asked.

"Yes, Your Honor," John replied.

He then smiled at Bethan and asked, "Miss Evans, how long have you been shooting a gun?"

161

"I was shooting a Winchester when I was eight, but didn't fire a pistol until I was ten, but that was only a .22 caliber Smith & Wesson Model 1. I didn't graduate to a .44 caliber Model 3 until I was thirteen."

"And how many guns to you have now?"

"I have a Winchester '76 chambered for the .45-75 cartridge and a '73 carbine that uses the same .44 rimfire cartridges that both my Smith & Wesson Model 3 and my Webley Bulldog also use. I have a twin-barreled 12-gauge Remington shotgun and a Remington .41 caliber derringer."

"Are you proficient with the guns?"

"Yes, sir."

John turned to the judge and said, "Your Honor, I can personally vouch for the accuracy of her use of her firearms and can produce a number of witnesses who can testify to that fact as well."

Judge Evers didn't comment as he looked at Bethan.

"Did you intentionally try to shoot the bootheel of Mister Lilly or Mister Rose, whichever name he's using today?"

"Yes, sir. I reasoned that it would stop him from firing and cause the least amount of injury."

John then glanced at the jury, realized that there was no point in asking any more questions, and said, "I have no more questions, Your Honor."

After the judge dismissed her, Bethan stood and walked calmly to her seat in the front row. Before she sat down, she spotted Martha sitting in the second row of seats between her father and Pete Towers, then noticed Garth and Al standing against the back wall in the packed courtroom.

She thought that the defense attorney hadn't done well, and when she looked at Kyle, and he nodded winked at her, she was sure that he hadn't.

As the defense had no witnesses, the closing arguments were all that remained for the two lawyers to do before the jury did what it had to do.

Bill Sanders tried dramatically to convince the jury that it was nothing more than a show trial to complete the conspiracy to railroad his clients rather than let the truth of Deputy Marshal Bryn Evans' murders see the light of day. It was a real stretch, and even Bethan could tell that it had no effect on the twelve men in the jury box.

The jury soon filed out of the courtroom before the judge left to go to his chambers.

She'd been surprised that her father hadn't come to the trial but figured that he had to mind the office with so many deputies gone. She'd have to go to the office to see him after the trial anyway.

While the jury was out, Kyle turned around from his seat at the prosecution table, then said, "You did a great job, Bethan."

"Thank you, Uncle Kyle. It really wasn't difficult. Mister Sanders went a little overboard."

Kyle grinned and said, "He always does, but this time I believe he was actually a bit more restrained. He wasn't threatened with a single contempt of court, which must be a record for him. Judge Evers may have been close once or twice but held back."

163

"How long before the jury is back?"

"It shouldn't be long, but you can never tell with a jury."

Bethan nodded then sat back in her seat and folded her hands on her lap. She was anxious to get started and each loud tick of the big clock on the wall behind the bench reminded her that the southbound train would be leaving in about seven and a half hours.

She then turned to Bryn and asked, "Bryn, can you describe the deputy down in Canon City who let those counterfeiters know you were coming?"

"His name is George Lynch and he's about five feet ten inches and slim, I'd guess around a hundred and fifty pounds. He's clean shaven except his sideburns are pretty long. He has light brown hair and blue eyes. His face isn't remarkable, but he has a small scar on the left side of his chin just above the jawline. He rides a light gray gelding with four white stockings. Is that enough?"

Bethan nodded, then replied, "Thank you, Bryn. How good is he with his weapons?"

"I don't know. I never got around to asking that question. I only met him once before about a year ago. How will you start your search?"

"Just like you would. I'll go to Canon City and check at the train station when I get there to see if he took a train out of town. If not, then I'll talk to the sheriff, get as much information as I can, then take it from there."

Bryn nodded and was about to answer when the bailiff trotted across the courtroom and entered the judge's chambers. The jury had arrived at a quick verdict, which didn't bode well for the defendants.

Five minutes later, the defendants were standing as the jury foreman announced the guilty verdict on both the murder and attempted murder charges.

Judge Evers looked at the two men and said, "I order that you both be hanged until you are dead tomorrow morning at nine o'clock."

Everyone, including the convicted men, thought he was going to rap his gavel, but he didn't.

As everyone remained standing, he said, "I further order than a thousand dollars of the genuine currency recovered at the time of their arrest be given to Mrs. Bert Hoskins. The remainder of the funds are to be returned to the United States Department of the Treasury."

Then he did crack his gavel, stood and said, "Court dismissed," and strode from the courtroom.

Bethan didn't wait to talk to anyone, but asked Bryn to help her get out of the courthouse.

Garth and Al joined her and Bryn as they exited the courtroom and merged with the outflow of humans leaving the building.

Once they stepped outside, she was surprised to see United States Marshal Dylan Evans standing on the sidewalk next to the buggy. Behind the buggy were the two horses and mule with all of the soon-to-be-hanged outlaws' possessions that hadn't been returned to the government or Martha.

As she approached, her father smiled and said, "I figured it wouldn't take long and you'd want to get out of here as soon as you could."

"Thanks, Dad," Bethan said before she kissed her father, then climbed into the buggy.

He handed her the reins and said, "Come and see me before you leave."

"Yes, sir."

She then turned to watch Garth and Al mount their horses before snapping the reins and driving west.

After she'd rolled away, Bryn, Dylan and Kyle all watched her leave with their arms folded.

"How did you talk Gwen into letting her go?" Bryn asked.

"It wasn't as hard as I thought. After Garth and Al told us, she wasn't very happy about it, but I pointed out exactly what she had used as her argument when she got back from Granite. Bethan is just as much her daughter as she is mine."

Kyle said, "I guess that's a pretty good point. I'm just surprised that you aren't having Lynn go with her."

"I thought about it, but it was Gwen who said that it was Bethan's choice, not ours."

"Now that, brother, is a real shocker," Bryn said before they waved goodbye to Kyle and headed back to the office.

———

Once she parked the buggy outside the barn, Al and Garth said they'd take care of the buggy and the critters while she changed and had some lunch.

Bethan thanked them, then quickly walked to the small house to change into her britches, boots and heavy flannel shirt. She'd pack normal women's things as well because she knew that the big disadvantage that her sex created for her could also be used as an advantage and she wanted every advantage she could get.

After she finished packing her two leather panniers, she lugged them out to the small kitchen and added her food supplies. She wasn't taking a lot with her today, but if she got to Canon City and had to trail that deputy, she'd buy more before she left. She wasn't packing heavy things like a cooking grate, either. She could handle cooking well enough on the trail to do without.

She did have a coffeepot, tin plate and cup with her as well as a spoon and a fork. She had her pocketknife and her real knife already but knew that there were two more big knives in the saddlebags, courtesy of the two outlaws.

Bethan took one more long look around the kitchen and was satisfied she was ready. She was wearing her Webley in her shoulder holster and had her derringer in her pocket. With her revolver at her hip, she had thirteen rounds of fire without reloading.

She hoisted the two panniers off the floor and waddled out the back door where she dropped them on the short porch before returning for her Winchester '76 and the shotgun.

When she returned to the porch, Garth and Al had led Nippy and the new gelding to the back of the house.

"How do you plan on hanging those packs on the horse?" Garth asked.

"With this," she replied as she pulled out a ten-foot length of heavy rope from the closer pannier.

Al looked at the rope and said, "You know that we won't be here to help you get them onto that saddle after you're gone."

"I know. That's why the rope is so long. I'll show you."

Garth and Al stood aside as Bethan moved one pannier to each side of the gelding, then tossed the rope over one side and looped it through the pannier's handle before tying it into a hard knot.

She then walked to the other side, slid the rope through the second pannier's heavy cloth handle, then left the end on the saddle and trotted around to the first side.

She grabbed the rope, pulled it taut, then leaned back and stepped away from the horse. Both panniers began to rise from the ground and soon their bottoms were just above the stirrups.

Bethan then kept the rope tight by wrapping it around her arm until she reached the horse, tied the rope around the saddle horn, then turned to face her brothers and put her arms out wide.

"Ta-da!"

Garth and Al both grinned and applauded their sister's effort and well-designed method for loading the supplies.

"I'll tie them down in a while, but I'm going to go to the big house and have lunch with mom. Did you want to come along?"

"Of course, we do. We're not going to miss it," Al replied.

Bethan turned and began walking to her parents' house as Al and Garth got in step alongside her.

She was already running through her basic plan for tracking down the traitorous deputy but knew that she'd have to talk to his old boss to find out more about him or where he might have gone.

When they entered the big house, the only one still there was her mother as Cari, Brian and Conway were all at school.

Gwen had four plates and flatware already on the kitchen table when they entered, and without looking at them, asked, "How did the trial go?"

Bethan smiled, then replied, "They're going to hang in the morning. It wasn't bad at all. As you have lunch already prepared, I guess you knew that it was going to be a quick one."

Gwen turned and smiled at her children, then said, "I knew they were guilty, and you and Bryn weren't going to quake on the stand. Are you ready to go?"

"I'm ready. I'll stop at the office and see Dad, Lynn and Uncle Bryn before I go."

"That's good. Have a seat and we can talk while we eat."

Bethan hung her hat and coat on a wall peg as Garth and Alwen did the same, but she left her shoulder holster and gunbelt where they belonged.

After they were all seated and having a well-prepared lunch that was closer to a full meal, Bethan studied her mother's face, wondering if she was really upset or accepted what her older daughter was about to do.

Gwen asked, "Tell me how you're going to chase him down."

Bethan explained her preliminary plan that would start in Canon City and talking to Sheriff Johnson to get a better understanding of the ex-deputy.

Gwen listened to Bethan as she outlined her steps and she heard what sounded like one of her husband's logical yet flexible plans for tracking down an outlaw. As much as her mother's instincts were screaming in the back of her mind, she was proud of her daughter.

When Bethan finished, Gwen smiled and said, "I think you'll be fine. Did you bring your field glasses and compass?"

"Yes, Mom. I have two boxes of .45s for the '76, four of the .44 rimfires, and one box of birdshot and another of buckshot for the shotgun. I don't have any spare rounds for the derringer for obvious reasons."

Gwen nodded, then said, "I can understand that. Do you have the spare horse and Winchesters?"

"Yes, ma'am. Two '73 carbines and I have their pistols, too. One is a Remington and the other is a Colt, but both use .44s. I gave the rest to those two lugs shoveling food into their faces."

Garth swallowed and said, "She's pretty loaded, Mom."

"I know that and if she wasn't so good with them, I wouldn't think of letting her go."

Bethan then said, "I'll be fine, Mom. I should be back in a week or so."

Gwen set her glass down, then replied, "I'll try not to worry, Bethan, but don't hold me to that. You may be every bit as good as your father, uncle, or oldest brother, but I worry about them too, so don't expect me to be calm while you're gone."

"I really do understand, Mom. But this is something I have to do."

Gwen then glanced at Al, who got the message, then stood and tapped Garth on the shoulder.

Garth looked up at his older brother, took one last bite of sliced beef, wiped his mouth using a napkin rather than his sleeve to avoid a motherly comment, then rose and followed Al to their jackets and hats.

After they'd gone, Gwen said, "You do know how difficult this is for me, Bethan. It's not as if I didn't know it was coming, but still, I was hoping that maybe you'd just marry and settle down."

"I still may do that, Mom. We've had this discussion more times than I can recall. One day, I'll find that man who can make me feel how you do about dad and then I'll be happy. For now, I just need to do this because I can. If I settled down, then I'd never know what I missed, and I'd regret it and probably resent my husband and children. I never want to do that, Mom."

Gwen stood and walked to her daughter, then as Bethan rose from her chair, had to look up to see her eyes. She was already six inches taller and might add another inch or two.

Gwendolyn rested her hands across Bethan's shoulders, feeling the leather of her shoulder holster's strap under her left hand.

"You know, Bethan, in a way, I'm very jealous of you. You're getting to make that choice that most women never have. I sometimes wonder what life would have been like if I had been allowed to choose what I would do when I was your age."

Bethan smiled at her mother, then replied, "You would have chosen to marry dad and become the rock for the entire Evans family, just as you are now. You may not have had the same few opportunities that I have, but I know that you've made the most of your life. I'm actually jealous of what you have and wish that I can be half the woman you are."

Gwen sniffed, then wiped away the threat of tears before she quietly replied, "You are my daughter and the daughter of the finest man I've ever met, and you're already the sum of both of us."

Bethan exhaled sharply, then embraced her mother. This was going to be a much more difficult departure than she'd expected.

She then kissed her mother, stepped back and said, "I'll be back as soon as I can."

Gwen just nodded before Bethan turned and stepped to the wall. She donned her coat, pulled on her Stetson, then looked back at her petite mother and waved before opening the back door and crossing the threshold.

Once outside, she stopped, sighed, then quickly stepped down from the porch and headed for the small house.

Gwen remained standing for a couple of minutes as she stared at the closed door. She knew that Bethan was much better prepared for her mission than Lynn had been, and it was much closer. But as much as she hated to admit it, Bethan was her daughter and not her son. She wished that it didn't make a difference, but it did.

She finally sighed, then turned to the table to begin the cleanup. She still had a house to run and her other children would be returning from school soon.

———

Bethan's parting from Al and Garth was much less stressful, so just twenty minutes after leaving the big house, Bethan was turning Nippy onto the road to Denver trailing the new gelding.

As she rode, she tried to think of anything that she'd missed. She wasn't planning on spending a lot of time on the trail, so that eliminated a lot of the items. She just had that nagging notion that there was something that she'd forgotten. It wasn't firearm or clothing related, so what was it?

She was almost to Denver when she figured it out and it wasn't anything dramatic. She needed a small notebook and a couple of pencils. She could pick them up at the marshal's office because her father kept a few in his desk. It was one of his many lessons; always write down notes of what happened. Her first note would be the description of Deputy Lynch that Bryn had given to her.

———

173

When she stepped down before the office, it was already late afternoon, but she still had a couple of hours before the train left.

When she entered the office, she found her father, uncle and brother in the main office, but none of the other deputy marshals were there.

"This is quite a gathering," she said as she closed the door.

"We were just getting ready to close up shop for the day but hung around until you showed up."

"I'm glad that you did because I forgot to include a notepad and some pencils."

"I'll get some for you," Lynn said as he left the front office and headed down the hall to Dylan's private office.

"How did it go with your mother?" Dylan asked.

"It went very well. I'm sure that she'll talk to you about it tonight."

"I'm sure that she will. After you get the notebook and pencils, are you all set?"

"Yes, sir."

As Dylan nodded, Lynn returned with the pad and pencils and handed them to Bethan.

Bryn then said, "Be careful that he doesn't join up with some buddy before you find him. Men don't like to go on the run alone because there's no one to watch their back."

"I already assumed that he had a friend. It's just a question of what kind of friend," she replied, then turned to her brother and asked, "Do you think that he'll be like that deputy that went rogue like Avery George did in Yankton, Lynn?"

Lynn's eyebrows rose as he asked, "You remembered that? I suppose that it's possible if not likely. Once he's been labeled as a man who can't be trusted, he'll need to either go far enough away that they won't know, or he'll just do what Avery George did and make that short trip to the other side."

"That's odd, isn't it? Lynch's first name is George and your ex-deputy's last name is George. I guess I'll get a better idea of what he might do when I talk to Sheriff Johnson."

Bethan slipped the two small notepads and pencils into her coat pocket, then said, "I guess I'd better get going."

Lynn gave Bethan a hug and a kiss, then Bryn did the same before each of them took his hat and coat from the wall of pegs and headed out the door.

Dylan then smiled at his daughter and said, "Stay put until I get my hat and coat from my office."

Bethan nodded, then watched him turn and walk down the hall, hoping that this wasn't going to be another heart-ripping departure at the train station. It wasn't as if she was leaving for China or anything.

Dylan returned just seconds later, wearing his new Stetson that he'd finally bought to replace his last worn-out flat leather hat. They'd even had a funeral service for the old headgear before burying it behind the marshal's office.

Once outside, Dylan locked the office, then mounted Raven and waited while Bethan stepped into the saddle.

They set their horses to a walk toward the large train station and neither spoke as they made their way in the busy thoroughfare.

When they reached the depot, they dismounted, and Dylan tied off Raven while Bethan led Nippy and the unnamed brown gelding to the stock corral. When she returned, they stepped onto the platform and walked to the ticket window where Bethan purchased her ticket and tags.

Dylan glanced at the train station's big clock, knowing he had another hour and ten minutes he could spend with his daughter, but wasn't about to make her that uncomfortable.

When Bethan approached him, he just smiled at her and said, "Well, I'll be heading back to the Double EE, Bethan. If you need anything, just send me a wire."

Bethan smiled back and asked, "No last-minute warnings or questions, Dad?"

"Nope. I'm more confident in your abilities than I would be for most of the deputies that I send out every day. You'll be all right."

Bethan didn't have to stand on her tiptoes to kiss her father's cheek, and after she did, she said, "Thank you for everything, Dad. I'll make you proud."

"You always have and always will, Bethan," he replied, then gave her a small salute, turned and strode from the platform.

Bethan watched her father untie and mount Raven, then she waved. He returned her wave, then swung his black gelding west and trotted away.

After he had Raven moving, Dylan let out a long breath and was pleased that he'd been able to avoid getting emotional. She would only be gone for a few days, but he had a bad feeling about her decision to chase down the ex-deputy ever since he'd learned about it. He knew that she was highly skilled and well-trained, but she wasn't even eighteen yet and she was his daughter. It had been bad enough with Lynn, but this was worse. Acknowledging that he was more worried now than when Lynn had gone to Fort Benton did bother him, though.

———

As Bethan sat on the bench in Denver waiting for her train, George Lynch was in his saddle and riding east. He wasn't taking the road to avoid bumping into anyone he knew. It made the trip more difficult, but it was safer. If he'd only had to worry about Sheriff Johnson or the other deputy, then it wouldn't matter. It was knowing that the U.S. Marshal's office was probably going to be looking for him that made him nervous.

He hadn't left the counterfeiters' house until almost noon because he'd overslept when the first two days of staying awake most of the time had finally caught up with him. He was still a bit drowsy, but at least now he was moving.

He'd swing north of Pinon, then after he crossed the tracks, he'd loop toward the southeast for Bishop. It was another good day's ride after the train tracks, and he hoped that Cody was still there. He'd never been to the small town before and assumed that they didn't have any law.

"Maybe I could offer my services and become the town marshal," he thought before he snickered.

All things considered, George Lynch was in a pretty good mood as he maneuvered his horse around obstacles on the rocky terrain.

———

Bethan sat at the west-facing window as the train rolled south. She was watching the last vestiges of the sunset over the Rockies after a particularly impressive show.

Even though she was wearing britches, a heavy coat and a Stetson when she entered the passenger car, she had attracted the attention of two men who were now sitting directly behind her. It wasn't as if she hadn't expected it; it was the norm, and not because she wasn't dressed like other young women.

Her hat sat on the bench seat next to her to keep anyone else from taking the spot, and her light brown hair was tied off with a short leather string in a ponytail. It allowed her to fold her hair under her hat when she was riding if she wanted to appear as a man at a distance. Once she was within fifty yards, even her bulky coat wasn't enough to hide her gender from watching eyes.

The two men hadn't spoken to her, but she could almost feel their eyes boring into the back of her head. She knew that they didn't know she was as well-armed because they couldn't even see her holster with her Smith & Wesson, much less her shoulder-holstered Webley Bulldog. She knew that both of them were armed because they left their jackets open when they entered the car. They didn't mean it as a threat; it was just that they might have been too warm once they were inside.

None of that mattered if they just left her alone, but it was another four hours before the train reached Pueblo after stops at Castle Rock and then Colorado Springs. There would probably be stops in smaller towns along the way, but only if the train had to stop to pick up or drop off passengers. The older wood-burning locomotives would have to stop much more often.

Bethan continued to stare out the window as the sky darkened and tried to concentrate on what she would do when she stopped in Pueblo. She'd leave her horses at the closest livery then stop at the nearest hotel and get a room. She'd get something to eat at Colorado Springs when the train made a thirty-minute stop.

———

She'd almost forgotten about the two men by the time the train pulled into Colorado Springs, but she couldn't ignore her growling stomach.

When the train had slowed to a walking speed, she stood, snatched her hat from the seat, and stepped into the center aisle.

When she turned to walk to the back of the car, she glanced at the two men as they stood, but didn't make eye contact before she began to step along the still rocking floor.

She stepped out onto the car's steel platform, then as the depot's wood platform slid into view, she hopped down and continued to walk without breaking stride.

Bethan didn't doubt that the two men were behind her as she entered the railroad's diner that was attached to the station.

She quickly took a seat at the counter and smiled at the young woman who approached and said, "I'll have whatever you're serving."

The waitress nodded, then as the two men sat on opposite sides of her as if they were her brothers, the one on the right said, "We'll have the same."

After the waitress left, Bethan pretended not to notice, but simply sat looking straight ahead. She didn't feel intimidated in the least and wondered what they were thinking other than the obvious.

The one who had ordered turned to her and asked, "Are you traveling alone, miss?"

Bethan turned to her right and asked, "Is that any of your business, mister?"

"We were just wondering. Young ladies shouldn't be unescorted. Are you some rancher's daughter?"

"No. My father is in a different line of work."

"Oh? What's that? Is he a farmer?"

"No, he's a United States Marshal."

Bethan could almost hear the impact of her reply on the two men as if she had just announced that she was infected with measles.

Neither man said another word as the waitress brought them bowls of beef stew and cornbread. She then poured cups of coffee for each of them and walked to another customer.

Bethan ate her food quickly, washed it down with the coffee, then left a quarter on the counter before standing and leaving the diner. She glanced at the reflecting window and noticed that the two men had remained at the counter.

It hadn't been much of a situation, and she'd experienced similar encounters in Denver, but was pleased to discover that the threat of having a United States Marshal as her father was just as effective here as telling men in Denver who knew Dylan Evans.

When the train began rolling again, Bethan noticed that the two men had chosen to use a different passenger car to resume their journey and didn't expect to meet them again.

———

George Lynch had already slipped into his bedroll to try and catch up on his missed sleep. It wasn't as chilly as it had been the last few nights and he was grateful for that. The sky was full of stars, so there wasn't going to be any rain either.

He guessed that he should be crossing those tracks by midmorning and might even make it to Bishop before nightfall.

———

Another hundred and twenty miles to the southeast, the three members of the Gentry gang were finishing off the last of their coffee at the McDonalds' kitchen table.

"Where do we go next?" Homer asked.

Avery replied, "There's a town called Bent Canyon on the Las Animas River. It's pretty small, so it doesn't have any law, but it does have a bank."

"I hope the damned townsfolk are more peaceful than that crowd in Kansas," Ted snarled.

"We won't be so obvious this time. We'll wear chaps and ride in separately, then scope the place first. We meet in the saloon and plan our move after that."

"Okay," Homer replied, "but I need to spend some time with a woman first. It's been too long."

"We can all do that before we do the bank."

"What if they don't have a whore house?" Ted asked.

"If they don't, then there's always whores around somewhere. We may just have to take a little while to find them."

"I hope so," Homer said, "'cause your mare is getting to look pretty good to me."

Avery and Ted laughed loudly as Homer grinned.

―――

Bethan settled into her bed at the Railway Hotel. It was almost midnight and she was more tired than she'd expected to be. Tomorrow would be a busy day, and hopefully, she'd find the ex-deputy within a day or two. But now, she just needed to get some sleep.

CHAPTER 6

Bethan was up at dawn, which surprised her as tired as she'd been, but she was grateful that she hadn't overslept.

She dressed quickly, then after a quick visit to the privy behind the hotel, she returned to her room to wash and prepare for her visit to the sheriff.

After she left her room and dropped off the key, she stopped at the nearby restaurant and had breakfast before picking up Nippy and the gelding from the livery. She did a quick inventory of her gear and weapons, found nothing missing, then mounted her mare and rode out of Pueblo. The train for Canon City wouldn't be departing until almost noon, so she decided to ride. The idea of spending four hours sitting at the station was irritating.

As she rode Nippy at a medium trot, she scanned the horizons just out of habit. She knew that there was no danger of an ambush, but it was something that her father had ingrained into her and had been emphasized after finding Bert's body on the mountain pass. The road was well traveled and she knew that she'd be passing a lot of traffic heading to Pueblo along the way, which made an ambush even less likely.

It was a good road and she guessed that she should spot Canon City just about the time that the train was leaving Pueblo, so she was happy with her decision to ride Nippy rather than a train.

———

The sun hadn't reached its zenith when Canon City began to rise in the west. It had been just ten days since she'd arrived in the town the last time to trail Bryn and Bert and so much had changed since that fateful trip. At least Bryn wasn't blaming himself for what had happened, although she wasn't sure if he still didn't harbor some sense of guilt.

When she entered the town, she headed straight for the jail and pulled Nippy to a stop, then stepped down.

She tied off her mare, then hopped onto the boardwalk and entered the sheriff's office.

Deputy Sheriff Matt Spangler looked up from the desk and blinked before he asked, "Can I help you, ma'am?"

"Is Sheriff Johnson in? I need to talk to him."

"No, ma'am. He's having lunch at home. Is there anything I can help you with?"

Bethan removed her hat as she stepped closer, then after she stopped before the desk, she replied, "My name is Bethan Evans, and I need to know all you can tell me about George Lynch."

"George? Why do you want to know about him? He doesn't work here anymore."

"I know that. I want to find him and arrest him for his part in the ambush that killed Bert Hoskins and almost killed my uncle."

Matt blinked again, then asked, "You're gonna arrest him? How can you do that? You're a girl."

Bethan simply opened her coat, displaying her U.S. Deputy Marshal's badge.

The deputy stared at the badge, then slowly lifted his eyes to her face again as he asked, "How did you get that?"

"My father, United States Marshal Dylan Evans, swore me in as a temporary deputy marshal so I could legally do what I was going to do anyway. So, could you please tell me all you can about him? I already have his physical description and his horse's as well. I need to know if he's married, has a family nearby, and those kinds of things that wouldn't be on a wanted poster."

"Um…okay. He's not married, and I don't think he's got any kin, at least not around here. He used to room over at Butler's Rooming House, but he cleared out of there when he left. We know that he didn't take the train, but we didn't go hunting for him after that."

Bethan cocked her head slightly, then asked, "Is he the kind that might turn bad or is it more likely that he'd try to get another job as a lawman somewhere else?"

Matt leaned back in the chair and had to think about it. It was a question that he'd asked himself more than once since he'd discovered that George had tipped off those counterfeiters.

"Well, if I had to guess, I'd reckon that he might use that badge he took with him to take advantage of folks. The sheriff thinks he was taking bribes from some shady characters just because he seemed to have too much money, but he never found anything."

"Okay. Thanks for the information. Tell the sheriff that I stopped by."

"Okay. Good luck, I guess."

Bethan nodded, then turned pulled on her hat and left the office. Once outside, she scanned the streets, then mounted Nippy and rode to the closest eatery for lunch.

————

As she sat at the table chewing her meatloaf, Bethan thought about how she could proceed without any hint of where he might have gone. She hadn't been surprised that the sheriff and his last deputy hadn't gone after him because he hadn't committed a serious crime in their county. He may have gotten a U.S. Deputy Marshal killed, but that wasn't their problem.

By the time she left the diner, she knew where she would begin her search. It was the only place where he might have gone if he'd stayed locally for a day or so.

She left Canon City and tracked northwest following the same route that she'd taken ten days ago when she'd trailed Bryn and Bert.

It was just forty minutes later when she found the counterfeiters' house and stopped two hundred yards away.

She sat in the saddle and examined the quiet house, then pulled her field glasses from her saddlebags and put them to her eyes. Nothing was moving, but she noticed that the front door was ajar. It hadn't been that way when she'd left it last and doubted if the sheriff or the other deputy had paid the place a visit.

Bethan returned the field glasses to her saddlebags, unbuttoned her coat and pulled her pistol before setting Nippy forward in a walk. She kept her eyes on the house as it grew closer but still didn't see any signs of life.

When she was just fifty feet away, she pulled up again and shouted, "Hello in the house!"

She waited for just thirty seconds before nudging Nippy toward the front porch and when it was close, she halted her mare and stepped down.

She didn't tie off the reins but stepped onto the porch with her pistol level but not cocked. After pushing the door open with her boot, she stepped inside the quiet house.

Once past the doorway, she spotted the printing press on a heavy table with all sorts of supplies, then she walked slowly down the hallway and quickly scanned each room. As she found one after the other to be empty, she was more convinced that it the house was vacant, but she still kept her pistol ready to fire.

It wasn't until she opened the back door before she lowered and holstered her revolver.

It was obvious that the house had been used recently as there were still dirty dishes on the table and a half-filled pot of cold coffee on the stove.

She stepped out the back door and found reasonably fresh hoofprints, so she assumed that the one horse that had been tied in back belonged to George Lynch. It was only an educated guess, but it was all she had, so she quickly passed through the house and after closing the front door, mounted Nippy, then rode to the back of the house to being following the single horse's trail.

After another fifteen minutes of tracking, she estimated that whoever was in front of her was about a day ahead. If it was George Lynch, she might catch up with him before long.

———

George hadn't awakened at the crack of dawn, but by the time Bethan had ridden out of Pueblo, he'd reached the same set of tracks that had carried her from Denver.

He was still in a good mood as he scanned his backtrail and found no one. He could see the smoke from a distant train coming north, but he'd be another mile away before it passed by, not that it made any difference.

He was more curious about the town of Bishop and what Cody Russell was doing now. He doubted if it was anything legal. Cody was one of those men who seemed be incapable of just working at a legitimate job. George had first tracked him down after he'd stolen a horse from a nearby ranch and when he caught him, for some reason, George had liked him. He'd let Cody go and even let him keep the horse. At the time, George thought he wouldn't see Cody again, but it wasn't long before their paths crossed again.

The second time was at Madam Humphrey's House when he had beaten one of her girls. It wasn't an uncommon occurrence and George hadn't been much out of line to let him walk again, but after that, he'd spent more time with Cody at the saloon and listened to his life story, which wasn't particularly notable. But it had given George some leverage, so he'd used Cody as a go-between for some of his protection collections. Cody was more than happy to take his cut and it was only when Cody had made the mistake of roughing up another whore and had been arrested by the sheriff that things got dicey.

As the prosecutor wasn't about to charge Cody for the assault, George thought that things would go back to normal, but Sheriff Johnson had pretty much ordered Cody to get out of town. Before he left, Cody had said something about returning to his hometown to see if he could get some cash from his father.

Now, George hoped that he was still there, but after the way Cody had described his father, George wouldn't be surprised if he found Cody already dead and buried by the time he arrived.

———

Cody wasn't dead or buried, but he was about to be tried for attempted murder. He was just waiting for the Bent County deputy to arrive from Las Animas to be tried at the county courthouse. He guessed that they weren't all that interested because it had been three days since he'd shot his father. That bastard wouldn't give him a dime without working on the farm, and he'd put up with it for as long as he could.

When he finished working on Monday, he'd asked his old man for a few dollars so he could go into Bishop's poor excuse for a saloon and get something to drink, but his grizzled, short-tempered father had laughed at him. He'd laughed!

Cody had first swung at him, but the old man was faster than he'd anticipated, and he'd missed. Then the old bastard had kicked him in his crotch and kept laughing as Cody had fallen to the floor grabbing his vitals.

His father had then made the mistake of walking away, still chuckling over what he'd done to his only son. Cody had waited until he was able to stand, then pulled his pistol, called out to his father so he could see his face and pulled the trigger.

189

The hammer had snapped back down, but nothing had happened. He had a misfire at the worst possible time, and before he could cock the hammer again, his father had ripped the pistol from his hand and hit him in the side of the head with the butt.

He woke up in the town's crappy cell and learned that his father had pressed charges for attempted murder. Now it was just a matter of waiting.

He knew he wouldn't hang, but his days of running free would be over for the next decade, if not longer. He only hoped he could live long enough to walk out of the state prison.

Cody looked over at the desk and asked, "Hey, Lee, when are you gonna get me some chow?"

Town marshal Lee Collins turned and said, "In about an hour. You know that and I would appreciate it if you kept quiet for once. I'm losing money by staying here just to watch over you."

Cody snickered, then replied, "No you ain't. Your hardware store is dead since that fire. I think one of your unhappy customers set it, too."

Lee didn't bother responding to Cody. Since the winter fire that almost destroyed the store and Lou's Livery next door, he'd hoped that the bank would give him a mortgage to allow him to rebuild, but they didn't think he'd be able to make a go of it as the folks could buy what they needed at the general store. It had been his father's store, and he'd grown up working there and even shared an apartment above the store with him.

He never remembered his mother, but his father had remarried when he was just five and he thought that his stepmother was like the evil stepmother in all those fairytales.

When she ran off five years ago, it had almost killed his father, which had surprised him because Lee thought that his father would see it as more of an emancipation. Instead, he became morose and hanged himself just four months after she had gone. He had no idea where she was living now and wasn't about to go looking.

He'd accepted the unpaid position as town marshal after they'd built the jail two years earlier because the mayor had told him that he was the best man for the job. He'd been flattered and accepted the badge, even though all it did was take time away from running the store.

They made him a badge of sorts, but it was an ugly thing. He believed that they had Will Josephs, the blacksmith, just cut it out of a flattened tin can. It sure smelled like beans if it was warm enough.

He was reasonably proficient with a pistol and rifle because they sold guns in the hardware store, but until his father died, hadn't been able to use much ammunition. After his father had killed himself, he'd been free to practice more often, and it had been his only real form of entertainment.

Then the fire came on the last day of the winter, he'd been fortunate that he was down in the saloon having a beer when the dreaded shout of "Fire!" sent him and everyone else in town into the streets. No one knew how the fire had started, but it looked as if someone had broken into the shed behind the store to help himself to some kerosene and the fire had quickly leapt onto the back wall of the store.

He'd had his personal Colt with him and salvaged one Winchester that still had a somewhat charred stock, but the rest of the guns had been destroyed in the fire and almost all of the ammunition had cooked off as well.

Now he was living on his savings and the sale of the rescued stock from the fire to Sid Lewis at the general store and had to decide what to do with the rest of his life soon. Once the bank turned down his request, he knew he couldn't make a living in Bishop.

Lee then stood, stretched, walked to the front of the jail, opened the door and stepped onto the dry boardwalk.

There was the usual paucity of street traffic and he wondered how much longer Bishop itself would survive. The Atchison, Topeka and Santa Fe had run their lines twenty-five miles south of the town and all the town was good for now was to provide basic services for the surrounding farms and ranches, but even they were shifting their business to the bigger towns near the railroad. It was one of the reasons that the bank gave for denying him the mortgage.

He glanced up at the afternoon's bright blue sky and said aloud, "At least spring is finally here," then he laughed and returned to the jail.

He hoped that the county deputy would arrive soon so he could get rid of Cody and then maybe he should finally leave himself. Maybe he should ride with the deputy to Las Animas and see about getting a job with the Bent County Sheriff.

———

Bethan had stopped twice as she followed the trail, still unsure of the man she was tracking. What made it more likely that it was Lynch was that the tracks hadn't turned south toward Canon City but continued east. There wasn't much in that direction, so that indicated that the man was trying to avoid being seen. She hadn't heard of any other serious crimes in Canon City, so the only person who should be doing that would be George Lynch, who also knew about the counterfeiters' house.

She had been making good time since leaving that house and soon spotted a cloud of black smoke to her left and guessed it was a coal train because there weren't any scheduled passenger trains at this time of day. That meant that she was nearing the train tracks, which gave her the idea that maybe George would then turn north to Wigwam to pick up the next northbound train. If he did that, then he might already be gone.

She was getting warm in her heavy coat, so she slowed Nippy to a walk, let go of her reins, the shrugged it free and tied the sleeves around her waist. She still wore her vest, just to keep her shoulder harness hidden from view. It was also why she was overly warm.

But once the coat was off, she nudged Nippy into a medium trot again and closed on the train tracks, hoping she didn't lose George Lynch.

———

George knew he was getting close to Bishop but didn't want to arrive after sunset and his horse was getting tired. He'd rather get there early in the morning with a fresh horse, so as the sun dropped low in the sky, George began hunting for a campsite.

———

After walking Nippy across the rails, Bethan had expected to see the trail turn north, but was surprised when it continued east. When it kept going for a few more minutes, she began to wonder exactly where the man was going.

She knew she couldn't keep going much longer before sunset arrived and she'd have to pull up for the night, but she'd press on for as long as she could.

She'd traveled almost another hour before she pulled Nippy to a stop at a small creek to spend the night. It would be the first time she'd get to unload her panniers from the saddle horse using her rope attachment system.

It turned out not to be difficult at all. The packs only weighed about forty pounds each, but it was the necessity to carry two of them that created the need for the unusual method of getting them on and off the saddle.

After Bethan had set up her camp, she began to think of some way to improve the device. She was going to keep a cold camp, despite her belief that George Lynch wasn't within ten miles.

George was actually more than twenty miles away as measured in a straight line, but the long curve to the southeast made that distance closer to twenty-four miles.

———

In Bishop, Lee Collins had returned Cody Russell's cleaned-off plate and cutlery to Alice's Diner and had dinner himself before making his rounds. Since wearing the misshapen badge, he'd made it a habit, even though he'd had no real incidents. He had just read it was what lawmen did, so he wandered the boardwalks each morning and evening and greeted the folks.

After he checked on Cody and locked the jail, he crossed the empty street and headed for his room.

Since the fire, he'd been renting the back room at Jasper Crowley's barber shop. It was just a small space, but he only had to pay Jasper three dollars a month. After that last beer, he'd had to economize and that included no more stops at the saloon or even target practice. His dwindling savings reinforced his decision to leave Bishop with the Bent County deputy when he arrived to pick up Cody. If that didn't work out, he'd try Pueblo and then Canon City. Somebody must need a lawman, or maybe he'd just have to go back to working in a hardware store.

———

Bethan was reasonably comfortable as she lay in her bedroll with her hands behind her head. The ground was hard, and she wished she'd brought a second bedroll to put underneath this one, but it was too late now. She just added that bit of knowledge to her experience bank.

She was thinking about how to approach Lynch. She had the double advantage of being both unknown and a young woman, so she knew that she could get close to him. But that meant that she'd have to ride with her hair out rather than tucked under her hat as she'd done today.

She tried to recall what towns were east of her campsite and had a hard time because she hadn't expected him to go this way. It was another shortcoming and she began to wonder what else she'd gotten wrong.

———

The full moon had set, and the sun was making its presence known when Bethan slid out of her cloth cocoon and quickly pulled on her boots in the morning chill.

She didn't bother hiding as she answered nature's call, then she walked to the small creek, dropped to her heels and washed in the cold water.

After returning to her camp, she brushed out her long hair, pulled on her Stetson, then took off her coat and vest, slid her shoulder holster in place and hurriedly put them back on. It wasn't freezing, but a warm coat was a real necessity.

She had a quick breakfast of smoked sausage and water, filled her two canteens with fresh water, then led Nippy and the gelding to the camp and saddled her mare first.

After saddling the gelding, she used her rope lift to get the panniers back in place then tied them down. She slid the two Winchester '73s into their scabbards on the gelding, then mounted Nippy and settled into the saddle.

Bethan then took a deep breath and set Nippy to a walk to resume tracking. The sun was in her eyes, so she had to use her hat's brim to block it as she looked down at the hoofmarks.

If she was riding into an ambush, she'd never know, even if her head was up because the sunlight was so intense, but she doubted if Lynch even knew she was there. Besides, she was just a girl; a girl with a pack horse carrying two Winchesters.

————

George Lynch had also broken camp early that morning as he was planning on having a real breakfast in Bishop. He estimated he was about another hour out of the town when he set his gelding to a medium trot.

He was already grinning when he envisioned the look on Cody's face when he saw him. He'd probably think that George had come to arrest him.

———

Cody was awake and already complaining to Lee about his lack of food as Lee took the chamber pot from the cell.

"Shut up, Cody! I'll get your breakfast after I dump this thing."

"When is that deputy from Las Animas coming to pick me up?"

"It beats me. I sent that telegram two days ago and the sheriff said he'd send a man as soon as he could. I reckon that you're just not that important."

Before Cody could whine anymore, Lee exited the jail's back door, walked about fifty yards away and dumped the chamber pot, then had to circle around the front of the jail to plunge it into the trough to clean it.

He returned to the jail, set the chamber pot on the floor near the door, then quickly closed the door, but didn't lock it.

Twenty minutes later, he reentered the jail with Cody's breakfast on a tray and headed for the cell.

"It's about time!" Cody snapped as Lee slid the tray through the slot in the bars.

Lee didn't reply, but sat down, took off his hat and set it on the desk. Maybe the reason that the deputy hadn't shown up yet was because the sheriff's office was shorthanded, which would be a real break. If that was so, he should send another telegram to the sheriff and tell him that he'd bring Cody to the town directly.

———

George Lynch rode into Bishop and spotted Alice's Diner as soon as he entered their main street, so he didn't bother going any further into town before he pulled up, then tied off his horse and stepped down.

After he'd taken a seat at a table, the waitress, who was probably the owner's wife, approached and asked, "What will you be havin', mister?"

"Give me a lot of bacon, four scrambled eggs with some biscuits and a lot of coffee."

She nodded, then before she turned away, George asked, "Ma'am, do you know where I can find Cody Russell?"

The waitress laughed, then replied, "Cody? If you want to see him, you'd better make it quick. He's over in the jail waitin' for the county to send a deputy to take him to Las Animas. He tried to shoot his father a few days ago."

George was surprised, but not as much as he should have been, before he said, "I didn't know you even had a lawman."

"We got a town marshal, but we don't pay him. That's not right, if you ask me."

George nodded, then watched her leave. This was a very interesting situation. He could just keep going, but he saw an advantage to getting Cody out of jail. That would put Cody seriously in his debt and he knew that Cody had a temperament that allowed him to do things that George could never do himself.

After the waitress brought him his breakfast, he took a sip of the hot coffee and began to eat as he thought of how he could spring Cody.

By the time he'd popped the last bit of his bacon into his mouth, his plan was set, and it wasn't even that difficult.

He dropped fifteen cents on the table, grabbed his hat, left the diner and mounted.

He wheeled his gelding down the street and set him at a walk as he scanned for the jail. When he spotted it, George snickered at the sight. The sign above the doorway read MARSHALL. He wondered if the man they gave the badge is the one who had misspelled it. He wouldn't be surprised, but if he was that ignorant, then he'd have no problem at all getting Cody out of there.

George stepped down, tied off his horse, then took off his coat and hung it on his saddle horn, pinned his Deputy Sheriff badge on his shirt and loosened his hammer loop.

He stepped onto the boardwalk, then opened the door and entered, closing the door behind him.

Lee looked up from the book he was reading, saw the badge on the stranger's chest, and said, "I'm glad to see you, Deputy. How'd you get here so early? That's about a three-hour ride from Las Animas."

George grinned, and replied, "The boss made me leave before the predawn because he wants me back today."

Cody heard the familiar voice and jerked his eyes toward the front of the jail and almost called George's name but managed to keep quiet. He knew why George was here, so he wasn't able to hide his smile.

George stepped closer to the desk and said, "Let's get that boy ready to move."

"Alright," Lee said as opened the desk drawer and pulled out the key ring.

After he stood and turned to step to the door, he heard the ominous double click of a Colt's hammer being drawn back and knew that he was going to die.

George had no intention of killing the town marshal, but said, "Open the cell door."

Lee slid the key into the lock, turned it and then swung the door wide with a loud squeal.

Cody bounced from his cot and exclaimed, "It's good to see you, George! Why are you here?"

"We'll talk about that later. Marshal, use your left hand to undo your gunbelt and let it drop."

Lee felt sick as he loosened his gunbelt, then let it slide to the floor.

"Cody, pick up the marshal's gunbelt and put it on. Then take out he pistol, cock it and keep it pointed at the marshal."

"Okay, George," Cody said before he snatched up the gunbelt, wrapped it around his waist and then pulled the Colt free.

Once Cody had the pistol pointed at the marshal, George released his own revolver's hammer, slid it home and then said, "Sit on the floor with your back against the wall, Marshal."

Lee exhaled, then took one long stride, turned and put his back against the wall and slid to the floor as he kept his eyes on George, examining every facet of his face in the unlikely chance that he would live to be able to live long enough to chase him down.

"Are we gonna kill him?" Cody asked excitedly.

"No, Cody, we aren't going to kill him. We don't need every damned lawman in Colorado looking for us. Right now, they won't even care about us at all."

"Then what are we gonna do with him?"

"I'll show you," George said as he stepped over to the cot, yanked off the sheet and began ripping it into long strips.

He quickly bound Lee's ankles, then he had Lee roll onto his side and tied his wrists behind his back before using another strip to link the wrists and ankles.

George then used the last strip of old cotton to gag Lee before standing and turning to look at Cody.

"You can holster that pistol, Cody. How often to folks come into the jail?"

"Not much at all."

"Okay. Where's your horse?"

"I guess he's at my old man's place."

"How about the marshal's?"

"He keeps him out back."

"Go and get him saddled. Is that Winchester the only other gun he has?"

"Yup. I'll take it, too."

"Get going. I'll see what else I can find around here."

Cody grinned, then grabbed his coat and shrugged it on before taking the flame-charred Winchester. He finally pulled on his hat and left the jail.

After he'd gone, George looked down at Lee and said, "Sorry, Marshal, but I need Cody and you don't. Just remember that I let you live when a lot of men, including Cody, would have been more than ready to put a bullet through your head."

Lee wished he could have asked a few questions, but was grateful that he would live, despite the humiliation of being fooled. He hoped that the Bent County deputy made it to town soon but guessed it wouldn't be for at least another four hours, if he was coming today at all.

George left the cell and closed the door before tossing the key ring to the back of the room. Then he began searching the small office but found nothing worth taking with them. He should have searched the marshal but guessed that the man didn't have much. He almost felt bad for doing it to the man, but he needed Cody.

George then left the jail, closed the door and walked to his horse. He donned his coat again, then mounted and walked his gelding around the jail and found Cody almost finished saddling the marshal's horse.

George said, "I wish that the marshal didn't ride a pinto. That critter sticks out like a beacon on a foggy night."

"Want me to take a different one?"

"No. Let's get out of here nice and quiet before anyone finds the marshal."

"Where are we going, George?" Cody asked as he finished adjusting the left stirrup.

"I think our best bet now is to head for Las Animas. I can't go back to Canon City."

"What if we run into the deputy that they sent to pick me up?"

"Unless he knows what you look like, I don't think he'll pay any attention to two riders."

"Okay," Cody said as he stepped into the saddle, then asked, "What about money or supplies? I don't have a damned cent."

"I'm okay for money and it's only about four hours to Las Animas. We'll figure out what to do on the way."

Cody grinned, then said, "Okay, George, let's get out of this fleabag town."

"Follow me. We don't want anyone to see us leaving."

Cody waited until George turned his horse east and then set Lee's pinto in line behind him as they rode along the back alley behind the buildings.

———

Bent County Deputy Sheriff Bart Williamson left Las Animas about twenty minutes after George and Cody left Bishop. He was a bit irritated for having to make the long ride after having just returned from Salt Springs yesterday, but he knew it wasn't the sheriff's fault that they were so shorthanded. Since Fred Latimore had left the job six weeks ago, they hadn't found a replacement.

He wasn't sure that he'd be able to make it back today unless that wannabe lawman in Bishop had the prisoner ready to go when he arrived.

––––––

Bethan was making good time as she tracked George Lynch. She still had no idea where he was going but noted his shift to the south so at least he seemed to know where he was headed.

It was almost noon when she first spotted Bishop in the distance and pulled Nippy to a stop so she could take a few minutes to prepare to encounter George Lynch.

She debated about removing her coat to have better access to her pistol but thought it might spook him. She thought about leaving the pack horse with its added firepower outside of town but decided she would stop at the first building and hope that he didn't spot her.

Bethan nudged Nippy into a slow trot and twenty minutes later, entered the quiet town. It may have been Saturday, but there should be more traffic.

She pulled up at the first building, Alice's Diner, then stepped down and tied off Nippy. Her stomach may be demanding that she go inside, but she wanted to find George Lynch. It was possible that he was already gone, but she wanted to do her search before getting something to satisfy her stomach.

She scanned the street, noted the burned-out store, and then was surprised to see a jail. It wasn't much, but even having any kind of lawman was a positive.

Bethan stepped quickly to the boardwalk and headed east to the town marshal's office, still letting her eyes wander in case George Lynch made a sudden appearance. She hadn't spotted his horse, so it wasn't likely.

She reached the jail, and after one last glance at the open road, opened the door and stepped inside.

After one step, she froze and quickly threw her coat open and pulled her pistol.

She did a quick scan of the small office, then walked to the jail cell that held a bound and gagged man who was obviously asleep, wondering what kind of lawman would do this to his prisoner.

She reached the door, found it locked, then looked for a key ring. It wasn't where she expected to find it, so she hurried to the desk and quickly checked the drawers. She was about to leave to ask someone where the marshal was when the prisoner groaned.

Bethan than turned and walked back to the cell door and looked at the man, then finally noticed that he was wearing a badge and realized that he must have been jumped by his prisoner who had then made his escape.

She then expanded her search for the keys and soon spotted them on the floor near the back wall.

After picking them up and opening the cell, she stepped inside, slid her pistol back into her holster, then pulled her knife from her gunbelt and sliced the long strip of cloth linking the bindings around his ankles and wrists.

Lee felt the release and was still groggy as the cold steel of a knife blade touched his wrists, cutting the fabric that bound them.

He opened his eyes and was stunned to see a very pretty young woman close and the first thing that entered his mind was that this only happened in cheap dime novels.

"Who are you?" he asked.

Bethan had moved to his ankles just before he asked, so she didn't look back when she replied, "I'm Bethan Evans. I'm guessing that you're the town marshal and you had a prisoner that somehow jumped you. Is that right?"

She then stood, slid her knife into the sheath and looked down at Lee who was struggling to get to his feet.

"Sort of. This man with a badge showed up and I thought he was the deputy from Las Animas who I was expecting to pick up a prisoner. He pulled his pistol and then he took my gun and gave it to the prisoner before he tied me up. I think they took my horse, too."

As he moved to the cot and rubbed his wrists, Bethan asked, "How long ago was this? Do you know where they went?"

"Why do you want to know? I'll send a telegram to Sheriff Allen in Bent County and he'll take care of it."

"The man who showed up here used to be a Fremont County deputy sheriff and that's why he had the badge. I've been trailing him for a couple of days, and I want to catch him first. It's personal."

"That's a bad idea, Miss Evans. You'd only get in trouble. Leave this to the law."

"I am the law," she replied as she opened her coat to show him her U.S. Deputy Marshal's badge.

"*Where did you get that?*" he exclaimed with wide eyes.

"My father swore me in a few days ago because he knew I'd just become a bounty hunter if he didn't. I'm not getting paid because the head office would probably fire him if they knew, but I'm still a sworn officer of the law."

Lee looked at her pretty, but determined face and said, "I guess he must know what he's doing, but I still want to notify Sheriff Allen because it's his jurisdiction. If those two bastards rode east, then they'd be heading into Las Animas, too."

"You can do that, but I need to get going. Where was your horse kept? I can start tracking them from there."

Lee stood then asked, "Can you wait until I find a horse? I'd like to go to Las Animas anyway."

Bethan looked at him and did a quick evaluation before she answered, "I have a spare horse and saddle outside, so you can use him. I've been using him as a pack horse, so that has to be altered."

"I'll do that. You wouldn't happen to have a spare gun, would you?"

Bethan laughed before she replied, "A few."

She waited while Lee walked to the far wall, took down and donned his coat and then pulled on his hat. Then they left the jail without even bothering to close the door.

Once outside, Lee stared at the two panniers and said, "That'll be easy enough. We'll just move it to the back of the saddle seat where you'd normally have the bedroll. Do you need to get anything out of those saddlebags?"

"Not right away. I have anything I need quickly in my own set. You can find a gunbelt and pistol in either of the saddlebags before we move the packs. We'll decide what to do if they split up as we go along."

Lee nodded, then noticed the Winchester '76 and shotgun on the mare and two Winchester '73s on the gelding and wondered why she had so many guns, but figured they'd have time to talk when they left Bishop. He wondered what she would do if one of them suddenly turned north or south.

He walked to the left saddlebag, opened the flap and removed the gunbelt and was pleased to find a well-maintained Colt '73 that was chambered for the .44-40 and not the .45.

He strapped it around his waist, then Bethan walked to the other side and after she untied the rope from the saddle horn, they simply lifted the two panniers and moved them to their new position. Lee then tied the rope to itself and snugged it down.

"I'll adjust the stirrups later," he said before he climbed into the saddle.

Bethan mounted, then looked at him and said, "You're only a couple of inches taller than me, so I don't think it'll be a problem. What's your name, anyway?"

"Lee. Lee Collins."

"Okay, Lee, send your telegram to the sheriff and then let's go see where those boys went after they took your horse," she said before she turned Nippy to the left and then curled around behind the jail with Lee trailing.

It didn't take long for them to spot the new tracks heading east, so they set off in that direction without further comment.

After Lee stopped at the telegraph office to send his message to Sheriff Allen, they rode out of Bishop. Bethan had thought about sending a telegram to her father but decided to wait until after she found George Lynch.

Lee expected to return in a day or so with his pinto, but still wondered if he shouldn't have picked up a change of clothes and his shaving kit from his room. It was too late now, but he'd be pretty scruffy looking when he got back.

———

George and Cody were trotting along the road to Las Animas as the temperatures continued to rise. George had already explained why he had to leave Canon City and Cody had to tell his story since arriving back at his hometown.

"Why did you come looking for me?" Cody asked.

"When I was sitting in that house waiting for my boss or those U.S. marshals to arrive, I didn't get any sleep at all and I didn't like it. At first, I was thinking that I might be able to catch on as a lawman somewhere else, and if I hadn't gotten that

U.S. deputy marshal killed by telling Irv Thompson that they were coming, I think it would have worked. So, by the time I left that place, I figured I might as well use this badge to my advantage, but I needed to have somebody I could trust to watch my back."

"And you chose me?" Cody asked with a grin.

"Yup. I figured you owed me before I even left town, but you really owe me big time now."

"You're right about that, George. I woulda spent a good part of my life behind bars if you hadn't sprung me outta there."

"Remember that, Cody."

"You bet," Cody yelled back.

Then George spotted a dust cloud ahead and said, "Do you think that's the deputy sheriff that's coming to pick you up?"

"Maybe. He shoulda been there yesterday."

"Well, let me handle it if he starts talking to us."

"Okay, but what happens when he gets to Bishop and finds Lee all trussed up in his own jail?"

George didn't answer right away as he stared at the dust cloud and the approaching rider. This was a problem he hadn't foreseen and even though he suspected that they'd find the town marshal soon anyway, the deputy might report to his boss that he'd seen two riders pass him.

He finally replied, "Let me do the talking, Cody. Just have your trigger loop off."

"It's already that way," Cody replied.

George glanced at Cody and hoped that he'd stay calm. It was one of Cody's many faults; he tended to act first and think second. It's what got him caught so often.

———

Bart Williamson had noticed the two oncoming riders before they'd seen him. They were still about a mile away, so he wasn't worried. He was wearing his badge on his jacket, so he didn't think that they'd be concerned about him either. They were just two guys headed for Las Animas.

When they were just two hundred yards apart, he thought that he'd seen one of their horses before but couldn't recall where or when he had. Pintos were unusual and this black and white one had a completely black head. He just couldn't match it to his memory.

The two men then slowed as he approached, and Bart was just curious enough about the pinto to ask about it.

He pulled to a stop as they drew near, and after they halted, he smiled and said, "Howdy. I'm Bent County Deputy Sheriff Bart Williamson, and I was curious about your pinto. How long have you had him?"

Unfortunately for George, the deputy's question was directed to Cody, so he had to hope that his new partner could provide a reasonable answer.

Cody replied, "Not long. I just got him from a feller in Bishop."

"That's funny because that's where I'm headed. I need to pick up a prisoner. How much did you have to pay for him? He's a handsome boy."

"Not as much as you might figure. The man I bought him from didn't need him anymore," Cody answered.

Bart nodded, then his mind made the connection to that unpaid town marshal in Bishop. He'd met him just about a year ago when he'd come to Las Animas to talk to the sheriff and Bart had talked to him about his horse. As proud as the man was with his pinto, Bart doubted if he would have parted with the horse for anything less than a king's ransom.

Bart didn't react as if he knew, but smiled and said, "Well, I guess I'd better get going. I wanted to get back by today."

As he nudged his horse to begin moving, Cody leaned over to George then waited until Bart was fifty feet away and said, "He knows about the pinto, George."

George was pretty sure that Cody was right and swiveled on the saddle to look back at the receding lawman.

Cody didn't waste time to just look but pulled the Winchester with the charred stock from the scabbard, then levered in a fresh round to be sure that one was in the chamber.

A .44 spat out of the carbine, but before it even touched the ground, Cody fired.

The bullet spun out of the barrel, crossed the hundred and eighty-one feet and punched into Bart Williamson's back just above his heart. The .44 shattered two ribs, then tumbled through his left lung before slamming into the same ribs on the front of his chest.

Bart rocked from the shock but as bad as the damage was, it wasn't fatal. He was pulling his own Winchester free when Cody fired a second shot.

That bullet stuck lower in Bart's torso, on the left side of his gut and just ripped apart his stomach before exiting through the front of his coat.

He still was able to get his Winchester's hammer cocked and was bringing it level when Cody fired a third time but missed.

By the time Bart was trying to aim, his horse was already panicking, and he was losing enough blood, but he still fired. Where his bullet went didn't matter.

George had watched Cody's reaction and wasn't shocked but was sickened when he watched Bart take the hits. He almost wished that Bart's lone shot killed him but didn't stop Cody when he sent the pinto back west to close the gap to the deputy.

Bart saw the shooter approach, but his vision was fading, and he was having a difficult time keeping his sights even close to the target when he saw the pinto rider fire again. He felt the hammer blow of the .44 when it struck the right side of his chest, then everything went black.

Cody watched him fall from his horse, but kept the Winchester pointed at the downed lawman until he was close enough to make sure he was dead.

He then lowered the repeater, released the hammer and slid it back into its scabbard before stepping down.

He quickly stripped the deputy of his gunbelt and his badge before going through his pockets. He found eleven dollars and some change, stuffed them into his own pocket, then dragged the body out of the roadway and dumped it off to the side.

Cody took his horse's reins then led it back to the pinto and was tying it to off when George stepped down and approached him.

"Now what do we do?" Cody asked.

George replied, "We can't go into Las Animas with that deputy's horse; that's for sure. Let's drag that body further off the road and cover it with prairie grass."

"Okay. So, where will we be goin'?"

"They can't hang this one on either of us if we get out of here before someone else sees us. Let's head south for a while. I don't want to go to a big town like La Junta. Let's go to Robinson. It's only about twenty miles south of here and we should be able to get rid of that damned pinto and get some supplies."

"Okay, George. You're the boss," Cody said before they walked to the deputy's body to move it another fifty yards.

George wasn't so sure that it was true, but he'd made his bed and now had to sleep in it.

It took them ten minutes to cover the body reasonably well, then George kicked dirt over the puddles of blood on the roadway just to be sure no one noticed. They mounted their horses, turned south and headed cross-country for Robinson.

———

Once Bethan and Lee were out of Bishop, the tracks stayed in the road, and as it wasn't well traveled, they were easy to follow.

Bethan then looked at Lee and asked, "How long have you been town marshal?"

"A little more than three years now. They built the jail first to try and impress the railroad, but that didn't work. They needed a town marshal but couldn't pay anything, so they offered me the job."

"Why did you take it if they weren't going to pay you?"

Lee shrugged and replied, "I guess I just wanted to feel important and impress folks."

Bethan smiled, then said, "That's an unusual admission, Lee. Most men would have said that they wanted to serve justice or keep the peace. Were you trying to impress some girl?"

Lee laughed, shook his head and replied, "Nope. Bishop was already dying by then and the only unattached young ladies were the girls of four of the local farmers and Abby Littlefield, the mayor's daughter. They were already spoken for, so having a badge wouldn't have made any difference."

"So, why did you stay in Bishop?"

"My father started and ran the hardware store, and I worked there since I was eight. He died a few years ago and I took over. I could see sales dropping even before the fire. Once it burned down and the bank wouldn't give me a mortgage to rebuild, I knew I had to leave, but I hadn't gotten around to it yet."

"I saw the ruins of your hardware store when I arrived. So, you're more of a shopkeeper than a lawman."

"Yes, ma'am," he replied, then asked, "Do you mind if I call you Bethan?"

"Not at all. I'm surprised you didn't ask if you could call me Beth or Bess."

"Why would I do that? You said your name was Bethan, so I assumed that's what you wanted folks to call you."

"Every boy or young man I've ever met has called me either Beth or Bess. Some even called me Bessie. It didn't go over well."

"Can you tell me how you got to carry that badge?"

Bethan was still scanning the ground as she began to tell Lee the story that began with her trailing Bryn and Bert to the counterfeiters' house. Just as she had when she made her report or her testimony at the trial, her narration was concise and exact.

When she finished, Lee asked, "What are we going to do when we catch up with those two?"

"That depends on where they are and if they're together."

"We should be able to spot Biff from a long way out."

Bethan turned and asked, "Biff?"

"That's what I named my pinto."

Bethan was smiling as she said, "You're going to have to explain that one."

Lee smiled back as he replied, "It's not hard to figure out if you see him. When I found him just after I was made the marshal, I thought he was as handsome a horse as I'd ever

216

seen. He was black and white, but his entire head was black. I was going to call him Blackface, but that was too long. I changed it to BF, but that sounded odd, so I called him Biff."

Bethan laughed, then said, "This girl I'm riding I call Nippy."

"Nippy?"

"When she was just a week old or so, my Uncle Bryn gave her to me so I could raise her as my friend. Well, the second day I was with her, I was giving her an apple slice, then dropped my pocketknife. When I bent over to pick it up, she decided to take a small nip out of me. She earned her name, but it was the only time she ever tried it. I guess she didn't like the taste."

It was Lee's turn to laugh before he said, "I guess her name was well-earned then. How about your name? Are you named after anyone?"

"Nope. It was just a Welsh name that my parents picked out. My mother told me that because there was a male curse in the Evans family, she only had a girl's name chosen before I was born. That way, she could break the curse. I'm not sure that it was completely successful."

"Oh, I don't know. Despite your dress, you don't seem exactly masculine to me."

Bethan was shocked to feel herself blush, but ignored the unexpected reaction and asked, "How about your name?"

"My father was an admirer of Bobby Lee and served with him in the army. My middle name is Robert, so that completes the explanation."

"Aren't you a bit too old for that? I mean, even if your father served with him when the war started, you'd only be about sixteen."

"He served with him during the Mexican War when he was a lieutenant colonel. I'm twenty-three now. After you explained how you got the badge, I got the impression that you have a large family up in Denver. Just how big is it?"

Bethan had to go down the list, family by family before she replied, "If you only count Evans, there are twenty-seven, but we have others that live at the Double EE and my brothers have two ranch hands at their ranch."

"My lord! How can you keep track of that many?"

"It's not hard."

"You said that there was a male curse in the family. How many of those twenty-seven are girls?"

"There are nineteen children and only six were girls. I have a sister, Cari, who is fourteen, and four cousins; Grace, who is almost ten, then eight-year-old Bess, three-year-old Meredith and sixteen-month-old Gwendolyn."

"That is odd, but I don't know if I'd call it a curse. I had a brother when I was young, but he died."

They continued to talk family as they rode in the afternoon sun. Each of them had to remove their coats and tie them around their waists after an hour just before Bethan handed Lee one of her two canteens.

———

George and Cody were making decent time, but because of the lack of landmarks, weren't heading due south, but more southwest. Neither of them believed that they were being tracked. If someone in Bishop had found Lee Collins by now, they'd probably just send a telegram to the Bent County sheriff, and he'd probably just send a reply that his deputy would arrive shortly.

By the time anyone realized that the deputy wasn't going to show up, they'd be out of Robinson on the next train. They didn't care if they went to Kansas or New Mexico, as long as they were out of Colorado.

———

Sheriff Allen had received a telegram, but it wasn't exactly as George and Cody had expected because it had much more information.

He didn't have any other deputies with Bart gone and the contents of the telegram bothered him.

He read it once more:

SHERIFF TOM ALLEN LAS ANIMAS COLO

PRISONER CODY RUSSELL ESCAPED
ASSISTED BY EX FREMONT DEP SHERIFF
STILL HAS BADGE
STOLE MY PINTO
BOTH HEADED TO LAS ANIMAS
WILL FOLLOW WITH US DEP MARSHAL EVANS

MARSHAL LEE COLLINS BISHOP COLO

If he had another deputy, he'd send him to Bishop to warn Bart, but he had to stay in town. All he could now was wait for the town marshal and hope he'd bring Bart with him. Until then, he'd keep an eye to the west to see who arrived first.

He wondered whether it was Bryn or Lynn Evans with Lee Collins and assumed that they'd been trailing that ex-deputy for something to do with the takedown of the counterfeiters. He'd gotten some official messages, but many more stories in the newspaper.

If the news about those two wasn't bad enough, he was still concerned about the Gentry gang who could be in his county by now.

———

Bethan hadn't spotted any changes in the two horses for over two hours and almost missed it. She and Lee had been talking almost non-stop and she was growing negligent in her tracking.

But even as she laughed when Lee was telling her the story about his big arrest of a cat thief, her trained eyes alerted her to the change on the road.

She abruptly stopped laughing, pulled Nippy to a sudden stop and exclaimed, "Hold up, Lee!"

Lee was still grinning when she yanked Nippy's reins, but quickly brought the gelding to a stop and trained his eyes to the road where she was looking.

"That looks like blood," she said as she dismounted.

Lee stepped down as well, then walked with her to the dark blotches in the middle of the road.

"Somebody tried to cover it up with dirt," Lee said.

Bethan nodded then began stepping further east along the road with her eyes focused on the ground. What she saw alarmed her.

"There is another set of hoofprints that were heading west. Do you think that they ran into that deputy you were expecting?"

"That's most likely. There isn't a lot of traffic between Bishop and Las Animas and this was just one rider."

She pointed to the jumble of hoofprints and said, "He wasn't alone very long. They came back here, and you can see footprints and signs of a scuffle all around the blood."

She then let her eyes drift south, then pointed and said, "It looks like they dragged his body over there."

They led their horses off road and soon reached Bart Williamson's body.

Bethan looked down at the dead deputy, then said, "I guess this changes our plans, Lee. We've got to take him to Las Animas."

"Okay. How do we do it?"

"We'll double up on Nippy and put the body on the gelding."

"Alright. We're only about an hour or so out of Las Animas, so we should make it before sunset."

"Let's get this done."

———

Just ten minutes later, Bethan was in her saddle with Lee sitting behind her as they returned to the road trailing the pack horse that now was draped with Bart Williamson's body.

"What do we do about those two?" Lee asked as he sat uncomfortably behind Bethan with his hands on her waist.

"I'm still thinking about that. Their tracks were heading south, which makes sense. They'd want to get on a train to get out of the state, but they probably won't go to La Junta. They'll want to find a smaller town without any law. You're more familiar with this area than I am. What's down there?"

"Well, if they're going to avoid going to La Junta, they'll head for Robinson. It's the closest stop on the AT&SF route just east of La Junta."

"But it's on the other side of the Arkansas River, isn't it?"

"Yes, ma'am. The tracks run along the south side of the Arkansas almost all the way to Pueblo. Of course, at La Junta they split and one branch heads southwest to Trinidad."

"Maybe they're headed for Mexico. When we get to Las Animas, we'll have the sheriff send telegrams to Pueblo and Trinidad."

"Then what will we do?"

"I'll send a telegram to my father and then I'm going to get something to fill my nagging stomach before I get a room."

"We're going to let them go?"

"I didn't say that, but there's no point in turning right around and chasing them in the dead of night. I need to come up with a revised plan now that there are two of them."

"It sounds as if you're planning on going alone."

"I thought you were going to ask the sheriff for a job. I hate to sound morbid, but with the deputy back there, he's going to be short-handed. How many deputies does he have left?"

"I think he only had two, but I'm not sure."

"As big as this county is, I would have thought he'd have more."

"He used to have four, but he lost two in one day when they decided to hunt for gold. I don't know if he hired any new men yet."

"Let's talk to the sheriff when we get there."

"Okay."

Bethan was formulating her revised plan for tracking down George Lynch and his partner but knew that circumstances were much different now. Not only were there two of them, they had murdered a lawman. Those bullet holes were in his back, so they had to have passed him on the road then shot him when he wasn't looking.

She may have wanted to find George Lynch, but she wasn't confident in Lee's ability as a lawman. He may have been a town marshal and said he was reasonably proficient with firearms, but he'd never been in a dangerous situation and even though she had, Bethan wanted better support.

She was trying to concentrate on the situation as Nippy trotted along the road but having Lee's hands on her waist was making it difficult. She admitted that she was already impressed with him for many reasons. Aside from the fact that he was easy on the eyes, he hadn't treated her like some defenseless damsel. Maybe it was because the first time he'd seen her, she was cutting off his bindings. But even then, he hadn't reacted with her expected, "You're a girl!".

It wasn't as if she hadn't been touched by a young man before, it was that she'd never been touched by a young man who had appealed to her.

Las Animas soon appeared on the eastern horizon and Bethan asked, "Where is the sheriff's office?"

"It's on the main street on the left side."

"You can tell the sheriff what happened. I've learned that men usually don't listen when I talk."

"I listened."

"You're different, Lee. You haven't treated me as most men have."

"It's just a matter of respect, Bethan."

"Well, I appreciate it," she replied and meant it.

―――

The sun was low in the sky as they entered Las Animas and pulled up before the county jail.

Lee slipped off the back of the saddle before Bethan dismounted and tied off Nippy. Then, they crossed the boardwalk and Lee opened the door before following Bethan inside.

After closing the door, they found themselves in an empty office, so Lee called out, "Sheriff Allen?"

Sheriff Tom Allen was at his desk in his private office when he heard the door open, so he was already on his feet when Lee called.

He hadn't recognized the voice, and his stomach already knotted because if it was the town marshal, then he should have been with Bart and the shout would be unnecessary.

When he entered the hallway, he spotted Lee with a handsome young woman and wondered how she was involved in this but didn't take much time to think about it as he strode into the front office.

"Where's my deputy, Marshal?"

"I'm sorry, Sheriff, but his body is outside. We found it about five miles west of town. He'd been shot in the back."

"Son of a bitch!" he exclaimed as he walked quickly past Lee and Bethan.

They followed him outside and watched as he quickly examined his deputy's body.

Sheriff Allen then turned and said, "Was it those two you mentioned in your telegram?"

"I'm sure it was. Their tracks headed south from the ambush site and they were leading his horse."

"I'll need to send telegrams to other law agencies right away. We can talk on the way."

"Okay," Lee replied, then glanced at Bethan.

She shrugged, then they quickly got in step with the sheriff as he crossed the street.

As they walked, the sheriff asked, "You said that you had U.S. Deputy Marshal Evans with you. Did he go after those two on his own?"

"No, sir. She's walking on your left. Bethan was deputized by her father a few days ago after that shootout west of Canon City and in Granite. She's the one who captured the last two."

They hadn't quite reached the opposite boardwalk, but the sheriff came to an abrupt stop, looked at Bethan and sharply asked, "*You're a United States Deputy Marshal?*"

"He had to make me a temporary deputy marshal so the head office wouldn't know about it. He wanted anything I did to be legal."

"Are you going to send a telegram to him now?"

"Yes, sir. Everything has changed."

"That's putting it mildly," the sheriff said as they resumed their walk.

As they stepped along the boardwalk, Lee began to explain what had happened in Bishop and didn't minimize his own failure.

"You didn't screw up, Lee," the sheriff said when they reached the Western Union office, "You were expecting a deputy sheriff and that bastard had one."

"He has two now," Bethan said, "They took your deputy's guns and badge as well as his horse."

"Bastards!" the sheriff spat under his breath as they entered the telegraph office.

As the sheriff wrote out his warning to other law enforcement agencies, Bethan wrote her own long message to her father and marked it urgent, so they'd send it to the Double EE if he'd already gone for the day. Unlike the Denver County sheriff's office, the United States Marshal's office wasn't open twenty-four hours a day. She showed it to Lee, who nodded before she handed it to the operator.

———

After they had ridden for another two hours, Cody asked, "Do you think we're gonna make it to that town before sundown?"

"I'm not sure. We might be drifting to the east or west and we won't know until we spot the river."

"I thought you knew where you were goin'."

"I know we're heading mostly south, but there aren't exactly a lot of landmarks out here. When we hit the river, we can cross and find a mile marker at the tracks and I'll have a good idea."

"What if we don't reach the tracks before it gets dark?"

"Then we'll set up a cold camp and start again in the morning."

Cody snorted then shook his head. He wasn't happy, but at least it was better than being in jail.

———

After writing their statements and having the body taken to the mortuary, it was more than two hours before Bethan was

227

able to leave Nippy and the gelding at the livery and she and Lee were finally able to get something to eat.

As they sat at the table, Lee asked, "What will we do next?"

Bethan swallowed, then replied, "We'll get our rooms at the hotel and then tomorrow morning, we have breakfast and then talk to the sheriff again. By then, I should have a reply from my father."

"Okay. What do you think he'll say?"

"I'm pretty sure that he'll tell me that he'll be sending help. When it was just one ex-deputy whose only crime was passing along information, he probably wasn't concerned. But now that there are two back-shooting murderers, he'll probably send someone."

"Even if you told him that I was with you?"

"No offense, Lee, but you're a town marshal and he may have let me chase down an ex-deputy, but I'm still his daughter, and he'll want someone he knows to help me. If it makes you feel any better, even if I was one of his real deputies, he'd probably still send someone."

"I've heard a lot of stories about your lawman family, and I didn't want to sound as if I was trying to impress you, but it was one of the reasons I accepted the badge It just wasn't as much as wanting to feel more important."

Bethan smiled and replied, "You were right about not telling me that in the first place. I've had a few boys use that as an excuse to get me to like them and it only made them less likely to be able to say anything else."

"Your whole family sounds as if it gets along really well."

"We have our moments, but overall, we're rather fond of each other."

Lee nodded, then stared at his fork as he said, "I wish that I'd known my father better. If I had, maybe I would have been able to like my stepmother. Sometimes I think that it was because I was so angry with her for taking my father away from me that I didn't like her. Then when she ran away, I was happy about it, but my father was heartbroken, and I didn't understand at all. I wanted things to go back to the way they were, but it didn't.

"He stayed quiet and morose and then he hanged himself. I never really talked to him and I regret those years. I still wonder if I had accepted my stepmother and not acted as I did, if he would still be alive."

Bethan looked across the table at his somber face and said, "You were just a kid, Lee. Did your father sit down with you before he married her to explain things?"

"No. I didn't even know he'd been seeing her. She was recently widowed, and when he told me three days before they were married, I was stunned."

"What if he'd involved you in the process? What if your father had told you at the very start that he was visiting her, and more importantly, why he was? He should have talked to you, Lee."

"He was always a quiet man, even when my mother was alive. He never beat me or anything, so I thought I was a lucky boy."

Then he looked at Bethan, smiled slightly, then said, "It's funny. I spent twelve to fourteen hours every day with him at the store and I'll bet we didn't pass sixty words between us that didn't involve business."

"Well, I'm glad that you're not that way. I don't mind some measure of silence, but when I have something on my mind, I want to tell someone. I noticed that you do the same."

"That's a bit odd, too. I never really had anyone that I wanted to hear things like this before. My father's been dead for years now, but I've never talked to anyone about it."

"We'll have more time on the train tomorrow."

"It's only three hours or so."

"We have more time tonight, Lee."

Lee nodded, then they both returned to eating their long-awaited meal.

―――

Dylan was still in the office because he hadn't heard from Bethan yet. With his daughter trailing that deputy in the area, he hoped to at least know where she was before he had to go back to Gwen.

Dylan was blowing out one of the two lamps in the office when the door opened, and Bobby Harrison entered.

"I got two telegrams for you, Marshal," he said as he held out the folded sheets.

"I hope one is from my daughter," Dylan replied as he took the papers and handed him a nickel.

Bobby accepted the coin and waited for the reply he knew was coming.

Dylan quickly opened the first message and read:

ALL COLORADO LAW ENFORCEMENT

**DEPUTY MURDERED WEST OF LAS ANIMAS
SUSPECTS CODY RUSSELL AND GEORGE LYNCH
RUSSELL ESCAPEE FROM BISHOP JAIL
CHARGED WITH ATTEMPTED MURDER
FREED BY LYNCH
HEADED SOUTH
MAY TRY TO JOIN GENTRY GANG**

SHERIFF ALLEN LAS ANIMAS COLO

Dylan avoided any expletives after finishing the first telegram before quickly setting it aside and opening the second one and quickly read:

US MARSHAL DYLAN EVANS DENVER COLO

**TRAILED LYNCH TO BISHOP
USED BADGE TO TRICK TOWN MARSHAL
FREED PRISONER AND RODE EAST
KILLED BENT COUNTY DEPUTY THEN SOUTH
WILL TAKE TRAIN TO LA JUNTA WITH MARSHAL**

BETHAN EVANS LAS ANIMAS COLO

"Damn!" Dylan swore then looked at Bobby and said, "Give me a minute to write my reply."

"Yes, sir."

Dylan walked to the front desk, took pencil from the cup, and quickly printed out his clear response in large block letters before returning and handing it to the boy.

"Have Wilbur mark this as urgent."

"Yes, sir."

Dylan guessed that it would be forty cents to send the message, so he handed Bobby Lee two quarters and said, "Keep the change. This is more personal than business."

"Thank you, Marshal," he replied then turned and quickly left the office.

After he'd gone, Dylan blew out the last lamp, then left the office, locked the door and mounted Raven to head home. He'd need to talk to Bryn and Lynn when he got back. He hoped that Bethan understood and followed his instructions. Now that she was a sworn deputy marshal, she had to obey his orders, or so he hoped.

He didn't understand why the sheriff believed that the two men were going to join the Gentry gang because no one knew where they'd gone to ground after leaving the Indian Nations. He wondered if he should have sent a query to Sheriff Allen along with the one that he'd sent to Bethan, but it was too late now. He needed to get Lynn and Bryn on a train to Robinson as soon as possible. If they pushed it, they could catch the night freight that would leave in six hours.

———

George and Cody had set up their cold camp and Cody was annoyed because they hadn't even reached the Arkansas River yet. *How could you not find a damned river?*

"We'll probably reach the river in the morning and then once we get across, we'll follow the railroad tracks into Robinson. We'll be out of Colorado by tomorrow night."

"Then what?" Cody asked sharply.

"I don't know yet."

"I figured that out already," Cody snapped.

George glanced at his new partner and wondered if he should just abandon him in the wee hours of the morning. He'd expected Cody to be a subservient follower, but something had triggered a monster. It must have been something to do with his father. Cody had just mentioned that he was in jail because he'd had a fight with his father but hadn't explained it much beyond that. After watching Cody quickly shoot that deputy in the back, George wondered if Cody was in jail for murdering his father and not just a simple fight.

He'd wait until they'd turned in for the night before he decided what to do.

Cody hadn't given much thought at all to the dead deputy other than anticipating what he could do now that he had the badge. He'd watched how George had simply entered the jail, smiled at Lee Collins and taken over, just because he had a badge. That simple method for breaking him out of jail had opened all sorts of new opportunities in his mind.

———

In Las Animas, Bethan and Lee had gotten their rooms and were sitting in the lobby when a critical and inevitable question finally arrived.

"Um, Bethan, I really hate to ask but this has been kind of bothering me."

"What do you want to know?" she asked in response.

"I didn't bring much money with me and I don't know if I can afford to pay for the train ticket to La Junta."

"It's only eleven dollars and fifty cents, Lee, but don't worry about it. I brought a couple of hundred with me, so I'll handle expenses. Does that bother you?"

"Of course, it bothers me. Other than my father, I've never had to ask anyone for anything before, but that doesn't include the bank when I applied for a mortgage."

"Well, you can pay me back out of your pay as a deputy sheriff when you take the job that Sheriff Allen will offer you. You know that he will, don't you?"

"I got that impression, but he was mad about losing his deputy and I'll see how that works out tomorrow when he's calmer. I do have enough to buy a new shaving kit and other things. I'll pick those up in the morning before we get on the train if the store opens early enough."

Behan smiled and said, "Strange as it seems, I have a shaving kit in one of those packs that you can use."

"Why would you have a shaving kit?"

"My father said that a razor is better for working on wounds than a knife and the soap cup and brush can be used to clean the area. I keep a small flask of whiskey with it too, for the same reason."

"Have you ever used it?"

"No, sir, so you can have it with my compliments."

"Thank you. I'll still buy a new one if I can."

"It'll be close. The train leaves at 8:50, but you can do some shopping in La Junta."

Before Lee could reply, the telegrapher walked into the lobby, spotted Bethan and headed towards them.

"This just came in for you, Miss Evans. My boy already went home, and this was marked urgent."

Bethan pulled a coin from her pocket, saw that it was a dime, then handed it to him after accepting the telegram.

He didn't squawk or wait for a reply, but tipped his hat, turned and left the hotel.

Lee watched as Bethan unfolded the telegram and read:

DEP MARSHAL B EVANS LAS ANIMAS COLO

**SENDING LYNN AND BRYN TO LA JUNTA
DO NOT PURSUE UNTIL HE ARRIVES**

US MARSHAL DYLAN EVANS DENVER COLO

Bethan grinned and handed it to Lee to watch his reaction.

He read the short message, then gave it back with a curious expression on his face.

"You're wondering why he sent it as the U.S. Marshal."

"That did strike me as odd after the way you talked about your parents."

"For the same reason he addressed it to Deputy Marshal Evans. He's hoping that by adding his new authority as my boss that I'd be more inclined to follow his orders. I've been somewhat of a rebel in the Evans home and he always found that he could keep me under control more easily if he gave me a good reason to be cooperative. He's run out of incentives now, so he's resorting to authority."

Lee shook his head, laughed, then asked, "Is it going to work?"

"Strangely enough, he didn't even have to try. It's in line with what we were going to do anyway. We'll go to La Junta and wait. If they're there, which I doubt, we'll come up with a plan to deal with them. If they aren't, we'll just wait for my brother and uncle and then we can start looking for them."

"Okay."

As much as Bethan wanted to stay and talk to Lee longer, she knew that they both needed some sleep. Tomorrow could be a busy day.

————

Lynn hadn't had to pack very much because he was accustomed to having to leave their home without much notice, but before he left his house, he kissed little Dylan, then Gwen and finally infant Nathan before he smiled at Addie, kissed her much longer and said, "I'll be back soon, sweetheart. This won't be hard. Bethan will probably already have them corralled by the time we get there."

"Maybe, but do you really think that the sheriff was right about them joining that bastard Avery George and his gang?"

"I doubt it. Even dad said that no one knows where they are, so I doubt if they do."

"If they do join up, are you going to still chase them all down?"

"It depends on the situation, Addie. Bethan is already traveling with a town marshal, so that would give us four lawmen if we do run across them. Most posses aren't that good."

"I still hope that you don't find the Gentry gang. I'm glad that Bryn's going with you."

"So, am I. He's bringing a pack mule, too. I think that's a bit of a stretch, but he likes to be prepared."

"Stay safe, Lynn," she said as she looked into his eyes.

He kissed her once more, then smiled and said, "I will, my wife," then turned and left the house.

Addie stared at the door for a few minutes, held Nathan to her shoulder, sighed, then turned to get the children back to bed.

Bryn had to spend a bit more time with his goodbyes as twelve-year-old Mason had once again pleaded with his father to come along, but Bryn had used the standard 'you're the man of the house now' argument. He then shook hands with Ethan, Huw and then Kyle before kissing the second light of his life, his only daughter, Grace.

She said, "Take care of yourself, Dad. No more adventures. They scare mom."

"I know, sweetheart, but I'll have Lynn and Bethan with me and another lawman, too."

"I don't worry about them as much as I do about you, Dad."

Bryn smiled at his blond haired, blue-eyed daughter, then turned and kissed the first light of his life, Erin.

"I won't give you any cause to worry, Erin. We'll be back in a few days."

"I know. We'll all be waiting."

Bryn smiled then pulled on his hat, waved to his family and left the house.

Erin watched him leave and had a sense of foreboding that she'd never felt before, even when he'd gone on much more dangerous missions. She didn't know why it was there, and hoped it was just a reaction to Bert's recent death when Bryn had been so close to dying himself.

CHAPTER 7

George had to kick Cody's bedroll to wake him up before he returned to the small fire he'd built while Cody had slept. He'd decided that even though Cody was a serious problem, he knew that, for better or worse, he was his partner now.

It still bothered him that Cody had made them both wanted men. It seemed as if he'd been sliding over to the bad side of that line of right and wrong ever since he'd first started taking small bribes to look the other way. Now he was a wanted murderer, even though he hadn't pulled the trigger. He knew that the judge wouldn't give him any leniency for just sitting in the saddle while Cody back shot that deputy. Besides, if they were captured, it was more than likely that Cody would give him up.

Cody stretched, then grinned up at George before sliding out of the bedroll and saying, "Mornin', George."

"Morning, Cody. We need to get moving. I reckon that they found the deputy's body by now and are probably following our trail. I'd guess they were about six hours behind us."

"We're okay, George. Once we find the Arkansas and get across to those tracks, we'll just head on down to Robinson and get on the train."

"We have to get going, Cody. We could be another six hours from Robinson, and we don't know when the train leaves that burg. I don't want to take the northbound train and head into Las Animas, so that reduces our chances of getting on the train by half."

"Whatever," Cody replied as he opened up his britches and relieved himself.

It took them another thirty minutes before they had the three horses saddled and rode south away from their campsite.

———

By then, Bethan and Lee were sitting on the train platform in Las Animas after having dropped Nippy and the gelding with the stock manager.

Since leaving the hotel just before sunrise, they had been in almost constant race against time. They'd had a quick breakfast, then met with Sheriff Allen and Bethan showed him her father's telegram. It was then when the sheriff let them read his message to all law enforcement in Colorado and they'd noticed that he'd mentioned the possibility of the two men joining the Gentry gang. The sheriff had also broached the subject of Lee joining the office, but Lee had just said that he'd give his answer when they returned.

Now, as they waited for the train's arrival, Bethan said, "I wonder if the sheriff's telegram is what spurred my father to send both Bryn and Lynn. I can't understand why the sheriff thinks that these two would join with that gang because the last time I knew, they had just left the Indian Nations, but no one knew anything else."

"Maybe he's just nervous. He did seem that way."

"I noticed. His other deputy hasn't returned yet and he's probably expecting the worse even thought he'd gone up to the north end of the county."

"How much do you know about that bunch?"

"Probably more than most lawmen do. My brother and his wife met the gang leader, Avery George, when he was a deputy sheriff up in Yankton."

"You'll have to tell me that story when we're on board."

"It might take the whole trip," Bethan replied with a smile, "It's just the latest of the almost mythical stories that I grew up hearing as a girl and thought they were all fairytales. It wasn't until I was around ten that I began to understand that they were all real and, if anything, the real stories were even more extraordinary."

Lee smiled at Bethan and asked, "You aren't planning on making one of your own fairytales now, are you?"

Bethan laughed, then replied, "Not one of them was planned, Lee, and I think if we tried, we'd probably wind up writing a comedy."

Lee laughed then stared east down the tracks wishing the train never came. He was enjoying every second he spent with Bethan and knew that once they caught the two men, she'd go back to Denver and he'd go to Las Animas and accept the deputy sheriff's job. He'd never met anyone, male or female, who had impressed him more and wondered if her brother and uncle would come close to matching her character.

———

Bryn and Lynn had taken a freight from Denver and had spent their night in the stock car with their horses. It wasn't as bad as it could have been because it had given them the time to talk and figure out what Bethan had gotten herself into.

They had to wait in Pueblo until the eastbound passenger train to La Junta departed at 7:10, so they had time to have breakfast before continuing their journey. Neither expected any serious difficulties, although knowing that at least one of the two men had already murdered a law officer did add a measure of caution.

———

"How are we gonna cross that?" Cody asked as he sat on Biff looking at the Arkansas River.

"You've never seen it before?" George asked, "I thought you lived here."

"I ain't never come down this far south."

"Cody, the Arkansas runs right past Canon City."

"Well, it wasn't this big up there, and there was a bridge, too."

"Let's look for a ford, but we'll turn back east. I think we're west of Robinson."

Cody didn't reply as he wheeled his horse to the left and trailed behind George.

Forty minutes later, they found their ford, if it could be called that, and had made it across the Arkansas River without too much trouble.

242

Once they were on dry land again, it didn't take long before they picked up the tracks and turned east. After a couple of minutes Cody spotted the mile marker.

"We're headed for La Junta and it's just another six miles."

"I noticed that. We'll have to swing south to avoid it and then ride another ten miles to get to Robinson."

"That's just great," Cody mumbled under his breath.

———

At what was now the Gentry farm, the three men were getting restless. They'd stayed at the farm for more than a week and needed action.

Their wish was fulfilled when in the mid-morning, a wagon turned onto their rutted, grass-covered access road being driven by the McDonald's closest neighbor, Willis Higgins.

They were lounging in the front room when Homer glanced out the front window and spotted the approaching wagon and stood.

"We got company. Looks like another farmer."

Avery and Ted rose and each of them walked to the windows.

"What do we do with him?" Ted asked.

"We don't have any choice," Avery said as he pulled his pistol and cocked the hammer.

Homer did the same and said, "I reckon not."

———

243

Willis was concerned about the family because they hadn't been to church on Sunday and they never missed a service. He'd spent all of Monday thinking about it and last night, he'd talked to Aggie. She had similar concerns, then suggested that he stop at the McDonald's on the way to town for supplies in the morning to see how they were. Their two boys could handle the day's chores until he returned.

He had driven the four miles with a good deal of concern, but not because he believed that the family had been murdered. He was afraid that some disease had overtaken them and that he might become infected himself. The thought of catching some hideous sickness made his stomach recoil.

So, when he turned his wagon onto the McDonald farm, he scanned the house and barn for signs of life. He felt a chill up his spine when he saw smoke coming from the chimney but nothing else moving. If they were healthy, they should be outside and working.

He kept the wagon rolling toward the house at less than normal walking speed as he began to think about turning around. Maybe he should go into town first, get his supplies and ask around. He then thought that he should at least call out.

He was eighty feet from the house when he pulled the wagon to a stop, then shouted, "Archie! Are you home!"

It was an eerie silence that enveloped him and the farm for thirty seconds, and Willis decided that he'd done his duty, snapped the reins and began to turn the wagon.

———

The occupants of the farmhouse had expected him to step onto the porch where they would have an easy target, but the farmer never got that close.

"He's leavin'," Ted said.

Homer then said, "I don't think we can let him go runnin' off and tellin' folks that somethin' ain't right over here."

"Nope," Avery replied as he hurried to the door and threw it open.

The three men bolted from the house just as Willis had started his wagon back down the access road. The creaking of his wagon and the noise from the mules' hooves drowned out the sound of the outlaws' noisy exit.

When they'd left the house, Willis was already fifty yards away and moving at a faster pace than he had earlier to put some distance between him and the diseased house.

Avery, Tom and Homer weren't runners, but still began to cut the gap to the wagon with their Colts ready to fire.

Willis was ready to make the turn onto the trail to town when Tom's first shot echoed across the Colorado ground and he whipped his head around to look at the source and knew he was going to die. His only hope lay with his two mules.

He bent over and snapped the reins. The mules didn't need much more incentive after hearing the loud report and the wagon lurched forward as Avery and Homer both fired.

Willis felt the smack of a .44 as it ripped across his left forearm, but he didn't slow down.

The three outlaws were winded as they stopped and began to fire at the fleeing farmer. If they'd taken just a moment to think, they would have targeted his mules, but they didn't.

Soon, their Colts were dry, and the farmer's wagon was beyond Winchester range, even if they had them.

"What…do…we…do…now?" Homer asked between breaths as he bent at the waist.

"We get our horses saddled and get out of here," Avery answered as he slammed his useless hunk of steel into its holster.

He then took one last look at the fleeing farmer and wondered if they could get mounted and run him down with their Winchesters, but thought it was too much trouble and he didn't know how far away the nearest town was or if they had law. Even if they didn't have a lawman, they probably had a telegraph office.

The Gentry gang walked back to the farmhouse to collect their things, then they'd have to pack and put some distance between them and the farmhouse. Whichever lawmen came to the house would find those poorly buried bodies and then all hell would break loose.

As they stepped onto the porch, Tom asked, "Are we going to head back to the Nations?"

"No. We're done hiding out. We need to get some money and maybe think about moving west again. We'll head north because there isn't a damned thing south of here."

"Okay, King," Homer said, "I wish we woulda killed that farmer, though."

"We would have had to leave right away anyway, but at least it would have given us more time."

Tom glanced back to the west one more time and watched the fading cloud dust being created by the farmer's wagon.

———

Willis slowed his mules when he saw that the men had started back to the McDonalds' farmhouse. His arm was bleeding, so he let the reins drop, then pulled his big handkerchief from his overalls' front pocket and wrapped it around his forearm. He wasn't sure if they would chase him down before he reached Liston, but all he could do now was to pray that they didn't go to his farm to do what they must have done to the McDonald family.

———

"I wish we could go into La Junta and get some food," Cody said as he looked at the buildings just a mile to the northeast.

George was already debating that it might be worthwhile to get rid of that damned pinto now and add some supplies rather than trying to do it in a small town like Robinson. Besides, he could use something hot in his stomach, too.

"Okay, Cody. Let's go into La Junta, get rid of the pinto and get something to eat before we head out of there. They probably haven't found that deputy's body yet."

Cody grinned, said, "Now, you're talkin'!", then angled his horse toward the town.

He had switched off the eye-catching pinto that morning but found the deputy's horse to be a bit more jarring. It was too bad that the pinto was so easy to spot.

———

They entered La Junta and headed for the first livery where George bargained for the sale of Biff and his tack while Cody waited outside the barn.

Cody paid particular attention to the town marshal's office about four hundred yards away. He wondered if this town marshal was like Lee Collins was back in Bishop, but he doubted it. They probably paid him, and he might have a deputy or two.

He didn't expect that they'd even recognize him or George once they got rid of the pinto, so he shifted his eyes to the train depot at the other end of town.

There weren't any trains there right now and didn't see any on the horizons, so he was disappointed. He would have preferred to just board the train here rather than ride another ten miles east to Robinson.

He was still staring at the station when George exited the livery wearing a grin.

"How much did we get?" Cody asked as he led his gelding alongside George.

"Would you believe I got a hundred and twenty? I guess he really liked the horse and the saddle was in great shape, too. He must have thought I was some rube because he offered me fifty dollars when I asked. That's what took so long."

Cody was about to ask when George handed him sixty dollars, which he quickly snatched and stuffed into his pocket.

"Let's get something to eat and then we'll check on the train."

"Okay," Cody replied as they continued to lead their horses down the road.

———

Bethan was sitting on the window side of the bench seat and Lee was on the aisle side. When she'd taken the seat, she slid to the window to see if Lee would join her on the same seat or take the one across from the aisle. It was a subtle thing to do and Bethan had been surprised that she had tried it because subtlety wasn't one of her strong points.

Why she had done it was another question altogether. She really liked Lee and had enjoyed talking with him. He hadn't tried to impress her with stories of his bravery or manliness, he'd simply talked to her and, even more amazingly, had listened to her.

After he'd joined her on the bench, he asked, "Do you mind if I sit with you, Bethan?"

She smiled and asked, "So you can protect me from evil men who might try to take advantage of me?"

"No, ma'am, I thought I'd protect the menfolk who entered the car from you."

Bethan laughed then said, "I see your point, sir."

"I checked the train schedules while we were waiting, and I didn't see any trains from Denver until this morning. When do you think your brother and uncle will get to La Junta?"

"They might not have waited for a scheduled passenger train. They use any rolling stock that passes through, even coal trains. If there was another train leaving Denver last night, they'd be on it, so they may get here today."

"Then what will we do?"

"That will be Bryn's call. The last we knew about the two killers was that they were riding south from about fifteen miles north of where we are now. They could have covered that already and might be continuing south cross-country, but most likely, they would have taken a train. If they did that, we just ask the ticket agents."

"I think that they'd probably want to get rid of Biff before they did either."

"You're right about that. Your pinto sticks out like a sore thumb. Maybe when we get to La Junta, we can check with the liveries while we wait for Bryn and Lynn."

"Okay. I miss Biff. He's a good horse, despite being a bit noticeable."

"Why did you buy such a conspicuous horse when you were a lawman?"

"Let's be honest, Bethan. I was more of a shopkeeper than a real lawman, so it didn't matter."

She looked at him, smiled and said, "I don't know, Lee. You're doing pretty well as a lawman and Sheriff Allen seems to think so, too."

"With as bad as a situation as he finds himself in right now, I think he'd offer Biff a badge."

Bethan's eyes crinkled as she laughed, knowing that he was probably just barely exaggerating.

———

With the stomachs full and money in their pockets, George and Cody headed for Cooper's General Store to pick up supplies. They'd already stopped at the train station to check on schedules after Cody had convinced George that going to Robinson was just a waste of time and their horses could use the rest.

George didn't take much convincing after he'd seen the town marshal's small jail but with each of them now having a deputy sheriff's badge, there shouldn't be any problem with the local law.

They'd been pleased to see that the next southbound train would arrive in just two more hours and the northbound train that they wouldn't be taking would show up just twenty minutes later.

———

"This is a lot better than that stock car," Lynn said as he stared out the window.

"I don't think it's a big step up, Lynn. The only real advantage is that we don't have to scoop out where we're going to sit."

Lynn grinned before he said, "I bet Bethan will be surprised to see us so soon."

"You know her better than that. She's probably going to be wondering what took us so long. I'm just curious about the Bishop town marshal who has been with her."

"You don't think that Bethan, um, you know? I mean, she's only seventeen."

"Let me see," Bryn said as he scratched his chin, "I seem to recall that you were sixteen when you left the Double EE and went a thousand miles to Fort Benton and then rowed down the Missouri chasing after Addie. Or am I wrong?"

"But that was different."

"Be careful, Lynn. You're sounding like those boys who called her Bessie."

Lynn laughed, then said, "I suppose you're right. I wonder if this guy calls her Bethan."

"Well, he's still with her, so if he hadn't before, he does now."

Lynn was smiling as he nodded, then returned to look at the passing prairie of eastern Colorado.

———

Willis had reached town and attracted a crowd with his story and his wound suffered at the hands of three men who had probably murdered the entire McDonald family. He left the wagon at the livery and borrowed a horse to go back to check on his family to make sure that they were safe. The borrowed horse had a Winchester in its scabbard.

As he raced out of town, telegrams were sent to the sheriff's office in Trinidad that described the three men and the likelihood that they'd murdered the McDonald family.

———

Cody and George stepped up to the ticket window and bought two tickets and horse transport to Trinidad. They would ride to Mexico or New Mexico, depending on what they heard in Trinidad.

After settling on a bench, they relaxed and watched the eastern horizon for their train. Soon they'd be out of this state and head further west, maybe to California.

———

The Gentry gang had packed what they could and taken one of the McDonald's mules before they left the farm riding north.

They didn't expect to see anyone following them but did notice a dust cloud in the distance which caused them to pick up the pace, not realizing it was Willis heading back to his farm.

They were already ten miles away when Willis reached his surprised but alive and well family.

They were about seventy miles due south of La Junta when Willis arrived at his home and told his wife and boys what had happened when he arrived at the McDonalds.

———

"Here she comes," Cory said as he pointed east at the black cloud on the horizon.

George stood, picked up his saddlebags and hung them over his shoulder before he scanned the street. His eyes stopped when they looked west and he spotted a man wearing a badge striding his way with a shotgun.

"Cory, we have a lawman coming down the road. We need to head over to the corral and check our horses."

Cory quickly turned, spotted the town marshal, and asked, "Check the horses?"

"We act like we're checking them and if that lawman keeps going, we come back here and board the train. We'll have plenty of time before it leaves."

"Okay," Cory said as he started walking toward the stock corral.

George avoided looking at the marshal, so he didn't attract his attention. He may just be on his rounds and it wasn't unusual to carry a shotgun. His years as a deputy sheriff was helping and as he thought about it, he slipped his badge from his pocket and pinned it to his coat before he stepped down from the platform.

Las Junta Marshal Bill Travers didn't even notice George or Cody as he walked along the boardwalk. He wasn't doing his rounds but responding to a report of an argument at the Purple Ace Saloon. He knew both of the men involved and wasn't particularly worried but took the shotgun anyway as a persuader depending on how drunk they were. It was pretty early in the day for either of them to be too bad, so he expected they'd calm down once they saw him enter the barroom.

————

Lee was laughing as Bethan told him the story of her first ride on Peanut when she was a little girl and his eyes were focused on her face as their car rolled past the stock corral. If he'd been looking past her out the window, he would have spotted Cody and George, but Bethan had his full attention.

George had kept his attention on the town marshal even after he'd entered the saloon, but Cody was watching the train as it passed.

When the train pulled to a stop just two minutes later, he was still watching as the passengers began to step down onto the broad wooden platform.

He spotted Bethan, smiled, then said, "Hey, George. Look at what just got off that train."

George turned to look at what had attracted Cody's attention just in time to see Lee step onto the platform behind her.

Cody noticed him at the same instant and cursed under his breath before turning back to George and asking, "What do we do now? Are we still getting on that train?"

"Wait until they leave," George replied as his eyes stayed glued on Lee.

Bethan had her saddlebags over her shoulder as she approached the schedule, then when Lee reached her, she said, "The train from Pueblo is scheduled to arrive in just twenty minutes. Do you want to go and look for your pinto or just wait to see if my brother and uncle are on the train?"

"Do you really think that they're coming this soon?"

"I'll bet you a dollar that they're on that train, Mister Collins."

"That'll be the best wager I'll ever make, Miss Evans," he replied with a grin.

She then asked the ticket manager, "Is the train from Pueblo on time?"

"Yes, miss. You'll be seeing her smoke pretty soon."

"Thank you, sir," she replied, then surprised Lee when she hooked her arm though his and guided him to the nearest bench.

After they sat down, she asked, "Do you have a dollar to pay off that bet, Mister Collins, or are you going to write me an IOU?"

"I'm good for it, Miss Evans. Are you?"

Bethan laughed lightly and looked west for the telltale sign of the approaching train.

"They're not leavin'!" Cody loud whispered to George.

"We sure can't board the train if they're sitting there, Cody. Let's get the horses and get out of here. With that marshal in the saloon, I don't like the odds."

"Alright, but we're gonna lose our money," Cody said as they approached the stock manager.

"We can use the tickets when we get to another station."

"Where are we goin'?"

"Southwest. We'll follow the tracks down to Trinidad, but we can stop at the first station and board the train there."

The stock manager didn't need to see their tags as they'd just left the horses, but just opened the gate and let them take their animals. If one of them hadn't been wearing a badge, he would have told Marshal Travers about the pair's unusual behavior.

They mounted, then walked their horses east on the road until they believed they were far enough away, then walked their horses across the tracks and trotted south. They'd pick up the tracks to Trinidad after they were out of sight of La Junta.

———

Neither Bethan nor Lee has spotted them as each was distracted by the other, but ten minutes later, they did see the smoke from the inbound train from Pueblo. It would have to be shunted over to the second set of tracks to allow their train to continue its journey, but they rose and walked toward the edge of the platform to watch it arrive.

"Last chance to get out of the bet, Bethan."

"I won't be the one paying up, Lee."

"If they are on the train, are we still going to look for Biff?"

"Absolutely. They could be sitting in the hotel right now."

Lee then said, "You know that I've never been in a gunfight before."

Bethan looked at him and said, "I guessed that. Why are you telling me now?"

"Well, if we do find them, I wanted to let you know that I might freeze. I didn't want you to get hurt because you depended on me."

"I'm not worried, Lee, and you shouldn't be either."

He nodded as the train approached but didn't feel any better knowing that they would soon be joined by her uncle and brother and both were tested lawmen. He hoped that his own lack of experience didn't create more problems when they encountered the two killers.

———

Lynn was still at the window as the train slowed and soon spotted Bethan on the platform standing beside a young man who appeared to be in his low twenties.

"I guess that's the town marshal from Bishop with my sister," he said.

"Unless Bethan is riding around collecting young men, I'd say that you're right," Bryn replied, "Let's get ready to go."

Bryn then stood, hung his saddlebags over his shoulder and pulled on his hat before he stepped into the aisle and waited for Lynn to do the same. He then began walking to the front of the car as it swayed, then had to grab a seat when it jolted to a stop.

Bryn soon stepped out into the bright sunlight and waved at Bethan.

Bethan waved back, then turned to Lee and said, "You can pay me later."

"Yes, ma'am."

Lee watched as U.S. Deputy Marshal Bryn Evans stepped down onto the platform and was followed by Bethan's deputy marshal brother, Lynn. Both men were taller than he was, but they seemed downright friendly; maybe because Bethan was waiting for them.

Bryn stepped close to Bethan, hugged her and then kissed her on the cheek before stepping aside and letting Lynn greet his sister.

He then offered his hand to Lee and said, "I'm Bryn Evans, Bethan's uncle. I'm guessing that you're the town marshal from Bishop."

'I was. I'm Lee Collins."

"Call me Bryn, and in case you haven't guessed, the young character behind me is her brother, Lynn."

"It's nice to meet you both, Bryn," he said as he shook Bryn's hand and then grasped Lynn's.

Bryn then turned to Bethan and said, "Now, tell us what happened while they unload our horses."

"Let's sit down and I'll give you the details."

"Good enough and maybe you can tell us why the Bent County sheriff thinks that they might be going to join the Gentry gang. I think that really spooked your father."

Bethan nodded as they walked to the longest bench and she took a seat. She almost laughed when Bryn sat beside her and Lynn then sat next to Bryn, letting Lee sit down on her other side. It was as if they assumed that she had finally found a man who appreciated her as she was, and maybe she had.

It took about ten minutes for Bethan and Lee to explain the situation, and when they finished, Bryn looked at Lynn.

"What do you think?"

Lynn replied, "I'd rather not ride up to Las Animas and pick up the trail, so I agree with Lee and Bethan that we do a quick search for his pinto before we do anything else."

"That won't take long and we can work from there," he said.

Then he looked at Bethan and said, "We brought a pack mule with us, so we have plenty of supplies because we weren't sure about the whole Gentry gang situation. Let's do a quick search for your horse, Lee, then we can have some lunch and talk about it, whether we find him or not."

"Yes, sir," Lee replied.

They rose as one, then walked to the stock corral and approached the manager who had just finished unloading their horses and pack mule.

Both Lynn and Bryn had their badges displayed, so when they handed their claim tags to the stockman, he grinned and said, "Sure are a lot of lawmen around here today. You chasin' some bad boys?"

"Maybe so, but we have to find them first," Bryn replied as he took Aesop's reins.

"Maybe those other fellers already know where they are, 'cause they dropped off their horses and then just picked 'em up again. I thought it was kinda queer, but when I saw one of 'em with a badge, I reckoned it was okay."

Bryn glanced at Lee, who asked, "What kind of badge?"

"I didn't look that close."

"What did they look like?"

"Well, the one with the badge was about average height and had nothin' special about him. The other one was a short feller with mousy hair and dark eyes. He looked kinda goofy."

Lee turned to Bryn and said, "It sounds like them. I don't know how I could have missed seeing them."

"Well, they didn't get on the train, so they must have ridden off," he replied, then turned to the stockman and asked, "Did you see which way they went?"

"They headed east. Are you tellin' me that they weren't lawmen at all?"

Bryn replied, "One was, but he did somethings he shouldn't have and then he and the other one backshot a Bent County deputy sheriff a few days ago."

"Damn! I shoulda told Marshal Travers!"

"It's just as well that you didn't. You wouldn't want a gun battle in the middle of town. We'll track them down."

"Good luck."

Lee then asked, "Did they have a pinto with them?"

"Nope."

Bryn then turned to Lynn and said, "Let's go find the pinto and have some lunch. We have plenty of time to track them and I want to do it right."

"Yes, sir," Lynn replied.

Bethan then said, "We're coming with you, Bryn."

Bryn smiled at his niece and said, "Of course, you are. You're the reason we're here and we can act as chaperones on the trail, so your father doesn't skin your brother alive when we get back."

Bethan grinned and replied, "He wouldn't, but mom might."

As Bryn and Lynn led their horses and mule away from the corral, Lynn said, "She'd more likely throw a party."

Bethan and Bryn laughed as Lee smiled but wasn't sure why they thought it was so funny.

––––––

"But I paid a hundred and fifty dollars for that horse and rig!" protested Charlie Fisher as he stared at Bryn.

"They were stolen from Mister Collins. It's those two characters who owe you your money and when we catch up with them, we'll be happy to restore it to you."

Charlie was annoyed, but as he looked at Bryn, he was pretty sure that he'd get his money back and maybe a bit more if the two men were killed first and couldn't say how much they'd gotten.

"I reckon that's the right thing to do, so you can take your horse and gear, young feller. He's a right pretty boy and I'm sure you're fond of him."

"I am," Lee said as he rubbed Biff's neck.

They left the livery leading Biff, the other horses and the lone mule and walked down the main street.

"We need to stop at the town marshal's office to let him know what's happening and then we'll send a telegram to the boss," Bryn said.

"You need to send a wire to my mother?" Bethan asked with a slight smile.

"Yes, Miss Evans, I need to tell your mother that she raised a daughter who can be a pain in the behind."

Bethan glanced at Lynn and then laughed as they approached the jail.

The showdown at the saloon turned out as expected, and Marshal Travers had put away his shotgun before taking a seat behind his desk and pulled out his pocket watch to check the time for his log.

When the door opened, he looked up and knew immediately that something serious was happening and he suspected that he knew what it was, but he was wrong.

He rose and asked, "How'd you get here so fast?"

Bryn was somewhat puzzled and replied with his own question, "Why would you even be expecting us?"

As they filed into the jail, the marshal said, "Because of what happened down in Liston. Didn't you get the telegram?"

"We've been on a train since last night. What telegram are you talking about? What happened in Liston?"

"A farmer was shot at by three men who might have murdered his neighbors. He was wounded but got away. I haven't heard anything else since then."

Bryn turned to Lynn and said, "That's almost a hundred miles south of here. If the farmer was right and there were three of them, then they were probably your old pal Avery George and his buddies."

"That makes sense," he replied, then turned to the Marshal Travers and asked, "Did he say which way they headed?"

"Nope. All I got was that the farmer was shot. He guessed that they had murdered the neighbors, but nothing has been confirmed."

Bryn nodded, then said, "We're here chasing down the two men that murdered the Bent County deputy sheriff a few days ago. They were in town and just left a little while ago. I guess they were planning on taking the train but changed their minds. We're going to get a quick bite to eat and then go after them."

"Are you going to keep going south to Liston after you catch up with them?"

"I think so. There isn't a lot of law down there. They probably headed back into the Indian Nations or south to Mexico. At least, that's what I'd do if I was in their shoes."

"Well, good luck."

Bryn nodded, then turned and led everyone back outside. Once on the boardwalk, he stopped and said, "This changes a lot of things, Bethan. I'd rather that you don't come along. Lynn and I can take care of it now."

Bethan's brow furrowed as she snapped, "It changes nothing, Bryn. You aren't going after those two and then possibly taking on three ruthless killers with only two of you. I don't care how good you are. We're coming and I don't want you to pull any of that ranking deputy crap, either. If you do, I'll give you my badge and still follow."

Bryn glanced at Lynn, who shrugged, then looked back into Bethan's fiery brown eyes.

"Okay, but you will do what I say when I say. Is that understood?"

"Yes, sir."

Lee watched them and didn't ask if he was going to come along. He knew that he was going as well, whether Bethan wanted him to come or not. He just hoped that she did.

————

It was early afternoon when they set out east from La Junta and picked up the tracks of the two riders.

Bryn glanced back at Lee, who was riding beside Bethan and wished he wasn't riding his pinto but figured it didn't matter as much once the two men spotted their dust cloud.

They were much better armed than the two killers that they tracked, and he was reasonably sure that they could outgun the Gentry gang if they were able to find them in the United States. He still believed that they were heading for either the Indian Nation or Mexico.

————

George and Cody had ridden south for two hours before shifting to the southwest, but their angle wasn't as sharp as it should have been, and they wound up riding parallel to the AT&SF tracks between La Junta and Trinidad.

265

It was late in the afternoon after they had stopped to give the horses water in a narrow creek when Cody took a deep drink of water from his canteen then scanned the horizon.

"Where are those tracks? We shoulda spotted 'em by now."

"They must be close. I guess we could shift to the right some more."

Cody snorted, then dropped to his heels to refill his canteen.

George looked at their shadows and figured that if he used them as a compass, they could ride directly into the sun which should take them west and they'd spot the tracks before sunset.

After the short break, they mounted and headed due west. Iron Springs was just seven miles away, but slightly south of their current direction.

_____

"They must not think anyone is behind them," Lynn said as he studied their tracks.

"It looks that way. They're riding straight and mostly south. I wonder where they're headed. I would have thought they'd go west by now."

Bethan then asked, "You don't really think that they are going to look for the Gentry gang, do you?"

"I doubt it. They don't even know where they are and probably don't even know who they are," Bryn replied.

"Just the same, I hope that we don't bump into that crowd," Bethan replied.

"Neither do I," Lynn said as he looked up from the trail.

———

'That crowd' was now riding northwest, hoping to reach Bent Canyon soon, so they could pick up some supplies and maybe some cash from that small bank.

They were just twenty-four miles from their target, but still weren't sure of its location. They'd reach the river and then pick up the road between Bent Canyon and Trinidad.

After they thanked the good citizens of Bent Canyon for their largesse, they'd take the road down to New Mexico.

———

"They must have figured out that they were going in the wrong direction," Bryn said as he stood over the spot where George and Cody had taken their last break.

Lynn put the cap back on his canteen and replied, "It looks like they're only a couple of hours ahead of us, Bryn. What's west of here?"

Bryn turned to Lee and asked, "You probably know this area a lot better than we do, Lee. What's west of here?"

"I rarely left Bishop, Bryn. I only went to Las Animas a few times, but never came south. I'm sure that Cody never came this way, either."

Bethan then said, "I looked at the map before I left Sheriff Allen's office and the closest town in that direction is Iron Springs."

Bryn looked west and said, "Okay, let's keep trailing until we lose our light and then we'll pick it up in the morning if we haven't spotted the town."

As he mounted, Lynn said, "I think we're moving faster than they are."

"Keep an eye on the trail and the rest of us will watch for their dust cloud. If we're gaining quickly, then we could spot it on the western horizon in the late afternoon sun."

They set off at a medium trot riding into that blazing sun, which was making it difficult to see anything more than a few hundred yards ahead.

———

"There's the rails!" Cody shouted.

"Let's turn left and ride alongside. We should get to Iron Springs before sundown."

Cody's mood had improved measurably when he'd seen the train tracks and anticipated spotting the buildings of the town soon.

George's concern about what kind of mess they'd stirred up by killing the deputy had been growing since they'd ridden out of La Junta. In his mind, he envisioned a massed horde of enraged lawmen searching the entire area for him and Cody. He'd seen Sheriff Bo Johnson's reaction when he heard about the deputy marshal's death in that mountain pass before he'd made his escape from Canon City, and didn't doubt that this would be even worse because Cody had shot that deputy in the back.

He let Cody keep his eyes trained ahead as he nervously scanned the horizons to the east and north expecting to see a posse appear at any moment.

––––––

"We're losing out light in another hour or so," Lynn said as he looked across at Bryn.

"I know, but they can't be more than a couple of hours ahead at most. I'm surprised we haven't spotted their dust cloud."

"We should reach the tracks soon."

"All we have to worry about is if they get on a train before we catch up to them, but I don't want a gunfight in town if we can avoid it."

"At least we can see a train coming from a long way off," Lynn replied, then grinned at his uncle.

Bryn then turned to Bethan and asked, "You looked at that schedule. Are there any passenger trains on this route in the next few hours?"

"Most of the traffic was to and from Pueblo. Only one train each way went through Trinidad, but both of them are night trains, so we might have a problem. I'm not sure of the times, but I remember that they were really late."

"Okay. I guess we might have to follow them into Iron Springs even after dark. I don't like it, but I don't want them to board a train and then just send a telegram to Trinidad. I wouldn't want to stick someone else with men who will shoot a deputy in the back."

Bethan nodded, then as she turned her eyes back to the front, thought she spotted a faint dust cloud on the southwestern horizon.

She didn't say anything for a few seconds as she stared into the reddening sky.

Then she pointed and said, "Is that them?"

The others all turned to look, and Bryn replied, "I see it, Bethan. Let's forget about the trail and head that way."

They turned their horses and set off at a fast trot to cut the distance.

Bryn knew that they'd be making a big dust cloud of their own but wanted them to see it before they entered the town. A shootout in a community was bad enough, but if it was at night, it could be a disaster. The memory of his last night shootout was still vivid in his mind.

———

Two miles away, Cody was happily riding along with the shining ribbons of steel on his right, expecting that he'd be sleeping in a decent bed tonight.

George was still anxiously watching their backtrail when he spotted a dust cloud at his seven o'clock position and slowed so his eyes weren't bouncing so much.

Cody noticed that George had fallen off, then slowed his horse, looked back at him and shouted, "What are you doin'?"

George pulled his gelding to a stop and without taking his eyes off the dust cloud, yelled, "We got somebody behind us!"

Cody then turned his horse around and walked him back until he was even with George, looked in the same direction, and then spotted the distant cloud of dust and the specks that were creating it.

"You sure they're followin' us? They could just be some cowpokes pushing some cattle."

"There aren't any ranches out this way. We haven't seen a soul since leaving La Junta. The only ones it could be is a posse."

"Why would a posse be there already? They probably haven't even found that deputy's body yet."

"I'd be surprised if they didn't. That was more than two days ago. If they found him that day, the sheriff could have formed a posse and lit out after us. That dust cloud is pretty big, too. I reckon there are at least six men coming after us."

"What do we do to throw them off?"

"It's almost sunset, so we keep riding along the tracks, then once the sun goes down, we cut east away from the rails. They won't notice the change until sunrise and by then, we'll be long gone."

"We need more supplies, George."

"I know. But we need to shake that posse first."

"We'd better start movin'."

Before George could reply, Cody had wheeled his gelding around and set off at a fast trot.

George took one last look at the growing dust cloud, cursed under his breath for ever thinking of looking for Cody, then turned his horse and chased after his useless partner.

————

"They're moving faster," Lynn said.

"I guess they finally spotted our dust cloud."

"Are we going to pick up our pace now?" Bethan asked.

"No. If they spotted us, then I don't think that they'll be going to Iron Springs now. They need to shake us loose, so they'll keep going that way until it's dark, then they'll turn either east or west."

Lynn said, "West would be their better choice."

"I know," Bryn replied, "and I hate to get into the 'I'll do what they don't expect us to do' game, and plan on them going east. We'll follow them as long as we can, then after we lose their trail, we'll go to Iron Springs to make sure they can't take that train. I'll send a telegram to the boss, then tomorrow morning, we pick up their trail."

"Aren't you concerned about an ambush now that they've seen us?" Lee asked.

"I'm always concerned about an ambush and maybe should have been more worried about one when we chased those boys over the mountain pass, but you're right, Lee. Let's spread out a bit and slow down to reduce the size of this dust cloud."

After they'd separated by a few yards and then slowed to a medium trot, the four riders and two trailing pack animals continued southwest as the sun touched the western horizon, illuminating the distant Rocky Mountains.

Bethan knew she should be looking for potential ambush sites but was attracted to nature's display and even at this distance, the mountains looked impressive.

Lee was off to her right and was included in her view, so she studied him for a few minutes as Nippy trotted along. He was unlike any other man she'd met, including the ones in her family. He hadn't even asked if she was married from the very first nor made any overtures to her since she'd discovered him in his own jail cell. She had no doubt that he was attracted to her because she was drawn to him. Yet for all her confidence and determination, she wasn't sure how things could progress, especially not with her uncle and brother riding with them.

Bethan began to regret sending that telegram to her father. Those two men they were chasing may be murderers, but she had no doubt that she and Lee could have captured them on their own. She couldn't ask Bryn and Lynn to go back to Denver but wondered what would happen after they caught the two men.

She knew that Lee wanted the deputy sheriff's job in Las Animas, and it was important for a man to make his own way. She had more than enough money to build a house on the quarter section of land on the Double EE that Bryn would give to her but knew that Lee would probably be almost offended by the idea.

Finally, she decided to let events unfold as they will and hoped that she would know what to do and when to do it, then turned her eyes to the front again.

———

George looked behind him one last time as the last vestige of dark red sunlight began to fade. The dust cloud was still there, but wasn't getting closer, which caused him some concern because he knew that they'd been spotted. The posse should have sped up, not slowed down.

Nonetheless, he turned to Cody and said, "Slow your horse to a walk, then after a minute, take a wide turn to the east and I'll continue for another minute and then turn east. That way, our turn won't be so obvious, even in the moonlight."

"You sure they won't follow us even with that damned full moon?"

"I doubt it, but if they do, we'll be waiting for them."

"Okay."

After slowing to a walk for that long, tense minute, Cody turned his gelding to his left and kept him going at a slow pace while George continued past.

George made his turn a minute later and after a couple of minutes, picked up his pace to a slow trot and angled northeast to meet with Cody again.

They were soon moving east at a slow trot while George kept looking northwest to see if he could spot that dust cloud in the dim light. If he couldn't see their big dust cloud, they wouldn't have seen the turn.

They rode for another ten minutes before George was confident that they hadn't been seen.

———

"Well, Lynn, it looks like we're heading to Iron Springs," Bryn said as the light faded.

"Why don't we just set up camp here and pick up their trail sooner?" Bethan asked.

"I want to send a telegram to the boss to let him know what we're doing," Bryn replied.

Lynn then said, "We can set up camp out here and you can ride to Iron Springs, send your telegram and then come back, Bryn. You'll be able to make better time without the pack horses."

Bryn thought about it and said, "That's only if they made the turn and didn't head to Iron Springs."

Then he turned and said, "Bethan, you and Lee set up camp here and keep both pack animals with you. Neither one of them has seen us before, so if they're in town, we can deal with them. If they're not there, then I'll send the telegram and we'll be back within a couple of hours."

"Okay, Bryn. We can set up camp over there," she replied as she pointed to a small stand of river birch beside a decent-sized creek.

All four turned toward the trees and soon pulled up. As both pack animals were attached to Bethan and Lee's horses, Bryn and Lynn stayed in their saddles as Lee and Bethan dismounted.

"We'll take care of setting up camp," Bethan said as he looked up.

"We'll be back in a few hours. Don't get any wild ideas in your head about trying to pick up those tracks in the night, Miss Evans."

Bethan smiled at her uncle and replied, "Believe it or not, I hadn't given it a thought. I don't want to bump into those killers in the dark."

"Good. Then we'll see you in a while," he said as he wheeled Aesop around and trotted away.

Lynn grinned at Bethan and said, "Don't do anything I wouldn't do, little sister," then turned his horse to follow Bryn.

As Lee began unsaddling Biff, Bethan watched them ride away and hoped that Bryn was right and that the two hunted men had turned away from Iron Springs. She didn't want Bryn and Lynn to capture them and end the search. At least she would have some time to talk to Lee in private now.

She began removing Nippy's saddle and soon she and Lee had all four animals cleared of their gear and watered at the nearby creek before setting them to graze on the fresh prairie grass.

Despite the plentiful supply of dry firewood lying about, they didn't even think of building a fire as they sat on the ground near one of the river birch clusters. None of them were single trees, and most had at least two trunks sprouting out from one set of roots.

"So, what do you think of my uncle and brother?" Bethan asked as she set her hat on her saddle.

"I like them quite a lot. They didn't talk down to me at all, despite my lack of experience. Most men like to show that they're more important, but even though Bryn and Lynn are

United States deputy marshals with impressive reputations, neither of them acted that way."

"They don't think they're important, and neither does my father, even though he's almost a legend already. Maybe it's because they know about the mistakes they made along the way and it keeps them level-headed. Besides, if you get that way, you'll cause more trouble when other hotheads show up in town."

"You're that way, too. When you told me about what happened in Granite, you talked as much about what you did wrong as what you accomplished. You're an amazing person, Bethan."

"I'll admit that I'm different, but then, so are you."

"Me? I'm not so different at all. I've done nothing remarkable in my life and just went wherever the wind took me. You are making your own way and I've spent almost all of my life in Bishop working in my father's hardware store."

"You can say that all you want, Lee, but I think you're very different, and a better different, too. We spent all that time on the trail already and you've talked to me like a good friend and not once treated me like a woman. You haven't even asked me the question that I expected you to ask me that first day."

"Which is?"

"If I was married."

Lee smiled and replied, "I was pretty sure that no man would allow his wife to ride off on her own with a pack horse to hunt down a bad man. That was obvious. I was much more curious about your motive than your marital status."

"So, if you knew I wasn't married and that I obviously liked you, then why haven't you even hinted that you might be interested in me as a woman?"

Lee stared at her for a few seconds before replying, "I suppose that I could say that I was just worried about offending you, but I don't think I could have done that after I got to know you on the first day. Am I right?"

"You are. You probably could have kissed me, and I wouldn't have been upset in the least. I've never felt that way about any boy or man before and it surprised me."

Lee let out a breath then said, "I have a reason for not acting as you expected, although I really did see you as an extraordinary woman right from the start. It's your family, Bethan."

"My family?" she asked with arched eyebrows, "I thought you liked my uncle and brother."

"I do, and after you told me about your family, I was almost in awe. It sounds as if each of them, and not just the men, is almost heroic. If anyone goes close to Denver, I'm sure that they know the Evans name. I'm just a burned-out shopkeeper pretending to be a lawman, Bethan. I'm not trying to be falsely modest about it, either. I'm just being honest."

"Before my mother met my father, he wasn't even a lawman; just a young man who worked on steam engines. My Uncle Bryn did the same work before he went off to war. My Uncle Kyle, who is now the assistant county prosecutor, had less than you did. He left Pennsylvania with nothing but eleven dollars and his baseball bat. What you are now doesn't mean it will always be that way. It's up to you, Lee."

"I'm not a kid, Bethan. I'm five years older than you and probably nowhere near as smart, either."

Bethan laughed, then said, "You're doing pretty well so far, Lee. I wouldn't be talking to you if I thought you were an idiot. I always told my mother that I wanted a man to challenge me, not act as if I was some porcelain doll. Do you believe that you can challenge me?"

Lee looked at her, then a smile grew on his face before he replied, "If you are the prize to win that challenge, Bethan, then I'll do the best that I can. I'm sure that you'll tell me if it's not enough. Okay?"

Bethan smiled back, then answered, "Okay. Now, let's forget about my scary family and wait for two of them to return."

"What do you want to talk about next?"

"How about your father? You seemed to blame yourself for what happened to him."

"Alright. It'll be kind of hard to separate the man from the father."

"It's that way for all of us, I think."

Lee nodded, then began to talk more about his father as Bethan watched and listened.

———

Cody and George had finally pulled up to camp after they'd crossed a wide, but shallow stream about nine miles from where Bethan and Lee were sitting.

They set up a cold camp in about fifteen minutes and were soon eating beans out of their tins.

Cody looked over at George and asked, "You know they'll be behind us pretty soon. Do you have any plans at all?"

George belched, then replied, "Yup. I think our best bet is to walk our horses south after a few hours and then make a big loop back to the west. We need to have a big enough gap so they can't spot us. They'll be riding east and we'll be going in the other direction. We should reach Iron Springs and get on a train south."

"That might work if the train was gonna leave in the daytime, but didn't you read the damned schedule?"

George hated to admit that he hadn't, so he replied, "It doesn't matter, Cody. If we keep riding east, they'll catch up with us, sooner or later. Do you have a better idea?"

"I may not know this country, but I know that the Las Animas River is only a few hours east of here. We could ride that way and then find a town on the river. I know there are a few still there, but I can't remember the names."

"What good would a town be? We'd still be trapped if that posse is behind us."

"We'd be able to get a pack horse, supplies and some more ammunition. Maybe we could add some cash to make up for those tickets we bought, too."

George was undecided and hated to let Cody think that he was now in charge, but there were definite benefits to his plan, especially as they each had badges.

"Okay, Cody. We head east early, find the river and then trail it north to find a town. We'll use our badges to calm the townsfolk down."

Cody grinned, then replied, "I bet those pieces of tin will get us some money, too."

"Maybe," George replied before he tossed the empty can into the creek to let the water take it away.

————

Bryn and Lynn rode into Iron Springs in the early evening and stopped at the small train station. Neither night train had passed through town yet, but the ticket agent said nobody had bought a ticket and he was closing the window in another thirty minutes.

Bryn sent his telegram to Dylan, then he and Lynn headed to the diner for supper.

As they sat at the table, Lynn grinned and asked, "What do you think Bethan and Lee are up to right now?"

"Not what you obviously seem to think they are. I imagine that they're just talking. She obviously likes him, which is a first, and he likes her, but I'm sure that Bethan wants to get to know him better before she lets him in close."

"I was just kidding anyway, Bryn. I know that you're probably right and I hope that she chooses him over being a lawman. I like him and I think he might make a good lawman himself. He didn't overreact to what happened to him in Bishop or finding that deputy sheriff's body, and if Bethan thinks he's worth her attention, maybe the boss could offer him a job. We're two short right now."

"Maybe three if Pete pursues Martha. I don't think she'd marry another deputy marshal after what happened to Bert and I don't believe Al is in the mix, either."

Lynn's eyes widened before he asked, "Do you really think that Pete would hand in his badge?"

"Bethan commented on it after the funeral, and I paid attention. In the office the next day, Pete was talking to Dylan about her and actually asked if Al was still interested."

"How come no one told me?"

Bryn smiled as the waitress brought them their baked chicken, then answered, "You weren't in the office when he asked, but I'm a bit surprised that Addie didn't pass along the gossip."

"I'll ask her about it when we get back," Lynn said before shoving his fork into his mashed potatoes and gravy.

————

Avery George, Homer Edwards and Ted Smith had set up their camp eighteen miles east of Bent Canyon, a town of less than two hundred residents on the western bank of the Las Animas River.

Unlike the other two camps, they had a fire going and were roasting a piglet that they'd butchered before leaving the farm.

"Do you know where we're headed?" Homer asked as he rotated the spit.

Avery replied, "East is our best bet. The Las Animas River should be ahead of us. I don't think anyone is going to be following our trail because there's no law back there. We just need to avoid any big towns."

"We could always get another farmhouse," Ted said with a snicker.

Avery just looked at him and shook his head without comment. It seemed as only disasters had followed them since entering Atherton back in Kansas. Their time in the Indian Nations hadn't been all that pleasant either as they'd had to keep someone on watch in case those Cherokee decided to walk off with their horses.

If they found a town, they'd behave differently, and he'd wear his badge to keep the folks from looking at them as potential danger. He wasn't about to have a repeat of Atherton.

———

Bethan and Lee had been talking for almost three hours when they heard hoofbeats from the southeast, and both stood immediately then faced that way.

The three-quarter moon was up, so it didn't take long for them to spot the two riders and Bethan quickly recognized Lynn and Bryn.

"Over here!" she shouted when they were about fifty yards out.

They turned their animals toward Bethan's shout and soon pulled up.

After stepping down, Lynn handed a bag to Bethan and said, "We brought you both some reasonably warm food."

"Thank you, big brother," Bethan said as she carried the bag back to the camp with Lee walking alongside.

As Bryn and Lynn unsaddled their horses, Bethan took her seat again beside Lee and reached into the bag. She pulled out a tin, then handed it to Lee before extracting a second. She set hers on the ground, then stepped to one of her packs, pulled open the flap and rummaged around until she found two table knives and two forks, then returned.

She handed one of each to Lee, then plopped down next to him.

He'd already opened both tins, so she could smell the baked chicken and said, "This was uncharacteristically thoughtful of you, Lynn."

Lynn laughed as he pulled off his horse's saddle blanket and replied, "It was Bryn's idea, so you can still think of me as being thoughtless."

Bethan already had a mouthful of chicken, so she couldn't reply, but she still managed to grin at her older brother.

"I wish you could have managed some hot coffee," Lee said after swallowing.

"Sorry, but I think Lynn drank all they had, so I don't think he'll be sleeping much, but probably peeing a lot."

Bethan then asked, "What did you find in Iron Springs?"

"It was only about another six miles or so south of here, so after I checked with the ticket manager to make sure that they hadn't bought a ticket, I sent the telegram and we had our supper. Once we were sure that they hadn't been in town, we were able to take our time on the way back, and with the moon higher in the sky, we had better light. We found where one of them turned off about eight hundred yards south of here and the other one headed east just a quarter of a mile or so from where we're sitting."

Lynn brought his canteen to Lee and handed it to him before sitting on his right.

Lee gave the canteen to Bethan, who smiled at him, took a long drink, then handed it back to him. He smiled back, then drank some water before capping it and setting it down.

Lynn looked up at Bryn and grinned before he said, "What's the plan now? Are we going to bother with setting up watches?"

"I think we're better off just getting some sleep. I want to be in the saddle by dawn."

"Sounds good to me. Do you think we'll catch up with them before noon?"

"Maybe. We know which direction they went, but if they were smart, they'd circle around and head in the opposite direction. They don't have a pack horse, so their supplies are limited, and they may not know of any towns to the east."

"How can we catch them if they do?" Lee asked.

"When we leave here in the morning, we won't bother heading south. Lee, you'll ride due east. Lynn, you'll angle northeast until you're about eight hundred yards away from Lee. Bethan, you'll head southeast until you have the same gap to Lee. I'll head even further southeast and then ride parallel to Bethan at eight hundred yards. That'll increase our visibility to about a six-mile spread. All we have to worry about is hills and gullies. But if you find a hill, then ride to the top and take a look around."

Bethan asked, "I assume that you want them to spot us, so if we see them, we'll fire a shot in the air."

Bryn grinned as he said, "That's the idea. Now when we leave, Lee and Bethan will trail the mule and pack horse. With any kind of luck, we should spot them by midmorning, even if they don't try to circle back west."

"Okay, boss," Lynn replied.

It wasn't until almost midnight before they were in their bedrolls. Both Bryn and Lynn had set their pocket watch alarms for 4:30 to ensure that they'd be able to get ready to move before the sun rose.

As she lay just three feet from Lee, who already had his eyes closed, Bethan looked across at him and smiled. She wondered how obvious she had been with her comment about not being offended if he kissed her. Maybe it wasn't as blatant a hint as she'd thought. As long as neither of them was killed tomorrow, she'd be a little less obtuse.

CHAPTER 8

The two pocket watch alarms didn't synchronize their dinging, but Bryn's alone was enough to stir them from their slumber. By the time Lynn's started chirping, they were all out of their bedrolls and stretching.

The men let Bethan use the creek and the cover of the birch trees to let her manage her personal toilette, while the males all used whatever ground was available.

None of the men bothered shaving to save time, and just twenty-five minutes after sliding from their bedrolls, they were mounting their horses.

After they were in their saddles, Lee headed due east, and Lynn headed sharply to the northeast while Bethan and Bryn rode southeast, but after a minute or so, Bethan turned east while Bryn continued on a southeast course.

Sunrise found them riding in a wide row that stretched across a mile and a half of eastern Colorado. They were moving at a slow trot to keep the horses from getting too tired.

They were blessed with a cloud cover that morning, so there wasn't the issue with having to look into the blinding sun. If the rains came, then they would have other problems, but for now, just not having the sun in their eyes was a blessing.

———

Dylan entered the office and found a telegram lying on the floor. After closing the door, he stepped slowly to the front desk as he removed his hat, dropped it on the desktop and took a seat.

He opened the telegram and read:

US MARSHAL DYLAN EVANS DENVER COLO

**MET WITH BETHAN AND BISHOP MARSHAL
TRACKED TWO MEN FROM LA JUNTA
WILL CAMP AND TRAIL IN MORNING
BELIEVE CLOSE**

BRYN EVANS IRON SPRINGS COLO

He set the telegram on the desktop and felt helpless. His daughter and son were out in the middle of nowhere chasing two killers and might be close to three more.

He wished he could send more men, but knew it was too late anyway. Besides, his best men were already there along with the best woman.

———

George and Cody hadn't awakened as early as their followers, but still were saddling their horses at daybreak. They hadn't had any breakfast and wanted to get to Iron Springs to get some supplies and then try to board that late train out of the area.

Once they were mounted, they rode east for another mile before turning south and picking up the pace to put some distance between them and that posse.

"How much do we head south?" Cody yelled.

"I figure about another thirty minutes or so. Then we head west with the sun at our backs."

"What sun? It looks like it's gonna rain."

"Just keep riding and turn when I do."

Cody didn't reply but wished they'd ridden to Iron Springs last night, posse or no posse. He didn't like this running and wished he'd never left Canon City in the first place. Even Bishop was looking pretty good to him now. Having that misfire still irked him. If only that cartridge had worked, then he would have owned the farm and could sell it. Now, he was on the run with a posse behind him just because some idiot at the factory screwed up when he made the cartridge.

Thirty minutes later, George made the turn back to the west and even if that posse was on their trail, they'd be at least three long miles north of their new path.

George had made his estimate assuming that they would be following the trail they had left behind when they were heading east, but they hadn't been riding due east. They had been riding east-northeast, so even if Bryn hadn't had them spread out, that gap would only have been two miles. With Bryn's plan to spread out, it was going to be much less. It would be less than a mile.

———

As they converged, the Gentry gang was cleaning up their campsite and saddling their horses.

They expected to be in Bent Canyon by noon and be headed out of Colorado before sunset.

———

289

It was Bryn who first spotted the two riders about two miles away riding east. They hadn't seen him yet, so he pulled up and rather than fire a warning shot, looked to his left at Bethan, took off his hat and waved.

Bethan had been scanning the horizon and soon saw Bryn's silent warning and waved back. She then looked north and wasn't surprise to see Lee already looking her way, so she waved and he waved back, but she wasn't sure if he understood what she was trying to tell him, so she pulled her Winchester '76 from its scabbard and waved it over her head, then pointed southeast.

Lee finally understood why she'd waved, then took off his hat, turned to his left and began waving it over his head. It took longer for him to get Lynn's attention, but when Lynn spotted him, he immediately understood and turned his horse toward Lee.

As soon as Lee saw Lynn turn, he wheeled Biff to the south and set off to meet Bethan.

Bethan waited for Lee, and when he was close, she said, "I think Bryn spotted them, but wanted to let them get closer."

Before he could reply, she turned Nippy south and nudged her into a fast trot. Lee quickly caught up to her and rode alongside as Lynn trailed by three hundred yards.

Once they'd started moving, Bryn turned to watch the two riders wondering how much longer it would be before they were spotted. It wasn't long.

––––––––

George was riding on the right and had been scanning the horizon for any signs of the posse, but because Bryn had stopped, there was no dust cloud or movement to announce his presence.

It was only when Lee and Bethan almost reached Bryn that their motion attracted his attention.

He quickly pulled up as he shouted, "Damn it! They're right there!"

Cody yanked his horse to a halt, then yelled, "What do we do?"

George almost panicked but noticed that two of the riders had pack animals, so he said loudly, "Turn around. They have pack horses and can't go that fast. They're still a good mile away."

Cody didn't wait to reply but wheeled his horse and pushed him to a gallop.

George swore, then ripped his horse around and followed, but at a canter. He needed to keep his horse from getting winded too quickly and began to hope that Cody's horse would falter soon to give him time to get away. Knowing Cody, he'd try to shoot it out with the posse and that might be just enough for him to make his own escape. He might even thin out their ranks a bit and dissuade them from following altogether.

————

Bryn started Aesop off at a fast trot before Lee and Bethan arrived, but they adjusted their angle and soon rode alongside, but Lynn hadn't closed the gap yet.

Lee shouted, "That's Cody who took off at a gallop."

"I figured as much. He'll run that horse into the ground soon enough. We'll slow down a bit to give Lynn a chance to catch up."

Two minutes after they'd all slowed, Lynn pulled up beside Bryn and said, "One of them is playing it smart. I guess he's your pal, George Lynch. Do you think he'll stick with his partner?"

"Only if he's stupid."

"What do we do if they separate?"

Bryn let Aesop take a few strides before he replied, "If he sets up, we'll have Bethan and Lee swing wide and chase down Lynch. I don't think he's the one who pulled the trigger on that deputy and might not be as big a problem as the little guy."

"Okay," Lynn said, then turned to Bethan and asked, "Did you get that?"

"I heard. We'll stay out of Winchester range if he gets off his horse and the other one keeps riding."

She then turned to Lee and asked, "Did you hear all of that?"

"Yes, ma'am. How much longer do you think he can keep that horse going at that speed?"

"Not much longer."

———

Cody could hear his horse's labored breathing before he swiveled in the saddle to look back at the posse. He was surprised to see that George was already four hundred yards away but pleased to see that the posse was still more than a mile back. He had no idea where he'd go, but even he understood that his horse couldn't handle the hard gallop much longer.

He was beginning to slow the horse when suddenly, it simply collapsed, and he found himself airborne. It wasn't a long fall, but when the horse fell to his right, Cody bounced hard off the soil and then rolled twice.

He quickly got to his feet and stepped to his exhausted animal whose chest was rising and falling rapidly but made no effort to stand, so he grasped the reins and began to tug.

"Get up, you nag!" he shouted as he tried to lift the horse's head from the dirt.

George had been expecting Cody to slow, but when he watched the horse go down, his biggest concern wasn't the horse, it was how Cody would react when he rode past without stopping. So, rather than take that risk, he quickly angled to the northeast.

Cody hadn't looked up from his horse's face, so he didn't notice George's shift, but continued to pull on the reins and curse the poor animal, as if it was to blame.

When he finally gave up hope that it would be of any use in his escape, he looked west for George and soon realized that his partner was going to abandon him.

"You son of a bitch!" he screamed as he pulled his Colt and cocked the hammer.

He was about to fire when he realized that he was now alone to face the posse and would need every bullet.

"Bastard!" he snarled as he turned back to his horse and dropped to his knees to pull his Winchester free.

George had heard the shout and expected to hear a gunshot but didn't even turn as he continued northeast away from Cody.

―――

"Go, Bethan!" Bryn shouted as soon as he saw George turn away from Cody's accident.

"We're going around!" she yelled back before she and Lee shifted to the northeast.

Their new path around Cody was in direct line behind the fleeing George Lynch.

He was still almost a mile ahead of them, but he was in clear sight and there weren't any good ambush sites on the surrounding landscape.

―――

When George felt that he was out of Cody's rifle range, he looked over his shoulder and spotted two of the posse still behind him and then noticed that one of them was riding the pinto that they'd taken from that town marshal in Bishop. *Was he one of the men in the posse?* If that was the marshal, then George knew he had an advantage, depending on who was with him. He guessed he was one of the deputy sheriffs from Bent County, and he had to assume he was reasonably proficient and competent, so George placed the second rider as the bigger threat. If he'd been closer, he would have seen Bethan's long brown hair and obvious feminine characteristics, even when wearing her coat. If he had, he might have decided to set up a defensive position in some creek, but he wanted to put as much distance between him and whatever was happening with Cody.

They were each trailing a pack animal, so they wouldn't be able to catch him and with two of the lawmen engaging Cody, he saw the slimmest possibility of a successful escape.

———

Bryn and Lynn were within five hundred yards of Cody and his still-breathing horse when Lynn asked, "How do you want to handle this, Bryn?"

"We'll split up about fifty yards apart, then when we're about two hundred yards out, we'll pull up and I'll let him know that there is a range advantage with the '76 and put a shot over his head."

"Sounds fair. You know he's going to duck down behind his horse."

"I figured that. I'll lay one into his behind if I have to, but we don't want to spend all day our here. We need to help Bethan and Lee."

"Do you want me to add to his discomfort?"

"Give me two shots and then let's see what he does. If he still insists on returning fire, then go ahead."

"Yes, sir," Lynn replied as he shifted slightly to the left while they continued toward Cody.

———

Cody watched the two lawmen approaching and then glanced at the other two who were following George. He briefly wondered if that wasn't George's plan; to break up the posse so they only had to face two guns apiece, but quickly dismissed the notion. But it did give him hope that he might get out of this mess. He only had two men to kill and they were on horseback.

He cocked his Winchester's hammer, then stood and watched the two riders, enticing them to get closer. As soon as they pulled their own rifles, he'd start firing, then drop to the ground. He didn't think about hiding behind his horse because if the horse took a bullet, he'd start thrashing around and one of those iron horseshoes might hit him.

———

When they were around two hundred yards away from Cody, Bryn shouted, "I'm United States Deputy Marshal Bryn Evans. You're under arrest for the murder of a Bent County deputy sheriff. Leave your guns on the ground and put your hands in the air."

Cody yelled back, "I didn't do that. The other feller, George Lynch, he pulled the trigger before I knew it. You better join the other two and chase him down before he gets away."

"He won't get away, and it doesn't matter who pulled the trigger, Cody. You're just as guilty in the eyes of the law."

"Well then, you'd better come here and try to arrest me, Marshal."

Bryn glanced over at Lynn, then looked back at Cody as he slid his Winchester from its scabbard and cocked the hammer as Lynn pulled his free.

Cody watched and was expecting the two lawmen to start riding again and was puzzled when he watched Bryn put his rifle's butt to his shoulder and then set his sights.

"What..." he began to ask himself when Bryn fired.

The .45 caliber bullet drilled through the five-hundred-and-eighty-four feet of thin Colorado air and yanked Cody's hat from his head.

As Bryn cycled in a new cartridge, Cody stood in stunned immobility with his eyes on Bryn. He had no idea why the lawman's Winchester had reached him but brought his level and fired.

His .44 punched into the dirt, just fifteen feet in front of Aesop's left front hoof, but his horse didn't flinch.

Bryn yelled, "Last chance, Cody! Drop your weapons!"

"The hell with that!" he shouted as he dropped to the ground and quickly set his sights on the lawman in the saddle. This time, he raised his sights before he squeezed the trigger.

Bryn was about to take his second shot when he felt the .44 slam into his right upper thigh.

He grunted loudly and let his sights drop as he grabbed the wound with his left hand.

Lynn had seen Bryn's reaction and didn't have to ask if he'd been hit, so he quickly brought his sights in line with Cody and squeezed his trigger.

Lynn's .45 spiraled out of his barrel at twelve hundred feet per second and about a fifth of a second later, crashed into the left side of Cody's spine near the third thoracic vertebra. It shattered two ribs before penetrating his left middle lobe and then plowed into his heart.

It was such an effective killing shot that Cody didn't scream or even feel the pain, but simply dropped his rifle and his head to the ground.

Lynn knew that the man was dead, and immediately turned his horse and rode to Bryn.

"How bad is it, Bryn?"

"Could be worse, I suppose. It's buried in my right thigh. I don't know how deep it is, but I need to get that bullet out of there and get it sewn closed."

"We'll head back to Iron Springs."

"No. You need to help Bethan and Lee. I'll ride back by myself. It's only about an hour or so."

"How about this? I'll come back with you to Iron Springs and then after I drop you off, I'll come back this way. They'll be okay."

Bryn didn't want to waste any more time arguing and knew that he needed treatment soon, so he nodded and said, "Okay. Let's get moving. I'll wrap something around hole to keep the blood from messing up my saddle."

After he slid his Winchester into its scabbard, Bryn pulled a towel from his saddlebag, wrapped it tightly around his thigh, then said, "Wave to Bethan and tell her to keep going and then let's head back."

Lynn removed his hat and waved to Bethan and Lee who had been watching since the first shot and motioned them forward. Bethan waved back, and Lynn waited until he was sure that they were continuing the chase before he turned to look at Bryn.

"Let's get you to a doctor, Bryn."

"Okay," he replied before getting Aesop moving.

He didn't want to worry Lynn, but he wasn't sure that he'd make it all the way to Iron Springs. He was losing more blood than he had originally thought.

Lynn glanced over at Bryn as they rode west at a fast trot, each of them hoping that Bethan and Lee wouldn't be in any real danger.

———

George was still riding northeast and checking his backtrail every few seconds. He wasn't gaining on his two followers, but they were still about a mile back, so he wasn't worried. But he did notice that two of the lawmen were riding west and he figured that at least one had been hit by one of Cody's bullets. He was pleased with his decision to split away and almost as pleased that he wasn't going to have to put up with his partner any longer.

He knew that the Las Animas River was ahead and that there were towns on the western bank, so he shifted slightly more to the north as he continued to lead the two lawmen.

———

As they rode, Lee asked, "Why did they head back?"

"I think Bryn took a hit and needed a doctor. He didn't want to lose Lynch, so that's why Lynn waved us on. I imagine that

Lynn will come back this way as soon as Bryn is with the doctor."

"Do they even have a doctor in a town that small?"

"I don't know, but the railroad goes through there, so it's more likely than in other small towns."

"Where is he going?" Lee yelled as he pointed at George Lynch.

"I have no idea. We'll just keep pushing him. If we have to, we'll slow down to keep the horses from tiring."

"You're the boss," Lee shouted back with a grin.

"Remember that after we're married," Bethan loudly replied.

Lee stared at her with big eyes before she burst into laughter, almost falling from Nippy.

Lee laughed, then shouted, "I'll hold you to that proposal, Miss Evans."

Bethan was still smiling as she turned her eyes back to the front and noticed that Lynch had changed his direction, so she shifted Nippy to her left and Lee matched her new track.

———

Bryn was getting wobbly after just twenty minutes of riding and wasn't sure he was going to make it. It didn't make any sense to him as the .44 that was buried in his leg couldn't have been very deep at that range.

Lynn noticed that Bryn was losing focus and shouted, "Are you all right, Bryn? Do you need me to tie you down?"

"No. I'll be okay. We should spot the town soon."

Lynn kept his eyes on Bryn for another thirty seconds, then turned his eyes back to the west and almost laughed when he spotted the cross atop the steeple of an Iron Springs church.

"We're almost there, Bryn!" he shouted.

Bryn just nodded, but his Stetson's brim was almost touching Aesop's neck as they continued toward Iron Springs.

———

At almost the same moment that Lynn had spotted the first signs of Iron Springs, George caught his first glimpse of Bent Canyon. He hadn't even seen the river on the eastern border of the town, but the miracle sight of those roofs ahead made him spur his horse to a fast trot to get there first. He moved his badge to his coat before taking another look at his backtrail and estimated he'd have enough time to disappear in the town.

When they tried to search for him, he'd be able to pick them off with his Winchester. It was just a matter of riding into town slowly and walking his horse into an alley. He wasn't going to have his Winchester in his hands until he was ready, so none of the townsfolk would be afraid of him. Let them worry about the two behind him.

———

Three minutes later, Lee spotted the distant buildings and yelled, "He's heading for that town, Bethan. How do you want to handle it?"

"Let's slow down and talk," she shouted back.

After they slowed their horses to a slow trot, Bethan looked at Bent Canyon and then said, "He's going to wait for us, Lee. He knows you and your pinto, so I think that our best option is for me to go in alone from the other end of town without the pack horse."

"He'll recognize Nippy, Bethan."

"Not if he doesn't see her. Let's keep going until he enters the town. I don't want him to think that we're planning something."

"Okay," Lee replied before he nudged Biff into a medium trot.

As she rode beside him, Bethan was formulating a better plan. They had never been within a mile of George Lynch and he probably didn't even know she was a woman. It was time to take advantage of his ignorance.

"How about this? Once he gets in the town, we stop and dismount. You switch to the pack horse and ride toward the town. I'll ride along the west side of the town about two hundred yards out, so he won't notice me. When I reach the northern end of town, I'll dismount, then tie off Nippy and leave my hat on my saddle horn. I want to look very girly, so I'll probably leave my coat and gunbelt in one of the packs on the mule."

"You don't need to take off your coat to look girly, Bethan, but it's still a bit cool, so you might look odd if you don't have your coat."

"Thank you for the compliment, Lee, but I'll still have my Webley in my shoulder holster, so I'll be okay."

"When do I enter town?"

"Slow down and watch me until I tie off Nippy. Then take your time riding into the town. Wear your badge on your coat and have your Winchester ready to fire. Remember that Lynch has a badge too, so he might pretend that you're a bad guy. You'll see me walking on one of the boardwalks and I'll see if I can spot him."

"I don't like it all that much, but it's pretty smart."

"Thank you for that even better compliment," Bethan replied with a smile.

Lee smiled back, then looked toward Bent Canyon and watched as George neared its outskirts.

———

George looked back once more before he rode into the main street and felt as if he was entering a sanctuary.

Once he reached the town, he looked for the saloon and trotted his horse to the place, stepped down and quickly tied him off.

None of the locals even seemed to care that he was there, even as he rode past the Bent Canyon Bank across from the barber shop. As he looked at the small building, he wondered if maybe he shouldn't take advantage of his badge and pay the place a visit after he eliminated the two lawmen.

There was minimal traffic, so he slid his Winchester from his scabbard, then stepped onto the boardwalk in front of the saloon, acting as if he was about to enter, then shook his head, turned and quickly crossed the street as if he'd forgotten something. He wasn't sure if the act was necessary as no one had even given him a second glance, which he found a bit odd.

After reaching the opposite boardwalk, he turned left, walked another fifty feet and turned into the alley between the barbershop and the hardware store.

Once inside the narrow alley, he turned and was pleased with his position. He could see his horse in front of the saloon and had a decent enough angle of fire. When those lawmen spotted the animal, they'd stop to check it out and would be sitting ducks.

————

Once George disappeared, Lee and Bethan pulled up and began to quickly modify their travel arrangements. They moved the two hanging packs that Bethan had created to Biff, while Bethan switched the mule's trail rope to the pack horse.

After they mounted, Bethan looked at Lee, smiled and said, "I'll see you in town, Mister Collins."

"Take care of yourself, Bethan," Lee replied.

"I will. Don't you go doing anything silly either."

"No, ma'am," he answered with a smile.

She wheeled Nippy to the north and rode away at a fast trot.

Lee watched her ride away and even though he knew that she was more than capable of dealing with Lynch, it still made him a bit nauseous.

He kept watching until she was parallel to the town before he started the gelding forward at a walk. He kept watching as she kept riding north, turned after passing the last building, then soon stopped and dismounted.

He nudged the gelding to a slow trot and almost forgot to move his badge to his coat because he'd been concentrating on Bethan. He rolled his eyes as he pulled the badge from his pocket, pinned it to his coat, and then slid his Winchester free.

Lee didn't cock the hammer yet but glanced at Bethan who was taking off her coat.

"I hope this works, Bethan," he said aloud before he shifted his eyes to Bent Canyon, now just six hundred yards away.

————

As Bethan had ridden past the buildings, she'd studied each one and checked the alleys in between and found nothing of interest. When she pulled up behind the last building which looked almost like a jail with barred windows, she quickly stepped down and unbuttoned her coat.

As she pulled it open, she thought of what Lee had said, then decided to leave it on, but leave it unbuttoned. She preferred to have the longer barrel of her Smith & Wesson if it came to that. Bethan hoped it would be more along the lines of what had happened in the hotel lobby in Granite when she surprised those two killers.

She did take off her Stetson and hang it on her saddle horn so Lynch would more easily identify her as a woman.

Bethan then glanced south, spotted Lee as he rode toward the southern end of town, then removed the leather strip holding her hair in place and fluffed it out.

She took a deep breath, then quickly strode around the outside of the building and soon reached the northern end of the boardwalk and stepped onto the elevated walkway.

When she glanced at the store that had the appearance of a jail, she smiled. It was a gunsmith's shop and she understood the need for the bars in the window.

She walked slowly, scanning the buildings and sparse traffic, but not seeing George Lynch's horse. Then, after passing a café, she saw the animal tied up before the saloon two blocks away.

She turned to her right to look in the window of the general store while she thought about the situation. If he was in the saloon, he'd be sitting with his back against the wall and probably have his pistol cocked and ready. He could also be in an alley across the street waiting for them to ride into the south end of town and wait until they entered the saloon. Of the two possible scenarios, she reasoned that his best option would be to stay outside in case things went badly for him.

She then turned, then took a few more steps before she hopped onto the main street and headed for the other side. She hadn't checked any of the alleys to her left, but they were at a bad angle for an ambush, so she didn't bother heading that way.

Once on the other side, she began to hum a Strauss waltz that always ended their family nights at the Double EE. The melody calmed her but reminded her that Bryn had been shot and she hoped that he was all right.

She continued to loudly hum the waltz as she stepped along the boardwalk, glancing at each of the side alleys as she passed.

———

George Lynch had shifted to the right side of the alley to give him a better view to the south. He knew that they had probably stopped before entering the town and began to think that they might split up and come from both directions. It really didn't matter, as long as they both stopped to look at his horse at the same time.

He was still staring at the saloon when he heard a woman humming a song and almost smiled but lowered his Winchester and turned around as she drew closer, so he'd appear to be relieving himself rather than trying to shoot two lawmen.

———

Bethan walked past George's alley and didn't miss a note when she saw him standing with his back to her. But she'd never been closer than a mile from him and wasn't sure if the man in the alley really wasn't doing exactly what he appeared to be doing, so she continued to walk until she passed the hardware store.

She hadn't even reached the hardware entrance when she cursed herself for making that mistake. It had to have been Lynch because the position was perfect. She'd missed a golden opportunity to capture him without a single shot being fired, and now she had to try again, but doubted if she'd be able to find him so vulnerable.

As she passed the doorway, she looked west and spotted Lee turning onto the main street and waved. He'd already tied off Biff and the pack mule, so he looked like a ranch hand. She noticed that he wasn't wearing his badge and guessed that Lee figured that because George Lynch had only seen him for a few minutes, he might not recognize him. It was a good modification to the plan.

Lee had already seen her, waved back and then slowed the horses to a walk as he waited for her to give him some sign of Lynch's whereabouts.

Once she had his attention, Bethan pointed to Lynch's horse before the saloon, then dramatically shook her head before shifting her arm to point back at the alley she'd just passed. Then she motioned that she'd circle around.

Lee nodded so much that he expected his head to fall off. He wanted to let her know that he understood.

Bethan nodded less violently, then picked up her pace, reached the next alley and turned left.

Once inside the dark space between the building, she pulled her pistol and cocked the hammer.

———

George had returned to his previous spot and had his Winchester loosely in his hands rather than letting his muscles get tight holding it level because he didn't know how much longer it would be before they arrived.

Then he caught sight of a rider coming in from his left where he expected to spot them, but George wasn't sure that he was one of the lawmen. He wasn't riding a pinto, leading a pack animal, and he didn't have on a badge, so George just kept his eyes on him until he got closer.

Lee walked his temporary ride down main street and felt like a target was painted on his coat as he kept his eyes looking forward. He expected that if he wasn't shot, Bethan would lay into him for not wearing the badge and riding too close to the saloon, but there was a reason he'd done it. He wanted George Lynch to spot him and keep his attention long enough for Bethan to get close.

Bethan had lost sight of Lee when she entered the alley but knew that she had to act quickly. She took rapid, long strides as she cleared the alley and turned left behind the hardware store. Her only real concern was that Lynch had a Winchester cocked and ready while she only had her pistol. The alley was a good eighty feet long and she wanted to get closer to negate the accuracy of his repeater.

She slowed as she reached Lynch's alley, then held her pistol level as she entered the shadowy space and spotted Lynch near the other end with his Winchester. She was almost giddy to see that he hadn't raised it to fire and began to quietly move down the alley.

George had been concentrating on that cowboy and there was something about him that looked familiar. Then, when he stopped by the saloon and began to dismount, it struck him. *He was that town marshal back in Bishop!*

He wanted to fire but had to wait until the other deputy arrived. *Where was he?*

He soon had his answer, and it was a genuine shock when he heard a woman's voice echo from the alley behind him.

"Drop the rifle, Lynch! You're under arrest for murder!"

George was still confused, but didn't bother with the woman, even if she was armed. She wasn't that close and the lawman across the street was already turning to draw his pistol after hearing her shout.

He ignored Bethan and snapped his Winchester to his shoulder. He barely felt the rifle's butt before he felt a bigger punch pound into the right side of his butt and screamed as the gunshot resonated through the alley.

He jerked his finger against his trigger, firing his Winchester, then fell to the ground as his smoking repeater dropped next to him.

Bethan raced to where he lay writhing in the dirt, snatched his Winchester from the ground, then holstered her own pistol before ripping his Colt from his holster.

She then looked at the alley's entrance and saw Lee sprinting towards her. He slowed as he crossed the boardwalk and looked down at Lynch.

"Where did you hit him?"

"I shot him in his behind. It's the best place to put a bullet if you don't want to kill him. He was getting ready to shoot you, so I had to fire."

"I heard you order him to drop his guns, but he still tried to shoot me?"

"I guess he figured that no girl would be a real danger."

"That'll teach him. What do we do with him now?"

"He's not a problem, so we see if there's anyone in town who can get that bullet out of there and then sew him up before we take him to Iron Springs."

Lee nodded, then took Lynch's Winchester from her as she slipped his Colt into her coat pocket and pinned her badge to her coat.

They then pulled George from the ground and half-carried him onto the boardwalk. As if by magic, the townsfolk that hadn't been seen in great numbers appeared all along the main street.

Bethan then looked at the closest bystander and said, "I'm United States Deputy Marshal Bethan Evans. This man is our prisoner and is charged with the murder of a Bent County deputy sheriff. His partner's body is a few miles southwest of town. I need to have someone pull my bullet out of his behind and sew it closed. Can you help us?"

The man blinked at her and asked, "You're a deputy marshal?"

"My father is United Stated Marshal Dylan Evans. Maybe you've heard the name."

"Oh, sorry, ma'am. The one who acts like our doc is Miss Lucy. She went to Denver and did some nursin' before she decided to come back here and be our schoolmarm."

"Can you take him to whatever you use as a jail and have her fix him up? We need to get our horses."

"We'll do that, ma'am," he said with a grin as he looked at George Lynch's bloody britches.

He and another man then took George's arms and led him away before she turned to another citizen and asked, "Where will we find him?"

"My place. My name's Lou Stanton, and I own the gun shop. The back room is empty, so we use it to lock folks up until we can get a deputy out of Walsenburg. Did you try to shoot that feller in the backside, Marshal Evans?"

Bethan smiled and replied, "Yes, sir. I was only about forty feet away, so it wasn't hard."

"I reckon not. Did you use that Winchester the other deputy is holding?"

"No, sir. That was the shooter's carbine. He was going to shoot my partner, so I had to take the shot with my Schofield."

"That's mighty impressive shooting, Marshal. I assume you and your partner will be taking him out of town and we won't have to ask for a deputy from the county to come and pick him up."

"We'll do that. And thank you for your help."

"You're welcome, Marshal."

As the crowd dissolved with most of them following the men carting George away, Bethan turned to Lee and hooked her free hand through his arm.

"Let's get our horses and wait for Lynn to arrive."

Lee smiled at her and replied, "I'll treat you to lunch after they're all in the livery."

"I accept your generous offer, sir," Bethan said as she returned his smile.

They had to separate to get their horses, and as Bethan walked north, she was already thinking about possibly giving up her temporary deputy marshal's badge.

———

"How is he doing, doc?" Lynn asked as the doctor left the examination room.

"It was a lot closer than you might have expected because the bullet nicked an artery that cost him a lot of blood. Luckily, the bullet kept it from bleeding him out. As soon as I pulled it free, I had to quickly close it before he lost too much. He'll be weak for a day or two, but he should recover."

Lynn blew out a long breath, then said, "Is there anything more I can do here, doc? I've got to help my sister."

"Your sister?"

"She and a town marshal chased down the partner of the man who put that bullet into my uncle. They were riding east when we left them. Are there any towns that way?"

"The nearest one I can figure is Bent Canyon. It's a bit more northeast than due east, though. You could ride east and pick up the road. It's right along the Las Animas River."

"Thanks, doc. I'll send a telegram to our boss in Denver, then see if my horse is up to the trip. He's had an hour's rest, so he should be okay."

"Good luck, Marshal. I hope things turn out okay."

"I should be back in the morning," Lynn said before turning and quickly leaving the doctor's office.

Once outside, he walked to the nearby telegraph office, sent his message to his father, then headed back to the livery to pick up his horse, hoping that the rest was long enough.

He was worried about his sister and hoped that Lee was as good as she seemed to believe.

———

313

Eight miles east of Bent Canyon, Avery George, Ted Smith and Homer Edwards were watering their horses in a small tributary of the Las Animas River.

Avery stood with his right hand resting on his pistol's butt as he said, "We'll just follow this stream until it reaches that river and then we'll cross over to the western bank and ride west until we pick up the road. It'll take us into Bent Canyon."

"What'll we do when we get to this burg?" asked Homer.

"I'll be wearing my badge and we'll just ride in like we own the place. We'll be talking and laughing to keep the townsfolk at ease and stop at the first saloon we see. We'll have a beer and find out what we can. We'll blend in."

Ted asked, "For how long?"

"Maybe a day. I've already concocted a story that should make you both laugh until your stomachs knot up."

"What's that?"

"If anyone asks what we're doing there, I'll tell them that we're chasing after the notorious Gentry gang. By now, even a town like Bent Canyon would have heard about what happened at the farm. They'll probably treat us like kings."

"Until we knock off their bank," Homer said with a grin.

"I reckon that might change their minds some," Avery replied, matching Homer's grin.

Ten minutes later, they were back in the saddle and following the stream as it flowed northwest toward the river.

———

After their horses and pack mule were happily munching oats in the livery, Lee and Bethan checked on their prisoner at the gunsmith's shop, then left to have some lunch.

As they walked to the café, Lee said, "I thought you'd chew me out for modifying the plan and not wearing the badge."

"I thought you had a good reason for doing it."

"I figured that he'd only seen me for a few minutes, so he might not recognize me on a different horse."

"That's what I thought, but why did you dismount in front of the saloon when you knew he was in the alley across the street?"

"I wanted to keep his attention on me to give you time to get closer. I was counting on his lack of recognition to buy the time."

"That was a big risk, Lee. He could have shot you, then turned around to make sure no one was behind him."

"I thought that even if he did recognize me, he'd spend a minute wondering where the second lawman was. It wasn't as risky as you think."

"Well, you did a good job and I'm glad that you changed the plan. If you noticed, I followed your advice and kept my coat on."

"I noticed. I also noticed that your hair isn't tied down now. It looks very nice that way."

"Is that a real boy-girl compliment, Lee?"

He smiled and replied, "Maybe. I hope that doesn't shift me into your typical man category."

"You can never be shoved into that group, Lee. You'll always be the only man who will be on the other side…except for the ones in my family, who don't matter."

Lee took her reply to heart and reached over and grasped her hand.

Bethan was a bit surprised, but when she felt his fingers wrap around her hand, she closed hers around his hand to let him know that she meant what she'd said.

The two young people walked toward Rosie's Café as if they hadn't been involved in a shootout just an hour earlier. There was still a dead body lying on the plains a few miles southeast of town, but it wasn't their concern at the moment.

———

Lynn was following his own tracks at a medium trot and expected that he'd spot Cody Russell's body in another hour or so.

He wondered how Erin would react to the news that her husband had been shot. In all the years that Bryn had been a lawman, he'd never been seriously wounded. The nearly fatal wound he'd suffered in the war was before he met Erin. He knew that Erin, just like his Addie and even his mother, worried about them whenever they had to pursue a killer.

Addie had told him that after the incident in the mountain pass, Erin had expressed her wish that he'd just hand in the badge and return to the ranch to raise horses and suspected that Bryn may agree with her now. Two close calls in less than a month is enough to put the willies into any man.

―――

The Gentry gang had crossed the Las Animas River without any difficulties, then continued east until they reached the road connecting Bent Canyon with Trinidad, sixty miles to the southwest.

Once on the poor excuse for a roadway, Homer asked, "Which way is that town?"

"It's got to be north because the road is still going. If it was south, there wouldn't be a road up here at all."

"Okay, boss, let's go have us a beer," Ted said before turning his horse north.

They were soon heading north trailing their pack mule, anticipating a nice quiet town with no lawmen.

―――

"How long before you take him out of here?" Lou Stanton asked as he stared at George Lynch.

George glared at the gunsmith but didn't comment as he lay on his stomach in the small room with his ankles bound, as if he could run.

"We're waiting for my brother, who's a real deputy marshal, to get here. I expect he'll be here within a couple of hours with news about my uncle."

"That was just bad luck to take a hit at that range. I don't figure it was too bad, though."

"If it wasn't serious, he wouldn't have headed back to Iron Springs."

Lou nodded, then asked, "Do you want to look at my inventory while you're here?"

Bethan glanced at Lee who laughed and replied, "She's traveling with two Winchester '73s, one '76, a shotgun, a Smith & Wesson, a Remington and two Colts. I'm wearing one of them."

Bethan then said, "Don't forget my Webley and my Remington derringer."

Lou's eyebrows rose as he said, "I reckon I won't be selling either of you any guns."

"We're going to just take a seat on the bench in front of the store to wait for my brother."

"Well, I'm glad things turned out okay."

"Me, too," Bethan said before hooking her arm through Lee's and walking with him through the shop.

Once outside, they crossed the main street and headed for the general store.

"After Lynn arrives, how do we get Lynch back to Iron Springs?" Lee asked.

"That's a good question. Maybe I should have thought of that before shooting him in the butt."

Lee laughed, then said, "We can always hang him over the saddle like he was dead."

"I'm sure that he'd be happy during that long, bumpy ride."

"The best way would be to shorten his stirrups so he can stand up as often as he could."

"I'm not sure that Lynn will care much about his comfort," she said as they reached the bench.

After they took a seat, Lee looked at her and asked, "Bethan, all joking aside, what do we do after we get to Iron Springs?"

"What do you mean? We'll all get on the train to La Junta, then they'll go back to Denver and we'll continue on to Las Animas. The murder happened in Bent County, so Lynch's trial will be there. If he gets off, and I doubt that he will, then we'll take him to Denver for trial."

"You won't be going back to Denver with your brother and uncle?"

"I'm a witness, Lee. I have to go back to Las Animas for the trial."

"But when the trial is over, you'll be going back to Denver."

"That's where I live, Lee," Bethan replied, knowing what he was really asking but wanted him to say it.

Lee then asked, "What if I asked you to stay with me in Las Animas?"

Bethan smiled and answered, "Why does it have to be Las Animas, Lee? You've proven yourself to be a good lawman already and a better man. With the recent loss of one deputy marshal, I think that you'd be welcomed in the U.S. Marshal's office."

Lee exhaled sharply, then said, "Bethan, I've never even fired a gun at a man. How could I possibly become a deputy marshal? And I don't want to be given the job just because your father is the marshal."

"He wouldn't do that, Lee. In fact, I'll promise that I won't even say a word on your behalf. If you come with me to Denver, I'll introduce you to my father and then we'll see where it goes from there. Don't worry about the lack of gunfights, either. There's a lot more to the job than shooting. You've already demonstrated that you possess a quick and logical mind."

Lee looked at her and asked softly, "What if I can't do it, Bethan? I don't know how I'd react if things get sticky."

"You were going to take that deputy sheriff's job in Las Animas, weren't you?"

Lee nodded, then replied, "But that would be different. If I failed there, you wouldn't know about it. I'd be able to just quit, and nobody would know."

Bethan sighed, then took his hands and said, "I watched you ride into town and you had the courage to dismount in front of the saloon when you knew that there was a Winchester aimed at your back. You don't have to prove anything to me, Lee. Besides, if you come with me to Denver and you don't want to be a deputy marshal, we have a big horse ranch to run."

Lee looked into her smiling brown eyes, said, "I forgot about the horse ranch," then without a pause, leaned across and kissed her.

Bethan was surprised when she felt his lips touch hers but was immensely happy as she slid her hand behind his neck and added more passion to the kiss. She felt a warmth flood from her shoulders down her back as their first kiss extended for another ten seconds.

Lee was lost in Bethan's response, almost expecting her to laugh because of the timing. Here they were kissing on a bench on the main street of a small Colorado town with strangers probably staring at the two young people who had just been involved in a shooting.

When they separated, Bethan smiled and said, "That was nice, Lee. I'm surprised that it took that long for you to take the hint."

"What hint?"

"The one when we were sitting in the dark waiting for Lynn and Bryn to return from Iron Springs. I dropped a pretty obvious one when I said that I wouldn't be offended if you kissed me, but you didn't even seem to pay attention."

"I definitely paid attention, Miss Evans. I just didn't want to be caught by your brother and uncle if I decided to take it further."

Bethan laughed, before saying, "I thought that I might have made it a bit more obvious by going behind the trees then undressed and walked into the camp like Lady Godiva."

"I would have forgotten all about your brother and uncle and ravaged you on the spot."

"I would have beaten you to it, Mister Collins."

Bethan then looked down the road, hoping to see Lynn when she spotted a dust cloud in the distance. It was too large for one rider, so she continued to stare.

Lee noticed the change and saw her eye focused south, so he turned and saw the distant dust cloud, then saw the dots from the horses that were creating it.

"That's not Lynn," he said.

"No. Where would they be coming from at this time of day?"

"They couldn't be coming all the way from Trinidad. It's too far away. I can't think of any other towns along the road that still exist after the railroad came through."

"You don't think it's that Gentry bunch, do you?"

"I'm not so sure that they're not. They hit that farm in Las Animas County, and that's where we are right now. It makes sense that they'd be looking to get more supplies and they might want to get some money, too."

"And just when we were having a good time, too. I don't want to get into a shooting match in town, but I think we'd better head down to the livery, get mounted, then set up on the south end of town to keep them from entering."

"Okay," Lee said before they stood.

Before they started walking, he took her hand and said, "We'll look like a normal couple if they see us."

Bethan smiled and said, "They're probably more than a mile out, Lee."

"I know."

They quickly walked slowly toward the livery, and Bethan wished there was more time to alert the townsfolk, but knew if she told anyone, there would be general panic. She was also concerned that Lynn would bump into them before they reached Bent Canyon.

———

Lynn had dismounted and stripped Cody's body of his gunbelt. His horse had recovered enough to stand and was grazing nearby when he'd arrived, and he thought about trying to get the body onto the saddle but didn't want to waste the time. He could pick it up on the way back after he was sure that Bethan was safe.

After shoving the gunbelt into his saddlebag and sliding Cody's Winchester into his bedroll, Lynn mounted and set Aesop to a medium trot heading northeast.

He had ridden just ten minutes when he spotted the same dust cloud that Lee and Bethan had seen, but from a different direction. With the late afternoon sun, he could see that there were three riders and a pack animal stirring up the dust.

"Damn!" he exclaimed as he made the same judgement that Lee and Bethan had made about the identity of the riders.

He nudged his gelding to a fast trot to get behind the group but knew that they'd reach the town long before he was within rifle range. He hoped that Bethan or Lee had noticed them but wasn't even sure they'd had time to deal with George Lynch yet.

———

When Lee and Bethan trotted into the barn, the liveryman was nowhere to be found, but their horses were still saddled, so they quickly took their reins and led them out the wide doors.

After mounting, they rode south down the main street at a medium trot.

Bethan moved her badge to her coat, slid her Winchester '76 from its scabbard, then said, "They're only about a thousand yards out, so we should be able to let them know we're here. Put your badge on your coat in the off chance that they aren't the gang. If they are those bad boys, they'll stop."

"Okay. What'll we do if they pull up?" Lee asked as he pinned his badge to his jacket then pulled his Winchester free.

"That'll be up to them. I hope that they didn't run into Lynn already. I didn't hear any gunfire, so I don't think they did."

Lee didn't reply as he stared ahead at the three riders and said, "They've got a pack horse with them."

"That reduces the chance that they're just a bunch of cowpokes."

By the time they reached the southern edge of town and pulled up, the Gentry gang was just six hundred yards out.

————

Homer was the first to pull to a stop as he yelled, "I thought you said there wasn't any law there, King!"

Ted and Avery both halted their horses and Avery replied, "They probably don't live there. I'll bet they're already out hunting for us."

Homer said, "They're not movin'."

While Homer and Avery were talking, Ted twisted in his saddle and spotted a rider about a mile down the road.

"I think there's another one comin' behind us!" he shouted.

The other two glanced back, saw Lynn, then Avery swore before loudly saying, "We can't go east with that river right there, so let's head west while we can."

"*We're runnin'?*" Homer exclaimed, "We can take out those two that are right in front of us and then get the other one later!"

"We'd be moving and they're just sitting there. They'd gun us down in a few seconds. Let's go!" Avery shouted before turning his horse west and setting him off at a fast trot.

The others followed and were soon racing across the open ground.

———

"There they go!" Lee shouted, then asked, "Is that Lynn out there?"

"That's why they didn't just turn back. Let's chase them down, Lee," Bethan said as she nudged Nippy into a fast trot.

Lee had Biff running alongside leaving a twenty-yard gap as they raced after the gang.

———

Lynn had been pushing his horse to get closer to the men and when they stopped, he didn't understand why until they wheeled their animals to the west, then spotted Bethan and Lee as they took after them. Lee's pinto helped with the identification.

He turned the horse to his left, leaving the road to cut off the angle to the outlaws. They were still a good eight hundred yards out and Bethan and Lee were already much closer, so, as much as he hated to do it, he set the tired horse to a gallop, hoping it wouldn't take long.

———

Homer yelled, "The other one's comin'!"

Avery glanced back to his left, saw Lynn's horse charging, then took another look at the first two.

He squinted, then shouted, "I think one of those two is a girl!"

Their animals were already tiring, and the realization that one of the two closest pursuers was a woman changed everything.

Avery screamed, "Hold up and let's take them!"

He was the first to pull his horse to a stop and as he was turning him to face the two riders, he pulled his Winchester and cocked the hammer.

As Ted and Homer did the same, they received another, unforeseen gift.

———

Lynn saw them turn, then looked to his right to see how close Bethan and Lee were when his horse's right hoof landed on an eight-inch thick chunk of rock. The iron horseshoe slid off its edge, snapping the ankle before the horse buckled and screamed as it rolled to its right.

Lynn had his Winchester in his right hand as the horse headed to the ground and didn't have time to brace himself before he slammed into the hard dirt, with the horse landing on his right leg. He felt his right wrist bend back as the rifle hit the ground and then a sharp pain shot up his arm.

The enormous cloud of dust enveloped him as the horse continued to scream in pain and writhe on the ground. Lynn was able to squirm free of the horse when it tried to stand on its broken leg, but as he crawled away from the injured animal, he knew that he was in trouble.

———

Lynn's accident provoked two very different reactions from those who had witnessed it.

Bethan and Lee both heard the horse's scream before they turned their heads and watched in horror as Lynn hit the ground.

Avery, Homer and Ted had seen it from the first stumble and knew it was as if God had smiled on them.

"He's down!" Homer yelled.

"Wait!" Avery shouted back, "Let them come to us!"

———

For another ten seconds, Bethan and Lee continued toward the outlaws.

But when they were just four hundred yards out, Bethan shouted, "Let's help Lynn!", and turned Nippy south.

Lee quickly matched her turn and slid Biff closer to her mare until he could yell, "When we get there, you check on Lynn and I'll keep an eye on the gang."

"Okay."

———

Lynn managed to stand but didn't bother picking up his repeater because his right arm was broken, and he couldn't use it if he tried. He pulled his pistol with his left hand, then before he shot his horse, he looked at the distant outlaws and then saw that Bethan and Lee had given up the chase and were coming to his aid.

He wasn't sure that it was the right decision but knew that those three didn't have anywhere to go now that they've been spotted, so it was likely that they'd attack rather than run.

He then cocked his pistol's hammer, walked to the head of his frightened, pained animal and pulled the trigger.

"I'm sorry for pushing you so hard," he said before he turned to face Bethan and Lee as they approached.

———

"Now what do we do?" Ted asked as they watched Bethan and Lee ride away.

"We can't let them send a telegram to let everyone know where we are," Avery replied.

Homer then asked, "Why don't we just head south into New Mexico? They won't care once we're out of Colorado."

"They'll follow us into Mexico if they have to, Homer. We killed a deputy sheriff and if we let those three live, then we'll just have to ambush them somewhere else and they might have more help by then. We'll never get better odds. One of them can't shoot and another one is a woman. That means there's only one real threat."

"You aim for us to kill a girl?" Ted asked.

"She's wearing a badge and carrying a rifle, so she's fair game."

"Where did she get a badge?"

"I've got no idea and we're just wasting time talking about it. Let's get over there before they can set up behind that dead horse."

"Do we split up?" asked Homer.

Avery paused then replied, "Yeah. I'll ride straight at them and Homer, you swing wide to the right and Ted will go left. When you get about three hundred yards out, slow to a walk, then start sending .44s their way from a couple of hundred yards out to keep their heads down."

"Okay. You're the king," said Homer.

Avery looked at Homer, didn't reply, then nudged his horse forward at a slow trot.

Ted disconnected the pack horse, then rode east at a fast trot while Homer headed west.

———

Bethan had dismounted near Lynn and quickly asked, "How bad are you hurt?"

"I broke my right arm and my right leg isn't too happy, but those boys aren't going to run, Bethan. Where's George Lynch?"

"He's in town with a bullet in his butt. I'll explain later," she said as she picked up Lynn's Winchester.

She then turned to Lee and handed him the repeater, saying, "Use Lynn's '76. It'll give you more range and power."

He took the rifle, then slid his '73 back into the scabbard before turning to check on the outlaws.

"They're coming back this way and splitting up."

"They'll expect us to hunker down behind my dead horse," Lynn said.

"You should do just that," replied Bethan, "You can only fire your pistol with your left hand, and I've seen you shoot left-handed."

Lynn knew that it wasn't the time to argue and it was the smart thing to do because he would only get in the way now.

"Alright. How are you going to face them? They're going to come at us from three different directions."

Lee suddenly replied, "I'm going to make them change their strategy. I'll ride at the one heading west and see how they react."

Bethan snapped, "That's wrong, Lee! They'll swing around and cut you off! They know that Lynn's hurt, and they're probably not worried about me at all because I'm a woman."

"That will give you a chance to get behind them, Bethan," Lee replied as he quickly stepped toward Biff and mounted.

Bethan knew it was futile to argue but even as Lee leaned forward and set his pinto away, she turned to Lynn and said, "I'll stay until they all turn to chase after Lee."

Lynn was watching Lee as he said, "Get ready."

―――――

Avery was the first to notice that one of them had mounted and it was the uninjured lawman, not the woman. He hesitated before shouting to Ted, "Get the one on the horse!"

Ted had watched Lee mount and thought it was a better chance to get the badge-wearing woman and the injured lawman, so he shouted back, "I'll get the other two!"

Homer heard Avery's shout, then turned his horse toward the oncoming rider, knowing that the King would be at the lawman's flank.

Avery didn't bother arguing with Ted but shifted his horse to get behind the riding lawman as he charged toward Homer.

––––––

Lee had heard Avery's orders and then Homer's defiant reply, so he knew that he had to keep heading for the one in front of him before the other one got behind him. He was about four hundred yards ahead and closing quickly, so he slowed Biff to a walk and then pulled up.

Homer was surprised when he saw the lawman stop but could see Avery about five hundred yards behind the badge toter and knew that he held all the cards.

He slowed his horse and cocked his Winchester's hammer as he watched Avery cut the distance to the lawman and wondered if the man even knew that he was about to be cut down from behind.

––––––

Bethan had been watching the drama unfold eight hundred yards away and wished she could help Lee, but knew that the third rider was getting close, so she turned to face the lone outlaw who had slowed his horse to a walk and was already two hundred yards out.

Ted remembered Avery's first instructions about firing at two hundred yards to keep their heads down, and thought it was still a good idea, so when he reached that distance, he let his reins drop, pulled his Winchester level and fired.

Bethan saw his muzzle flash and smoke as the rifle's report reached her ears. She didn't know where the bullet went but brought her Winchester to her shoulder and set the sights on the oncoming rider.

He fired again, and this time, she heard the bullet ricochet off a nearby rock, but still held her fire.

Ted was surprised and impressed that the girl hadn't flinched after his first two shots but levered in a third round as his horse continued to carry him closer to the downed horse and the standing woman.

He set his sights on the lawman behind the horse, estimating the range to be about a hundred and forty yards, and was about to pull the trigger when the girl fired.

Ted didn't have time to wonder if she was any good with the rifle when Bethan's .45 arrived. It rammed into his chest on the left side, right where a badge would have been worn if he'd been a lawman. The slug of lead then drilled through the center of his heart, exploding the critical muscle before it crashed into a rib and stopped.

Ted wobbled in the saddle before he slowly rocked to his right, released his Winchester, then tumbled to the ground.

Bethan didn't waste time, but hurtled toward Nippy, flew into the saddle and set her off at a gallop to chase down the outlaw who was behind Lee.

————

Avery hadn't turned to see what had happened to Ted but was focused on Lee, just three hundred yards ahead.

Lee was still almost two hundred yards from Homer and the gap wasn't closing quickly enough, so he turned, saw how close Avery was, but also spotted Bethan coming quickly behind him.

He then set Biff forward at a fast trot to close the gap to the one in front of him, which took Homer by surprise.

Homer had seen the girl chasing behind Avery and knew that he should warn him because he'd just seen her shoot down Ted. But the other one was coming right at him, so he pulled his horse to a stop and raised his Winchester.

Just as Homer brought his repeater to bear, Lee whipped Biff to the left and then yanked him to a sudden stop.

Homer had to swing his sights to Lee before he quickly fired his first shot, knowing that he'd probably miss, but expected the lawman to duck or run.

Lee knew that the man would be shooting at him, but at that range with the sudden change, it was an iffy proposition at best.

He hoped that the newer model Winchester was as good as Bethan had claimed as he set his sights on the shooter but took an extra heartbeat to let them settle before he held his breath and squeezed the trigger.

After Homer had levered in a new round, he saw the lawman aiming at him, and quickly took his second shot, but missed again.

Lee's .45 sped across the four-hundred and thirty-seven feet of ground in its tiny arc, barely dropping a few inches before it punched into the right side of Homer's gut just below the ribs. It had enough power to mangle his liver and rip apart blood vessels before it exited his back and buried itself in the Colorado dirt.

Homer was losing blood rapidly as he tried to work his Winchester's lever action, but his vision began to fade, and the repeater fell from his hands as he tried to focus on the man who had just killed him.

He began to blink before his chin dropped to his chest and then he just fell over his horse's neck as he took his last breath.

Lee didn't have time to think about his first gunfight before he turned Biff and set him off at a medium trot to trap the last one between him and Bethan.

———

Avery had seen the gunfight in front of him and had slowed his horse to give him time to think. He still hadn't looked back, so he wasn't aware that Bethan was just a couple of hundred yards away, but it really didn't matter to him now. He knew that Homer and Ted were both dead and he was alone.

He could have thrown up his hands and extended his life for a few weeks at the most, but he wanted to go down fighting, and the only danger was in front of him now.

He suddenly wheeled his horse back to the east and spotted the woman charging at him. He hadn't seen her shoot Ted but believed that she had gotten off a lucky shot, so he continued to ride straight at her to get a better shot before the other lawman could get close.

As soon as Avery had turned towards her, Bethan pulled Nippy to a stop and brought her Winchester's sights to her eyes.

Lee was just two hundred yards behind Avery and knew that Bethan would have a better shot from her stable horse but pushed Biff to close that gap. He wanted to get a shot off to distract the last outlaw and maybe get a hit if he was lucky.

Avery glanced back at Lee and knew that it was going to be close. Once he shot the woman, maybe that other one would stop to help her and become a target instead.

He then slowed his horse when he was less than two hundred yards from the woman who was already aiming at him, then brought his repeater level and set his sights on the woman, but when he saw her face, he dropped them slightly to her horse's head. She may be wearing a badge, but she was still a woman.

Bethan saw the slight change, but it didn't affect her decision as she squeezed her trigger.

Avery saw the bloom of smoke and heard the report as the bullet exploded into his right shoulder. As the joint splintered, he screamed, and his Winchester plummeted to the ground.

Lee lowered his rifle, then continued to ride to the stricken outlaw, watching for any sign that he might try to pull his pistol with his left hand.

Bethan had already slid her repeater into its scabbard and pulled her Smith & Wesson from its holster as she approached Avery.

He was still in his saddle but was leaning to his right and grasping at his torn, bloody jacket with his left hand.

When Bethan was close, he shouted, "You missed! Why don't you just kill me now and get it over with?"

Bethan pulled Nippy to a stop and replied, "I didn't miss, mister. You're under arrest and you're going to hang."

"You can't wear a badge, girl. Who the hell do you think you are?" he snarled.

"I'm United States Deputy Marshal Bethan Evans."

Avery stared at her and asked, "Evans? You aren't related to Lynn Evans, are you?"

"That's him near his dead horse over there. He's my brother."

Despite his pain, Avery glanced at Lynn in the distance and laughed as he said, "Now doesn't that take the cake."

Lee rode close, then pulled up and asked, "What do we do next, Bethan?"

"We'll take this one into Bent Canyon to see that lady, then we'll have to borrow a wagon to get the bodies moved, including Cody Russell's."

"Do you want me to take him into town while you help Lynn?"

"Go ahead," she said before adding, "You were really impressive, Lee."

Lee smiled and replied, "Thank you, ma'am. You were just your usual spectacular self."

Bethan returned his smile, then turned Nippy back toward Lynn.

Lee then walked Biff to Avery's right, pulled his Colt from his holster, then, after dropping the pistol into his coat pocket, took the reins and started riding toward Bent Canyon.

———

As she rode, Bethan had alternated looking at Lynn and then back to Lee. She had been more than just impressed with how he had performed today. She had been falling in love with him from almost that first day. Now, as she watched him lead the prisoner away, she knew that she had to make a choice about what she would do about it.

She had always been so frustrated with her lack of choices in her life, and now that she'd finally proven herself to be the equal of any man wearing a badge, she wondered if it really mattered how good she was with a gun.

She remembered the conversations she'd had with Addie and her mother about being a wife and a mother, and at the time, it had just been a discussion that hadn't risen to the level of reality. Now, it was here and very real.

She pulled up next to Lynn, dismounted and said, "Lee is taking the last one into town to get fixed up and then we'll need a wagon to pick up the bodies. Can you get into the saddle?"

"I think so. I wish I could have been more help, but Lee did a great job. I admit I thought his idea was risky, but it worked out well. You have quite a man there, sister."

Bethan didn't argue with him, but simply said, "Go ahead and step up. I'll get behind you."

Lynn nodded, then glanced back at his dead horse, sighed, and had to walk around Nippy to mount on the left side. He grabbed the saddle horn with his left hand and mounted without a problem.

Bethan put her foot in the right stirrup, swung her leg behind Lynn and grasped the reins.

After they set off, Lynn asked, "How did you take down Lynch?"

Before she explained, she asked, "What happened to Bryn?"

"That's right. I haven't had a chance to tell you in all the excitement. He took a lazy .44 in the right thigh, but it bled a lot more because it nicked an artery. The doc said the bullet must have plugged it up, but he still lost a lot of blood. He's doing okay now, but he's going to be laid up for a while."

"Hopefully, we'll see him tomorrow," she said, then began her explanation of the takedown of George Lynch.

When she finished, Lynn said, "Well, little sister, you did a great job and it sounds like you found yourself a keeper."

Bethan smiled and replied, "I think so."

———

The rest of the day was spent cleaning up the aftermath of the shootout. Miss Lucy began to set Lynn's arm before beginning to work on Avery George because Lynn just needed a quick splint.

While she was working on her two patients, Lee and Bethan borrowed a wagon and with the assistance of four grateful townsfolk who understood what Lee and Bethan had prevented from happening.

After they'd gone and Lynn had his broken forearm splinted, Lynn watched as Miss Lucy worked on Avery's mangled shoulder.

Avery grimaced as she washed the blood from the wound but looked up at Lynn and asked, "You don't remember me, do you?"

"I remember you. You were the one who tried to blame Addie for what happened and then covered up your pal's mistake. If you had just come clean back then, you would have lost your job, but you wouldn't hang."

Avery winced, then said, "I was doing all right in getting out of Yankton, but when my old man still wouldn't give me a job, I didn't care anymore. That old bastard thought I wasn't man enough to wear a badge. Well, I showed him that I was more of a man than he was."

"You think killing people makes you a big man? What kind of crazy talk is that? How much fight did that farmer and his family put up before you murdered them all? You're nothing but a coward and not close to what I consider to be a real man. I'll be more than happy to see you walk up those gallows steps."

Avery was about to deliver an angry retort when Miss Lucy exclaimed, "Damn!", and blood squirted out from his shoulder.

She pushed her fingers into the wound to staunch the bleeding, but the blood kept pulsing through her fingers.

"One of the broken bones must have cut an artery!" she said loudly as she tried to locate the source of the bleeding.

Avery was getting woozy and losing focus as he smiled and whispered, "I guess you're going to be cheated out of your entertain…"

Miss Lucy felt the flow of blood slowing, then stop before she stepped back, wiping her hands on her bloody apron. She knew the battle was over.

Avery's eyes stared lifelessly at the ceiling as she turned to Lynn and said, "There was nothing I could do."

"It's all right, Miss Lucy. He was going to hang for what he did anyway. In a way, it's probably a more merciful way for him to die, even though he didn't deserve it."

"We all deserve it, Marshal," Miss Lucy said as she looked at him.

"Tell that to the family that he and his friends murdered, ma'am," Lynn said, before turning and walking out of the gunsmith shop.

––––––

Lee and Bethan rode with two other men while two of the helpers drove the wagon. When they reached the site of the gunfight, the men handled the bodies while Lee and Bethan rounded up the four horses and their weapons. The men then removed Lynn's saddle from his dead horse and tossed it and the rest of his gear into the bed.

Once that was done, they headed southwest to where Cody's body still lay in the sun. The circling vultures identified the location, so they didn't have to follow any tracks and soon found his body. His horse had wandered to a tiny creek and was now grazing on the new grass when Lee reached him and added him to the herd.

By the time they returned to Bent Canyon, Lynn was waiting outside the general store, sitting in the same bench where Bethan and Lee had shared their first kiss just before engaging the Gentry gang.

He stood as the wagon rolled past to take the bodies to the mortician, then waited for Lee and Bethan to dismount.

As soon as they were close, Lynn said, "Avery George died when a bone severed an artery. I guess that makes things a bit easier when we finally leave."

"You're in charge, Lynn. How do you want to handle this?" Bethan asked.

"Let's get something to eat and we can talk then. I already sent a telegram to the boss."

"Supper sounds like a good idea," Lee said as he hooked his arm through Bethan's.

Lynn smiled at his sister before they stepped away and headed for the café.

––––––

In Denver, Dylan had received the first telegram that Lynn had sent from Iron Springs and was worried. He now had his son and daughter in a dangerous situation with no way of knowing what was happening. It was infuriating and the idea that the Gentry gang was in the area didn't help.

He reread the telegram:

US MARSHAL DYLAN EVANS DENVER COLO

TRACKED LYNCH AND RUSSELL
RUSSELL DEAD IN SHOOTOUT
BRYN SHOT IN LEG
WILL BE OKAY
BETHAN AND LEE STILL TRAILING LYNCH
WILL ASSIST

LYNN EVANS IRONS SPRINGS COLO

He assumed that Lee was the Bishop town marshal that had been mentioned in previous telegrams and wasn't sure of his abilities. He hoped that Lynn would arrive to help them before they caught up with Lynch.

It was already late and he wished he could hang around for more information, but had to leave to tell Erin about Bryn, so he locked up the office, then headed for the Western Union office where he told them to send any messages from Lynn to the sheriff's office.

He rode Raven to the sheriff's office and told the deputy on duty about the situation and that if they delivered a telegram from Lynn to have someone bring it out to the Double EE.

Dylan soon left Denver behind and rode his black gelding at a faster pace than normal. Gwen had told him that Erin had a sense of foreboding about the mission before Bryn had gone, and he could at least tell her that her husband was going to be all right. He may be a bit gimpy for a while, but he was okay, and she didn't have to worry.

———

After Bethan had cut Lynn's meat, they enjoyed their well-deserved meal of thick steaks and baked potatoes, as Lynn explained what they should do tomorrow. He didn't even feel odd knowing that he was three years younger than Lee, and Lee didn't seem to mind either.

"The four bodies will be buried here, but we need to get George Lynch to Las Animas for trial. Can I assume that you and Lee will handle that?"

Bethan replied, "You already know the answer, Lynn. How do we get him back with his butt in that condition?"

"I was going to borrow a wagon, but I don't want to have to move that slowly. I think we can put him in a saddle backwards, so he leans on the horse's rump. It seems appropriate, somehow. We should get to Iron Springs around noon and then we'll check in on Bryn."

"What about their horses and gear?" Lee asked.

"We'll string them along, too. I think they're yours now, Lee. You surely earned them."

"I appreciate it, Lynn, but I don't have anywhere to put them."

"No? Well, we can take them to Denver and keep them on the Double EE until you and Bethan get there," he replied, then said, "You know, Lee, we're going to be awfully shorthanded in the office now and we could really use you. Bryn won't be working for at least a month and I won't even be able to write for a month, either. With Bert gone, we'll be really hurting. I think that our boss, also known as our father, would really appreciate it if you'd join us."

Lee glanced at Bethan, then asked, "You're not asking me because of Bethan. Are you?"

Lynn grinned at his sister before replying, "Nope. If anything, that was a point against you for poor judgement. All kidding aside, Lee, you really impressed me today and if Bethan thinks that well of you, I'm sure that you'd make a great deputy marshal."

"I'd be honored, and I appreciate your confidence. I imagine that Lynch's trial won't take long, so we should be in Denver by next Tuesday."

Lynn smiled at Bethan and asked, "Will you be arriving as Bethan Evans or Bethan Collins?"

Bethan held a piece of steak before her lips and laughed before replying, "Don't get ahead of yourself, brother. Just think of how you're going to have to explain your broken arm to Addie."

Lynn grimaced as he said, "I hadn't thought about that. I guess that means that I won't be changing any diapers for a while."

Lee and Bethan laughed, then shared a quick look before they returned to the task of devouring their steaks.

———

Dylan had found Erin at his house when he entered the kitchen and wasn't surprised. When he was gone, which wasn't that often anymore, Gwen would visit Erin.

"Did you hear anything?" Erin asked anxiously when Dylan entered.

"I received a telegram from Lynn a little while ago," he answered as he hung his hat and began removing his jacket.

"Well?" Gwen asked.

Dylan hung his coat, then turned to the two anxious women and replied, "All four of them tracked George Lynch and Cody Russell east of Iron Springs. There was a shootout, and Cody was killed, but he put a .44 at long range into Bryn's leg before he was shot. Lynn took Bryn back to Iron Springs and the doctor said he'll be fine. Bethan and the town marshal went after George Lynch, but that's all I know. I left instructions for them to send any more messages to the Double EE."

Erin sat down hard on a chair and said, "I've had this feeling of dread ever since he left. At least he's all right as long as it doesn't become infected."

"Lynn got him to a doctor right away, Erin. I'm sure he'll be okay."

"He won't be able to work for a while."

"No. He'll be your problem for a few weeks."

Erin then looked up at Dylan and said, "I don't want him to go back. That shootout at the mountain pass was bad enough, but to be shot just a couple of weeks later is getting too much. I want him to stay here and raise horses, Dylan."

345

"I can understand that, Erin, but it's his choice. If you can convince him to hand in the badge, then I'm not going to try to change his mind. But just remember who you're dealing with. Your husband left Omaha when he didn't need to go just because he wanted to make a difference. He almost died in the process, but when he returned, he could have just started his horse ranch, but he still wore the badge. Maybe he'll be happy just raising horses now that he's older, I don't know. I guess we'll just have to find out how he feels about it when he gets back."

Erin nodded, then looked at Gwen.

Gwen smiled at her and said, "Just be happy that he's coming back to you, Erin," then she turned to her husband and asked, "Bethan is chasing down a killer by herself?"

"No. She has the Bishop town marshal with her. He's been with her since she found him tied up in his cell."

"That doesn't speak well of his abilities as a lawman," Gwen replied.

Dylan stepped over to the kitchen table, took a seat and waited for Gwen to sit down.

"I can understand how it would have happened, Gwen. He's in a quiet town with a prisoner and in walks a man with a badge. He's expecting a deputy sheriff from Las Animas and probably didn't know who was coming. By the time he even gets to ask the man with badge his name, Lynch draws his pistol and he's got no choice."

"That still doesn't mean he's good enough to help Bethan."

"No, but if Bethan thinks enough of him to keep him along, that alone should give you some confidence in him."

"I suppose you're right. Maybe I am being a bit harsh, but she's our daughter, Dylan."

"She is, and that's why you shouldn't worry about her. Now before we talk anymore, could I please have something to eat?"

Gwen laughed, then stood and walked to the cookstove as Erin stood.

She smiled at Dylan and said, "I'm going to go back to the house and tell the children and then send yours back home. I'll start building my case for Bryn to stay with the horses, too."

"Good luck, Erin," Dylan said as he smiled back at his sister-in-law.

After she'd gone, Gwen looked at her husband and asked, "How long before you retire, Dylan?"

Dylan blinked, then stared at her before exclaiming, "*Retire?* I'm only thirty-nine!"

Gwen smiled, then simply said, "Yes, dear," before turning around and sliding a pot from the cookstove's hot plate.

———

It was two hours later when a rider turned down the Double EE access road, then angled to the big house south of Bryn's place. He stopped at the front porch, dismounted and trotted up the steps.

He had barely knocked on the door when it swung open and Cari smiled, then asked, "How are you, Deputy?"

John Carruthers smiled back at her and replied, "I'm fine, Cari. Is your father home? I have a telegram for him."

Before she could answer, Dylan trotted across the parlor and entered the foyer.

"This just arrived, Dylan, and I thought it was important enough to run it out here myself."

Dylan took the single folded sheet of paper and said, "Thanks, John."

John tipped his hat, smiled at Cari again, then turned, crossed the porch and was mounting his horse when Cari closed the door.

Dylan almost ripped the paper as he opened the telegram and read:

US MARSHAL DYLAN EVANS DENVER COLO

LYNCH SHOT AND CAPTURED
ENGAGED GENTRY GANG NEAR BENT CANYON
ALL THREE DEAD
HAVE BROKEN RIGHT ARM AFTER HORSE FELL
WILL RETURN TO IRON SPRINGS TOMORROW
DENVER NEXT DAY
BETHAN AND LEE TAKE LYNCH TO LAS ANIMAS
LEE COLLINS WAS HEROIC
RECOMMEND FOR BERT REPLACEMENT
BETHAN AGREES

LYNN EVANS BENT CANYON COLO

He stood frozen in place as he reread the message and really wished he could talk to Lynn for more details, but the abbreviated news that he had received astonished him on several levels.

"What is it, Dad?" Cari asked.

He looked down at his daughter and replied, "Come with me into the kitchen and I'll tell everyone at the same time."

Cari took her father's hand as they entered the parlor, then walked down the hallway.

When they entered the kitchen, Gwen, Brian and Conway were all looking at Dylan.

He stopped, smiled at them, and read the telegram.

Conway had wide eyes as he exclaimed, "They shot the Gentry gang!"

"I don't know the details, but it seems that way."

Gwen was concerned about Lynn's broken arm, but immensely relieved that Bethan wasn't hurt. She was also curious about why Lynn had added the last line that Bethan would approve of the Bishop town marshal being made a U.S. deputy marshal.

After the chatter between their two youngest sons subsided and the three children had left the room, Gwen asked, "Lynn actually described the town marshal as heroic?"

"I assume that he didn't want to use longer words, but it must have been impressive for him to recommend him as a replacement for Bert. Besides, with his broken arm and Bryn's wound, I really will need some more bodies. If he's as good as Lynn seems to believe, then I'll hire him a heartbeat."

"What about that last line? Am I reading too much into it in believing that Lynn seems to think that our Bethan is smitten with Lee Collins?"

"That's the way I read it, too. So, maybe, my beloved wife, you'll finally get your deepest desire and Bethan may surrender her ambitions to be a lawman and settle down to live on the Double EE."

"I'll admit that I've been hoping that she'd do that, but it's not my deepest desire."

Dylan smiled at her and asked, "Oh? And what, pray tell, is your deepest desire?"

Gwen smiled back and replied, "I'll show you when the children are asleep."

Dylan laughed lightly, then said, "As if that's stopped you before."

"I intend on making more noise than usual this time, sir."

"My lord, that'll wake Erin from a sound sleep!"

"I want to wake Bethan from hers."

Dylan rose walked behind Gwen, then kissed her upside down as he let his hand slide behind her dress, not wanting to wait until the children were asleep or even in bed.

————

Bethan, Lee and Lynn had rented rooms in the Bent Canyon Hotel and turned in for the night.

Lynn was having difficulty sleeping because of his throbbing right arm. Miss Lucy had only put it into a splint but told him he'd need to see a doctor in Denver to see if his bones needed to be aligned.

Lee was finding sleep elusive as well for many reasons. He was relieved that he'd faced danger and hadn't screwed up and admitted that he had done well when he needed to perform at his best. He was more than just pleased with Bethan. She was such a presence that she overwhelmed him sometimes, and he was still trying to understand her better. He hoped that what they had started would continue for the rest of his life because he knew that he'd never meet her equal.

The only thing that really bothered Lee was his underlying concern that if he went to Denver and accepted the position of U.S. deputy marshal, it wouldn't have been earned. He still had that nagging thought that Lynn had recommended him because he knew that Bethan wanted to be with him.

By the time he finally drifted off, he decided that he'd return to Denver with Bethan and meet her extraordinary family. He especially wanted to meet her father. It was only when Dylan Evans looked him in the eye and still offered him the position that he would believe that he deserved it.

Bethan, lying on her bed in the adjacent room, had no such concerns. She knew that Lee was better than any of the other deputy marshals not bearing the name Evans. Even as they had been riding with the wagon retrieving bodies and horses, she could see his power and authority, even if he couldn't.

When they had gone out to retrieve the bodies and horses, it had been difficult for her to shift into the role of assistant just to watch if Lee would take charge, and he had. The local men who joined them invariably believed Lee to be in charge, so they asked him questions. After the first one and he'd looked at her, she hadn't said anything or even nodded. He then answered that question and took the lead.

Bethan smiled as she looked at the dark ceiling and thought that she might enjoy doing the same job that her mother and Erin had explained to her. She'd be Lee's guide and help him to reach his enormous potential. When they had first explained it to her, she'd laughed and thought it was a silly thing to imagine. She could understand raising children to behave properly, but not a grown man. Now she understood. It wasn't a matter of changing behavior as much as it was providing support and guidance. A little nudge to prevent him from doing something stupid wasn't a bad idea either.

Once she'd realized the reason for the advice from her mother and aunt, she was able to spend more time just imagining her life with Lee. She had thoroughly enjoyed their kiss on the bench and even though it wasn't her first, it had thrilled her. Now she was able to drift into much more exciting fantasies about what would happen when they were alone again.

CHAPTER 9

It was almost midmorning before they set out from Bent Canyon. Lynn was riding Bethan's pack horse as they led their caravan west toward Iron Springs. One of the horses had Lynn's saddle strapped onto its own, and all of them carried Winchesters.

As it turned out, George Lynch preferred to sit in the saddle but had them adjust the stirrups so he could stand. His bullet wound was on his right butt cheek toward the outside, so he could sit in the saddle if he leaned forward and off to the left. It may not have been comfortable, but no one else cared.

Bethan and Lee rode behind Lynn and their prisoner and each had a string of horses trailing, but Lee had one mule at the end of his line. Even though they'd had the support of many townsfolk, they'd been so busy getting packed that they hadn't had much time to talk.

But once they'd settled into their long ride, Lee asked, "Why did Lynn say that all of the horses and the mule were mine? You did more than I did."

Bethan looked across and replied, "I don't think so, but we have too many already. You forget that Bryn bought the Double EE to raise horses and has been doing it for a while now. I noticed that two of your new horses were very nice young mares, so you might get a good price for them if you sell them and the mule to my brothers. Their horse ranch isn't as well-stocked as the Double EE, and they're always looking for new stock."

"I couldn't sell them the horses and mule, Bethan. I'd just give them to them."

"Trying to ingratiate yourself with my brothers, Mister Collins?"

Lee grinned and replied, "Maybe."

"I'll tell you what. How about if my brothers pay for shipping all the horses and the mule to Denver? That way, they'll get the mares and the mule, and you don't need to spend anything to get them there."

"How would we manage that?"

"I'll pay for the shipment and then they'll pay me back."

Bethan was expecting an argument, but Lee just nodded and said, "That sounds fair."

Bethan then just smiled and turned her eyes to Lynn, who was riding thirty feet in front of her. She was sure that he'd heard the conversation and didn't mind if he thought that she and Lee were making plans after they left Las Animas because she had already made many more.

———

Over the long ride, George Lynch shifted from standing in the stirrups to sitting awkwardly in his saddle but was surprisingly silent. He knew what was awaiting him in Las Animas and even the pain in his behind didn't take his mind off his fate.

His silence was appreciated by the others as Lee and Bethan continued to talk about the Evans family, the Double EE, and Denver. Before they'd reached Irons Springs, they'd even managed to squeeze in some chat about the marshal's office.

They only took one break and George Lynch remained in the saddle rather than dismounting and then having to swing his leg around again.

By mid-afternoon, they spotted Iron Springs and picked up their pace slightly, arriving in the town twenty minutes later.

Before they even went to the local eatery, they stopped at the doctor's office, and Lee stayed with George Lynch and their equine collection while Bethan and Lynn went inside to check on Bryn.

When they entered the parlor, the doctor's wife recognized Lynn and said, "He's in the room across from the surgery. Follow me."

Bethan and Lynn then followed her into the small bedroom and had barely crossed the threshold when Bryn asked, "What happened?"

"You seem a lot better than when I left," Lynn said as he and Bethan approached the bed.

"I'm all right. What happened? Did you get Lynch?"

"He's outside on his horse and not comfortably, I might add. Bethan shot him in the right butt cheek when he was about to shoot Lee."

"Thank God for that! I was worried about her."

Bethan then smiled at her uncle and asked, "Do you want to hear about the Gentry gang?"

"*What?*" Bryn exclaimed, then finally noticed that Lynn's arm was in a sling, and asked, "*Did you get shot?*"

"No. My horse fell when we were in pursuit and I broke my arm. Lee and Bethan took them down. Avery George, the one I ran into in Yankton, survived the gunfight, but died when they were fixing him up. We had them all buried in Bent Canyon, including Cody Russell."

"Damn! If I'd have known they were that close, I would have gotten out of this bed and ridden over there."

"You were barely awake, Bryn. Listen, we've got to get something to eat and then get Lynch into a jail or just tie him up. We'll be back in an hour to fill you in."

"Okay. Sorry about your horse and your arm, Lynn. Where's Lee?"

"He's outside watching the prisoner and the horses. I told him that he could have all of the outlaws' horses and gear. He was something to watch out there, Bryn. I was out of action before bullets started flying, but he and Bethan did everything right."

"I'm glad to hear it. You know, we're already shorthanded, and neither of us will be any good for a while. Do you think he might be interested in joining our merry band?"

Bethan laughed, shook her head then replied, "We've already practically sworn him in, Bryn. He was worried that he might not be good enough because he'd never even been in a gunfight while he was the town marshal, but I wasn't worried about it even before we ran into Lynch. The courage and logical mind were there and when they were needed, he showed them both to perfection."

Bryn looked up at his niece and said, "It sounds like you're smitten, Bethan."

"I hate that word, Uncle Bryn. I love Lee Collins, and I'm going to marry him."

Lynn's head whipped to his right before he asked, "Does he know it yet?"

"He knows, but he hasn't asked me yet. I'll let him have the honor when he's ready. Speaking of Lee, I think we should get back outside and get things moving."

Bryn then said, "Get going and don't forget to send an update to the boss. I wouldn't mention your surprising news, Bethan, but we'll be back in Denver before you will, so is it okay to mention it to the family?"

"Just tell them that I'm very fond of Lee and that they'll all meet him next week."

"He's going to miss our Sunday get-together."

"I'll send a telegram before we leave Las Animas and we can have a Wednesday Sunday."

Bryn laughed, then said, "Get going and get back here as soon as you can. I need to get out of here and you need to tell me how you eliminated the Gentry gang."

Bethan walked to his bed, kissed Bryn on the cheek, then she and Lynn exited his recovery room and soon left the doctor's house.

After they mounted, Lynn looked across at Lee, smiled, but didn't say anything before they pulled their horses away from the house and headed for the telegraph office.

While Lynn sent the telegram, Lee asked a local where they could incarcerate George Lynch until the train arrived. It turned out that, like Bent Canyon, they didn't have a proper jail, but used an abandoned workshop to keep miscreants from wandering the streets.

So, when Lynn exited the telegraph office, they headed for the abandoned shop where Lee pulled Lynch from the horse and led him inside with Lynn and Bethan following. The residents had boarded up the windows, and there was just a cot and a chamber pot in the room. There was only one outside door and the back room had been sealed.

"We'll bring you some food in a little while," Lynn said.

"How about some water? It's already hot in here."

"I'll get a canteen," Bethan said before turning and leaving.

"They're going to hang me. Aren't they?" George asked.

"If they find you guilty and the judge give you that sentence. You know, you could have gotten off easy if you hadn't planned on shooting Lee and Bethan. Your lawyer could argue that you were shocked when Cody suddenly shot the deputy in the back, but you didn't turn yourself in. You ran and then tried to shoot it out. That was really stupid."

"Yeah, I suppose. It didn't seem stupid at the time, though. It seemed like each mistake made the next one worse."

Bethan entered with the canteen, handed it to George, then hooked her arm through Lee's, and they left the small, dark room with Lynn trailing behind.

Once outside, they barred the door, then mounted and rode to Janie's Diner, just three blocks away.

———

An hour later, a messenger delivered Lynn's telegram to the U.S Marshal's office.

Dylan was sitting in his office when Pete Towers entered and handed him the sheet, saying, "This just came for you, Dylan."

"Thanks, Pete," Dylan replied as he opened the telegram.

"More news from Lynn?" Pete asked.

"Good news. They're in Iron Springs and Bryn is anxious to leave. Bryn and Lynn will be coming here directly and should be here on tomorrow's evening train. Bethan and Lee Collins will be taking George Lynch to Las Animas for trial."

"We're going to be really short on bodies, boss."

"I know, but both Lynn and Bryn have recommended that I hire Lee Collins when he arrives. Lynn said he was the one who took down one of the Gentry gang and Bethan shot the other two."

"If they think he's good enough, then that says a lot."

Dylan looked up at Pete and said, "Bethan seems to think he's more than good enough."

Pete's eyebrows shot up as he asked, "Bethan likes him?"

"It sure sounds like it. We'll meet him next week when he and Bethan return from Las Animas."

Pete grinned and replied, "Unless he meets the real Bethan."

It was Dylan's turn to raise his eyebrows before he replied, "She's always the real Bethan and that's what drove those young men away, including you, if I recall. If he's still with her, then he already knows and appreciates the real Bethan. I'm just impressed that she found a young man who she appreciates as much."

"Um, you're right, boss," Pete said before turning and leaving the office.

Dylan watched one of his four remaining functional deputies leave and understood why he passed the remark. He'd been one of Bethan's rejects and he'd placed his failure on Bethan, not on himself.

He reread the telegram, then folded it and slid it into his pocket. He had been quietly pleased that his daughter had rejected Pete's overtures, and was curious to meet Lee Collins.

––––––

After leaving a tray of food for George Lynch and waiting until he finished so he wouldn't be left with any cutlery, they headed for the train station.

When they stopped at the ticket window, Lynn stood before the agent, showed him his badge and said, "I need two tickets to Denver with horse transport for ten animals and three more tickets to Las Animas."

The agent studied the badge and said, "I'll need you to sign a chit, Deputy."

"It won't be pretty, but I can manage."

"You break that arm chasing down that Gentry gang?"

Lynn nodded and replied, "My horse went down in pursuit. My partners who are standing behind me took them down."

He grinned as he looked at Bethan and said, "I heard some pretty gal was in the shootout, and I kinda thought it was just a tall tale, but I guess it was true after all. Just tell me your name and I'll write it in."

"Bryn Evans."

The ticket agent filled in the chit and had Lynn scrawl his initials before he issued the tickets and the horse tags.

"Thank you," Lynn said as he accepted the stack of heavy paper.

"No, sir. I'll be thanking you and your partners for keeping us all safe."

Lynn smiled, said, "You're welcome," then turned and walked to Lee and Bethan.

He handed them the tickets and tags and asked, "Can you sort these out and just give me the two Denver tickets? I'll need you to tag the animals, too. I figured that you two wouldn't need horses until you got to Denver."

Bethan replied, "We won't."

Lee took the stack then handed the two Denver tickets back to Lynn, who then stuffed them into his jacket pocket.

"I'll go and tag the horses," Lee said before Bethan took his arm and escorted him from the ticket window.

As they walked, Lee said, "I thought you said that you'd pay for the shipment of the horses."

She shrugged, then smiled and replied, "I wasn't sure if Lynn would be using his badge to pay for the tickets or not. I guess he figured that this was official duty."

"You paid for our tickets to La Junta."

"That's because I'm only a temporary deputy marshal."

As they untied the horses from the hitchrail, Lynn asked, "How temporary?"

"Very temporary," Bethan answered.

Lynn and Bethan both had smiles on their faces as they led the long line of horses and one mule to the stock corral.

———

After they spending some time with Bryn explaining what had happened at Bent Canyon, Bryn finally dressed and was given a crutch to help him leave the doctor's house.

The sun was setting when Lynn and Bryn walked to the diner while Bethan and Lee went to pry George Lynch out of his temporary residence.

George was quiet as Lee helped him walk to the diner where they joined Lynn and Bryn.

The train wasn't going to depart for another four hours when they finished, so they stayed in the diner and had coffee which gave time for each of them to write their reports. Lee and Bethan only wrote the reports that would be going to Denver, believing that they'd have more than enough time to write their statements for Bent County later.

George Lynch just sat quietly and listened, and wished he had some way to make an escape, but knew it wasn't possible. He had no gun, no horse and no money. That girl's butt shot was the clincher. He couldn't walk without assistance and he almost wished that she'd aimed at his heart.

As they wrote, he stared at the top of Bethan's head and wished there was some way he could pay her back for putting that .44 into his backside. It was downright humiliating to have that Miss Lucy messing around down there.

The longer he sat and watched her, the angrier he became. It was bad enough to be shot in the behind, but to be taken down by a damned girl was going to hang over him long after he dropped down through that trap door. They'd probably be singing bawdy tunes about how George Lynch was shot in the ass by a pretty lass all across the West.

George was sitting on the opposite side of the table from Bethan, with Lee on one side and Bryn and Lynn on the other. It was a heavy table and he knew that two of the men were injured, so maybe he could get his payback now.

Lee flipped his sheet over to continue on the back page and glanced at George Lynch just as he began to move.

Everything shifted into slow motion, as he watched George suddenly begin to rise with his hands grasping the edge of the table.

As the table's oak surface began to tilt, Lee knew what would happen if the heavy piece of furniture was flipped onto Bethan and without hesitation, pushed himself to his feet.

He could see the startled look on Bryn's face as he realized what George Lynch was doing, but by then, his own arms were already reaching for George and he felt his leg muscles coil before they released and sent him flying across the tabletop.

George hadn't even looked at Lee as he was concentrating on Bethan, but when his end of the table was six inches off the floor, he saw Lee flying at him with his fingers stretched as if to strangle him.

George was still yanking on the table when Lee slammed into his chest and they both flew backwards, tipping over George's chair, which added some height to their combined arc before they slammed into the diner's floor and slid into the adjoining table amid the sound of shattering wood.

Lee quickly stood, grabbed George's jacket and jerked him the floor.

"*What were you doing, you bastard?*" he shouted just inches from George's face.

George's eyes were wide when he saw the fury in Lee's face but didn't say a word as he began to shake.

Bethan had shot to her feet just before Lee had pulled Lynch from the floor and raced around Lynn to stand behind Lee.

Lynn left his seat and returned George's chair to the table and then stepped around Bethan.

Lynn said, "Lee, I think we can take him to the train station now, but I suggest we let him change into some clean britches before we do."

Lee was so angry that he hadn't noticed the foul odor that rose from George Lynch, but said, "Maybe we should just let him ride to Las Animas in the stock car with the other animals."

Lynn glanced at Bryn, then said, "Let's get him out of here at least, Lee. He's offending the diners."

Lee nodded then ungently led his prisoner out of the diner with Bethan following.

After they'd gone, Bryn left two dollars on the table, then pulled on his hat, stood and put his crutch under his arm.

He grinned at his nephew and said, "That was impressive."

Lynn nodded, then replied, "I didn't even notice he was moving until Lee left his feet."

Bryn thumped his way out of the diner with his crutch and Lynn followed.

When they got outside, they were a bit surprised to see that George was still standing as Lee had him firmly in his grip while Bethan smiled at her uncle and brother.

They made their way to the train station but stopped at the makeshift jail to allow George to change his clothes, leaving his malodorous clothes in the room.

When they arrived at the train station, they took two of the benches with George sitting by himself because of his lingering bad scent.

"Your train leaves almost two hours after ours, Bethan," Bryn said.

"We'll be okay. I don't think George will try anything and we'll tie his wrists when we get on board."

"I think Lee wouldn't mind shooting him if he tries anything like that again."

Lee looked past Bethan and said, "I'd like to, but I probably would just tackle him instead. I don't know if he has another pair of clean britches though."

Lynn snickered, then said, "You know why he did that, don't you?"

"I figured that he was mad because Bethan was writing about how she shot him in the butt, and he didn't want everyone to know about it."

"Imagine how they'll react when you add that little incident in the diner to your statement when you get to Las Animas."

Bethan then took Lee's hand and said, "Thank you, Lee. I might not have been killed if he tossed that table on top of me, but I'd be joining the ranks of the walking wounded."

Lee just nodded and smiled at her, not wanting to imagine seeing her hurt or even worse.

The train to Trinidad which would then turn north to Denver arrived forty minutes later. Lynn and Bryn shook Lee's hand and kissed Bethan before they boarded the train leaving them with George Lynch.

Lee watched the parade of horses and the mule being loaded into the stock car and wondered how he'd manage to give the two mares and the mule to Garth and Al without expectation of payment now that Bethan didn't need to pay for their shipment.

After they watched the train pull out of the dark station, Bethan and Lee returned to their bench.

"Now that we're alone, Miss Evans, maybe we should discuss more personal topics."

"Such as?" Bethan asked with a knowing smile.

He took her hands and said, "I know we've only known each other for a few days, and they were all filled with distractions, but I have no qualms about telling you that those days were the most fulfilling time of my life. It wasn't because of the danger; it was because I spent them with you. I want to spend the rest of my life with you, Bethan."

Bethan felt her heart skip a beat before she said, "Can I tell you something, Lee?"

"Of course."

"As long as I can recall, I've wanted to be a lawman like my father and uncle. I learned all of the skills that they could teach me and I'm not ashamed to admit that I've learned them well. But one thing that always bothered me was that I knew that no matter how good I became I could never wear the badge because I was a woman. That's why I followed Bryn and Bert to the counterfeiters and then chased after George. I was frustrated and wanted to prove that I could do the job as well as any man.

"Of course, my mother wanted me to marry and have children because it was expected. I love and respect my mother and it's a measure of how strong a woman she is that she let me go to Canon City the second time. Even as I walked into the jail in Bishop, I still had no intention of marrying and starting a family. It wasn't as if I'd ruled it out and part of me did want that, but not for a while.

"That all changed after I cut those bindings on your wrists, Lee. You never once treated me as if I was some pretty,

367

vacant girl that you wanted to bed. You talked and listened to me and sometimes, you even challenged me. Believe it or not, it was when you did that you really won my heart.

"When we get back to Denver, I'll hand my badge back to my father and we can start down the road to spending our lives together."

Lee glanced over at George Lynch who was sleeping, then pulled Bethan close and kissed her even more passionately than they had with their first.

Bethan was already emotionally charged when his lips pressed against hers and she thought she might explode as she wrapped her arms around him.

When they parted, Lee smiled and said, "Bethan, I don't think you should give your badge back."

"No?" she asked with wide eyes.

"You aren't getting paid and having it might come in handy if you need to exert even more authority on our rebellious daughter."

Bethan laughed, then kissed him again.

After they parted lips once again, Bethan said, "I think you're right about the badge. Now that we're engaged, I can tell you about some other things that I haven't mentioned yet."

Lee grinned and asked, "You're not going to tell me that you're a nun. Are you?"

Bethan laughed again, then replied, "No. It's actually good news. Remember when I told you about Lynn's trip to Fort Benton?"

Lee nodded and Bethan continued, saying, "Well, he sold the bank and split the proceeds of the sale giving each of us four thousand dollars. I still have that and whatever I earned for stopping the counterfeiters. I don't know how much it will be, but I had another five hundred or so in the bank already."

"That doesn't bother me, Bethan."

"I'm glad about that because a lot of men seem to resent it when the woman in their lives have more money, unless that is their primary interest in the first place. Anyway, the other item is that when Bryn bought the Double EE, and that's an interesting story in itself, it was sixteen sections. A few years ago, he had it surveyed, then the southern sections were broken into quarter sections. Each of the Evans offspring can have one quarter section when they turn eighteen if he or she wants it. Lynn and Addie did when they married and live west of the family cemetery."

"And what, Miss Evans, will I be contributing to our new home?"

Bethan smiled as she rubbed his hands and replied, "You, Mister Collins, have given me a completely different direction in my life and I can't wait for it to start."

Lee studied her brown eyes and knew that she believed what she'd just said because she would never say a word that she didn't mean, but he knew he needed to work. Without work, a man is nothing. He wanted to be sure that her father genuinely wanted him to become a deputy marshal. If that didn't happen, he'd have to find another job, maybe even as far away as Las Animas.

"I guess we'll have a lot to talk about on the train and while we're in Las Animas."

"We will. I wonder what Bryn and Lynn will tell my parents when they get back."

"You don't think that they'd dare to disobey your request, so you?"

Bethan laughed and replied, "They're Evans just like me and just as hardheaded."

"I almost wished that I could change my name to Evans rather than have you change yours to Collins."

Bethan tilted her head, batted her eyes and asked, "Would you mind it if you become Lee Evans?"

Lee stared at her face for ten silent seconds before Bethan bent at the waist and began laughing.

As she laughed, Lee looked at the back of her head and thought that the rest of his life would be more than just interesting. It would be an adventure.

———

The train journey to Las Animas was uneventful, and because Lee had sent a telegram to Sheriff Allen when they'd stopped in La Junta, when he and Bethan escorted George Lynch onto the platform in the first hour after sunrise, they were met by the sheriff and his lone deputy.

"We'll take your prisoner, Lee," the sheriff said as he grabbed George's arm.

"Thanks, Sheriff. We already wrote our statements and we'll follow you to the jail."

"Do you have to wait for your horses?"

"No, sir. They're on their way to Denver with U.S. Deputy Marshals Bryn and Lynn Evans."

"I read about you taking down the Gentry gang in that law enforcement telegram Bryn sent. You'll have to tell me and Fred about it."

"It was Bethan and I who did the shooting after Lynn's horse broke his leg and he fractured his right arm when he hit the ground. She's also the one who took down George when he was planning on backshooting us."

Sheriff Allen looked back at a smiling Bethan, then said, "I gotta hear this one."

He then had his deputy take hold of George's other arm before they led him across the platform.

Lee linked his arm through Bethan's before they followed with their saddlebags filled with personal items over their shoulders. Neither had a Winchester or even spare ammunition. It wasn't as if they were unarmed. Lee carried the Colt he'd gotten from Bethan while Bethan still had her Smith & Wesson, the Webley and the derringer.

After entering the jail, George was deposited in the second cell as the first was occupied by a rather shabbily dressed man who was still sound asleep.

The sheriff held out a chair for Bethan, who sat down while Lee pulled another straight-backed chair and set it next to her before taking a seat.

The sheriff sat behind the desk, which mean his deputy was left to plant his butt on the corner of the desk.

"So, tell me what happened down in Bent Canyon," the sheriff said as he removed his hat.

Lee slid his and Bethan's reports across the desk as he said, "These are our statements for everything from what happened when Lynch arrived at the jail in Bishop until we put him in a locked room in Bent Canyon. It was just after we did that, when Bethan and I were sitting on a bench waiting for her brother, Lynn, to arrive, that we noticed a dust cloud..."

The sheriff and deputy listened without asking as single question as Lee told the story. He deferred to Bethan often when she was the primary actor in the engagement.

When the tale was finished, the sheriff leaned back and asked, "So, are you gonna take me up on my offer to become my deputy?"

Lee glanced at Bethan, then smiled and replied, "Sorry, Sheriff, but I have a better offer.

————

The trial was set for Monday morning at ten o'clock, which gave Lee and Bethan the weekend to spend some relaxed time together.

They got two rooms at the Argyle House with neither asking about the sleeping arrangements beforehand.

While Bethan headed for Luella's Dress Shop, Lee visited the barbershop where he invested thirty cents in a shave, haircut and a hot bath.

When he left the barbershop wearing his clean clothes and a clean face, he felt like a new man as he strode to the dress shop, not really expecting to find Bethan there because he'd taken over forty-five minutes in the barbershop.

But when he looked through the window, he spotted her talking to an older woman and didn't see any difference in her clothing.

He was debating about going inside when the woman must have said something to Bethan because she turned, smiled and waved at him. He waved back and then took a deep breath and entered the shop.

"I was just getting ready to leave, and don't you look all shiny and clean," she said as he stepped closer.

Lee grinned, took off his hat, and replied, "Yes, ma'am. Didn't you buy anything?"

"I did. Mrs. Atchison already has them in a bag, and we were just talking when you arrived at the window, but we're finished."

Mrs. Atchison smiled at Lee, then hoisted a large cloth bag from the floor and held it out to him.

Lee accepted the bag and was surprised at its weight as it could only hold cloth.

Once he had the bag, Bethan said, "Thank you, Charlotte," then hooked her arm though Lee's free arm.

Lee stepped with her to the door, swung it open and let her exit before following her outside and closing it behind him.

"What did you buy? It seems heavier than I expected."

"It's just packed tightly. What do you want to do now?"

"Well, it's too early for lunch, so we could just go back to the hotel and sit in the lobby."

"Alright," Bethan said, then as they began walking, she asked, "Do you want my Webley and shoulder holster?"

"Right now?"

"No," she replied with a light laugh, "Later. I've only used it for target practice, but now that you're going to be a deputy marshal, it would be a good thing to have."

"You know that I've never seen it? You've either had a coat or your vest on and to be honest, I've wondered how you could manage to wear a shoulder holster at all."

"Is that because I have obstacles in the way?"

Lee laughed and replied, "I'd hardly call them obstacles, but yes."

"I did have to alter the straps to avoid those obstacles, but it wouldn't be difficult to change them back. Do you want to see how it fits later?"

"Very much."

"When we get to our rooms tonight, you can come into mine and I'll show you."

Lee didn't answer but looked at her smiling eyes and wasn't sure exactly what Bethan would show him.

———

That night, after supper, Bethan showed Lee her shoulder holster and he was impressed with her alterations and her obstructions as well now that they were no longer hidden by her coat or vest.

But after she removed her shoulder holster, they sat on her bed and Bethan returned the harness to its standard configuration then adjusted it to fit Lee.

He stood, strapped it on, then felt the weight and said, "I'll have to get used to having the pistol there, but that shouldn't take long."

"It doesn't. Remember that the Webley is a double-action revolver, so you don't need to cock the hammer. It's not as accurate as a Colt or any other pistol with a longer barrel."

"I understand that, ma'am. Do you want it back now?"

"No. It's yours. I have my derringer if I need a backup."

As Lee sat back down on the bed beside her, Bethan said, "To be honest, it'll feel good not having to wear that shoulder holster all the time. It was almost like wearing a corset, which is something I will never wear. I never told anyone that even with my modifications, it still was somewhat, um, restricting. I was too stubborn to admit that it was uncomfortable after buying it. I confess that I hate to admit it when I'm wrong."

"Most people are that way. I once made a seriously bad decision and knew it even before I acted on it, but never said a word and had to live with it for a week."

"Are you going to tell me what it is?"

"If you insist, but it's still embarrassing."

"I insist."

"I was twelve years old and just becoming aware of girls. We had a small schoolhouse and only four girls that had developed obstacles. One girl, Priscilla Henderson, was especially noticeable, but she wasn't very pretty. She liked me and one Friday afternoon, she asked to meet me in the woods near the creek outside her farm. Now, I knew that the woods were covered with poison ivy, but I thought if I wore my boots it wouldn't be a problem."

Bethan was already grinning when she said, "But it was."

"It was a big problem. When I met with Priscilla, we made small talk for a few minutes and then we, well, showed each other our new equipment, as it were. I was very impressed with hers and when she wanted to touch mine, I was horrified. When she reached for me, I quickly stepped back and fell on my naked behind into a nice patch of poison ivy."

Bethan was giggling as Lee finished his confession, saying, "What made it worse was as I sat in the poison ivy, Priscilla stood there laughing at me as she pulled her dress back on. She left me sitting there and at the moment, I was more concerned about her telling the other kids what had happened than I was about the poison ivy's effect on my posterior. My area of concern changed after a very short time when the itching began in earnest."

Bethan's giggles progressed to full laughter as Lee watched.

When she quieted, Bethan said, "Well, now that you've admitted to behavior for a typically sex-crazed young man, I'll tell you my own real secret that borders on lawbreaking."

Lee's eyes widened as he asked, "Really? An Evans broke the law?"

BETHAN'S CHOICE

"At the time, I knew it was wrong, but it was almost a tradition among some of the girls in my school and I didn't think it really hurt anyone. We never told any adults about it and I don't think that anyone in my family knows about it to this day."

"This ought to be juicy," Lee said with a grin.

"In Denver, there was this shop near the school that only sold sweets. It was called Baldthrush's and was owned and run by Mrs. Baldthrush, who was a widow. We all called the place Baldy-Bean's, and she was Lady Baldy-Bean. Anyway, we thought she was really old, but she was probably around fifty. Mrs. Baldthrush had a habit of taking her medicine beginning in mid-afternoon. By the time we finished class for the day, she was usually pretty soggy.

"We discovered that if we went into her shop just before she closed, we could put a penny on the counter and begin pointing to different jars of penny candy and say, 'I'd like some of those, and some of those,' until she filled a bag. She'd hand it to us, and we'd leave the store giggling knowing that we'd gotten ten cents worth of candy for a penny."

Just when Lee was about to comment, Bethan dropped her eyes to the floor and said, "It wasn't until I was a couple of years older that I realized it wasn't really a funny game and that I was essentially robbing Mrs. Baldthrush and taking money from her that she probably needed. So, when I realized what I had done, I went to her store late one afternoon and put a golden eagle on the counter and bought a penny's worth of candy. I never told anyone, and it still nags at my conscience."

When she looked up and turned her eyes to Lee, he said, "I'm sorry for asking, Bethan. But that story tells me a lot about you. You didn't have to go back to the store and make amends, but you did. I'll bet that none of your friends did.

You're a very special person, Miss Evans. You're the best human being that I've ever known."

Bethan smiled and replied, "It was such a silly thing to get so serious about, but I'm still glad that I told you. Now that we've gotten our deepest secrets out of the way, give me a goodnight kiss and take your scratchy behind to your room."

Lee smiled, then kissed her longer than most goodnight kisses before he stood, adjusted his new shoulder holster, and said, "I'll knock on your door in the morning to take you to breakfast."

"I'll be ready."

"Goodnight, Bethan."

"Goodnight, Lee."

Lee wanted to give her one more kiss but was already uncomfortable and knew that he needed to leave quickly.

After he'd gone, Bethan smiled, then slowly laid on the bed and put her hands behind her head. She had as big a need to have Lee leave as he had. It was going to be a long four days before they returned to Denver.

————

In Denver, Lynn and Bryn met their wives and their boss at the train station, everyone moved to a bench so Bryn could sit before he and Lynn gave their verbal reports to Dylan.

Dylan was wise enough to let Erin and Addie question their husbands before he would ask about the mission, so he remained standing while the two couples sat.

Erin stared at his leg but couldn't see the wound as she asked, "How bad is it, Bryn?"

"I'll admit that it hurts, and the doc said to keep an eye out for infection, but he said it'll heal completely in about eight weeks or so. I'll be a bit gimpy until then."

"When we get home, we need to talk."

"I know."

As Erin was interrogating Bryn, Addie was doing the same to Lynn on the adjoining bench and received pretty much the same responses.

When the wives were somewhat satisfied, Dylan said, "Give me a quick rundown of events from when you met with Bethan and Lee."

Bryn began his report and had to let Lynn take over after he'd been shot. As Lynn talked, Bryn noticed that their animals had been moved into the stock corral.

After Lynn finished, Bryn said, "We need to get those horses and the mule to the Double EE, Dylan. Did you bring any help?"

"We can manage, Bryn. Your thoughtful wife drove the buggy, so you don't have to ride. I'll get them strung out behind Raven."

"Okay, boss," Bryn replied as he took his crutch then stood.

Dylan let Bryn and Erin drive away with Addie, then after he'd connected the long string of animals, he waited until Lynn was in the saddle before mounting and setting off for the Double EE.

They wouldn't get back to the ranch until late in the night, but he was sure that Bryn wouldn't be getting any sleep for a while.

CHAPTER 10

Saturday morning was quiet and after they'd had their breakfast, Lee and Bethan walked to the sheriff's office to make sure that there hadn't been any change in the trial date and to answer any questions that the sheriff may have.

As they approached the jail, they noticed a group of men coalescing near the opposite boardwalk.

"They don't look happy," Bethan said.

"The sheriff said that Deputy Williamson was well-liked in the community and that some of his friends might start trouble."

"With the trial only a couple of days away and an almost certain verdict, I'm a bit surprised that they would stand watch like that."

"Maybe they don't trust the system to hang Lynch."

"I won't make the obvious pun, but do you think that they might try to yank him out of the jail?"

"I doubt it, but you can never be sure."

"Let's ask the sheriff when we get there," she said as they stepped across the dusty street.

When they reached the jail's door, Lee turned the handle and found it locked, so he knocked and waited.

The sheriff's face appeared in the window, then disappeared before the door opened and he said, "Come on in, folks."

Bethan stepped inside and as soon as Lee passed through the doorway, the sheriff closed and locked the door.

When the sheriff turned, Lee asked, "Are you expecting trouble from those men across the street?"

"I don't think they'll do anything other than stare, but I'm not taking any chances."

Bethan then asked, "Where's your deputy?"

Sheriff Allen snapped, "He claimed he had a bellyache. I reckon he saw those boys across the street, and it was more of a weak spine than an upset stomach."

"Do you need any help?" Lee asked.

"No. I'll be all right. The missus is going to bring us chow when we need it, and I reckon those boys will break up soon enough."

Bethan sat down and asked, "We thought we'd stop by to check on the trial and see if you or the prosecutor needed any more information."

As the sheriff walked behind the desk and took a seat, he replied, "The trial is still at ten o'clock on Monday, and the prosecutor was very pleased with your statements. I wish that the deputy marshals could be here, but I can understand why they couldn't. I don't think you'll find a single man in this town who won't vote to convict before the man enters the courtroom."

Lee sat down before Sheriff Allen asked, "What was the better offer that you talked about, Lee?"

"I've been told by Miss Evans and her two deputy marshal brothers that I should see Marshal Evans about becoming a United States Deputy Marshal. It seems that they're even more shorthanded than you are."

"I'll admit that it's a better offer, but I might be able to swing some more pay in light of running down Lynch."

Lee glanced at Bethan, then said, "It's not just the money or even the position that made it a better offer, Bob. Bethan made me an offer that I couldn't refuse. Or I made the offer, I can't remember which."

Bethan laughed and said, "I can't recall how it happened either. It just did."

Sheriff Allen grinned, then said, "Well, I can tell that you two are a pretty good match. Congratulations."

"Thank you."

"I'd like to talk to you, but I want to keep an eye on those boys until they break up and go home or to back to work."

"We'll see you on Monday, Bob," Lee said as he stood.

The sheriff followed them to the door, then after they'd stepped onto the boardwalk, they heard the door lock behind them.

After they turned and began walking, Lee asked, "Did the sheriff seem more worried than he let on?"

"I was about to ask you the same thing. I think that having his deputy run off and hide didn't help. He might believe that his deputy knew something that he didn't."

"We can keep an eye on things while we spend the day wandering the town."

"I'll agree with that."

"I need to pick up some things at the general store first."

"Nothing exotic, I hope."

"No, ma'am. Just a new toothbrush and some powder and a new shaving kit."

"You look quite nice to me, Mister Collins."

"Why, thank you, Miss Evans, and I honestly say that I find you quite fetching as well."

They shared a smile as they continued to step along the boardwalk to Feinstein's Dry Goods and Sundries, momentarily forgetting the cluster of angry men across the street from the jail.

———

On the Double EE, Bryn was alone in the kitchen with Erin after the children had all gone to visit Gwen's youngsters.

As they sat at the table having coffee, Erin asked, "How much arguing will it take for me to convince you to hand in your badge and just stay here to raise your horses?"

Bryn looked up from his cup and answered, "Not as much as you might expect, sweetheart. When I took that bullet in my thigh, I wasn't that worried and actually thought about staying with Lynn to finish the fight. But after I began to feel a bit out of sorts enough for Lynn to notice, I knew I had to get to Iron Springs for treatment. I must have looked worse to Lynn because he escorted me back and I felt horrible knowing that Bethan and Lee would be going after a killer on their own. But it was when we were riding back to town and I was losing more blood than I expected and had to lean over Aesop's neck to keep from falling that I realized what I might lose if I didn't make it.

"I'd lose you, Erin, and that thought terrified me. It's kind of odd when you think about it. I didn't mind dying nearly as much as knowing that I wouldn't see you again. Later, after the doc removed the slug and sewed me up, I was resting and all of it came back, the gunfights and the brushes with death. It was then that another revelation struck me even harder. I have put you through so much over the years and all you could do was sit at home waiting for a telegram or for Dylan to walk through the door with bad news. I'm sorry, Erin."

Erin set her cup down, took his hands and said, "You don't have to apologize, Bryn. I was very proud of you for what you did to keep everyone safe. I was worried and I'm sure that Gwen told Dylan about it. I'll even admit to feeling a sense of doom when you and Lynn rode away for this job. But if you do hand in your badge, I want it to be your decision, not mine."

Bryn nodded, then smiled slightly as he said, "We have a few weeks to think about it. Don't we?"

"We do and by the time you can walk normally again, you may decide to run as fast as you can back to the office just to get away from me."

"You'll have to put up with having me around the house all the time too, Erin."

"I can live with that," she said before letting his hands go and picking up her cup.

————

Lee and Bethan were sitting on the bench in front of the tobacco and pipe shop just after sunset when the men who had been across from the jail but then dissipated returned in greater numbers.

Bethan stared across the street and said, "There are more of them now. I counted seventeen."

"More than the numbers, it looks as if a few of them have spent the afternoon in the saloon."

"Do we go to the jail to help the sheriff?"

"Not yet. Let's see if they just stand there making noise. The sheriff didn't light a lamp, but he's still inside."

"I wish I had my shotgun."

"The sheriff probably has a couple, so we could borrow one if it gets ugly. I'm sure that he'll have one if it does."

They continued to watch as did many of the residents as a few more men joined the boisterous gathering.

"This doesn't make any sense," Bethan said, "They have to know that Lynch will probably hang on Tuesday morning. I wouldn't be surprised if a few of them aren't on the jury."

Lee looked at Bethan and said, "Let's end this now before it gets out of hand."

"How do you want to do it?"

"Take off your coat and put your badge on your vest. I'll do the same. Then we'll just walk over there and start talking."

Bethan smiled and said, "And tell them a story."

"Yes, ma'am. The story of how you shot George Lynch in the butt."

"And how you made him soil himself in the diner."

Lee nodded, then stood, removed his coat and pinned his sorry-looking Bishop town marshal badge to his vest while Bethan attached her much nicer United States Deputy Marshal badge to hers.

Lee looked at her with her pistol at her hip and said, "You are something to behold, Bethan."

She smiled then she and Lee stepped into the street and angled toward the crowd in the shadows.

When they were approaching the group, Bethan could see their eyes turning toward her and Lee, so when they were about twenty feet in front of the nearest man, they stopped.

The loud, angry chatter ceased as if the wind had carried it away. Each of the men stared at Bethan and almost ignored Lee in the low light provided by the lamps in the nearby shops.

Lee said loudly, "My name is Lee Collins and I used to be the town marshal in Bishop, which is why my badge looks homemade because it was. Beside me is United States Deputy Marshal Bethan Evans. I'm sure that you've all heard that we were the ones who captured George Lynch. Do you want to hear how he wound up with a .44 in his right butt cheek?"

The question had a mollifying effect on their anger, and one of them replied, "We heard he been shot, but not in his behind."

Lee looked at Bethan, who then said, "I was the one who put it there. Here's what happened."

She then told her part of the story, which captivated the would-be lynch mob as much by its narrator as they were by its content.

After she finished the last part of her tale, she said, "If you think getting shot in the behind is embarrassing for a tough man like George Lynch, wait until you hear what happened when we were having dinner at a diner in Iron Springs before we got on the train for Las Animas."

Lee then took over, telling about the violent ending to what had been a peaceful supper. By the time he'd finished his description complete with wrinkled nose and waving hands to ward off the stench, the group was laughing and adding their own somewhat off-color comments.

Then he paused and said, "Now, boys, Miss Evans and I are only here to testify at his trial in just about thirty-six hours. We'd appreciate it if you'd let us tell the judge and jury what happened so we can go home."

One of the men then loudly asked, "Did you really try to shoot him in the butt, ma'am?"

"I always put my shot where I want it to go."

"But you're a girl!" shouted a different man.

Bethan had already picked out her target before hearing the shout, and said, "See the A in the saloon sign about sixty feet away?"

Their heads uniformly turned and looked at the sign that they'd all seen for years when Bethan pulled her Smith & Wesson, cocked the hammer and fired in less than four seconds.

The sound echoed across the street as a hole appeared in the space in the center of the letter.

Bethan had her pistol holstered by the time their eyes all returned to stare at her.

"Damn! That's fine shootin'!" exclaimed the man who'd commented about her sex.

"Thank you," Bethan replied, then said, "We'd appreciate it if you could all just go home now so Lee and I can get some rest before that trial."

"Yes, ma'am," the leader of the group replied.

Some began wandering away, but more approached Bethan and Lee to shake their hands and even thank them for what they did before leaving.

When the boardwalk was empty, they turned and walked to the jail, but before they stepped onto the boardwalk, the door flew open and Sheriff Allen stepped out.

"That was something worth watching! At first, I thought you might be trying to yell at them to break them up, but then when you started talking, I opened the window so I could hear better. That was the first lynch mob I've ever seen and if I ever see another one, I'll know how to handle them."

"Will you be okay now, Bob?" Lee asked.

"Oh, sure. I'll sleep here but I don't think I'll have a problem on Sunday. I really appreciate what you did."

Bethan replied, "We were glad to help. We're going to get our coats and head back to the hotel. We really do need to get some rest."

"Thanks again and good night to you both."

"Good night, Sheriff," Bethan said before taking Lee's arm and walking to the tobacco shop.

Sheriff Allen watched them leave, then turned and entered the jail, but still locked the door.

———

Sunday morning, Lee tapped on Bethan's door and then stepped back, waiting for her to exit, but after almost a minute with the door still unopened, he began to grow concerned.

He knocked more loudly, then waited for another fifteen seconds before loudly asking, "Bethan? Are you all right?"

"Just a minute," Bethan replied from the other side of the door.

Lee relaxed until the door finally swung wide and Bethan stepped into the hallway.

After she closed the door, she turned and looked at Lee who was staring at her. It wasn't as if she wasn't expecting his reaction, and in fact, had been hoping that he would be impressed.

Lee finally said, "I haven't seen you in a dress before."

Bethan smiled and replied, "This is what I bought at the dress shop. I have some dresses at home, but I wanted one that I thought you might like. Do you like it?"

Lee blinked, then answered, "That's a silly question, Bethan. I do believe that you're just trying to make a point."

"Maybe," she said, "Let's have some breakfast and then you can escort me to Sunday services."

"Yes, ma'am," Lee said as he hooked his arm though hers.

They walked down the hallway and crossed the lobby before stepping outside to a glorious morning on the last day of April. It was still a bit brisk, and Bethan knew she should have worn a jacket, but she did have the woolen shawl that she'd bought along with the dress, so she wasn't that cold.

Lee had been a bit surprised by his own reaction because he had seen Bethan in just a shirt and her britches, but somehow seeing her in a well-fitted dress had stunned him. He wondered if it was her less feminine attire that had allowed him to see her more as a person than a woman. Regardless of the reason, he was actually glad that he hadn't seen her dressed this way until now. He might not have been able to talk to her so freely.

After breakfast and church, they spent the rest of the day just strolling and talking or sitting and talking. Because of her large and interesting family with their many adventures, Bethan found herself dominating the conversations, but Lee didn't mind at all. He was actually enthralled by each of them, from her father and mother's meeting to Kyle's arrival and Lynn's canoe trip down the Missouri.

As Bethan spoke, Lee could already hear the voices of their children talking about how their parents met and adding it to the family history.

———

Monday, May 7, 1877

After that pleasantly quiet Sunday, Bethan and Lee had a normal breakfast, then, after getting some welcome news from the desk clerk, checked out of the hotel, and walked to the county courthouse. They spent half an hour with the prosecutor before going downstairs and taking their seats in the witness row in the already crowded courtroom.

After the drama with the lynch mob, the trial turned out to be almost mundane. The trial began in the accepted manner and each attorney presented his arguments. The defense attorney's angle for inserting reasonable doubt was that his client wasn't even with Cody Russell when he'd killed the deputy. It was really his only option.

Lee was called as a witness first, and his testimony was factual and unassailable because he knew both Cody and George Lynch. The fact that he had broken Cody out of jail was just another nail in George's coffin.

The defense attorney tried to rattle Bethan by pointing out that she had mistakenly shot George Lynch because she had never seen him before, but that was a weak argument at best. Even if she didn't know him from Adam, he was pointing a Winchester at Lee Collins.

The judge's seat was probably still warm when the jury returned their guilty verdict and George Lynch was sentenced to hang the following morning.

BETHAN'S CHOICE

As Lee and Beth stood outside the courthouse waiting to talk to Sheriff Allen, the deputy that had abandoned him the day before escorted George Lynch past them. He didn't even look at them, keeping his head down as he shuffled past in his manacles.

Sheriff Allen was just a few feet behind them and stopped when he spotted Bethan and Lee, then said, "I hear you got lucky about the train."

Lee grinned and replied, "The hotel manager told me before we left. I guess the Atchison, Topeka and Santa Fe knew that we wanted to leave so they arranged for that broken switch."

"Well, I hope everything goes well for you both, and, Lee, if it doesn't work out for you, you can always come back here."

"Thanks, Bob, but if it doesn't work out, then I'll just get on my horse and ride to China."

The sheriff laughed, then shook Lee's hand before Bethan leaned across and kissed him on the cheek.

He gave them a short wave, then trotted away to catch up to his deputy and their prisoner.

Bethan said, "Let's get our things and get to the station. We can send the telegram to my father when we get to La Junta."

Lee nodded, then they quickly returned to the hotel lobby, snatched their saddlebags and the two cloth bags with their recent purchases and hurried to the train station.

The delayed departure was longer than the railroad expected, so after buying their tickets, they had enough time to get a quick lunch before the train finally pulled out of Las Animas.

———

It was mid-afternoon when Dylan received Bethan's telegram and quickly left the office to ride out to the Double EE. He had Raven moving at a fast trot, so he made short work of the four-mile ride.

He stopped at Bryn's house first to let him know the news before riding the four hundred yards to his home.

Rather than telling her its contents, Dylan let Gwendolyn read the telegram so he could watch her reaction.

Her face exploded with joy as she read:

US MARSHAL DYLAN EVANS DENVER COLO

**RETURNING TODAY WITH LEE
LYNCH FOUND GUILTY
PLAN ON MARRYING SOON
LOVE TO ALL**

BETHAN EVANS LAJUNTA COLO

"She's already planning on getting married!" Gwen exclaimed as she stared at the short message.

"It's kind of frightening, but not out of character. Once she makes her mind up, she goes with her decision without hesitation."

Gwen looked up and said, "We need to meet this young man. I know that both Lynn and Bryn thought he was a real match for Bethan, but I still need to make my own judgement."

Dylan grinned and said, "You always do, sweetheart. Just remember what Bryn and Lynn told us about him. He even saved Bethan from at least a few broken bones. He sounds like an exceptional young man."

"I guess I should be grateful that she finally found a man who she met her standards. I thought that it would never happen."

"I wasn't so sure myself. Anyway, we need to get everything ready to meet them in a few hours. Can you go tell Lynn and Addie? I've got to tell Garth and Al that they're going to have a roommate when they come back to visit. I figure he can stay in the small house and Bethan can move back here until they're married."

"Garth and Al will be leaving shortly, so you'd better hurry."

Dylan kissed her, then hurried from the house to let Garth and Al know that they might be getting their first brother-in-law in a few weeks.

———

As their train rumbled north out of Castle Rock, Lee asked, "How many Evans will be on the platform when we arrive?"

"I hope it's not all of them because no one would be able to leave the train. You're not nervous, are you?"

"No. I'm just curious more than anything else. You've been telling me stories about your family ever since we met, and I can't imagine that one family has had so many adventures. It's like they were all characters in some long saga. Most folks live and die within five miles of where they were born, but your family seems as if they've been everywhere in the country."

C. J. PETIT

"Most of us haven't been outside of Colorado since we moved here. As far as the adventures go, we seem to have already had our own share, don't you think?"

Lee smiled and replied, "I think you can say that. Have you decided about whether or not you're going to keep your badge?"

"I think I will, at least for a while. In fact, if you do become a deputy marshal, maybe I'll join you on your missions."

"Really? I guess that would be all right, at least until you started swelling around the middle."

Bethan grinned before she said, "That would be a sight, wouldn't it? A pregnant woman wearing a gunbelt."

"I think it would be more restrictive than your shoulder holster was. I just can't imagine you being unarmed."

"I will never be unarmed, Mister Collins. I may only have a derringer, but I will never be without a pistol of some form."

"Why am I not surprised?" Lee said before he leaned over and kissed her.

———

It was late in the afternoon when the Evans who would greet Bethan and Lee assembled on the platform. It wasn't as many as Bethan feared. Only Dylan, Gwen, Kyle, Garth and Al were on the platform. Lynn and Bryn were back on the Double EE with their families. Garth and Al were preparing to leave the ranch to return to their own place when Dylan told them that Bethan was returning with her suddenly discovered fiancé. They weren't about to leave when they heard the news.

Garth was staring down the tracks looking for the train as Al asked, "What do you think he looks like, Dad?"

Dylan replied, "I can't believe that he'd be some fat old codger with white whiskers, although I don't believe that his appearance is what won your sister over. After what Lynn and Bryn told us on Sunday, I'll admit that I'm pretty impressed."

"We were, too. Are you going to make him a deputy marshal?"

"It depends. I need to meet him and make my own judgement, but after listening to how he performed, I'd be surprised if I didn't. We were already shorthanded before Lynn and your uncle were temporarily put out of commission, so now I'm down to just four."

Al then said, "You may be down another one soon, Dad."

"You mean Pete?"

"Yes, sir."

"You think that because he seems to be interested in Martha that he might quit? Bethan mentioned it to Addie before she left, but I can't see it."

"It's not just that. I reckon that if you bring Lee on board, that there might be some hard feelings between him and Pete."

"I hadn't thought about that, but I should have. He made a snippy comment about Bethan when I mentioned that she seemed to like Lee. Luckily, he didn't know about Bethan's telegram. At least not yet," he replied, then looked at his wife and asked, "Gwen, what do you think?"

"I agree with Alwen. Pete was really smitten with Bethan and couldn't understand why she'd so quickly rejected his attentions. He probably believed that she'd never find a better man and thought she would just wind up as an old maid. Now she returns and announces that she's going to marry a man she's known for less than two weeks. It will be a hard pill for him to swallow."

Dylan scratched the side of his neck as he said, "If Lee makes a good impression, then before I even think about offering him the job, I'll have a long talk with Pete."

"What if he says that he won't work with Lee?" Al asked.

"I don't believe that he'd say that, but I'll have to watch how he says it. If I think that he's going to harbor a grudge, then I'll have to decide, one way or the other."

"Is Pete a good lawman?"

"Honestly? He's about average. He makes his share of mistakes, but overall, he's doing a good job."

"I don't envy you, husband," Gwen said as she looked up at him.

"I hope I don't have to choose between losing Pete and hiring Lee."

Al said, "He could always just work on the Double EE with the horses. He already has a few of his own and one mule. You could swear him in as a temporary deputy just like you did with Bethan. Uncle Bryn only has Lucas and Roger to help him with the herds right now and they're stretched."

"That's not a bad idea, Al, but it'll only push the issue to the back of the stove for a while. All we can do is wait to meet Lee and then see where it goes from there."

Garth rejoined them and said, "Those horses that they sent back with Uncle Bryn were pretty nice. Even the mule was top notch. I wonder if Lee would consider parting with those mares."

Dylan grinned at his son and replied, "If Bethan even suggested it in a passing remark, I imagine that he'd give them all to you and Al."

Garth chuckled, then said, "We wouldn't want the geldings, Dad, but Ripper wouldn't mind a couple of more nice mares to add to his harem."

"When are you going to add a filly or two to your all male domain?" Gwen asked.

"Aw, Mom, we're doing okay. We only have the one house now anyway."

Al then said, "We still have most of the money that Lynn gave us, so we can build another house whenever we want to. It's just a matter of finding the right girls."

"It doesn't help that you two spend most of your time on your ranch or visiting Morrison. You both need to come to Denver more often where there are many very nice young ladies."

"There are nice young ladies in Morrison, too, Mom."

"I don't care where you meet them, but if Bethan can find a husband while she's out chasing outlaws, then I hope that you can find wives somewhere."

Garth laughed, then looked at his brother and said, "I guess we have our orders, Al."

"We've had the same orders for a while now, Garth."

They were interrupted when Kyle said, "There's the train," and everyone turned and looked southwest down the tracks and spotted the telltale sign of a black cloud on the horizon.

"Well, this should be interesting," Dylan said as he soon spotted the speck of the locomotive creating the cloud.

———

Ten minutes later, the train slowed as it rolled into the ever-expanding Denver station. With three different railroads now operating out of the burgeoning city, it seemed as if the tracks were being laid in a constantly widening series of parallel lines of iron as new routes were being created.

Lee stood, hung his saddlebags over his shoulder, then picked up both of their cloth bags before stepping into the aisle and letting Bethan exit the seat. She was wearing her britches and coat simply because she expected to be riding back to the Double EE.

The car banged into the coal car as the train came to a halt, but each of the passengers were already holding onto a seat as they anticipated the jolt.

Once the car had overcome its inertia, the departing passengers queued to exit the front door. Lee followed Bethan as they slowly made their way out of the car.

He wasn't nervous at all because he knew that Bethan had made up her mind and wasn't about to change it, even if her parents somehow disapproved of him. He didn't believe that was likely but did want to like them as much as he'd liked Bryn and Lynn. As he hadn't met an Evans yet that he didn't get along with, he would be surprised if her father and mother would be an exception.

As Bethan stepped onto the platform, she was almost immediately captured by her mother, who wrapped her arms around her much taller daughter. Bethan hugged her mother, then as she stepped back, she put her hand out to Lee.

Lee took her hand as she said, "Mom, this is Lee Collins."

Lee smiled at Gwen and said, "I'm pleased to meet you, Mrs. Evans."

Gwen's reservation immediately evaporated as she looked into his warm hazel eyes, then smiled and replied, "I'm even more pleased to meet you, Mister Collins. May I call you Lee?"

"I'd be honored."

Bethan could see that her mother was more than pleased already, then she looked at her father and said, "Lee, I'd like you to meet my father, the famed United States Marshal, Dylan Evans."

Lee released Bethan's hand, then shook Dylan's as he said, "I'm glad to meet you, Marshal."

"I've heard nothing but good things about you since my brother and son returned, Lee. I hope my daughter hasn't filled your head with fables about me."

"They didn't sound like fables, sir. Whenever she talked about you or anyone else in the family, it was like an official report without embellishment."

401

"Call me Dylan. Despite what my wife thinks, I'm not that old."

Lee smiled then replied, "Thank you, Dylan."

Bethan was enormously pleased with her father's reaction before she said, "Those two are my older brothers, Alwen and Garth, and this is my Uncle Kyle."

Lee shook each of their hands before Dylan said, "Let's head back to the ranch. The rest of the family is there already and we're pretending this is another Sunday."

"Did you bring Nippy and Biff?" Bethan asked.

"They're at the hitchrail on the other side of the station with our horses."

Bethan then slid her arm through Lee's before they crossed the platform.

Once mounted, the six Evans and one Collins trotted down Lawton Street and continued west until they reached Argyle Street where they headed south. They soon left Denver and were on the road to the Double EE.

As they rode along in a somewhat disorganized group, Bethan turned to Lee and asked, "What do you think?"

Lee smiled and replied, "I see you in both of your parents."

Bethan was incredibly happy with his response. He couldn't have paid her a higher compliment, even if he'd told her she was the most beautiful woman in the world.

―――

When they turned down the access road thirty minutes later, Lee was struck by the size of the layout and the number of buildings, even though Bethan had described the ranch in detail. He saw the herds of horses in the distance and some in the corrals near the two big barns. There was one big house and one small house in front of them and another, even bigger house to the south with another small house. Bethan had drawn the layout of the ranch on the train, so he knew which Evens family occupied each of the houses. He could see a third house and barn to the west and knew that it was Lynn's place.

Dylan's house already had a crowd outside, gathered around what appeared to be almost an outside café with six large picnic tables. There was even a large stone firepit for cooking off to the side that was already smoking.

"This is really impressive, Bethan," he said as he continued to stare at the setup.

"You'll get used to it. You'll be staying in the small house over there. Right now, Al and Garth are there, but they'll be leaving soon to return to their own ranch about thirty miles southwest of here. I was surprised a bit that they were still here. They usually leave right after the Sunday gathering."

"I need to talk to them anyway," Lee said as they turned to head toward the big house and the big group of Evans.

He soon found Bryn sitting at one of the picnic tables and then spotted Lynn with his new cast on his right arm standing with whom he assumed was his wife Addie. She had a baby in her arms and everywhere he looked, he saw more children of all ages.

When they pulled up at the back of the big house, Bethan hopped down from Nippy before Lee slowly dismounted from

Biff as he was still in awe of the large family, despite knowing what to expect.

Bryn's older sons, Mason and Ethan trotted over and one took Biff's reins and the other took hold of Nippy's, then they led the horses away without saying a word as the rest of the hoard of Evans looked at Lee.

He would normally have felt uncomfortable being under such scrutiny, but none of the faces that were turned towards him showed a hint of distrust. It was as if they were all anxious to just meet and talk to him.

As Lynn was still mobile, he was the first to step forward and rather than try to shake his left hand, he just grinned and said, "It's good to see you again, Lee."

"It's good to see you too, Lynn. I noticed that you're wearing a cast now."

Lynn looked at his heavily wrapped arm and said, "It's more annoying than the splint and Doctor Corbin had to reset the bones because they weren't straight. That wasn't any fun, but he said the itching is going to drive me crazy after a while."

As Lynn talked, Addie stepped to his side and when he finished, she offered Lynn her hand and said, "I'm Addie Evans, this clumsy oaf's wife. He told us how you stopped those killers from taking advantage of his bad situation, and I'm very grateful to you for keeping him safe. He may be a clumsy oaf, but he's my clumsy oaf and I'm rather fond of him."

"I like him myself, ma'am," Lee said as he looked at the baby she held in the crook of her left arm.

"Call me Addie, Lee. I'm probably younger than you are. I think I can safely recommend that you address each of us by our Christian names. From what Dylan told us, you're going to be joining the family soon."

"That's what Bethan told me, but I haven't agreed to the marriage yet."

Bethan had arrived halfway through the conversation and as soon as he passed the remark to Addie, she smacked him in the right arm with her fist.

Lee grabbed his arm, then turned and grinned at Bethan.

"I'm sorry, almighty and powerful empress of all the dominions under the sun, and beg that you forgive this humble, wicked and ignorant peasant for denying your imperial designs."

Addie laughed as she looked at Bethan who was already smiling before she took Lee's hand and said, "You are forgiven, unworthy supplicant. Now, you will agree to my desire to join me in matrimony."

Lee bowed his head, then replied, "I agree with only joy in my heart and a promise of constant devotion for eternity, my beloved empress."

"Then it shall be so. I shall set the date for our joining to be the twenty-fifth of this month, the same day as the anniversary of my exalted birth."

Lee then said, "In all of our other talks, I forgot that it's your birthday."

"To be honest, I almost forgot about it myself until just now. But it's not a bad idea."

"I think it's a great idea."

Before they could continue, more Evans began to arrive, and the introductions began. It took a good twenty minutes for Lee to meet each of them, including Mason and Ethan who had returned after taking care of their horses. He met Lucas Fairfield and Roger Birch, the two wranglers who worked on the Double EE after he'd been introduced to all of the Evans.

Lee knew that it would take a while to remember all of them, but for now, he concentrated on the adults.

As the sun dropped lower in the west, they enjoyed a barbecue and by the time sunset had ended, the family began to disperse. Kyle and Katie had to return to Denver, then Lynn and Addie had to take their buggy to their house.

After everyone who hadn't lived in Dylan and Gwen's house had gone, Bethan asked, "Al, can you and Garth help Lee get situated?"

"Sure. We'll be leaving in the morning after we get mom to feed us."

Cari then said, "I'm the one who's been doing most of your cooking, Alwen Evans, and you'd better not forget it."

"I know that, dear sister, and we do appreciate it."

Bethan then turned to Lee, and before he could even think about how to say goodnight to her with her parents eight feet away, she took one step closer, then wrapped her arms around him and kissed him.

When they separated, she smiled and said, "Good night, Lee. I'll see you at breakfast."

Lee smiled back, no longer caring if her parents and the rest of her immediate family were watching, then said, "Good night, Bethan."

After she released him, she turned to her mother and said, "I need to move my things to the big house, but that can wait until tomorrow."

Gwen smiled at her daughter, then hooked her arm through Bethan's and without replying, walked with her to the back of their house. Dylan followed them before Cari, Brian and Conway trailed behind.

Al then grinned at Lee and said, "Let's get you moved in before we move out, Lee."

The three young men then headed for the small house and before they reached the front door, Garth asked, "Say, Lee, what are you planning to do with those horses of yours?"

———

By the time Lee finally crawled into his new bed, he'd given the two mares and the mule to Al and Garth. They had insisted that when he came to their ranch, he could take whichever gelding he wanted or even one of their stallions. They suggested that taking one of their young ungelded males would save them some work.

As Lee laid in the bed, tired yet not sleepy, he was almost overwhelmed after meeting Bethan's extended family. After growing up with just him and his father and no other family at all, it was a real adjustment. But as unsettling as it may have been at times, it was also a very warm and pleasant experience. Each one of her relatives had seemed genuinely pleased to meet him. He wasn't sure if it was just because they liked him or if it was because Bethan had appeared to be giving up her desire to wear a badge.

Whatever the reason, he was still more than happy to be on the Double EE and knowing that in less than three weeks, he wouldn't be sleeping alone any longer.

––––––

Two hundred and forty yards away, Bethan was finally under her covers in her original bed. She had spent more than two hours talking to her parents about everything that had happened since she left. Most of their discussion didn't center on the gunfights or the chase, but on her relationship with Lee.

They hadn't asked if it had progressed beyond the kissing stage, which didn't surprise her because they knew her well enough to understand that if it had, it was her business. She was pleased to see that both of her parents not only approved of her decision, they seemed to genuinely like Lee. That wasn't a surprise either because she loved Lee, and her mother and father were so much like her, just as Lee had already noticed.

So, as she awaited sleep to take her, she was far more than just content. She was very happy knowing that before the month of May ended, she would be joining Lee in the small house. That thought began to generate more lust-filled visions and she began to wonder if she'd made a mistake choosing her birthday as their wedding date. Maybe she should have suggested May 15th...or maybe May the 9th.

––––––

After breakfast the next morning, Garth and Alwen made their farewells, then left the Double EE trailing their two new mares and one mule.

Once she finished waving to her departing brothers, Bethan turned and asked, "What did they give you for the horses and the mule?

"They said I could pick out any gelding or stallion that I wanted when I visited their ranch. I think they'd actually prefer that I take one of the stallions."

"Really? You might want to talk to Bryn before we go to the A-G Connected. He'll help you out. You could talk to Roger or Lucas, too."

"We have time for that. What do we do today?"

"My father is going to go to work shortly and then we need to go into Denver so you can buy some more clothes and anything else you need. I can give you a tour of the Double EE this afternoon, if you'd like. We can pick out our quarter section for our house, too."

"I'd forgotten about that, but I'd like to see the rest of the ranch."

Bethan smiled at him, then said, "Let's go back inside and have some more coffee before we go."

He nodded, then took her hand before they entered the back door.

———

An hour later, Dylan was at his desk reading some of the messages, letters and requests from various agencies needing assistance when Pete Towers rapped on the doorjamb then entered his personal office.

Dylan looked up and asked, "What's up, Pete? I thought you'd be on your way to Golden already."

"I'll be heading out in a little bit, but I just heard that Bethan was planning on getting married in just three weeks. Is that right?"

"That's what she told us yesterday."

"Have you met this Lee Collins? I mean, she's only known him for a couple of weeks."

Dylan thought he may as well have his conversation with Pete as he'd already broached the subject.

"I spent a few hours with him yesterday and again this morning. He impressed me as a very thoughtful and confident young man. I have no objections or doubts about Bethan's decision and neither does my wife."

Pete's jaw muscles tightened before he said, "I heard that you might be offering him a job here."

"That's possible. After talking to Bryn, Lynn and Bethan, I was convinced that he had great potential. I haven't asked him yet, but there's a good chance that I will pretty soon. We're really shorthanded right now and we could use some help. I don't want you, Benji, Thom and Jesse to spend all your time in the saddle or on trains. It was getting difficult before Bryn and Lynn got laid up."

Pete didn't say anything, so after a pregnant pause that lasted ten seconds, Dylan asked, "Pete, I know that you were sweet on Bethan and might not understand her well enough to realize that once she's made up her mind, she won't be dissuaded. If I decide to hire Lee, are you going to have a problem with him?"

Pete hesitated for another few seconds, then shook his head and replied, "No, sir. I'll be okay."

"Good. Tell Cal howdy for me when you get to Golden," Dylan said

Pete nodded, then quickly turned and left the office.

Dylan then leaned back in his chair and sighed. He knew that Pete would be anything but okay with having Lee in the office and that was now as big a problem for him as losing Bryn and Lynn. The other problem was that he wasn't sure that Bryn would be returning at all. He knew that Erin had left it up to her husband to decide, but Bryn would still have to weigh her concerns against his preferences. That gunshot to his thigh was another factor in making that critical decision, and Dylan began to believe he'd soon lose his brother's service.

———

Pete rode out of Denver forty minutes later, heading west to Golden to assist Jefferson County Sheriff Cal Burris. After Cal's initial issues after taking the job, he'd added two deputies, but lost one, so he requested help fairly often in his rapidly growing county. Because he used to be a deputy marshal, Dylan tended to give him aid more quickly. This wasn't a big problem; just an issue about a contested border between two ranches. The reason for the request was that one of the ranches crossed county lines, so Cal had asked for a U.S. deputy marshal to avoid jurisdictional problems.

As he rode at a medium trot, he still thought about that town marshal winning over Bethan. He hadn't really even paid much attention to her after she had expressed her lack of interest, but it had irked him. After Bert's recent death, he'd focused on Martha. He'd always liked Martha and it was pretty obvious that she and Bert were having marital problems, and he'd been spending more time with her than was probably proper.

After that deadly shootout that claimed Bert's life, he'd spent even more time with Martha and despite the fence of the mourning period, she'd quietly suggested that she wouldn't mind if he made his visits official. The fact that she had one baby and was already pregnant with Bert's child didn't bother him. She was still younger than he was and very attractive. She had become the centerpiece of his nighttime fantasies and he had already expressed a willingness to become better acquainted with her. *Everything was going so well, so why should he care about Bethan at all? If she wanted to marry this hick town marshal, then, so what?*

Pete was still in a grumpy mood when he arrived in Golden shortly before noon. After a quick lunch he and Cal Burris left the town and rode north to talk to the two ranchers.

———

As Bethan and Lee rode past the last structure on the Double EE heading south, Bethan said, "I was impressed that you didn't complain when I paid for your things."

"Why would I complain? I don't have any money to speak of and I don't have a job yet. I know that I needed some more clothes and you have a large bank account. No misguided sense of pride can change the facts, Bethan."

"That's what makes you so special to me, Lee. You don't have a phony bone in your body. Besides, you have some big rewards coming your way."

"Rewards? For what?" he asked as he looked at her in surprise.

"For taking down the Gentry gang. Didn't you know that they all had impressive rewards on their heads?"

"No. I knew that they were wanted, but I never got any posters. Besides, I only took down one of them. You shot the other two."

"I can't get a reward because I was acting as a temporary U.S. deputy marshal, so my father sent out a notice to those that offered the rewards to send payment to you. He said that they came to just over eleven hundred dollars."

"That's a surprise. I guess I can pay you back after all."

Bethan grinned and said, "I'd rather you pay me back in service, Mister Collins."

"That won't work, Miss Evans. That would make me a man-whore and that would ruin my standing with your family."

Bethan laughed, then said, "We can't have that now, can we?"

"No, ma'am," he replied as they continued riding south.

After another ten minutes they headed west for another twenty minutes and Bethan pulled Nippy to a stop.

She didn't say anything, nor did she need to as Lee sat in the saddle and scanned the landscape. It wasn't ranching or farming ground, but there was more than enough flat space for a house and barn. There was a decent creek that flowed from the foothills then turned northeast, and along the west there was a good-sized forest of pines. It was a rugged, but beautiful terrain that appealed to him.

"This is our place, isn't it?" he asked.

"I thought you'd like it. I used to come out here all the time, but thought I'd never have a home here because I didn't think that I'd ever get married and have my own family. It's a little out of the way compared to the other houses, but it's where we can be happy, Lee."

"Wherever you are is where I'll be happy, Bethan, but this place is special. How do we go about making it ours?"

She twisted in the saddle, pointed to the northeast and said, "We'll need to have a road of sorts carved out of the ground between here and the rest of the ranch. That's not too bad because there aren't any real obstacles. We can have that done soon and it won't take long. After the road is put in, we can have the house and barn built."

"Let's walk for a while," Lee said before he dismounted.

They let Biff and Nippy graze while they explored the site of their future home.

———

The problem between the ranch owners, while not settled, was at least defused when they realized that the U.S. Marshals were watching.

As they rode back toward Golden, Pete asked, "So, Cal, I noticed that you're short a deputy. You find anybody yet?"

Cal grinned and asked, "Are you applying for the job, Pete?"

"Hell, no! I was just wondering because that town marshal that Bethan is thinking of marrying is looking for lawman work and he might be a good hire."

"If he's such a good hire, then why doesn't Dylan hire him? I mean, if he's going to marry Bethan, I would think that he'd be a good choice, especially with you guys being so short. With Bryn and Lynn laid up, that's got you down to just four deputies."

"I think Dylan doesn't want to appear to be playing favorites."

Cal laughed, then said, "You mean like hiring his brother and then his son?"

"It's not the same thing, Cal. He knew both of them really well before he brought them on board. He doesn't know this town marshal at all."

"Then why do you think he's good enough for me to hire on?"

"Come on, Cal. Be honest. How long did it take for you to hire the first two? And now, one just left, so you're desperate. You'd probably hire an Indian if he wanted the job."

"Things are better now that I've got more folks moving into the county. But if he's interested, send him over and I'll talk to him."

"I'll mention it when I meet him."

"I appreciate it, Pete."

Pete nodded and figured that he might just mention to Dylan that it would look bad to the big boss if he hired Lee Collins and then became his son-in-law. Then he'd add that Cal was looking for a deputy, and that might get that town marshal at least out of Denver. He could marry Bethan and then they'd both be far enough away so he wouldn't have to see them together.

He just hoped that he would have his chance to talk to Dylan before he offered Lee Collins a position.

––––––

When Dylan returned that evening, he joined the family for dinner in the dining room because there was more room. He had decided that he wouldn't talk about Pete until he was alone with Gwen that night, so it was a pleasant supper as Bethan talked about her choice for their new home.

Lee talked with Brian and Conway as well as with Cari, who was shorter than Bethan and almost as pretty. It didn't take him long to feel like part of the family. Maybe it was because each of them seemed to have been raised by two exceptional people who ensured that that they didn't wear disguises to mask their true character. It helped that those characters were well founded.

He and Bethan spend some time alone after dinner when they rocked on the front porch. The weather was warming nicely, so could avoid heavy jackets, but Bethan still wore her shawl, even though she was wearing her britches and heavy flannel shirt.

When it was time to turn in, Bethan escorted Lee to the small house and once inside, she tossed the shawl aside then attacked.

As she pushed him back toward the couch, Lee almost lost his footing when his heel hit the rug as she kissed him and still maneuvered him across the floor.

Finally, the kiss ended before she shoved him onto the couch then sat on his lap with her arms around his neck.

Lee stared wide-eyed at her grinning face and sharply asked, "Are you trying to get your father to shoot me already?"

"He won't, but you might have to worry about my mother."

"Have you no shame, woman?"

"I'm not sure if I do or not because I've never wanted to do anything like this before. I have to admit that I've been thinking of little else for a few days now, at least when I'm alone."

"We can't go any further, Bethan."

"I know. But tell me that you don't want me as much as I want you."

"You're sitting on my lap. You should already have your answer and I'm sure that you've known it for some time now."

Bethan kissed him again before replying, "I was pretty sure that you did, but you hid it well."

Lee smiled, then gently slid his fingertips across her cheek as he said, "I love you, Bethan. I wasn't sure if I should tell you after just a few days, but I've known it for some time, too."

"I love you, too, Lee. But I think that I'll give you one more kiss before I scamper back to the big house. I don't want my sister asking too many questions."

"I'm still worried about your father asking those questions."

Bethan kissed him once more, then slid from his lap, smiled and said, "Don't try to stand, Lee. I don't want to cause you any more pain."

"That's very thoughtful, Miss Evans."

Bethan laughed, then quickly exited the house before her wall of restraint collapsed under the massive pummeling from her growing desire.

After the door closed, Lee remained sitting on the couch for more than ten minutes before slowly rising and heading into his bedroom.

———

An hour later, Gwen lay snuggled in close to her husband when he finally asked, "Gwen, I need your opinion about a problem in the office."

"That's why I'm here, Dylan."

"No, sweetheart, that's about the ninth reason on the list for your presence, but I need it now."

Gwen smiled as she asked, "So, what is the trouble?"

"There isn't one yet, but I have a real dilemma on my hands about Lee."

"Lee? I thought you really liked him, and so do I. What's the problem with him?"

"I do like him. I think he's an exceptional young man, and even if he wasn't going to marry Bethan, I would have hired him in a heartbeat. But marrying Bethan is the heart of the issue."

"How can that be a problem?"

"It's Pete Towers that's the problem, not Lee. You know how everyone, including me, thinks that he's sweet on Martha?"

"I think it was that way before Bert died. I don't believe that he did anything about it, but we all knew that he was fond of her."

"Well, that was only after Bethan turned him down. She didn't think much of it, but I believe that he did. Anyway, this morning, before he left for Golden, he came in and asked if Bethan was marrying Lee. After I told him that she was, he then asked if the second rumor that I was thinking of hiring Lee was true. When I said that I was thinking about it because we were so low on manpower, I could see his jaws tighten.

"Then, I asked him if he had a problem if I hired Lee, and there was a significant pause before he said that he didn't. It wasn't hard to see that he wasn't happy with the prospect and that's my problem."

There was a delay of a few seconds before Gwen said, "Then let me ask you this. Just going by how Lynn, Bryn and Bethan described Lee's performance over the past two weeks, how does it compare to Pete's? I know that's a bit difficult, but you've worked with him for years now."

"There really isn't any comparison, Gwen. Pete's a good lawman, but about average. I see enormous potential in Lee, and I know that he'd be an invaluable asset to the office."

"Then why not hire him and then if Pete starts misbehaving, fire him."

"I wish it was that simple, sweetheart. There are two problems with that solution. First, we're not in the ranching business. We're in the business of enforcing the laws of the

United States. I can't have one deputy harboring a strong dislike for another. What if I send them both out on a job and Pete decides not to back up Lee at a critical moment? I don't want to add more risk to an already risky business."

"What's the second reason?"

"Benji. If Pete begins visiting Martha, which might be as early as June, then that will put Benji in an awkward position. Who would he support if there was a giant rift in the office? What I'm looking at is a serious problem with my deputies if I hire Lee, and with my lack of functioning deputies, I can't afford it."

Gwen sighed, then said, "You might lose Bryn permanently too, you know."

"I know. He's right on the edge right now and I wouldn't blame him if he decided to stick to the horse ranching business."

"Why don't you explain it to Lee and ask him what he thinks?"

"I'll do that, but not for another couple of days to let me get a better read on the situation. Pete might just be in a foul mood because he was stunned by the news. He may mellow once he gets used to the idea."

"What if you can't hire Lee? What would he do if that happens? I don't think that he'd be satisfied going back into the hardware business after he gets the reward money."

"I don't think so, either. Let's just hold on for a few days and then, hopefully, things will work out."

"So, after all this talk about asking my opinion, all you did was procrastinate."

"No, Mrs. Evans, all I did was defer my decision until I had more facts. And, I might add, I did appreciate your input. I just hope that Pete comes around."

"Maybe Martha will make him forget his pride. He never had a chance with Bethan anyway."

"I thought he might quit after Bethan mentioned that she'd turned him away. Maybe he'll turn in his badge now, but that would be another problem."

"Just get some sleep, husband. You may need it over the next two weeks until you walk your daughter down the aisle."

Dylan kissed Gwen on her brow, then pulled her closer. Sleep would be difficult, but she was right. It would be a tense couple of weeks that might last beyond that.

CHAPTER 11

Friday morning, Dylan rode into Denver, still unused to riding by himself. He'd been going to the office with Bryn and then Lynn for a long time, and even when one or the other was on a mission, it was rare for him to go to work by himself. Now it would be routine, at least until Lynn returned to the job. He was reasonably sure that Bryn would never ride with him each day, but his brother hadn't said anything about it yet.

After he'd put Raven away in the marshal's private barn in the back alley, he entered the office and found Pete Towers already there, which was highly unusual. If anything, Pete tended to be the last one to arrive.

"Morning, Pete," he said as he removed his hat, "How did it go with Cal?"

"It wasn't a big problem. We just talked to the two ranchers and they got the message. Could I talk to you for a minute, boss?"

"Sure," Dylan replied, "What do you want to talk about?"

"Yesterday, when we were riding out to the ranch, I told Cal about everything that happened down south and when I mentioned that Bethan was marrying Lee Collins and that you might be hiring him, he said something that I didn't think about."

Dylan took a seat near the front desk and wasn't surprised at all when Pete had broached the subject, just that he was claiming that it was Cal who brought it up.

"What did Cal say?"

"He asked me if it might raise some attention back in Washington City about hiring a man who then marries your daughter."

"They didn't mind when I hired my brother and then my son, Pete. I don't think they'd care a bit and besides, he's not an Evans."

"That's what I told Cal, but he figured that even if they didn't care, other folks in Denver might not see it that way. Of course, he might have been hoping that he gets a chance to hire Collins. He's down to one deputy again."

"I heard that. I haven't even mentioned offering Lee the job yet, so I'll add Cal's concerns to my decision."

Cal nodded, then said, "I'll go ahead and write my report now."

Dylan stood before saying, "Thanks, Pete," then strode down the long hallway to his office.

Once he sat behind his desk, he knew that the problem with Pete wasn't going to go away. He was sure that Cal hadn't even though about nepotism, but Pete obviously didn't want Lee in the office.

He'd talk to Lee when he returned that evening, then after that conversation, he might have to have a much more intense talk with Bethan.

As the other three deputies drifted in, he heard them chatting about Bethan and Lee and it put him into a grumpy mood before he left his office to issue the day's assignments.

———

Shortly after Dylan had ridden out of the Double EE, Bethan and Lee walked to Bryn's house.

After his only daughter, ten-year-old Grace had opened the door, she walked with her cousin and Lee into the parlor where Bryn sat in his easy chair as Erin entered from the hallway.

"What brings you here this fine morning?" he asked with a big smile, "I figured you two would be off in some dark place where us old folks couldn't find you."

Bethan and Lee sat on the couch while Erin took the chair closest to her wounded husband.

"Yesterday afternoon, we rode south on the ranch to pick out the section where we would build our home and we found it. We just wanted to let you know which one."

"I can guess which one you chose. It's not attached to any of the occupied sections. Is it?"

"No. It's south of Lynn and Addie, but there's another quarter section in between."

"I figured that would be your choice, Bethan. It's pretty, but not very practical. A small herd couldn't live on that grass for more than a month."

"I know, Bryn. We aren't going to raise horses anyway. We already have you, Al and Garth doing that."

Bryn grinned, then said, "I'll tell you what, Bethan. I'll have that quarter section put in your names when you're married, then I'll add the quarter section that connects it to Lynn's place."

Bethan glanced at Lee before saying, "That's not necessary, Bryn. You are being very generous to each of us by giving us a quarter section. It wouldn't be fair to the others if you gave us two."

"I'm not giving you two quarter sections, Bethan. I'm giving one to you and one to Lee, and I don't want to hear any arguments about it. He earned it. There's more grass on the other section, so if you do want to have a few more horses, I'm sure that they'd appreciate it."

"Then all I can say is thank you, Uncle Bryn."

"Oh, so now I'm back to being Uncle Bryn again, am I?"

Bethan laughed, then as she took Lee's hand, she said, "I still sometimes have a hard time just calling you by your Christian name, I guess."

"That's alright. Are you going to ride out there again? You might think of moving the location of your house now that you have a mile by a half a mile to work with."

"We were going to head there anyway. We have a lot to do over the next two weeks."

"I'm sure you do. It's a lot more than I'll be doing, that's for sure."

Bethan then asked, "Are you going to go back to work after you're able to walk without pain?"

Erin looked at Bryn as he replied, "I haven't decided yet, but I have some time to make up my mind."

Erin then turned to Bethan and said, "I'll help him to make the right decision."

"I'm sure you will, Aunt Erin," Bethan replied, then stood, taking Lee with her.

Bryn looked up at Lee then said, "It was nice talking to you, Lee."

Lee laughed before replying, "I do tend to dominate conversations."

Bryn and Erin both laughed, but Bethan only smiled as she guided Lee across the parlor and then out of the house.

Once outside, she hugged Lee and exclaimed, "Two sections! Can you believe it? I was more than happy to have the one, but the other one is almost as pretty."

Lee smiled at her, then said, "Let's go and see if Bryn was right about moving the location for the house."

Bethan released him from her tight grip, then they quickly trotted from the porch and headed to the barn to saddle their horses.

————

Two hours later, as they strolled on their second section of land, Bethan said, "I can't believe how much my life has changed in just a couple of weeks. Exactly two weeks ago I rode out of Canon City trailing George Lynch just to prove that I could do anything a man could do. Then I found you all tied up in your cell and since that moment, my view of the world and what I intended to do with my life has been shifting."

"You never really had to prove yourself to anyone, Bethan. After getting to know your family, I could see that each one of them respected you as a strong, independent person. For many women, that would mean an argumentative, difficult person. Probably because of they were just as frustrated as you were. Even then, I don't imagine that you ever reached that stage because of your parents and the rest of your family.

"You may be assertive, but you're still compassionate and thoughtful. It helps that you're also brilliant and have a wicked sense of humor. They'll keep me on my toes for the rest of my life and they're what attracted me right from the start."

Bethan smiled and asked, "It wasn't my obstacles or the smoother hills on my backside?"

"No, ma'am," Lee replied with his own smile, "I didn't even see them for some time, if you recall. In a way, I'm glad that I didn't. I think it helped me get to know you better."

"There is that. So, where do we put our house now?"

"Let's keep searching. I can see Lynn's house from here, so maybe we're too close."

Bethan laughed, then pulled Lee closer.

———

That night, after they were alone, Dylan told Gwen about the meeting with Pete.

"He's not going to mellow at all. Is he?"

"I don't think so. I'll talk to Lee tomorrow when I get back to see what he thinks. Maybe it would be better if he took the job in Golden."

"You're not going to give in to Pete's blackmail, are you?" Gwen askes sharply.

"I may not have a choice, Gwen. I'll just have to hear what Lee thinks."

"Don't expect me to explain it to our daughter, husband. That will be your job."

"I know, and hopefully, it won't be as bad as I expect. Do you think I should talk to them together?"

"I think it would be better to talk to Lee first. If Bethan is in the room, then she'd exert her considerable influence."

"Just as you have often done, my dear wife."

"And it was always necessary, my manly husband."

Dylan smiled, but wasn't happy knowing that this was a no-win situation and he was now worried that no matter what he did, there would be severe ramifications.

———

Saturday was usually less busy for the U.S. Marshal's office as they didn't have to deal with the rowdy, drunken cowhands and miners that kept the men assigned to the Denver City Marshal's office on their toes.

After all their paperwork was done, Dylan closed the office just before noon and headed back for the Double EE to have his dreaded conversations. Pete hadn't mentioned Bethan, Lee or Cal Burris that morning, mainly because Dylan didn't give him the opportunity. He'd spent most of the morning in his office with the door closed, so he could only be bothered if it was something important.

After unsaddling Raven and releasing him into the corral with Lee's horses, he walked to the small house and knocked on the door. He was relieved when the door remained closed even after a second round of louder knocks, then turned and headed for the big house.

When he entered, he asked Cari, "Have you seen Lee or Bethan?"

Cari grinned as she replied, "You mean Leethan? It seems as if they're bound at the hip, Dad. Brian came up with that one."

"Very cute, but do you know where they are?"

"They're visiting Lynn and Addie."

Dylan nodded, then hung his hat and left the kitchen to find Gwen. He didn't have anything more to add to the situation but wanted to talk to her again to reinforce his decision. He couldn't hire Lee and would ask him if he'd consider working with Cal Burris. Golden wasn't a long ride from Denver, and with Bethan's bank account and his rewards that were already arriving, they could buy a nice house. It wasn't a palatable solution, but it was the best he could manage. His biggest concern was Bethan's reaction.

———

"That's wonderful!" Addie exclaimed after Bethan had told her and Lynn about their adjoining quarter sections.

She had just put two-month-old Nathan into his cradle and their other toddlers were napping as well.

Lynn asked, "Have you found the site for your house and barn?"

"We have and it's just far enough away so we won't be annoying."

Erin then asked, "Lee, has Dylan mentioned anything about filling one of the vacancies?"

"He doesn't know me well enough, Erin. As far as he knows, I could still be married with four children after escaping from the state prison."

Bethan smacked him on the arm before saying, "I don't care if you escaped from prison, mister, but you'd better not have some other woman stashed somewhere."

Lee laughed as he rubbed his left bicep, then replied, "I'm just saying that there's no reason for Dylan to even think about it yet. We're going to be pretty busy for the next two weeks anyway."

"He'd be making a big mistake not to hire you," Lynn said, "When I was on the ground next to my horse, I knew we were in a really bad spot. I was stunned when you rode right at them, but it turned out to be the right decision. Even if Bethan hadn't told me the other stories, I would have recommended you for the job. Marrying Bethan would have no bearing on it, either."

"Thanks, Lynn. I appreciate your confidence."

Bethan said, "We're going to head back now. I just wanted to stop by to give you the good news that we're going to be your neighbors. If you consider a half a mile away to be neighbors."

She then stood and after Lee took her arm, they made their farewells and left the house.

After mounting, Bethan asked, "Did you want me to ask my father about it?"

"Absolutely not. This isn't a personal or family decision, it's strictly business. Dylan will do what's right for the office and I really don't want to make it seem to be anything less."

Bethan nodded, then said, "I'm proud of you, Lee. Let's go back."

Lee smiled at her before they wheeled their horses away from the house and headed northeast.

———

Dylan had been pacing in the kitchen because it had the best view of the small house, and every time he reached that end of the room, he'd glance out the window.

Gwen was sitting at the table with a cup of tea and had been watching him for almost thirty minutes and had tried to convince him to just sit down and relax, but she'd given up after fifteen minutes.

Dylan kept his eyes focused outside after he spotted them and said, "Well, they're back. I'll need to get out there, so they don't disappear again."

"You can wait until tomorrow, Dylan."

"I'd just as soon get this over with."

"So, would I."

Dylan took a deep breath, blew it out, then snatched his hat, pulled it on before he opened the door and walked onto the back porch.

Bethan was the first to spot him and as soon as she did, she waved.

Dylan waved back, then stepped off the porch and walked about fifty feet before stopping.

Bethan turned to Lee and said, "I think he wants to talk to us."

"He doesn't have a shotgun, does he?"

Bethan laughed as she replied, "No, but he's still armed and dangerous."

They were still in a cheerful mood as they approached Dylan and their optimistic happiness didn't allow them to notice his serious demeanor.

That changed when they dismounted, and Dylan managed a weak smile before he said, "Bethan, can you see your mother? I need to talk to Lee."

Bethan quickly glanced at Lee, before looking back at her father and replying, "Alright. Do you want to unsaddle Nippy for me?"

"I'd be happy to," he said as he accepted her mare's reins.

Normally, Bethan would have kissed Lee before leaving, but her father's serious face concerned her, so she just took one last look at Lee before heading for the house.

After she'd gone, Dylan said, "Let's get these horses unsaddled. We can talk on the way."

"Alright," Lee replied as they headed for the barn.

He could sense Dylan's tension as well, and whatever it was, he hoped it didn't have any impact on his and Bethan's plans.

"Lee," Dylan began, "I can't tell you how impressed I am with everything that you've done and your character. I know that Bethan made the right choice when she decided to marry you. I'm sure that you'll make her happy."

"She makes me happy, too."

"I can see that. It's an amazing turnaround from how she was before she left. Anyway, this isn't about Bethan, at least not directly. Did she tell you about Pete Towers, one of my deputies?"

"She told me that he'd asked to visit her, and she'd turned him away."

"That's right. He's already moved on, but for some reason, he seems to resent the fact that she's chosen you. He's already mentioned it more than once and even asked if I was going to ask you to become a deputy marshal. When I told him that I was thinking about it, I could tell that he wasn't happy and then when I asked him if it was going to be a problem working with you, he told me that it wouldn't, but he wasn't being truthful."

They reached the barn doors and went inside as Lee said, "That would be a problem for you if you had two deputies who were really at odds. Wouldn't it?"

"It's even more than that. Pete is probably going to pursue Bert Hoskins' widow, Martha. She is the daughter of one of my oldest deputies, Benji Green. You can imagine the chaos that it could create in the office if Pete complains to Benji."

"I can see that. I don't want to cause any kind of disruption among your deputies."

"I'm glad that you understand my dilemma, Lee. If you still want to be a lawman, Jefferson County Sheriff Cal Burris over in nearby Golden really needs a deputy."

"I appreciate the offer and taking the time to explain the situation," Lee said as he slid the saddle from Biff.

"I'm really sorry about this, Lee. I don't like it at all and if I had my druthers, I'd hire you and let Pete go. You're already a better lawman than he is, but it's not that simple."

"I really do understand, Dylan. Did you want me to tell Bethan?"

"No, I'll talk to her in a minute. I deserve to absorb her wrath as penance."

Lee removed Biff's bridle, then turned and smiled at Dylan.

"Can you send her to the small house when you've finished talking with her?"

"I don't think I'll have to send her. She'll fly out the door with wings on her feet and probably horns coming out of her head."

Lee nodded then began to brush Biff's coat.

Dylan didn't brush Nippy but set her into a stall and headed out of the barn.

As he slid the brush over his pinto, Lee wondered what he would do now that he no longer had a future in Denver. He wasn't sure about going to Golden because he was unfamiliar with the sheriff. It may be a relatively short ride from Denver, but it was still too far for them to build a house on their chosen site.

He began to think that maybe he should go back to Bent County and work for Sheriff Allen. He liked the man and knew that he was probably even more shorthanded than the sheriff in Golden.

————

Bethan sat in her chair fuming as her father continued to explain his reasons for not hiring Lee. If it had been because Lee wasn't qualified, she couldn't have cared less, but this was just pettiness.

When Dylan finished, Bethan asked, "Can I talk to Pete? I'll straighten him out."

"No, you may not. That will only make things worse. He'll deny that he was trying to keep Lee out of the office, but after you leave, he'll be angrier and more of a problem for me even after hearing that Lee wasn't coming on board."

"So, Lee's going to have to go to Golden just to keep Pete from whining every day. Is that right?"

Dylan wanted to deny the somewhat insulting way she framed it, but simply nodded and said, "Pretty much."

Bethan looked at her mother and snapped, "Men! I'm going to go and talk to Lee!"

She then popped to her feet and marched from the parlor and exited through the front door, leaving it open.

Gwen then looked at her crestfallen husband and asked, "After all you've done in your life, why do I think that this was the most difficult?"

"Because it was. I'd rather be facing a gang of outlaws who were intent on shooting it out rather than hurt Bethan. Lee took the news well, but I know that he was more than just disappointed. He may have understood why I had to do it, but that doesn't mean I was happy about it."

Gwen stood, walked to her husband, then sat on his lap before kissing him gently.

"It'll work out, my love."

"I hope so, because it looks downright gloomy right now."

————

Lee was sitting on the couch in the front room, examining Bethan's Webley Bulldog as he waited for her to make her dramatic entrance.

The five .44 cartridges were on the side table as he dryfired the pistol to get used to the double action when the door flew open and Bethan strode across the room.

He tried to smile but her fierce visage made it impossible.

"I can't believe it!" she exclaimed as she practically threw herself onto the couch beside him.

"He didn't have a choice, Bethan. He has to keep his office running as smoothly as possible. He can't fire a deputy just because he's unhappy and it's much easier not to hire someone when you don't have to."

"He's already short two deputies and that was before he lost Lynn for a month and may lose Bryn altogether. He needs you, Lee, almost as much as I do."

"Let's just deal with his decision rather than get mad about it. Okay?"

Bethan sighed, then said, "Alright. What are we going to do now? Maybe you could hire on at the sheriff's office or with the city marshal. That way, we could still build our house on the Double EE."

"I'd still have to deal with Pete Towers if I was a lawman in Denver, Bethan. You know that."

"You aren't thinking of taking that job in Golden, are you?"

"No. Golden may be close, but we couldn't live here if I took that job."

"That's good. Are you just going to do something else other than working as a lawman?"

"I was leaning toward accepting Sheriff Allen's offer."

Bethan's mouth dropped open before she exclaimed, "*Why would you go to Las Animas?* That's two hundred miles away and much worse than Golden!"

"I said that I was just leaning that way. I haven't made up my mind yet because I wanted to talk to you first."

Bethan was speechless as she stared at Lee. Her entire new world was crashing down around her simply because of Pete Towers' injured pride. She doubted that he even cared about her at all. It was nothing more than his petty jealousy that was ruining everything.

Lee looked into her troubled brown eyes and said softly, "We have some time to think about it, Bethan."

Bethan blinked then asked, "But what about the house? What about the wedding?"

"What do you mean? We can get married and then move to Las Animas or Golden or anywhere else."

Bethan's mind was still reeling with a jumble of conflicting thoughts and emotions and found that for the first time in her life, she couldn't think straight.

"This isn't right," she finally said quietly.

"I know that it's not right, but it's what we need to face and handle. It's not a horrible problem, Bethan. Most people have much worse issues than this."

"I know that, but this is our issue and there's no reason for it."

Lee took her hands and said, "Things will work out, Bethan. We didn't go through all that just to have this ruin everything."

"That bastard!" she snapped under her breath.

"Did you want to talk some more?"

"No. I'm going to go for a ride to work off my frustrations."

"You're not going to go to Denver and talk to Pete Towers, are you?"

"No. My father laid down the law about that."

"Alright. Do you want me to come along?"

"I need to be alone," she said before standing then striding rapidly to the door and leaving the house.

Lee stared at the closed door and wondered if he should go and talk to Pete Towers. He picked up the Webley, loaded the cartridges and then slid it back into the shoulder holster. Rather than leaving the house, he walked to the kitchen to make some coffee. On that short walk, he decided that finding Pete Towers would be a bad idea and would probably only make things worse.

———

Bethan quickly saddled Nippy and soon rode out of the barn and down the Double EE access road before she turned north toward Denver.

———

Dylan and Gwen were still talking when Brian entered the parlor biting into an apple.

As his parents looked at him, he asked, "Where is Bethan going without Lee? She's not Leethan anymore."

Dylan asked, "Which way did she go?"

"She turned left after she reached the road, so she's probably going to Denver."

Gwen quickly asked, "You don't think she's going to talk to Pete, do you?"

"She may be obstinate, but I don't believe she'd break her word."

"Then why did she go to Denver without Lee?"

"I don't know, but we're going to have to trust her."

"She was pretty angry, Dylan."

"I know she was, but she's still got a good head on her shoulders and we have to believe that she's going to use it."

Gwen nodded then said, "Maybe you should go talk to Lee again and find out what he told her."

"That's a good idea," Dylan replied before standing, then patted Brian's head before stepping across the room and leaving the house.

———

As her father was on his way to talk to Lee, Bethan had Nippy at a fast trot riding to Denver. She had calmed down somewhat but wasn't sure that she was going to get anywhere with her plan. When she left Lee, it had been the obvious path to clear this obstacle, but after giving it more thought, she wasn't so sure.

She had reasoned that if she talked to Martha about the situation, she could influence Pete to back down. The problem was that it would require Martha to admit that Pete mattered to her, and even if she did and was able to convince Pete to get along with Lee, the undercurrent would still be there. Sooner or later, it would resurface, and it might be at a very inopportune time.

Bethan reached the outskirts of Denver and pulled Nippy to a stop. She thought that maybe she could see Kyle and ask if there was anything that he could recommend that would keep Lee in Denver without causing a problem, but decided that, in the end, it was a joint decision for her and Lee to make.

She turned Nippy around and headed back to the Double EE at a slow trot, frustrated in her inability to resolve the issue.

———

"She headed for Denver, Lee," Dylan said after Lee had repeated their conversation.

"I thought so. She said she wasn't going to talk to Pete Towers, so I don't know where she would go when she got there."

"She might have gone to talk to Katie, or maybe even Kyle, but I don't think they can help."

"I know. Maybe I should have just told her I'd think about taking that job in Golden. At least she wouldn't have been quite as upset."

"I don't think it would have mattered much. I'm pretty sure she's as mad at me as she is at Pete."

"How can I make this better?"

"I'm not sure that you can, Lee."

"Do you think I'm in danger of losing her?"

"No, I don't. I believe Bethan will go with you wherever you decide to go. I just wish that it wasn't so far away. I agree with you that taking a deputy sheriff or deputy city marshal job would still be a problem."

Lee nodded, then said, "We have a few days to let things calm down. Maybe next week, I'll take a ride to Golden and see Sheriff Burris."

Dylan stood, then rested his hand on Lee's shoulder as he said, "You're a good man, Lee. If Pete was more like you, then there would be no issue at all."

"Thanks, Dylan."

Dylan tapped his shoulder once, then turned and left the house.

————

An hour later, Pete Towers entered the Green home to join the family for dinner. Martha had moved back to her family home, and he had been a regular visitor for the past week.

After he closed the door, Benji said, "Let's go to my office and talk, Pete."

"Sure," Pete replied, then followed Benji out of the foyer and turned into his office.

Benji closed the door then walked behind his desk and sat down while Pete moved the straight-backed chair to the front of the desk and took a seat.

Benji glared at him and asked, "Okay, Pete, what's going on?"

Pete swallowed hard, believing that he was objecting to the attention he had been paying to his recently widowed daughter.

"What do you mean?"

"As long as I've known Dylan, I've never seen him stay alone in his office with the door closed for more than a few minutes. He was in there most of the day and when he was in the office, I could feel the chill between you two. What's the problem?"

Pete almost sighed in relief before replying, "I don't have a clue, Benji."

"That's a bunch of horse manure, Pete. What did you talk to him about that caused this? I have never seen him this way, even when Bethan was down in Bent County fighting off those killers. Is it something to do with Bethan or Lee Collins? Be honest with me."

"All I did was to ask him if Bethan was going to marry Collins."

"Is that all?"

"Well, I asked him if he was going to hire him, too."

Benji studied Pete and knew there was more to it, so he asked, "What did Dylan say?"

"He said that Bethan was getting married on the 25th and after he said he was considering hiring Collins, he asked me if I would have a problem working with him."

"Why would he ask you that?"

"I don't know. I told him that I wouldn't, then he said okay and I left. That's all that happened, Benji."

"Do you have a problem working with him if the boss decides to swear him in?"

"Not at all. If he's as good as everybody says he is, then I'm okay with it."

Benji suspected that there was a lot more to it, but nodded and said, "Let's go have supper."

———

Bethan turned onto the Double EE and headed for the barn, but kept her eyes focused on the small house. She may have wanted to be alone when she left, but she desperately wanted to see Lee now.

She abandoned going to the barn and turned to the small house, then pulled up in front and dismounted.

As she stepped onto the porch, the door swung open and Lee stepped outside with a warm smile.

"Welcome back, Bethan. Did you have a good ride?"

"Can we go inside?"

He took her hand, led her inside, then closed the door.

They walked to the couch and slowly sat leaving no gap between them.

Lee put his arm around her shoulders and as she laid her head on his right shoulder, he asked, "Are you all right now?"

"I'm better. I'm still unhappy, but if you decide to go to Las Animas, then I'll go with you. I love you, Lee, and you're my life now."

"It's not written in stone, Bethan, but I told your father that I'd head out to Golden next week and talk to Sheriff Burris. At least you'd only be a few hours away from your family."

"I'm not going to lie to you and tell you that it doesn't matter because it does. I still wish we didn't have to leave just after finding the perfect spot for our new home."

"Neither do I, but we'll find someplace that we can turn into our home and raise our family."

Bethan smiled, then kissed him and said, "I can't wait for our wedding night when we can start making our family."

"We can start early, if you'd like."

She laughed and replied, "Oh, that wouldn't be noticed by anyone when I go back to the big house. I'll bet that even Conway could tell that we've had a grand time over here."

"Not if you don't go back at all."

"You evil, ravenous man! I'm shocked!"

"Shocked, but not appalled."

She laughed again, then said, "I'll never be appalled when you make those suggestions."

"Let's go to the big house and talk to your parents so they don't worry so much."

"We've got to take care of Nippy first."

"Are you trying to trap me alone in the barn, lusty lady?"

Bethan laughed, then wrapped her arms around Lee's neck and kissed him as if it was the last that they would ever share.

When they parted, Lee let out a long breath, then said, "We'd better leave before Conway gets suspicious."

As they stood, Lee looked at Bethan and was enormously relieved that she was happy again. The question of which badge he would wear was now irrelevant. All that mattered was that Bethan was back to being Bethan.

———

That night during the family dinner, no mention was made of Pete Towers or even Bethan's ride to Denver. Her buoyant mood kept everyone from even think of raising the topic.

After the sun had set, Lee and Bethan were on the big front porch using two of the six rocking chairs when Dylan and Gwen stepped onto the porch.

"May we join you?" Dylan asked.

"It's your house, Dad," Bethan replied.

"We just don't want to interrupt anything," said her mother.

Bethan laughed, then when Lee said, "We can always go to the small house and give you your privacy," she laughed harder.

After he and Gwen sat down, Dylan said, "We're glad to see you in a good mood, Bethan."

"We decided that it really isn't important where we are as long as we're together. Lee is going to see Sheriff Burris next week."

"Make it no earlier than Wednesday, Lee."

Lee didn't ask why the delay was necessary, but simply replied, "Alright."

"Are you going to get married in the church or in the courthouse?" Gwen asked.

"We think that getting married by Reverend Hughes would be nice."

"We can talk to him tomorrow after services to start the process. They like a little bit of warning."

"That's a good idea."

"That's settled. Now we need to do some serious planning, but we do have a lot of help."

"Yes, we do. I think that Addie's going to be a bit tied up, though."

"Enjoy your freedom while you can, young lady."

Bethan smiled at her mother, then said, "This from a woman who constantly espoused the joy of motherhood."

Gwen laughed, then shrugged and said, "Hoisted on my own petard."

After some more wedding conversation, Dylan and Gwen thoughtfully returned to the house leaving Lee and Bethan alone.

Lee asked, "Why did he ask me to hold off going to Golden until after Wednesday?"

"I honestly don't know. He seemed pretty set in his decision about Pete Towers. Maybe my mother suggested he rethink his position."

"I don't think so. While you were riding into Denver, he stopped by and said that it was the right thing to do. Maybe he wants to talk to Sheriff Burris before I go there."

"Maybe that's it. I suppose I'm going to have to let you leave now."

"Alas! I must make the dangerous journey across the deadly plains to find refuge in my sanctuary, at least until I see you in tomorrow morning."

"Don't forget to shave. Your beard almost scratched my cheek off a little while ago."

"Sorry. I forgot this morning."

Bethan stood, kissed him, then said, "Good night, Lee. And thank you for being so patient with me."

As Lee rose, he replied, "I'd do anything for you, Bethan."

She smiled, then turned and went into the house.

Lee watched her leave, then let out a long breath before leaving the porch to head for his sanctuary.

––––––

Sunday's church services at the Second Presbyterian Church had ended and Lee had the privilege of seeing Bethan in a dress for the second time.

After the service, Lee was introduced to Reverend Hughes at the church entrance, then he and Bethan walked with him to the minister's house to make their arrangements.

As the rest of the Evans family returned to their horses and buggies to make the return trip to the Double EE, Gwen nudged Dylan in the arm and pointed down the road.

She said, "I think one of your deputies wants to talk to you."

Dylan turned his head and spotted Benji Green waving to him.

"You go ahead, Gwen. I'll ride back."

"I hope it's not bad news," she replied before joining Erin and Bryn as they walked to their buggy.

Dylan stepped quickly toward Benji, who had stopped before the nearby schoolhouse. It was a sign of the rapid growth of the city that it was already the sixth primary school to be built and there were two high schools that were almost filled as well.

He was glad to see Benji because he'd already made up his mind about hiring Lee and had wanted to talk to his senior deputy first thing tomorrow to ask what he thought of the issue before reading the riot act to Pete. Now he could avoid that meeting and go right for the serious interrogation and setting down his law. *What was the advantage of being the boss if he couldn't do what he thought was right?*

When he reached Benji, he stopped and asked, "What's wrong?"

Benji replied, "It's nothing to get all flustered about, but this has been nagging at me since suppertime and I wanted to talk to you about it before you got into the office tomorrow."

Dylan asked, "Is it about Lee Collins?"

"Kinda. It's more about Pete than Lee."

Dylan was surprised that it had become an issue so quickly as he asked, "What's wrong with Pete?"

"Yesterday, I noticed that you stayed in your office most of the day, which I've never seen you do before. And when you did come out to talk to us, you and Pete seemed to at odds."

"We had a talk that seemed to annoy him, and I didn't want to rekindle it."

"I reckoned it was something like that, so I asked him why you two were acting like strangers."

"And?"

Benji's seasoned lawman mind repeated the conversation almost verbatim, and when he finished, he looked at his boss.

"That's what he said, but it didn't strike me as being all that honest. Was it?"

"It was probably how he remembered it, but he left out a few things. I first became aware of his unhappiness with Bethan's marriage before I even met Lee when he made a comment about Lee making a mistake for marrying Bethan because he didn't know the 'real' Bethan.

"He brushed that off as a joke, but then, just before he left to go to Golden, he came in to talk to me and asked if I was going to hire Lee and I told him I was just leaning that way and I could tell he wasn't happy about it. So, I asked him if he would be able to work with Lee and he said that he could, but if you had seen his face, you'd know that he wasn't being honest in his answer.

"The next morning, after he returned from Golden, he was in the office before I got there, which we both know is rare. He asked me about hiring Lee again and then suggested that if I did, it might look bad because he'd be my son-in-law. He didn't even take credit for the notion, but said it came from Cal Burris. Then he mentioned that Lee could go to Golden and work with Cal."

"I figured it was something like that. Pete was a bit put off when Bethan turned him down last year. You're not going to give in to him, are you?"

"After talking to Pete, I realized that I had a dilemma on my hands. I couldn't have any personal issues causing a disruption among the deputies, Benji. How could I send Pete and Lee out on a job when I'd be concerned that Pete wouldn't back him up in a critical situation? But to be honest, the other concern I had involved you."

"Me?" Benji asked with raised eyebrows.

"I'm sure you know that Pete has his sights set on Martha."

"I think it's been that way since Bethan turned him down. I don't know if you were aware of it, but Bert and Martha were having some problems with their marriage and I'm not sure if Pete wasn't one of them. He's been coming by more often, and even Alice reckons it won't be much longer before he asks her to marry him. Why would that be a problem?"

"That isn't it. I was concerned that if I hired Lee, it would put you in a bind if Pete expressed his dislike to Martha and then she and Alice put pressure on you to side with him. I can live with one disgruntled deputy, but I can't abide having two when we're already down to just four that can still go out in the field. Besides, I've known you for far too long to make your home

451

life uncomfortable. I was going to talk to you about it tomorrow morning."

Benji snickered, shook his head and replied, "Dylan, for somebody who's spent more time with me over the years than anyone but Alice, you should know better. I can handle anything at home, and I can't imagine my Alice ever siding with Pete even if Martha began weeping and begging. You do what you think is right and if Pete can't handle it, then it's his problem."

Dylan grinned, then said, "I'm glad you think that way, Benji, and I was hoping that you did. After I talked to you first thing tomorrow, I was planning on having a come-to-Jesus meeting with Pete right afterwards. I had already decided to hire Lee and not because he was marrying Bethan. Well, that's not quite right, either. She's marrying him for the same reason that I want to hire him.

"He's an exceptional young man, Benji. Ever since she met him, he's shown to be a confident, intelligent and courageous man who hasn't even reached his full potential. He's already well beyond Pete's abilities and after a few months, he'll probably be right there with yours, Lynn's and Bryn's."

Benji nodded, then said, "I'm glad to hear you stopped acting like an old spinster, Dylan. I've been hearing whispers that Bryn might hang it up. Is that right?"

"I've heard them as well, but he hasn't said anything."

"Do you want me to talk to Pete? He's already at my house."

"Just let it slide. Don't tell him that I'm going to hire Lee. I'll bring Lee with me tomorrow to introduce him to everyone."

"Okay, boss."

"You know what makes Pete's attitude even more petty? Here he is intensely disliking the man, and he hasn't even met Lee yet."

"It's got nothing to do with Lee. If he wasn't marrying Bethan, Pete would've welcomed him with open arms."

Dylan grinned, smacked Benji on the arm, and said, "You've got the right of it, Benji. Thanks for hunting me down. I've got to get back to Gwen before she goes home without me."

"See you in the morning, Dylan."

The two lawmen parted, and Dylan's step was lighter as he strode back to the church. His decision to hire Lee was based on a very simple question. Who would be the better lawman?

The answer was Lee Collins and if Pete Towers couldn't work with Lee, then it was Pete who would be heading to Golden. Once he'd made up his mind last night, his only remaining concern had been about Benji, and now, that was gone.

———

While Dylan was having his chat with Benji, Bethan and Lee were having a much more boring conversation with Reverend Mortimore Hughes.

He was delighted with the news of Bethan's pending nuptials, and if it had been any other young woman marrying a man whom she'd only known for two weeks, he would have suspected that she was already carrying the man's child. But

453

he had known Bethan for years and was sure that her parents had raised her properly.

They set the time for eleven o'clock on Friday, the twenty-fifth of May.

With the groundwork done, they left the reverend's house and stepped outside, then mounted their horses to return to the Double EE for the Sunday family gathering, even though they'd had the midweek get together. There had been some discussion about postponing it, but the children were adamant mainly because they hadn't played a game of baseball on Wednesday.

———

So, that afternoon, Lee was introduced to baseball and struck out every time he was at the plate. When Bethan got three hits out of her four plate appearances, she had the good grace not to gloat.

After the game, Lee received another surprise when the family collected in the original Double EE house owned by Bryn, and he saw the player piano. Bryn was in no shape to dance, so he had to watch the others, and Lee was able to turn a few steps with Bethan without tripping.

It wasn't until the dancing was over when Dylan called for everyone's attention.

He stood in the center of the crowded room and called Lee and Bethan to his side.

"On the twenty-fifth of May, Bethan celebrates her eighteenth birthday. Most young ladies are already married when that anniversary arrives, but we expected that she would probably reach her eightieth birthday and still be looking for that elusive beau."

There was the expected tittering and giggles in the room as Dylan smiled.

"But she shocked us all when she left us two weeks ago to track down one man, but before she found him, she discovered Lee, and when she did, Bethan did what she has always done since she was a toddler; she made up her mind and never faltered. In less than two weeks, Bethan will be the first Evans to change her name when she marries Lee and I believe that I can speak for the entire family when I tell Lee that even as she becomes Bethan Collins, he will become an Evans in spirit."

Everyone broke into applause as they smiled at Lee and Bethan, expecting Lee to say something. Bethan was expecting it as well and gazed at her fiancé.

Lee smiled at her, then took a breath to make his own much shorter speech when Dylan held up his hand.

"I'm going to interrupt the newest member of the family to add one more tidbit of information. I've been riding to the office each morning with Bryn and Lynn for some time now. But as they both decided to become housemaids for a while, I've been making that ride alone and I didn't like it. So, after some deliberation, I figured that the best way to avoid those lonely journeys each morning and evening, I'd just have Lee ride with me."

He then turned to Lee and asked, "So, Lee, tomorrow morning, would you mind riding with me to the office?"

Lee smiled and replied, "I'd enjoy that, Dylan."

Dylan returned his smile then said, "Of course, I wouldn't expect you to come along and then turn right around and ride back. That's just a waste of your time. When we get there tomorrow, how about if I swear you in as a United States Deputy Marshal?"

Bethan and Lee both stared at Dylan in stunned silence for ten seconds before Lee replied, "I thought you were concerned about Pete Towers."

"I was and it was poor judgement on my part. So, will you accept the position, Mister Collins?"

"Yes, sir," Lee said before turning to look at Bethan's beaming face.

"We can build our home now," she said softly.

Lee nodded and took her hands as Gwen said loudly, "Oh, kiss her, for God's sake!"

Lee glanced at his future mother-in-law, then willingly complied with her order to another, even louder round of applause.

When the kiss ended, Lee scanned the smiling faces that crowded around them and said, "A few days ago, I joked to Bethan that as proud as she was with her family that maybe I should change my name to Evans rather than having her change hers to Collins. She turned the table on me and asked me seriously if I would mind. She was having fun with me, of course, but now, after I've met each of you, I don't think it was such a silly idea at all. The law may not allow that to happen, but even before we're wed, I feel honored to be part of the Evans family."

This time, in addition to the clapping, each of the family members that was old enough to talk, approached the couple to offer their congratulations.

After almost twenty minutes of pats on the back, handshakes and kisses, Lee and Bethan managed to spend some time with Dylan and Gwen. Dylan explained his thought process that led to his decision and the meeting with Benji.

When he finished, Lee asked, "Do you think that there will be a problem tomorrow?"

"No. It will be a crowded office, even beyond the lawmen that work there. We'll have Bethan, Gwen, and Kyle join us and I imagine there will be others as well. After you've been sworn in, I'll have a private talk with Pete. Just flow with the situation and it'll be fine."

"Thank you for everything, Dylan. I won't disappoint you."

"You're marrying Bethan, and I know you won't disappoint her, so how could you possibly disappoint me?"

Lee had his arm around Bethan's waist as he turned to look at her, expecting a quick comment, but she just smiled back at him.

"We'll be going to the small house to talk for a while. We interrupted our plans when we thought we'd be moving and I'm sure that Bethan would like to get them back on track."

Gwen smiled as she replied, "Enjoy your private time when you can get it."

Bethan grinned at her mother, then swung Lee around before they passed through the crowd of Evans to make their way to the front door.

As they wound their way past the smiling faces, more than one of the adults winked as they passed, making Lee blush.

Once they reached the porch, Lee asked, "Do they expect us to, um, you know, be together already?"

"That's what I thought, but I'm sure those winks were meant almost as a joke."

They walked quietly until they were halfway to the small house before Lee asked, "How serious was Pete Towers? When you told me about him, I thought it was a quick request and rejection."

"Are you worried that I may decide to give in to some deeply disguised longing to be with him?"

"No, ma'am. I was wondering what to expect tomorrow when I meet him. I don't want to have to worry about turning my back on him."

"It wasn't really that much at all, at least as far as I was concerned. I knew that he was interested since I was fifteen, but he was just friendly. Then he became more flirty than friendly when I was sixteen and then when I was seventeen, he finally asked if he could visit me socially. I didn't laugh or demean him at all. I never did to any of them, but he did seem somewhat surprised when I turned him down.

"I don't know why he was, either. I'd never been anything more than polite to him because he worked for my father. Maybe he misinterpreted politeness for affection. But after that, he left me alone. Whenever we met, he was polite but not overly attentive."

As the approached the small house, she said, "I don't think he'll be at the wedding, though."

Lee opened the door, then as Bethan passed, he said, "I guess I'll just have to do as your father recommended and flow with the situation."

―――――

After the unexpected shift back to their original plans, they spent more than two hours chatting about the new house, his new job and the wedding, but not all of it was spent just talking.

Lee finally escorted Bethan back to the big house late that night and after he kissed her goodnight, she smiled at him.

"Goodnight, Deputy Marshal Collins."

"Goodnight, Mrs. Collins."

She laughed lightly, then opened the door and disappeared into the house.

Lee let out his breath, then turned, trotted off the porch and headed back to the small house. He was excited about tomorrow, but his excitement was tinged with a bit of apprehension about Pete Towers.

―――――

Pete had returned to his room after spending most of the day with the Green family. Benji hadn't mentioned his meeting with Dylan, so as far as Pete knew, tomorrow would be just another Monday.

―――――

The next morning, Bryn was driving his buggy with Gwen and Erin sitting beside him as he trailed Dylan, Lee and

Bethan. Lynn was riding behind the buggy with Garth and Alwen, who had postponed their return for one day.

As they rode out front, Lee asked, "Will the deputies be there when we arrive?"

"Usually I'm the first one in the office, but we're running a bit late this morning for some reason, so they should all be there."

Bethan grinned at her father as she asked, "Can I go in first?"

"That might not be a bad idea, even if it was meant as a joke," Dylan replied.

————

So, after the entourage arrived at the office and either dismounted or exited the buggy, they loosely assembled, and Dylan let Bethan take the lead.

She opened the door and the four deputy marshals all turned, expecting to see their boss.

"Morning, Bethan," Benji said with a grin.

"Hello, Benji," Bethan answered as she matched his grin.

Before any of the other deputies could add their greetings, Dylan entered leading Gwen, Lee, and the rest of the family.

"What's the occasion, boss?" Benji asked, knowing full well the reason.

"Before we start the day, we're going to have a short ceremony, Benji," Dylan replied before removing his hat.

Lee hadn't met any of the deputies, but it didn't take long for him to realize which one was Pete Towers. Pete wasn't glaring at him, but there was an almost disparaging look on his face, as if Lee wasn't worthy to enter the office. He removed his hat as Bethan turned, walked beside him then took his arm.

Dylan then said, "As you can see by Lynn's cast on his right arm and Bryn's desperate need to find a chair, we're now short two deputies, at least for six more weeks. After losing Bert last month, we're very shorthanded. That being said, even if we only had one slot to fill, I wouldn't have hesitated to give it to Lee Collins.

"By now, you all have heard the stories about the work he did down in Bent Canyon with the Gentry gang. Bethan recognized his abilities before that shootout, and on the 25th, she'll be marrying him at the Presbyterian church. You're all welcome to attend of course.

"But before that happens, he'll be participating in another ceremony that we'll be having shortly. I've offered him a position as a deputy marshal, and he's accepted. After he's sworn in, you can all meet him. He'll be here all day, so there's no rush."

As he'd spoken, Dylan had let his eyes bounce to each of his deputies but spent more time on Pete to read his reaction and it wasn't difficult to read his displeasure. The swearing in ceremony would be short, and then he'd have his pow-wow with Pete.

He reached into his pocket, pulled out a U.S. Deputy Marshal badge, then said, "Gentlemen, let's get this show on the road."

As Bethan stood with her arm through Lee's left arm, he raised his right hand and repeated the oath that Dylan had recited many times before, but never with as much concern as he had now.

After administering the oath, Dylan handed the badge to Bethan.

She released her grip on Lee's arm, then stood before him and smiled as she pinned the badge on his vest.

"Congratulations, Deputy Marshal Collins," Dylan said before he initiated the applause.

Lee smiled as he scanned the faces but left his eyes on Bethan. He wished this joyous occasion wasn't marred with Pete's ill will, but he hoped that he'd be able to smooth their relationship over the coming days. He owed it to Dylan.

After he kissed Bethan, the other Evans shook his hand before leaving the office to return to the Double EE. Kyle only had to walk across the street and then another block over to get to his office.

Dylan then introduced him to Benji, Jesse Van De Berg, Thom Smythe, and finally, Pete Towers.

Lee shook each of their hands and was received warmly by each of them until he greeted Pete. Pete smiled, but it was almost a grimace as they shook.

Dylan then said, "Okay, boys, the party's over, so let's get to work. Pete, I need to talk to you in my office."

When Bethan had entered the front door, Pete had expected that he was going to be warned about not making any more comments about her marrying Collins. But when he'd seen her with a man he hadn't met before along with other family members, he realized that Dylan was going to give him a slot.

He walked down the hallway behind Dylan and made his decision before he was halfway there. He'd been mulling it over since he'd had that short talk in his office and the boss has asked him if he could work with Collins. At the time, he wasn't sure that he would hire the man, but now, Pete felt as if he had no alternative.

Dylan entered his office, stepped past his desk, leaving his hat on the desktop, then took his seat and waited for Pete.

Pete stepped inside and before Dylan could ask, he closed the door before sitting down.

Then, before Dylan could begin his prepared argument, Pete said, "Boss, I've been doing some thinking since I got back from Golden, and I think I'll head back there today and see about taking the job as deputy sheriff."

Dylan was surprised but relieved as he asked, "Why have you decided to leave, Pete?"

"Just for the change, I guess. I liked the town and Cal, too."

"Well, I'm sure that you'll do a good job. Hang onto your badge until Cal offers you the position."

"Okay, boss," Pete said, then stood and without another word, opened the door and left the office.

Dylan shook his head and even though it would leave him short again, he knew of a few candidates for the open positions. None of them were named Evans, but he had been studying the deputy sheriffs and the city deputy marshals for a while now to fill his first two empty positions.

Benji then entered and closed the door but remained standing as he said, "That didn't take as long as I expected."

"I never got the chance to start. He beat me to the punch and said that he was going to head over to Golden and take a job with Cal."

"You're kidding!" Benji exclaimed, "I didn't see that coming!"

"That means we'll still be pretty understaffed, so I'll see what I can do. How is that going to affect your home life?"

"You mean with Martha? I haven't got a clue. I'd better get back out front to see if Pete's heading straight to Golden or he's going to stop at my house."

Dylan nodded before Benji made a hasty exit, leaving the door open. He then stood and walked slowly out of his office and walked to the main office where he spotted Lee talking to Thom and Jesse while Benji exited the office to chase after Pete.

When Dylan stepped into the big office, Thom turned and asked, "What was that all about?"

"Pete just told me that he's going to Golden to see about working with Cal as his deputy. I imagine that Cal will jump at the opportunity, so I'm not sure if he'll be back."

Jesse then asked, "Can I guess that Benji is heading home to deliver the news to Martha?"

"I'm not sure, but he probably wants to talk to Pete anyway. Anyway, we have work that needs to be done, so I'll be right back after I get the assignment sheets from my office."

"Okay, boss," Thom replied.

When Dylan returned just a minute later, he handed one sheet to Jesse, then a second to Thom.

"Jesse, I need you to head over to Boulder and see the postmaster. He thinks that someone is helping himself to two of the mailboxes."

Jesse looked up from his assignment sheet and said, "Got it."

"Thom, I want you to take Lee with you and start his education about our many regulations and rules. He's already skilled enough for the dangerous aspects of the job, but he needs to be filled in on the boring stuff. You won't have to take a train on this job. Just ride over to Box Elder and see a ranch owner named John Coolidge. He says that he's losing a bunch of cattle each month."

"Isn't that the county's job, boss?" Thom asked.

"It would be normally, but he claims that a band of renegade Arapahoe is responsible for the thefts. We haven't had any problems with them for a few years, so he's probably wrong."

"The army isn't interested?"

"Apparently not. If you find that he's really right after all, then we can pass the word onto the army and they can get them back onto the reservation."

"We're on our way, boss," Thom said as he snatched his hat and headed for the door, assuming Lee would follow.

Lee trotted behind Thom, then closed the door behind him.

Dylan stood alone in the office with one more assignment sheet in his hand for Benji when he returned. He hoped that Lynn recovered quickly because he was certain that Pete was gone. He may not have been as good as the others, but he was still good enough to earn the badge.

He turned and then took a seat behind the front desk. Lynn would be back in the office next Monday but would only be able to handle administrative jobs and even those would be limited by his difficulty in writing, but at least he could man the desk.

————

As Lee rode, he listened as Thom began his instruction. He didn't review the regulations in any particular order but chose those that he felt were the most important. He also mixed in stories that were inspired by some of the rules.

The twenty-two-mile ride to Box Elder seemed to fly by and before noon, they'd reached the town where they received directions to the Coolidge ranch.

It was just twenty minutes later that they turned onto the ranch's access road and headed for a fairly large house.

By the time they reached the house, the ranch's wrangler was already walking toward them from the nearby corral.

"Howdy! You come about them Injuns?"

Thom asked, "Have you seen them?"

"Nope. They're too cagey and only take cows from the outer herds at night."

"How do you know they're Arapahoe?"

"The boss asked the neighbors if they'd seen the cows or anybody out there who didn't belong, and one of 'em said he saw an Injun scoutin' the southern pastures that bordered his place."

"How many cattle have you lost altogether?"

"You'd have to ask the boss, but I reckon it's about forty head or so."

"Is he in?"

"Yup. Just go on up there and knock."

"I appreciate your help," Thom said before nudging his horse closer to the hitchrail.

Lee brought Biff alongside, then they dismounted, tied off their horses and stepped onto the front porch.

The door opened before Thom knocked and John Coolidge stepped outside.

"You boys gonna get those Arapahoe?"

"We're going to investigate the problem and determine how many are involved. If it's more than we can handle, we'll notify the army."

"I reckon that's all you can do."

"What's your brand?"

"The Circle C. It's easy to spot."

"Alright. Who can show us to the place of the last theft?"

"Hobart, the wrangler you boys were talking to can do that."

Thom tipped his hat, then he and Lee left the porch and had barely settled in their saddles when Hobart arrived on a stubby gelding.

"I reckoned that the boss would ask me to show you around."

"Then show us around, Hobart. Take us to the last place that you lost cattle."

"Let's go," he replied, then wheeled his horse around and set off at a medium trot.

As they caught up with him, Lee glanced at Thom, wondering if he noticed anything odd about the situation. *Even if Arapahoe were responsible, why would they take so many animals?* That many cattle would feed a village of a hundred for a month. Thom must have had the same thoughts as he seemed to be deep in thought rather than just riding along.

They rode south into the rolling hills of prairie grass and he could see one of the herds to the east with six ranch hands working the critters. Then, he swiveled in his saddle to look north and spotted another, smaller herd, that four more hands were driving to join the bigger herd.

Thom then asked, "Hobart, who owns the land south of here?"

"Bob Quimby."

"Is he the one who saw the Arapahoe?"

"Yup. You wanna go and talk to him?"

"Maybe."

Lee suppressed a smile as he understood why Thom had asked the question. The only evidence that the Arapahoe were involved was from a single sighting of a single Indian by the neighbor. The question now was whether Mister Quimby was rebranding the cattle or selling them straight away to an unscrupulous buyer.

They reached the edge of the ranch and Hobart said, "Well, I'll leave you boys. If you need to see Quimby, his place is over yonder about a mile or so."

"Thanks, Hobart. We'll take it from here."

The wrangler waved, then started back to the ranch house.

As soon as he was fifty yards away, Thom asked, "What do you think, Lee?"

"I think we might want to take a quick look at the butt end of Mister Quimby's cattle before we pay him a visit."

Thom grinned and replied, "So, do I. The odds of those critters being taken by Arapahoe are getting lower by the minute."

————

On the Double EE, the womenfolk were busy preparing for Bethan's wedding. There was a lot to do and not much time to get it all done.

Sprinkled in the planning and marital conversations were asides concerning Lee's new position and Pete's reaction, but none of them had guessed that Pete would be leaving.

————

They may not have known, but Martha did. After her father had watched Pete ride out of town, he headed home to break the news to his daughter.

She was more upset when he told her the news than she'd been at her husband's burial. Her parents spent time with her to remind her that she was still an attractive young lady, but even as distraught as was, she believed that Pete would come to the house when he returned and then promise to take her with him.

By the time Benji left the house to return to the office, it was almost noon.

When he entered the office, Dylan asked, "Can I guess that Pete rode out of town without stopping?"

"Yup," he answered as he hung his hat, "Then I had to spend a couple of hours with Martha to settle her down. She was still complaining to Alice when I left."

"There's no point on going out on a mission now, so why don't we just go over some paperwork and get ready for tomorrow. Then I'm going to head over to Kyle's house to have Katie fix me some chow."

"Okay, Dylan. Sorry it took so long."

"I'm sorry everything has to be so damned much trouble."

Benji shrugged, then said, "It's not all bad. I like Lee and I think he and Bethan make a fine couple."

"So, do I. Let's get started on tomorrow's assignments."

―――――

Two hours after arriving in Box Elder, Lee and Thom were riding back to Denver. After having their talk with Bob Quimby, they had stopped at Mister Coolidge's house to let him know that his neighbor had been in error in his observation, and after a short search, they had discovered the Circle C cattle at the far end of Mister Quimby's ranch. Bob hadn't confessed any wrongdoing but attributed it to wandering critters. He promised that he'd have his hands drive the missing cattle back later that day.

As they rode, Thom continued Lee's education, so Lee's first mission turned out to be far from exciting. But he got to know Thom Smythe better and learned a lot about the duties that the job encompassed as well as the restrictions on what he could do.

———

While they were riding back from Box Elder, Pete was heading east from Golden. He was already wearing a Jefferson County Deputy Sheriff's badge and had his U.S. Deputy Marshal badge in his pocket.

Accepting the new position wasn't the only decision he had made since leaving Denver. He decided that he wanted nothing to do with any of them any longer, and that included Martha.

He'd transitioned from almost proposing to her to regarding her as a pathetic figure with her young child and Bert's unborn baby in her womb. He thought he could do better in Golden once he was established.

Pete wasn't even going to visit the Green home again. He'd return to the office, drop off his badge, then go to his room and pack. He'd pick up his pay the next morning, then ride out of Denver. He may visit the city if he needed to buy something that he couldn't find in Golden, but nothing more. He surely wasn't going to attend that wedding, either.

———

Early in the evening, when Lee and Dylan entered the house for dinner, they had barely had time to hang their hats before Bethan asked, "What happened when you talked to Pete, Dad?"

Dylan was unbuckling his gunbelt as he replied, "I barely got in a word before he told me that he was going to Golden to take the deputy sheriff's job with Cal Burris."

"*He quit?*" she asked with big eyes.

"He hasn't turned in his badge yet, but I'm pretty sure that he'll do it tomorrow."

Gwen asked, "What is he going to do about Martha? Has she been told?"

Lee stepped over to the table and sat beside Bethan when Dylan answered, "Benji told her and then he and Alice had to spend a couple of hours consoling her."

Bethan tilted her head and said, "I wonder if he's going to take her with him."

"I have no idea, but let's forget about Pete and you should ask your future husband about the dangerous mission that he and Thom had to handle on his first day on the job. I was relieved when they returned without wounds."

Bethan quickly turned to Lee who was already grinning before he even began to describe the far from harrowing episode.

Dinner was a very loud affair as Cari, Brian and Conway bombarded Lee with questions about everything from his childhood up to his arrival on the Double EE. None of them had enjoyed much personal time with Lee, and they were determined to make the most of it.

––––––

An hour later, Lee and Bethan walked with hands firmly linked as they strolled to the small house.

"I won't see you much now that you're officially a deputy marshal. I was spoiled by spending almost every minute with you for two weeks."

"I think that I got the better part of that bargain, but we can make up for it after we're married and then you'll be begging your father to send me on missions down to La Plata County."

Bethan laughed and said, "I doubt it, but once I'm pregnant, you may be the one doing the begging to go to that distant part of the state. I've been with Addie through all three of her pregnancies and I hope I don't get that emotional. I'd even prefer the morning sickness."

"Knowing you, Bethan, you'll probably set your mind to being rational and keeping your stomach calm."

"We'll see," she said as they stepped onto the porch, "I'd go inside with you, but I'm worried that I might get carried away."

"And I would let you, ma'am."

Bethan then pulled Lee close and kissed him with all the love and passion she possessed, which was considerable.

Lee was almost overwhelmed but lifted her from the wooden surface as he added those same feelings that he felt for her.

When he lowered her back to the porch, she whispered, "I'm glad that you lifted me, Lee. I thought my knees would fail me."

"I was worried that I'd drop you, but I think you're right about not going inside. We might not make it to the bedroom."

Bethan sighed then said, "The next eleven days are going to be absolute torture."

"But on that night, I'll make it worth every one of those frustrating seconds."

"I'd expect nothing less, but I'd better go."

He kissed her once more before she scurried back to the big house.

After Lee entered the house and closed the door, he began to worry that Pete might be a problem sometime before the wedding. If he was upset enough to quit, then how much more would it take for him to cause some disruption? He didn't believe that it would take the form of violence, but there were other ways of creating havoc.

———

Just a few minutes after Dylan and Lee arrived in the office the next morning, Pete walked through the door and just tossed his badge on the desk.

"I need to collect my pay, Dylan."

"Sure. Come on back."

Lee watched Pete follow Dylan into his office and last night's concerns resurfaced. Not only had Pete not even looked at him, he'd used Dylan's Christian name, which wasn't done when others were around. To Lee, it was more of a measure of Pete's discontent than anything else he had done.

Pete soon exited Dylan's office and was stuffing some currency into his pocket as he passed by.

After he'd gone, Lee asked, "Why does he seem even angrier today that he did yesterday?"

"I guess he's just had time to stew. He rode alone to Golden and back, and probable let it simmer all that time."

Lee nodded as he looked at the closed door, wondering how hot that simmer would go before it reached boiling point.

———

Within the next fifteen minutes, Thom and then Benji arrived but Jesse was stuck in Boulder, which meant that he was still looking for the mail thief.

As they shared coffee, Dylan said, "Just to let you know, Pete handed in his badge a few minutes ago. He'll be a Jefferson County deputy sheriff now."

Benji shook his head, then said, "Martha was waiting for him to stop by all night and was unhappy when he didn't. Did he say he where he was going after he left the office?"

"He barely spoke at all. He tossed the badge on the desk, asked for his pay and left."

"Mind if I go and check on Martha, boss? I don't want her running off with her baby. I don't reckon she would, but I need to know what's going on at the house."

"Go ahead and let me know if you have a problem."

"Thanks, boss," Benji said before handing his cup to Thom and quickly exiting the office.

After the door closed, Thom said, "Boss, I don't like the way things are headed. First Boris goes to Kansas City, then we lose Bert and now Bryn and Lynn are laid up. We're bleeding too much. It's like God won't be happy until this office is empty. Even with Lee, those requests are going to keep stacking up."

"I know. I've been prioritizing them and almost ignoring a lot of the more routine jobs. I've already decided to offer jobs to Les Templeton from the city marshal's office and Harry Shoemaker from the sheriff's office. I didn't want to raid just one of the departments. I've already cleared it with their bosses, so I'll go and ask them shortly."

"That's good news, boss. Les and Harry are both top-notch lawmen and good guys."

"That's one of the reasons that I selected them. There were more talented lawmen available, but those boys tended to be a bit too pompous to suit me. I wanted to avoid a potential office problem like we had with Pete, and I know that Les and Harry will fit in well."

"Any word from Bryn yet?"

"Not a whisper. He's got a couple of weeks before he has to decide, but both he and Lynn will be coming to the office starting Monday. Neither of them will be able to go on missions, but they can help with the routine stuff that I've been pushing off."

Dylan then set his cup down and said, "I've got assignments for each of you and I'll give Benji his when he gets back."

He handed a sheet to Thom and said, "You're getting the harder nut, Thom. The mayor of Greeley claims that the town marshal is crooked. Now we all know that it's a fairly common problem, and so does he. But Marshal Ralston has gone beyond simple graft. The mayor says that he's moved into a serious extortion racket and everyone's afraid of him. What the mayor is most concerned about is that one of his citizens may attempt to backshoot the marshal and then all hell will break loose."

"Okay, boss. Any word on how good this feller is with a gun?"

"The mayor described him as a sharpshooting scoundrel, so you may want to keep your badge hidden, buddy up and then make your play."

"That's what I was thinking."

Dylan then handed Lee his first solo job, saying, "You'll be heading east to Hugo. Two men robbed a stagecoach on the road between Hugo and a smaller town named Ranch three days ago. No one was hurt, but it was the second time that the shoestring operation had been hit, so they're on the edge of failing and if they go, then the town will probably dry up altogether.

"You might want to take some grub with you, Lee. Elbert County Sheriff Wannamaker isn't very mobile anymore, so you'll probably have to track them on your own."

Lee nodded as he studied the information.

"Okay, boss. If I have enough time, I'll head back to the Double EE to pick it up, but if the train leaves early, I can grab what I need in Hugo before starting to track those boys."

Thom then said, "Let's check the train schedules. I need to load up, too."

The office had copies of the train schedules, so Thom handed Lee one for the Kansas Pacific Railway, while he studied the Denver Pacific Railroad's brochure. He quickly tossed the schedule onto the desk before snatching his hat.

"Gotta go!" he said quickly before hastening through the door.

Lee then said, "My train doesn't leave until 11:10, so I'll head back to the Double EE, boss."

Dylan nodded, then said, "Lee, just because they haven't fired a shot in those holdups, don't take it for granted that they'll throw up their hands when you find them. Play it safe."

Lee grinned and replied, "Trust me, I'll be careful. I have a wedding to attend in ten days."

Dylan nodded, then watched Lee pick up his hat and leave.

———

Lee made short work of the four-mile ride to the ranch and headed for the small house.

He dismounted, removed his saddlebags, then hustled into the house and walked to the kitchen where he added some smoked beef and a few of Gwen's biscuits.

He turned to go to his bedroom to toss in an extra shirt and a pair britches in case the ones he was wearing were damaged, when he saw Bethan enter.

"Where are you headed, Deputy?" she asked with a smile as she drew closer.

"I'll be going to Hugo to track a couple of highwaymen."

"Who's going with you?"

"It's my first solo mission. My train leaves in two hours, so I've got to get moving."

"At least you're not going with Pete."

"He quit this morning to be a deputy sheriff in Golden," he replied as he stuffed his spare clothes into his saddlebags.

"That's not a surprise."

Lee hung his saddlebags over his shoulder and stepped close to Bethan, wrapped her in his arms and smiled.

"Come to give me a warm send off?"

"No. I came to tell you that I'm ready to go."

"What? What do you mean that you're ready to go?" he asked with bulging eyes.

"I figured that with so few deputies, you might want company if you had to go alone, so I was packed in case you stopped by to tell me where you were going. As I'm still carrying my temporary U.S. Deputy Marshal badge, as suggested by my very smart fiancé, I have the authority. Besides, we work together rather well."

Lee looked into those beautiful, but very determined brown eyes and knew that he'd lost the argument before it even started.

"Alright, Miss Evans. I'll agree to your offer, but only because I'm sure that you aren't in a motherly way."

Bethan laughed, then kissed him before replying, "And whose fault is that?"

Lee laughed as he shook his head. How he was able to win Bethan would probably be the biggest mystery he would ever know and one that he would never solve.

———

After they returned to Denver, they stopped at the office to let the boss know that his older daughter would be accompanying his future son-in-law.

Dylan hadn't raised too loud of an objection because he knew Bethan better than anyone and knew there was no point. After they'd gone, he even admitted that he was somewhat relieved that she'd decided to go along. They really did work well together, but just wondered how Gwen would take the news.

Benji had returned before Lee and Bethan arrived and told him that Pete hadn't even stopped by the house, which put Martha into a deep funk, but he'd left his wife to handle it.

Benji's job was more local, so he just had to ride to Pine Grove to arrest a moonshiner who was avoiding paying his liquor tax.

———

The sun was almost directly overhead when Lee and Bethan stepped onto the train platform in Hugo.

They had to wait for Biff and Nippy to be unloaded, and as they waited, Bethan said, "You might want to think about using of your more nondescript horses for jobs now that you have a bigger selection."

"I was thinking the same thing. Biff is a great horse, but he does stick out. Maybe we can ride out to Al and Garth's ranch and I can collect my equine payment."

"We can do that on Saturday."

They led their horses from the stock corral, then mounted and headed for the sheriff's office. Sheriff Bill Wannamaker was almost sixty years old and had only one very young deputy, who they soon discovered was his grandson.

Sheriff Wannamaker told them that the robbery had taken place about halfway between Hugo and Ranch just after the road dipped into a gully. The two gunmen wore full masks and said nothing, letting their shotgun and Winchester do the talking.

———

Twenty minutes later, they were on the road heading southwest. The landscape was almost like a mix of desert and plains, but there was enough water to provide for some trees.

"That trail may be hard to pick up," Bethan said as they rode along the crude roadway.

"We haven't had any rain, so they should still be there, but the advantage is that they probably stayed in that gully to make their getaway."

Bethan then grinned at Lee and said, "Isn't this fun? It's just like the old days."

Lee laughed then replied, "Old days? Like two and a half weeks ago? Why, that's ancient history now and it's hard for me to remember that far back."

Bethan laughed and was pleased that she'd come along. She would have followed him if he hadn't agreed, but it wouldn't be the same.

She then said, "I've been thinking about these boys. They've got to be local because no highwayman in his right mind would come down this way to hold up a third-rate stage. The money just isn't there."

"I know. That's probably why they don't talk. I mean, even Hugo has less than two hundred resident and Ranch has less than a third of that. If they were local boys, then even their voices would give them away."

They soon spotted the dip in the road where the builders had cut into the walls of the gully so wheeled traffic could pass. After they walked their horses into the gully, and dismounted, Lee and Bethan pulled off their canteens while they had the time.

Lee screwed the cap back onto his canteen then said, "I'll head south looking for tracks and you head north."

"Yes, boss," Bethan replied with a smile before heading north.

Lee shook his head, then started south along the gully. He didn't see any hoofprints for almost a hundred yards and was about to head back and check the other side of the cut when he took one last look further down the bed of the dried-up creek and thought he saw some about twenty yards away.

He jogged to the marks and was gratified to spot two sets of hoofprints continuing along the gully's floor.

Lee turned and whistled, then when Bethan looked his way, he waved. After she turned, he continued following the tracks on foot knowing she would bring Biff with her.

When Bethan arrived on Nippy, she handed Biff's reins to Lee who mounted before they set off at a slow trot, keeping the clear trail in sight.

"They must have cleared the tracks for the first hundred yards before mounting. That meant that they probably knew Sheriff Wannamaker and expected that he wouldn't look very far, if at all," she said as she scanned the horizons while Lee focused on the prints.

"That means that they're not idiots."

They followed the tracks for another ten minutes before the trail suddenly turned left and climbed out of a natural cut in the wall.

He waited while Bethan climbed Nippy out of the gully before he nudged Biff up the incline. Once they were back on level ground, the tracks headed almost due east.

Lee pulled up alongside Bethan and said, "Hugo lies northeast, so they didn't go back to town. If they were, the smart thing would have been to head for the roadway and let their tracks get mangled by traffic."

"I wonder if they're in town now."

"I hope not. We'd lose them in town because we have no idea what they or their horses look like."

"Then all we could do is tell Deputy Sheriff Wanamaker to let his grandpa know that he had two highway robbers in town, and he'd have to take it from there."

"You know that he probably wouldn't look too hard, and his grandson didn't impress me much."

"Maybe we'll get lucky and somebody will mention that they saw two of their fellow citizens ride in that day."

"Maybe," he replied as they continued to ride east, and just five minutes later, they spotted a building on the horizon.

It looked like an adobe structure, but it wasn't that large. There were no outbuildings that they could see, but if they were in that house, it would be hard to get them out if they didn't want to leave. Those walls made it a tiny fortress.

Lee pulled up, then looked at Bethan and asked, "Do you think that they're still in that place after three days?"

"I don't see any movement or smoke, but I think we have to approach it as if they were inside and already watching us."

"We can't pretend to be innocent young people out for a romantic ride because we're coming from an odd direction and we have too many guns to boot."

"Besides, they probably know most of the folks in the area."

"And they really would have noticed you, Bethan."

"Don't forget Biff, sir," she replied.

"That place is in pretty bad shape. I imagine somebody tried to make a go of a ranch out here and failed. Let's put our badges in plain sight, then head that way. If there is anyone inside who isn't an outlaw, then they won't be worried."

"And if they are outlaws, they'll get ready to shoot us off our horses."

"Yes, ma'am. Let's not give them that chance."

Bethan nodded, and they started their horses toward the adobe house at a slow trot, leaving their Winchesters in their scabbards.

———

Inside the house, Lou and Joe Dempsey were sitting at a small table as they prepared for what would be their last robbery.

"If we'd gotten just another seven dollars the last time, we woulda been all set," Joe said as he pulled his mask from his saddlebag.

"We shoulda had Mrs. Townsend empty her purse, Joe."

"She was always nice to us, Lou. It doesn't matter now. Tomorrow, we'll hit the stage and should get a good thirty dollars and then we'll be done. Nobody got hurt and we'll be okay."

"Then what happens next year?"

Joe sighed then replied, "We'll come up with somethin'. I reckon we can find some mustangs or mavericks and start up from scratch."

485

Lou nodded, then set the shotgun on the table, still worried about next April.

———

Bethan and Lee pulled up about two hundred yards from the house, dismounted, then slid their Winchesters from their scabbards. They just let their horses' reins drop as they began to walk toward the house.

After a few seconds, Lee whispered, "I can see a horse's behind in back of the house, so they're inside."

"After three days, that's a bit of a surprise."

"It's better than having to depend on Sheriff Wanamaker to flush them out of town. If we don't spot anyone in the windows, I'll just open the door and warn them while you cover."

"It's your mission, Deputy."

Lee glanced at Bethan without comment before they continued toward the house.

They reached the front of the house without spotting any movement in the windows, so Lee readied himself before the door while Bethan cocked her Winchester and leveled it to his right because the door opened to the left.

Lee didn't cock his repeater but held it in his left hand as he reached for the door handle. Once it was in his grasp, he looked back to Bethan who nodded.

He quickly rotated the handle, then threw open the door and stepped into the dark room as he brought his Winchester to his shoulder, pointed it at two men sitting at a nearby table, and shouted, "United States deputy marshals! Put up your hands and step away from those guns!"

Joe and Lou were stunned but quickly threw their hands above their heads, hopped to their feet and backed toward the center of the room.

Bethan entered and even in their shocked state, both men stared at her in disbelief.

"I'm arresting you both for armed robbery," Lee said as he lowered his Winchester, then asked, "What are your names?"

Joe replied, "I'm Joe Dempsey and this is my brother Lou."

Neither man was wearing a pistol, so Lee said, "You can put your hands down."

As they slowly lowered their hands, Joe said, "We didn't hurt nobody. Our guns weren't even loaded, and I don't reckon that they'd work if we even had ammunition."

Lee looked briefly at Bethan, then walked to the table, leaned his Winchester against the edge, then picked up the shotgun. But before he could crack it open to check if there were shells inside the breech, he knew it wasn't possible. The catch that held the barrels was rusted to the point that it would probably snap off if he tried to break it free.

He set it down and then inspected the Henry rifle that they had used in their robberies. The lever was stiff yet still worked, but no cartridge was expelled, so it was empty. He stepped past Bethan, who still had her Winchester on the two men, then into the bright Colorado sunshine. One quick look down the barrel confirmed that what Joe Dempsey had told them was accurate. The barrel was heavily corroded and would be dangerous to fire.

He returned to the room, then picked up the shotgun and stepped to the fireplace. He swung the shotgun once, actually bending the barrels as chips of rock flew across the hearth. He then hammered the lever action of the Henry into the fireplace and then tossed it to the floor with the useless shotgun.

Lee returned to Bethan, who lowered her Winchester.

"Why did you boys rob the stage? You couldn't have gotten much money, but you took a real risk that you'd either get shot or arrested."

Joe replied, "Clyde Stadler, he's the coach driver, never had a gun and we knew that the sheriff wasn't gonna come lookin' for us."

"You're going to spend a few years in the state prison for what, fifty dollars?"

Lou quickly said, "We got sixty-four dollars and fifty-five cents. All we needed was seven more dollars and then we'd stop 'cause we'd have enough."

Lee looked at Bethan who had the same look of curiosity on her face that he knew he must have on his before he turned back to the Dempsey brothers.

"Why do you need exactly seventy-one dollars?"

"We really needed a hundred and eighteen dollars, but me and Lou been doin' odd jobs for a while, so we already had forty-seven. We did some figurin' and knew that we'd never get that much before the end of May, so we reckoned that the only way we could do it was to hold up the stage."

"Why the end of May?" Lee asked.

"If we don't pay the taxes on the ranch, then the county is gonna sell it."

"This ranch?" Bethan asked.

"It was our pa's place. He started it, but after our ma died, he got all sad and didn't feel like workin', so he began sellin' the critters. When he died, we moved to town for a couple of years, figurin' we could get hired and get some money to get it goin' again, but that didn't work out. Then the sheriff told us that the county was gonna sell the ranch if we didn't pay the taxes. We couldn't figure another way to get the money that fast."

Lee looked back at Bethan, then reached into his pocket, counted out a ten and two five-dollar notes, then handed them to Joe Dempsey.

"Now I want you both to understand this, and the only thing that saved you both from being sent to prison is the condition of your guns. Go pay your taxes and that will buy you a year. I'll wire the sheriff in a couple of days to make sure that you did and have him notify me personally if there are any more holdups. Do you understand?"

Joe took the bills from Lee's hand and stared at the crumpled currency before he looked up and replied, "You ain't gonna arrest us?"

"No, but don't make me come back here. My partner and I are planning on getting married a week from Friday and I don't want to have to chase you both down again. Besides, I know where you are."

Lou had been staring at Bethan while Lee had been talking, but finally shifted his eyes to Lee before asking, "Is she really a deputy marshal? I ain't never seen a woman with a badge before."

"She is, and her father is the U.S. Marshal, so she's very good at the job because he's been training her since she was waist high."

"I reckon so."

"We're heading back to Denver now, so you both remember what I told you."

"Thanks, Marshal," Joe said, "You're a right nice feller."

Lee picked up his Winchester, then as he turned, Bethan took his arm before they walked out the door.

———

After sliding their repeaters where they belonged, they mounted, and Bethan said, "I'm proud of you, Lee. I was going to suggest that we at least let them go, but you one-upped me. That was just about the last of your money, too."

"I haven't picked up those vouchers yet because I didn't want to open a bank account until I was sure that we'd be living here. I guess I'll have to do that when we get back. I just hope they can figure out how to make this place work after we're gone."

After she nudged Nippy into a trot then waited for Lee to catch up, she asked, "What do we tell Sheriff Wanamaker?"

"I have no idea. Can you come up with something?"

She paused for a few seconds before answering, "Let's just tell him what really happened without telling him their names.

After we tell him that believe it won't happen again, but to let you know if it does, then we can ask him if he really wants to know the names of two of his town's citizens."

"Now that, Miss Evans, is an excellent suggestion. I don't think that he'll need to hear their names anyway. I imagine that once we explain what happened, he'll have a good idea of the two thieves. I'll add that when we write our report to the marshal, we'll include that we chose not to arrest them, just in the off chance that he might throw them in his jail."

"Maybe your first two missions are setting a pattern. It sounds bad, but then it finishes with a strange ending."

"It's better than getting shot in the butt."

Bethan laughed but didn't reply as they continued toward Hugo. They picked up the pace knowing that they had a good chance to catch the evening train to Denver.

———

The meeting with Sheriff Wanamaker went as they had anticipated, and before the sun had set, they were on their way back to Denver after sending a telegram to Dylan.

As the train rolled northwest, Lee asked, "Are you going to make this a habit?"

"Do you mean coming with you on your missions?"

"Yes. I know that you're very good at this and I really do enjoy having you with me, but after we're married, then things will change."

"I know, and that's why I wanted to come with you on this job. It's not as if I plan on making a career of wearing the badge, but I did want to help while the office was so shorthanded. Dad says that he's hiring two more this week, so that'll help. Would you mind if I still joined you until we create a baby?"

Lee smiled before he replied, "That sounds like a good offer to me, but we'll have to get you father's approval."

"It'll be more difficult to get my mother's, but I can manage."

With that issue settled, they changed to the very different topic of Pete Towers and Martha.

_____

It was the middle of the night when they rode out of Denver and headed for the Double EE.

After putting away their horses, they slowly walked to the big house. There was light coming from the windows, so Bethan knew that her parents were waiting.

The night meeting didn't last as long as either of them had expected, but Gwen laid down some rules. Bethan could still accompany Lee on assignments, but with one restriction. She could go with Lee to the office, but it would be up to Dylan if she could accompany him when he left. She was mollified when Bethan explained the agreement that she and Lee had made that as soon as she discovered that she was pregnant, she'd stay home.

Dylan had only asked for their report, so everyone was in a good mood before they turned in.

_____

Over the next five days, Bethan joined Lee on four jobs, but only two were far enough from Denver to have them ride rails instead of horses. Dylan denied her one assignment and sent him with Thom. Bethan may have objected but kept her arguments to herself before she rode back to the Double EE.

Les Templeton and Harry Shoemaker were both sworn in on Thursday morning and were sent out on jobs on Friday.

On Saturday afternoon, Lee and Bethan rode out to the A-G connected so Lee could pick out his horse. They'd stay the night and ride back with Al and Garth in the morning.

As they rode, Bethan asked, "You aren't going to take a stallion, are you? They can be just as annoying to a lawman as your pinto. I'd recommend a nice, brown gelding."

"I already have a nice, brown gelding. I think he was Avery George's horse. The light brown with the dark brown mane and tail and the four black boots. I think if I get a stallion, maybe we can introduce him to Nippy."

Bethan laughed, then said, "I've been saving her from Bryn's stallions, but maybe it's a good idea to keep the mating in the family. It'll just be a race to see which of us foals first."

Lee grinned at Bethan and hoped that she would beat Nippy by more than just the added time for Nippy's gestation.

When they arrived at the A-G Connected, it didn't take long for Lee to choose a handsome young light gray stallion that was probably too bright to use when chasing outlaws anyway.

———

Everything seemed to be aligning and going well until Sunday's family get together. The usual cheerful mood dominated the afternoon with most of the discussion about Bethan and Lee's wedding on Friday.

The gray stallion had been introduced and obviously accepted by Nippy. Before he named the stallion, Lee christened his new lawman gelding King, believing that the horse had earned the moniker more than his previous rider. The stallion was awarded the clerical name of Bishop, although, in this case, it was more of a geographical reference than religious.

Kyle's family arrived later than usual and after they put away their buggy, Kyle watched his children and Katie join the crowd while he looked for Lee.

Once he spotted him with Bethan, he took a breath before he began walking toward them.

When he was five feet away, Lee greeted him with a smiling, "Howdy, Kyle."

Bethan then said, "You must have been busy, Kyle. You're usually here by now."

"Could I talk to you both in private?" he asked.

Bethan saw his troubled face and asked, "What's wrong?"

"Let's go to the small house and I'll show you."

Bethan looked at Lee, then took his arm as they walked with Kyle to the nearby small house.

Once inside, Kyle pulled a folded sheet from his jacket pocket and said, "This arrived at my boss's office on Friday. He wasn't sure what to do with it, so he gave it to me. It's about you, Lee."

He handed the sheet to Lee who read:

Dear Mister Jones,

I am writing to you rather than anyone named Evans because I don't trust them to do anything to make things right.

I read in the newspaper that Lee Collins, who used to be a town marshal in Bishop, is marrying the marshal's daughter. If he does, then he will be a bigamist.

Three years ago, while he was living in Higby, he married my daughter, Eloise and a year later, she gave birth to a son they named Richard. Soon after he was born, Lee Collins abandoned her and the baby.

She has been living with us since he left, and we didn't know where he had gone until we read the newspaper story.

I never want to see that horrible man again, but if he is still allowed to marry that girl, then that lying scoundrel will be breaking the law and you need to have him arrested and thrown in prison for the rest of his life!

If she comes to her senses and turns him away, then the only law he will have broken is God's law that he provides and protects his wife and children. He may not go to prison, but I know that he will burn in hell.

Eloise begged me not to write this letter, but I wasn't about to allow that miserable man enjoy himself while his real wife and son suffer.

Sincerely,

Mary Hotchkiss

When he finished reading, he handed the page to Bethan, then asked, "Do you have the envelope?"

"No. My boss tossed it after he read the letter. I asked him where it had been posted, but he hadn't noticed. Unfortunately, our trash is picked up quickly and burned out back because of confidentiality concerns."

Bethan then asked, "Why would anyone send something like this?"

"Obviously, she didn't want you to marry Lee."

"Well, this changes nothing," she spat as she handed the letter back to Lee.

"It may not be that simple," Kyle replied.

"You don't believe this!" Bethan exclaimed.

"No, I don't, and I'm sure that no one else in the family will, either. But you have to realize that by tomorrow, the contents of this letter will be the hot topic among the gossips."

"How is that possible? Only you and the prosecutor saw it before you let us read it."

"Yes, that's true, but Walter may be a good prosecutor, but he's a charter member of the gossip club. I'm sure that he's told his wife about the letter and by tomorrow, it'll be all over town."

"So? I still don't see a problem," Bethan replied sharply.

"The problem is that Reverend Hughes may balk when he hears about it, and I'm sure that he will."

Lee finally replied, "I'll bet if we had the envelope, we'd see that it was posted in Golden, or maybe Denver."

Kyle asked, "Do you think Pete Towers would really do something like this? If you look at the handwriting, it's pretty delicate. If you compare it to some of Pete's reports, then you know that he didn't write this letter."

Lee had seen some of Pete's reports and had to agree with Kyle.

Bethan then said, "Maybe he paid a prostitute to write it for him."

"I suppose that's possible, but the letter seems to be filled with venom that appears genuine. It's a lot more difficult to fake than you might think. Whoever did write this letter really doesn't like you, Lee. Or at least, doesn't want you two to get married."

Lee looked at Bethan and said, "I still have to go to work tomorrow, so will you handle the detective work on this?"

She snatched the letter from his hand before she replied, "With pleasure."

They left the small house, corralled the adults, and let them know about the damning letter. In a measure of respect that they already had for Lee, not one of them gave the claim any credence.

Bethan told Kyle that she'd be riding into Denver with Lee in the morning but would come to his office to talk to the prosecutor to start her investigation.

Despite the interruption, the rest of the day progressed along its accustomed path. In the afternoon's baseball game, Lee got his first hit to the cheers of the entire family.

After the player piano dance, Lee and Bethan walked to the small house.

As they stepped along, Lee said, "Thank you for not doubting me, Bethan."

"Do you know what's odd about that?"

"No."

"I haven't known you for a month, but not for an instant did I believe it to be true. As soon as I read that accusation, I was angry at the letter's author. I've trusted you since that first day because you never pretended to be anything other than who you are. Remember when I first asked you why you became a town marshal if you didn't get paid?"

"Yes, ma'am."

"You told me that you wanted to feel important and that told me of your true nature."

Lee smiled and said, "If you remember, I did add that secondary reason for my taking the job."

"That was just another example of your character, Lee. You didn't have to confess it to me at all. You are an honest man, Lee Robert Collins, and I want to spend the rest of my life with you.

"It will be an interesting life if our first month together is any indication."

They stepped onto the porch, and Bethan kissed him goodnight before saying, "I'll find the person who sent this letter, and even if I can't and the Reverend Hughes won't marry us, we'll have Judge West perform the ceremony."

Lee kissed her again, then replied, "You'll find her."

Bethan nodded, then turned and trotted back to the big house.

Lee watched her fade into the night before going inside.

Twenty minutes later, he was stretched out on his bed wondering who would make the effort to interfere with his and Bethan's marriage if it wasn't Pete Towers. He drifted off to sleep without coming up with any suspects.

―――――

Kyle's prediction that the letter's contents would soon be common knowledge was proven to be correct shortly after Lee, Dylan, Lynn and Bryn entered the office.

They'd barely had time to hang their hats when Les Templeton entered the office and added his hat to the line of pegs on the far wall.

He grabbed the coffee cup that he'd taken with him from his old job and walked to the heating stove to add the morning's brew.

As he poured the coffee, he smiled at Lee and said, "I hear that you're getting married again, Lee."

Lee didn't think that Les was being malicious with the comment, so he just asked, "Where did you hear that?"

"My wife told me she'd heard it from one of her friends after church yesterday. She said that our county prosecutor had gotten some letter claiming you left a wife and kid to go to Bishop. I reckoned that it had to be nonsense, because nobody in his right mind would go to Bishop if he didn't have to."

"Bethan is over in Mister Jones' office right now trying to find who had sent the letter. I thought it might have been Pete because he wasn't happy with me marrying Bethan, but Kyle pointed out that the letter had been written by a woman."

Les took a sip of his coffee, then said, "Maybe he had a whore write it for him."

"That's what I thought, but Kyle suggested that the author seemed really mad, and that it was hard to fake. I think that any woman can get mad enough to fake it, but then, I'm not a lawyer."

Les chuckled, then replied, "I'll go along with you, Lee. Mary could probably write a letter accusing me of being the devil himself when she's unhappy with something I did."

When the other deputies filtered in, each of them admitted to hearing the rumor, but the work still needed to get done and soon the entire office was empty except for the boss and his two injured deputies.

"Dad, do you mind if I help Bethan to find the woman who sent that letter?"

Dylan replied, "Wait until she gets back from the prosecutor's office. Maybe she already found out."

Bryn then asked, "Are you really thinking of sticking me here at the desk all day?"

"No, sir," Lynn replied, "Just for most of it. At least I can walk."

"I'll be walking before you get that rock off of your arm."

"Don't remind me. This thing is already itching, and I have to tie it down every night, too."

"Why?"

"I almost whacked Addie with it the first night when I rolled over in my sleep. That scared the devil out of me, so I tie it down now."

Dylan returned to his office and had just read the first three requests for assistance from other law agencies when he heard the door open.

When he heard Lynn ask, "What did you find out, Bethan?", he stood and walked to the front office.

Bethan saw her father walking down the hallway, so she paused until he entered the room before replying, "Almost nothing. Mister Jones couldn't add anything that we didn't already know, but I could tell that he felt a little guilty for starting the rumor. I didn't push it, though, because he's Kyle's boss."

"What are you going to do now?" Lynn asked.

"I have the letter, so all I can do is take it apart word by word and see if there are any clues that I missed."

"Want my help?" Lynn asked, "I'm already bored, and I just got here."

She pulled the letter from her pocket, then looked at her father and asked, "Can we use the interrogation room?"

"Go ahead. I've got to get to work on the incoming requests and orders from the boss back in Washington City."

"Thanks, Dad," she replied before following him down the hallway and turning into the small room that they used for interrogating suspects and witnesses and where the deputies would write their reports.

After more than thirty minutes of examining the letter, neither of them had identified anything that gave them a hint of who had written it or even where she lived. They had only agreed in Kyle's original assessment that it had to have been a woman's hand to set the smooth script to paper.

———

Over the next two days, no progress was made in discovering the author of the disruptive letter and the wedding was just two days away.

Bethan had visited Reverend Hughes to assure him that the letter was nothing more than an attempt to start trouble, and while he still agreed to perform the ceremony, the reverend admitted to a certain amount of trepidation. What added to his concern was that he might face some backlash from the women's group that provided much of the church's financial support. He didn't even mention the intense interrogation his wife had put him through.

After she left the reverend's house Wednesday afternoon, she rode back to the Double EE at a fast trot in utter frustration. She knew that she would marry Lee come hell or high water but knowing that so many people probably believed that the rumor was true bothered her immensely. It seemed that the more salacious the gossip, the more some people accepted it as fact.

———

After dinner that night, Bethan and Lee made their anticipated slow walk to the small house, but this time, after they reached the porch, Bethan didn't stop and embrace Lee. She opened the door and walked inside and waited for him to enter.

Lee wasn't surprised because Bethan had been in a dreary mood since he returned from the office and he was sure that he knew why.

After closing the door, he asked, "Why did you come inside tonight, Bethan?"

"I want you to make love to me. Is that plain enough?"

As much as he wanted to do as she asked and despite understanding that Bethan shared his desires, he could tell that she really didn't mean what she'd just said.

"No, it's not plain enough. Let's sit down and talk."

Bethan nodded, then stepped to the couch and took a seat before Lynn tossed his hat onto another chair and joined her.

"You're angry about that letter. Aren't you?"

"Of course, I am. What makes me mad is that so many people want to believe it. Even if we did find who wrote it, it might not matter."

"So why did you want to join me in bed?"

"I guess I wanted to prove that I was going to be your wife despite what those people thought. I wanted to be your wife tonight."

"Bethan," Lee said as he took her hands, "you and I will be married on Friday. I want that night to be special because we both want it so badly. I don't want anything to spoil that day."

Bethan sighed then replied, "I suppose you're right, but this letter creature is really annoying. Why would anyone want to hurt you like this? I don't believe that even Pete would do something like this. Only a woman could have this kind of vindictiveness. Men are a lot more direct."

Lee smiled as he said, "You're direct, Bethan, and I can assure you that you are all woman."

Bethan managed a smile before saying, "I'm glad that you noticed, and even more pleased that you turned down my request."

Lee then asked, "Bethan, I know this may sound silly, but we've been looking at this as a plot aimed at me. What if it's really meant to hurt you?"

"*Me?*" she asked with big eyes, "*Who would want to hurt me?*"

"I have no idea. I've only been here for a few weeks, so I'll let you go now, and you can think about it."

After her perspective change, Bethan was already deep in thought. *Who would be trying to hurt her, and why?*

Bethan slowly stood and walked with Lee to the door. After he opened it, he gave her a quick kiss before she stepped across the porch and headed for the big house, still contemplating the new angle.

Lee closed the door and let out a long breath. He'd been so close to just scooping Bethan off her feet and taking her to the bedroom and it had taken every bit of his will to talk instead.

He doubted that anything would change in the next day, but if anyone could come up with a way to do it, it was Bethan.

———

Bethan hadn't said much to her parents, brothers, or sister when she returned, but walked to her room and lit a lamp so she could read the letter yet again.

As she studied the words even more closely, she left the world of those who would harbor a grudge against Lee and focused on those who knew her.

She started by writing the names of women she knew alphabetically. Some of them may not have been friendly, but none were openly hostile.

When she finally reached Verna Woods, she set the pencil aside. She'd hoped that just by writing the names, one of them would jump off the list, but they all stayed on the page.

She set the letter beside her list and tried to connect a name to the paper, but that didn't work either.

Suddenly, her eyes stared at the name on the bottom of the letter and quickly shifted back to her list.

Once she made that tenuous link, she leaned back and smiled. Tomorrow, she'd follow the tiny clue and see where it took her. She may be wrong, but the more she thought about it, she was convinced that she knew who had authored the vindictive letter.

———

Bethan didn't disclose her possible solution, not even to Lee, as they rode toward Denver the next morning. She could be wrong, and if she was, then it could hurt innocent people that they'd known for years.

After entering the office, Bethan joined her father, uncle, brother and future husband with a cup of coffee.

Lee said, "You seem a lot better this morning, Bethan."

"We're getting married tomorrow, Lee. Why shouldn't I be in a good mood?"

Lynn remarked, "I expected you to stay at the ranch this morning so you could put the finishing touches for the ceremony."

"We're as ready as we'll ever be, brother."

They were still chatting about the wedding when Thom entered the office with Benji.

"Morning, all," Thom said as he headed for the coffeepot still wearing his headgear.

"Morning," Benji added as he removed his hat.

After Lee and the four Evans all returned their greetings, Thom asked, "Still can't find the one who sent that letter, Bethan?"

"No," she replied as she pulled the offending missive from her pocket, "Maybe I should have you two old lawmen examine it to see if I missed anything."

Bethan then offered it to Benji.

"Sure thing," Benji said as he accepted the letter.

Bethan watched him unfold it and after just a few seconds she saw his eyes grow wide and she knew she'd been right.

When he continued to stare at the sheet of paper, Bethan said, "We're sure that it was written by a woman, but we all thought it was an attempt to discredit Lee. Last night Lee suggested that it might be aimed at me and not him. What do you think?"

Benji slowly turned to Bethan and said, "I...I'm sorry, Bethan. How can I make this right?"

The other men in the office all stared at Benji in confusion, as Bethan replied, "It was only when I realized that the author and Martha shared the same initials after she married Bert. Once I made that tenuous link, I realized that Martha must have blamed me because Pete had asked to visit me and then she added more blame when Pete left Denver rather than work with Lee."

Benji replied, "She always crosses her small t at the top rather than across. I've never seen anyone else do that. I'm sure that this was written in her hand. How can I make this right, Bethan?"

Bethan was relieved but was now concerned that anything that they could do to rectify the situation might make it worse.

Lee then said, "Why don't you have Martha write another letter from Mary Hotchkiss? Have her explain that she'd lied and only wanted to hurt me because I'd turned her down when I was in Bishop."

Bethan turned to Benji and asked, "Can you have her write one today? That way, we can let Mister Jones read it and compare it to the original. Then he can gossip all he wants. I know that some people will still think it's true, but it will die out faster."

"She'll write it and I'll make sure that it's heartfelt," Benji replied with more than a trace of anger in his voice.

Bethan then said, "Don't be too hard on her, Benji. She's pregnant and her emotions probably had a big impact on her decision to write that letter."

"I reckon so," Benji said, then looked at Dylan and added, "I'll be gone for a couple of hours."

"Go ahead. We'll manage."

Benji quickly walked to the wall, snatched his hat and was out the door.

Lee then turned to Bethan and said, "That was good work, ma'am. You'd make a damned good lawman."

Bethan smiled then replied, "Right now, I'd rather make a damned good wife. I've got to get back to the ranch and help with the last-minute preparations. I'll let you boys handle the letter issue."

Lee kissed her before she turned and left the office.

Dylan then said, "I wish I didn't have to send any of you out until after Benji returned, but I have a couple of jobs that are out of town. Lee, I'm keeping you in town today because you have to do some preparations that you need to take care of yourself."

Lee nodded as he watched Les and Harry enter the office and thought that it was going to be an interesting day, but tomorrow was going to be even better.

———

Benji returned with the apologetic letter in less than an hour and had made sure that it matched the first letter in style and even the same type of envelope, but it was addressed to Kyle and not his boss.

It had been an emotional discussion with Martha while Alice sat with her daughter as she admitted to sending the letter. She was weeping as she explained that she was jealous of Bethan and that when Pete left without even saying goodbye, she was angry and upset. She said that after she posted the letter, she regretted it almost immediately, but even then, hadn't expected that it would cause such an impact. She said that she though Mister Jones would just give it to Kyle and then its vicious content would die.

So, after her father told her what she had to do to rectify the damage she had done, she was pleased that no one would ever know that she had been the instigator. She wrote the letter quickly and her father agreed that it was even more believable than the original.

Lynn carried the letter to the county courthouse and gave it to Kyle, who opened it and then walked to Mister Jones' office to let him read it.

By the time Lee returned from serving his three subpoenas, the new letter's contents were already entering the gossip chain.

_____

Friday, May 25, 1877

The morning of their wedding was far from a delightful, sunny spring day. There was a low cloud cover that dropped the temperature into the low forties and threatened a chilling rain, but the weather didn't affect the joyful mood on the Double EE.

When Bethan appeared on the porch wearing her wedding gown, Lee thought he sun had suddenly blasted through the clouds.

Bethan smiled at him as he stood beside their buggy, then tried to be as elegant as possible as she stepped down the four stairs.

Lee didn't care how she walked, just that she was walking to him before they rode to the church.

After he helped her into the buggy, which she really needed this time because of her voluminous gown. She didn't have a train, but she found the petticoats awkward.

The long caravan of Evans departed the ranch before ten o'clock and reached the church forty minutes later.

Lee left the buggy and entered the church with Lynn, who would be his witness. Addie would be Bethan's witness and after Lee and Lynn had disappeared through the church doors, she assisted the bride from the buggy.

Dylan waited at the back of the church for his daughter with Gwen. The pews were soon filled with the large number of Evans, but one seat was left for Gwen on the end of the front pew.

As other guests began arriving, Gwen smiled and greeted each of them as they passed while the bride and her father waited off to the side of the church out of view.

When Reverend Hughes finally walked onto the altar, the ceremony officially began.

As the organist played the traditional wedding march, Lee looked down the aisle.

Bethan took her father's arm, and he said, "There were times that your mother and I thought we'd never see this day."

She smiled and replied, "Neither did I."

He smiled back, then they stepped forward and turned onto the aisle.

Lee saw her and found it difficult to believe that such an amazing woman would choose to spend her life with him.

As Bethan stepped down the aisle, her eyes were hidden by a thin veil, but she focused them on Lee. For so long, she had thought that this day would never come because she was determined to prove that she was the match for any lawman. Even as late as last month, after she had made that decision to follow Bryn, she was satisfied that she had chosen the right path. But now, as she approached the altar and looked at Lee's loving eyes, she realized that her new choice was much better because she had chosen the right man.

EPILOGUE

After the wedding, the couple moved into the small house while construction began on the road and then the house and barn that would be their new home.

Bryn finally announced his retirement on the thirteenth of June, and Dylan then raided the town marshal's office to hire a replacement two days before Lynn convinced the doctor to remove his cast.

The biggest surprise that month was when Pete Towers had second thoughts about how he had treated Martha and returned to Denver a week later and asked her to forgive him. When she did, he then proposed to her and she married him on the twenty-fifth of the month. Bethan and Lee attended the wedding and the rift between the couples, while not completely repaired, was restored to civility.

Not surprisingly, Bethan announced her pregnancy in July and unknown to Lee, didn't discuss a boy's name as she hoped that she would have a girl. It had worked for her mother and Erin, so she thought she'd at least give it a chance.

On March 4, 1878, Bethan went into labor and nine hours and eleven minutes later, gave birth to a very healthy baby girl they named Hope Gwendolyn. It was only then that she confessed to Lee that she hadn't chosen a boy's name but found that he had recalled the story about how her mother had used it before Bethan had arrived, and was more than pleased with her decision and their new daughter.

As Bethan held her daughter to her breast for the first time, she remembered when Addie had told her that having a baby was so incredibly joyful and she had found it hard to believe.

But as she looked at Hope's blond head, she felt a swelling of happiness engulf her that was different than any she'd ever felt before and knew that the man who had given her his love had also given her this perfect child.

She looked up at Hope's smiling father and whispered, "Thank you, Lee."

Lee just nodded and smiled as he fought back tears, still finding it difficult to believe that this extraordinary woman had chosen him.

Author's Note

Before writing the fifth book in the saga, I had intended to write a book of short stories because I had one in mind, but after writing it, I realized that each of them would take as much time as I'd spent writing some of my earlier books. So, after finishing the short story that had inspired the idea, I started on this one. My daughter had warned me that it would be difficult writing from a woman's perspective because, well, I'm not. She was right, of course. She usually is. But it's done and I'll be doing some editing for a while.

When I start the next book, I'm leaning toward a standalone story before I return to the Evans saga, but at least I'm not going to attempt a collection of short stories again.

That being said, the first and only short story, which about a character who appears in all of the first five books, is included following this monologue. It's also in the first person, which is different, as is the perspective, which is even more different from that of a woman. You'll see what I mean.

So, with an accompanying drumroll, I present:

THEY CALL ME...PEANUT

I wasn't always called Peanut. In fact, when I was born...I hate to use the word 'foaled' because it sounds as if I was just unceremoniously dropped onto the dirt... the name given to me by my proud parents was the much more impressive 'Augustus'. It was obvious that they had great expectations for me and my future.

I can still remember seeing the pride in my father's eyes when he gazed upon his firstborn son. He was convinced that I would become the greatest donkey ever to set hoof on the Great Plains.

My parents thought I was the cutest youngster ever to take a breath, and with all due humility, I'll admit that it was well-deserved. I was beyond cute. I was adorable.

That extraordinary cuteness remained with me for a year before my father began to question when my adorability would be replaced by a more mature, stud-like handsome. My mother, of course, never wanted me to stop being her sweet, cuddly Babboo.

As much as I appreciated my mother's attention, I was beginning to worry about my lack of growth. It wasn't as if there were any other donkeys on the farm for comparison, but compared to my father, I was a midget. It was getting embarrassing.

If that wasn't bad enough, my coat wasn't nice and short-haired like my parents but was as curly as a damned dirty brown sheep before shearing. I began to wonder if I could cut it all off but figured that it would probably grow back even worse. Besides, managing scissors was a bit of a problem. You can figure out why.

It was hard enough to pretend that I would eventually grow to be worthy of being called "Augustus" in any sense of the name. What made it worse was that just a few weeks after I was "foaled", …there, I used it. Happy? … the small humans that shared my farm began calling me "Peanut".

At first, I was thrilled to be such an object of attention as all the humans crowded around and said how cute I was. One of their male children became particularly attached to me and it was he who christened me with the human name. This was despite my persistent attempts to tell him that my name was Augustus. No matter how hard I tried, the stupid little human would just point at me as he laughed at my very clearly enunciated correction.

I wasn't offended by the mis-appellation for the first few months because I didn't know what the hell a peanut was. For that matter, I didn't even know what a pea or a nut was either.

It was when the boy was in the barn showing me to another boy that I finally realized that the new name wasn't anything to wear proudly.

"That's Peanut," my boy said.

The other, taller boy, laughed and said, "He sure is small like a peanut and I'll bet if I crack open his head, I won't find a brain in there either."

"*Crack open his head?*" I thought as I looked at the strange boy, "*What kind of monster are you?*"

My boy was obviously of nobler stock because he smacked the other one on the arm and said, "He may be small, but he's my friend and nobody is going to hurt him!"

I thought that the mean boy would strike my protector, and I was preparing to come to his defense by smashing my rear hooves into the head-cracker's behind when the threatening boy laughed.

"I didn't mean nothin'," he said, complete with the double negative, which I chose not to correct. I ain't never used "ain't" neither.

My human smiled at me, then said to him, "Just don't say anything bad about Peanut."

"Who cares? Speakin' of peanuts, do you figure we can ask your mom for some of her pecan pie?"

"Let's go ask her," my boy replied, then waved and said, "Goodbye, Peanut. And don't worry, my mother doesn't make pies out of peanuts, just pecans."

As I watched the two laughing boys leave, I finally began to realize what a peanut was and how I was perceived by humans. I'd been given pecans as a treat before, so I knew what they were. I could have asked my father back then, but he was already ashamed of me, so I didn't talk to him much. I suspected that if I asked my mother, she would tell me that a peanut is something grandiose like a tiger just to make me feel better.

The only good thing to come from that visit was when I heard the boy call me his friend. In my world, I only knew my parents, a pair of stupid cows that gave the humans milk every day, and two mules that shared our barn, and none of them could even remotely considered to be my friend.

In fact, the two mules did more than just literally look down on me; they acted as if they were some superior relatives. It was another question that I should have asked my father before I disappointed him.

My father, whose name was Jack, was tall for a donkey, and so was my mother, Jenny. I thought their names suited them, and it wasn't until late one spring day that I discovered that jack and jenny were what humans called all donkeys, depending on their sex. It was a sad revelation and was even sadder in the way that I learned about it.

It was the day that a strange big man arrived at the barn with my boy's father, who was the boss.

My boy's father pointed to my parents and said, "I'll let you have the jack for twenty dollars and the jenny for fifteen."

I was stunned when I realized that he was selling us to the other man but still noticed that he'd referred to my father as 'the' jack and not 'Jack', then did the same for my mother.

If that had surprised me, it was made much, much worse when I heard the strange man say, "If all they can produce is that scrawny little critter, I ain't gonna pay that much. I'll give you twenty-five for both of 'em, but I ain't takin' that sorry excuse for an ass."

"*An ass? Did you just call me an 'ass'?*" I asked myself in righteous indignation, ignoring the ominous threat of possible separation from my parents.

"Peanut is my son's pet, so he'll stay with us anyway. Make it thirty and we've got a deal."

"I'll give you twenty-seven, but that's my final offer."

My eyes were shifting back and forth as the humans dickered on a price for my parents while my mother and father sat behind me listening as if they didn't understand what was happening or didn't care. I guessed that they thought it was just their lot in life.

"Okay, Fred, we have a deal. Did you want to take them with you?"

While they shook hands, the other man said, "Let's get ropes on 'em and I'll take 'em along."

I sat there dumbfounded thinking that they could be so heartless to take my mom and dad away yet hoping that they were just putting on some thoughtless play for my benefit.

Then the stranger gave my human some paper, and after he pushed it into his pants...I've never been able to figure out why humans wear them in the first place. I can understand the need to keep their hairless bodies covered, but why pants?... he and the other man put ropes around my parents' necks and led them away. My father never looked back, but my mother gave me one last, sad glance before disappearing.

I never saw them again, and now I was alone; or at least I was alone with the stupid cows and haughty mules. I didn't find out why the mules were acting all superior until much later in my life. When I did figure it out, I was almost sick to my stomach knowing that my father had been unfaithful to my mother – and with a horse, for crying out loud!

I was still pretty tiny when they were led away, and maybe it was because they were both above average in size that my small stature became so obvious so quickly. Whatever the reason, before I celebrated my next birthday, I had finally accepted that I would never be the tall, handsome jack worthy of my august name...that was almost a pun, by the way.

But after that first visit by the boys, my small human, who was ironically named Jack, began coming to the barn more often and soon, he would let me accompany him when he walked around the farm. He'd let me wade in the creek and even dunk myself in the cool water when it was warm.

I followed him into the house once but was immediately banned by the adult male and female humans because I used it like they used the smaller house in the back yard. I couldn't understand why they got mad because they wouldn't let me use the small house either. What did they expect me to do, use my own home? How barbaric! The cows and mules did, but I always considered myself to have better manners than either of them. I didn't recall my parents ever using the barn, but then, I might have chosen to not notice.

That first summer, even though the tips of my magnificent ears barely reached Jack's elbows, he brought his sister out to the barn and asked me if it would be okay if she rode me. Now I'd seen humans riding the mules and even watched Jack riding my father, Jack, but I was still surprised that I was being asked.

But because I was being asked politely by my only friend in the world, I didn't object. His sister, who was named Allie and not Jenny as one might expect, wasn't very big either, so when Jack helped her onto my back, her short legs didn't touch the ground.

When she began to giggle, I thought she was cute, even for a human. So, I began to carefully walk around the barn while she held onto my mane. It didn't hurt much because she was so small, but I knew that if she slipped, it would hurt like the devil.

———

For the next year, Jack, and sometimes Allie would visit me and began treating me like family rather than some scruffy cow or mule. They'd talk to me and soon, I began to forget all about wanting to be Augustus and was proud to be Peanut. Augustus sounded big and important, but also cold and unreachable. Peanut, on the other hand, was anything but important. The name created a happy, gentle image which matched my own nature.

I was a content donkey despite my size and wooly coat. I had two small friends now and thought it would never change.

But it did.

———

Near the start of my second summer, something happened on the farm that I couldn't understand. The adults hadn't planted any crops and as the summer went by, there were a lot of visits by strangers. I tried to ask Jack or Allie what was going on, but all I could do was bray.

It wasn't until late in the summer when I saw them drive a bizarre, large wagon into the yard with a huge cloth cover over the top like a round barn roof that I knew something bad was happening. It was being pulled by the mules and there were four more mules in front, too. Then, over the next few days, they started moving things out of the house and into the big wagon. I began to realize that they were leaving, and I'd probably be left behind because no adult humans wanted me.

I was growing despondent when Jack trotted into the barn and dropped to his knees so he could look into my eyes.

He smiled and rubbed my head as he said, "Peanut, we're leaving here soon, and I had to convince my father to bring you along. He was going to give you away, but I told him you were my friend, and he said okay."

I exhaled sharply and wanted to kiss Jack, but I didn't have the lips for it.

Then he said, "You're going to have to walk, Peanut. My father says that you'll just poop in the wagon and if you did it once, he'd throw you into the nearest river. It's going to be a long walk, Peanut, but I know you can do it. You may be small, but I know you have a big heart."

I thought that big heart was going to explode with pride, but then Jack hugged me, and I wished I could manage to hug him back, but well, you know.

———

Three days later, I was led behind their new wagon with the stupid cows and even four of the fat hogs who had inhabited their own place far enough away from the barn so that we didn't have to smell it. Talk about a pigsty! They weren't haughty like the mules, but they scared me because they were so mean and even though I hated to admit it, they were pretty smart, too. They were all much bigger than me and the biggest of the lot, an oinker named Pinky, would look at me with his beady eyes and let me know that they were omnivores and could eat anything, including donkeys. As I was barely a snack for the four hogs, I kept my distance.

The humans' wagon was soon joined by others and our traveling menagerie kept growing and soon consisted of more cows, pigs, goats, sheep and even some horses. I was the only donkey in the mix which was awkward. I was taunted constantly by the others as we made our way, but sometimes Jack would walk and talk with me. I didn't add anything to the conversation, but when he was there, I felt safer and a bit more important, too.

———

I was already beginning to lag behind by the fourth day of the trip, but I'd catch up by the time the sun went down and they'd stopped for the night. When Jack had said it was a long journey, he hadn't been very specific, so after a week, I began to wonder just how long it really would be.

By then, I thought my short legs would fail me and I'd never reach wherever we were going. Jack tried to inspire me to keep up the pace by telling me that his father was threatening to leave me behind again. It was more of a kick in the butt than an inspiration.

As we walked, I began to scan the area for other farms, wondering if I'd be able to find a new home on my own if I failed to keep up. But none of them seemed inviting, and with my past experience with adult humans, I didn't think it was likely that any would be happy to see me and take me in. They'd probably just feed me to their own mean hogs.

———

It was on the eleventh day of the trip that everything changed in a way that I could never have expected.

We'd only been moving for a little while when I was given a clue that this wasn't going to be just another boring day when one of the bullying hogs snuck up behind me and took a nip at my tail. Before he could start snorting in derision, I let him have a taste of Peanut hoof when I smacked his already flat snout.

I may have gotten my revenge, but instead of gloating or trying to act bravely by glaring at the hogs, I took the smart way out and immediately scooted to the front of our walking zoo to put the sheep between me and the hogs for protection. The woolies had two dogs with them, and they didn't like the hogs either.

I may be small, but I'm not an idiot. I suspected that the evil hogs would extract their own revenge soon, though. As I mentioned before, unlike the cows, they weren't stupid, and they would plot to exact their payback.

A short time later, even though it wasn't their normal time, the humans stopped their wagons. So, being the curious creature that I am, I walked past the last wagon and saw that we'd reached a big river. I was impressed and wondered how the humans would get their wagons and us across when some of the men got out of their wagons and walked away to talk to other men near the river.

That's when it became more interesting. The two groups of men began yelling at each other, and when I saw some of the other ones pull guns, I hurried back to the sheep. I've seen what those things can do when humans get angry.

As I trotted back to the woolies, I saw another man whom I'd never seen before on a tall black horse pass in the other direction. He was a big man and wore an odd, flat hat that sagged a bit.

He ignored me as he passed and I turned around, wondering what he was going to do. I didn't think he had a gun until I looked at his back and noticed one stuck in his pants. I thought that the man must be loony or something to keep his gun there. He could shoot his behind off if he wasn't careful.

I wanted to walk closer to the angry men to hear what they were saying, but my curiosity didn't overcome my good sense, so I stayed with the sheep.

After our angry men got back in their wagons, the tall man dismounted and began to talk to the other angry men, but he wasn't angry at all. I was very confused with the man, but then he said something to the leader of our group, and they began to turn the wagons around.

Then the other angry men got mad at the tall man and I thought they were going to shoot him, but whatever the tall man said to them made them laugh instead. Then I watched him pull his gun from his pants and made the angry men stick their hands in the air. This was human behavior well beyond what I'd seen before, and I really wanted to know what was happening, but the tall human had his gun out and I wasn't about to get close.

Then our wagons stopped, and I after the tall man talked to the man in the first wagon, I noticed two other strange men ride in from the side to talk to the tall man who still had his gun pointed at the four river men who now seemed more sad than angry.

The other men then began to tie up the angry men as if they were going to get them ready for butchering, and I thought about going to tell the hogs to pay attention because that was their future but thought better of it. As I watched, the three strangers then put the four angry men on their horses.

I thought everything was done for the day, but then I noticed Jack approach the tall man and begin to talk to him. Jack's father then talked to the tall man and soon, they were walking back towards me.

I suspected that my day of reckoning had arrived. Reckoning for what was a mystery to me, but I could see them all staring at me and I knew I was the reason for whatever they were planning.

The tall man looked down at me, then smiled and asked Jack, "That's Peanut?"

I should have felt insulted, but he seemed to be a good human, so I just looked back up at him.

Before I knew what was happening, I was stretched out across the tall man's saddle atop his big black horse and heading back the way we came.

I could see Jack waving as I bounced along and knew that I would never see my first and best friend again. I would have waved back, but, well, you know.

The two men who seemed to be friends of the tall man rode alongside and began talking about me. Even though all of them looked alike to me, I did notice that one of the two seemed to look a lot like the one who'd plucked me from the ground as if I was a frog or something. It didn't take me long to figure out that he was the tall man's brother.

They were joking about me and asking if he was really going to take me back to his house or just drop me off at some farm or town. I wasn't terrified at the prospect, but I wasn't overly pleased either.

I wasn't sure of the tall man's decision until after we'd stopped at some town and he left me with his horse in a livery and I heard him tell the man in charge to give me oats. It was then that I relaxed and began to wonder what my new home would be like.

———

It wasn't until we'd stopped at a really big town the next day that the tall man left with me and his brother and rode to his home. By then, I'd also come to know their names. The one who rode with me seemed to be in charge and was named Dylan and his brother was named Bryn. I'd never heard names like that before, but they were both still better than Peanut.

He even talked to me as we trotted up and down some hills. He said that his children would be happy to see me, so I wondered if they'd be as kind to me as Jack had been. If they were like their father, I was sure that I'd be treated well.

When we arrived at his place, I was surprised how big everything was. The barn was a lot nicer than Jack's and there were horses in a corral nearby with no mules, cows or hogs to be found. I wondered what the man did to survive because he surely wasn't a farmer.

We hadn't reached the barn before I saw his family waving to him, but his children were all smaller than Jack. Two of them were taller than me, but the woman held a baby and another woman held another, longer one in her arms.

Then he turned and waved to a different house as other female humans left the place and began walking toward us. My curiosity about my new home continued to climb, but I hadn't found anything that gave me concern.

Before I knew it, I was back on the ground and surrounded by the mass of humans and the two tallest of the short ones were the first to touch me when they both scratched my head just like Jack used to do.

I quickly learned that their names were Lynn and Al, but sometimes they called him Alwen. They would become my new best friends and I'd be there to watch them grow until they were as tall as their father.

But now they were small enough for me to give them rides, although that didn't happen for a few days. I was given my own stall next to Dylan's black horse named Crow. The brother's horse was named Maddie, but neither of them paid me much attention.

Over the next few weeks, I explored the place that was on the top of a hill and when I crossed the road, I could see an even bigger river than the one we'd tried to cross. There were smoking boats that went up and down the river sometimes and I wondered where they were going.

Over the next few months, Lynn and Al visited me often, but usually with one of the women from the other house and sometimes, the women would bring strange men into the barn to look at me, or at least that's what they said. I think it really was to get away from the older adults. There was sure a lot of giggling when they did, too.

Winter passed and then the next spring, Bryn went away on one of those boats and everyone seemed sad. I didn't know where he went, but they didn't know if he'd come back at all, and that made me sad because I liked him.

I learned that Dylan was in charge of stopping bad men from doing bad things and sometimes he'd be gone for days at a time. I thought I'd be in charge while he was gone, but no one else seemed to share my opinion.

Lynn and Al grew fast and soon were too big to sit on me without their feet touching the ground. It was just another reminder of why I deserved to be called Peanut. But their little sister, named Bethan, which I thought was a wonderful name, was deemed old enough to take their place. Her brothers would always be with her to help, but she seemed to be pretty sure of herself and was soon bouncing onto my back on her own.

———

During the next two years, something was going on that I couldn't understand, but Dylan's wife, whose name was Gwen, had another baby and everyone seemed happy about that.

It was in the summer when Bryn came back that I found out that he'd been shot and almost died. He didn't seem any different, but before he'd returned, something had happened with one of the women that seemed to make him sad. I just couldn't figure it out.

After he came back and began to work with his brother, it wasn't long before he moved into the house where all of the other ladies had lived and married the female that Gwen had brought there to help her with her litter. Her name was Erin. I never could figure out how all of that worked, either. I thought that maybe Gwen had bought her for Bryn, but Erin didn't seem to mind. How it happened didn't matter, but Bryn wasn't sad anymore and I thought he'd stay in the house for a long time.

But after he and Erin had their own baby, he left for a while, then just a little while later, he and his new family packed up and moved away. I was sad because I was expecting to give their new baby a ride when he was big enough. I thought that I'd never see them again, but that turned out to be wrong.

———

Just when I thought things had begun to settle down, there was another shock when I heard that Dylan would have to uproot everyone then move to a new home, and he wasn't happy about it at all. He left to look at the place, and then, just after he returned and said he wasn't going to go there was an even more surprising development.

When he rode back to the house, he had another man with him who was younger and looked like his brother, but I'd never heard anyone say anything about another one.

He seemed to fit in quickly though, and almost immediately after he arrived, Dylan changed his mind about not moving and I learned we were leaving after all. Not only that, but we were going to be living near Bryn again. I was excited with the news because I wanted to see how much bigger Bryn's boys were and if he had any more children. I don't call them 'kids' because I had a bad experience with a gang of young goats that was almost as bad as my problem with the hogs.

The new man, who I learned was named Kyle, didn't stay long before he went off with Dylan. He seemed okay while he was here, but even though he didn't have a gun when I saw him, he carried this big stick that gave me the willies. If he was as mean as those hogs, I swear I would have run all the way to Pennsylvania where he came from...wherever that was.

———

When they returned from looking for our new home, it wasn't much longer before I was packed into a big wooden box with the horses and was horrified when it began to move. Some of the horses were pretty upset too, so I didn't feel particularly cowardly when I began to shake. We eventually all adjusted to the sensation but weren't happy about being cooped up in that rolling prison. I wished that the humans cleaned the place out more often, though.

When we were finally freed from the dark jail, I was the last one to leave, but soon found that I wasn't going to have to walk with the horses, but I'd be riding with Lynn and Al in the back of a wagon. I was warned about using the wagon for my personal privy, but by now I was well aware of that apparently unwelcome behavior.

So, off we went on our journey to our new home with Bryn and his family. Most of the adults had already left in a closed wagon that looked like a small house on wheels, but we were the last wagon in the line with the snooty horses hooked onto ropes behind us. I didn't laugh at them because I got to ride while they hoofed along because I'm not that kind of donkey. But I did think it might be worthy of an occasional grin or a wave as I sat while they walked and probably would have done it too, but, well, you know.

The first night of the trip, Dylan and one of the other men rode into the dark and I heard gunshots before they came back. I don't know what happened, but Al and Lynn seemed excited. I only learned later that some bad humans were planning on taking everything for themselves, but Dylan and the other man stopped them then left them for the coyotes and wolves. They added some more horses to Dylan's herd, too.

A few days passed without anyone else starting trouble and then I saw my new home for the first time. It was where I still live and this time, I didn't believe that I'd be moving again.

It was there that the two families were together again, and I met another adult male. He was older than Dylan and was another Jack. I was wondering why the name seemed to be so popular when I heard him called Flat Jack, which really puzzled me. He seemed perfectly round to me. His head wasn't like a plateau either. I would have asked him, but despite his job of caring for the horses, he couldn't speak donkey.

I hadn't quite trusted Kyle with that big stick of his before he left with Dylan, and once I was reunited with him, I became downright spooked. I had barely settled into my very nice private stall in one of the two big barns when he showed up.

He still didn't have a gun, but after he took off his shirt and stretched for a little while, he picked up that stick and I thought he was going to beat me with it, so I was ready to race away like the stallion I dreamed I was, but he didn't.

Instead, he began to swing it around as he twirled. I was still confused as to his purpose but watched in fascination. He'd stop from his turning at times and poke the stick, then sometimes, he'd swing it over his head. There seemed to be a rhythm to what he was doing, and I'll admit that it was pretty impressive. Why he was doing it still made no sense, but he began to slow and finally slammed the big stick into the barn floor and stopped. I kind of jerked when he rammed it hard, but he should have warned me. At least I didn't poop in the barn.

He'd come into the barn once a day to do his swinging stick routine, and each time, I'd watch and try to figure out its purpose. As he almost danced around the barn floor, I would begin to guess what he'd do next and got pretty good at it.

I thought that I had finally realized why he did it when one day, as he began to swing and poke, I saw Katie, Erin's younger sister, arrive at the door and watch him. He pretended that he didn't see her, but I could tell by watching her that she was looking at him as a potential mate. It was then that I realized that Kyle must be performing a human ritual mating dance to attract a female. It was the only thing that made sense to me, even though I had never seen Bryn do one to attract Erin. Maybe it was different for each human mating pair.

Right after he pounded the stick to the floor, she let him know that she approved of his mating dance by clapping her hands and smiling. Then I was certain of its purpose when, after a little while, they performed the same movements together, only without the stick. I felt like a furry voyeur and thought that they'd be mating on the barn floor soon, but luckily, I didn't have to endure that embarrassment.

The mating ritual was immediately forgotten when there were hoofbeats outside, and Kyle stopped Katie from leaving, then snatched his big stick from the floor and began limping out of the barn. I hadn't seen him fall or anything, so I trotted to the open barn doors and watched what he was doing. What I witnessed was the bravest thing I'd ever seen.

Two bad men had ridden in on their horses and Kyle kept limping toward them when one turned his horse at him and as he rode at Kyle, he began firing his gun. Kyle just stood there with his stick over his head as if the man was just waving at him. Then, just as the riding man passed, Kyle hit him in the leg with his stick and the man dropped his gun and began screaming.

Kyle then turned and walked straight at the other man who pulled out two shiny knives. I didn't think that Kyle's stick was going to matter if the man threw one of his knives, but instead, they had a fighting kind of dance and Kyle won.

Flat Jack came back, and soon Dylan and Bryn returned to talk to Kyle, Flat Jack and the women. As I listened, I was shocked to learn that the two bad men were going to kill everyone on the ranch, including the children. Kyle acted as if he hadn't done anything brave at all, but everyone knew that he'd risked his own life to protect the family. I was proud to give up part of my barn to Kyle from then on, now that I knew the real purpose for his stick.

It wasn't much longer before I discovered that his stick was also used in this bizarre game that the humans played when they used a stick to hit a ball that someone threw at them. And if they did hit it, they'd run to white pads while those not playing cheered. I swear, the longer I'm around humans, the less I understand them.

The stick dance may not have been a mating ritual, but Kyle and Katie began spending more time together and soon mated anyway.

But shortly after that scary day, Flat Jack and Kyle brought some new horses into the corral and that's when I first saw her.

She stood out among the others because she was the most beautiful creature my eyes had ever seen. She was so incredibly perfect with her silky, tan coat and blonde tail and mane that I found it hard to look at her without having my heart pound out of my chest.

She was a young filly and they called her Lulu. I thought the name was ill-fitted to such a goddess-like creation, but she didn't seem to object.

I didn't expect her to notice me right away because there were so many horses around her, but I decided right then that she was the only girl for me. I suddenly had new respect for mules and wanted to produce a whole herd of them with Lulu.

Over the next few weeks, I ignored everything else that was happening around me as I tried to get Lulu to notice me. Once, I even tried scraping my curly fur on a stall post, but that turned into a disaster when all that happened was a clump became tangled in a big splinter and I had to wait until Kyle showed up and pulled me free. It was embarrassing, to say the least.

The weather was growing colder, and Lulu still hadn't paid me much attention. I was growing desperate as I noticed that they'd introduced a young stallion into the corral, and he was making big eyes at her. I know. I know. They all have big eyes, but you know what I meant.

I had never expressed my devotion to Lulu, but I was convinced that once she knew how I felt, she would put the stupid stallion in his place and return with me to my barn where we would start our mule family.

So, one afternoon, I crawled under the bottom corral fence rail, which wasn't difficult for me, then stood as tall as I could and strode majestically with my head held high toward Lulu.

After weaving around the hooves and legs, I finally stood in front of Lulu and gazed up at her. She hadn't seen me yet, but I could almost feel that jealous stallion approaching me from behind, so I had to announce my love quickly.

I took a deep breath and out it came…an annoying, off-key bray.

Lulu looked down and, instead of giving me an approving nicker, she snorted derisively, and I knew that she would have laughed if she had the ability.

Then I heard the stallion behind me snort loudly with true malice and any façade of bravery evaporated when I suddenly found myself in much more danger than those hogs had ever presented.

Before the stallion could raise one of his big hooves, I shot straight between his four legs and thought about giving him a passing kick into his stallion parts, but I don't think I could have reached them anyway. I raced around the other horses and almost slid beneath the fence rail to make my hasty escape.

Once on the safe side of the corral, I stopped to catch my breath and when I turned, I expected to see an agitated herd of horses pressing against the rail in frustration for being denied their opportunity to crush me. But not a single one was even looking my way, not even the stallion or Lulu. It was as if I didn't even exist and that was much more painful than incurring their equine wrath. I wasn't even worthy of their attention. I was a nobody.

I thought that I couldn't feel any worse when my horrified eyes witnessed the stallion mounting Lulu as if to mock me. I wanted to scream and run away, but I couldn't. I was stunned when she let him have his way with her and then I realized that I meant even less than nothing to Lulu, if that's even possible.

I finally turned and walked back to the barn with my head down and my spirit crushed. I was just a small, insignificant donkey that would never know what it was like to love another and have a family. I'd just give rides to small humans and make them laugh. I was just a short, four-footed clown with a wooly coat designed to be nothing but a source of amusement.

By the time I reached my stall, my mood was lower than I was. I just plopped on the floor and didn't care about anything anymore.

———

Over the next few weeks, I slowly got over the Lulu debacle but never chased away the feeling of hopelessness. I had become a pessimist for the first time in my life and thought I was just being honest with myself.

The children still visited me and that helped my mood somewhat, even though I understood that I was still just another toy to them.

Kyle came every day to exercise and was often accompanied by Katie, which didn't surprise me at all. I became jealous of Kyle because he had found what I knew I could never have in my life.

The snows began to arrive and that made my mood even worse because it limited how far I could wander around the ranch. If I had been my previous optimistic self, I would have enjoyed romping in the white fluffy stuff, but now I saw it as a cold nuisance.

It was then that Kyle and Flat Jack began planning something that didn't make much sense to me at all. They'd come into the barn and point at different spots and say that Joseph would go there, or the manger could be put there. It sounded as if they were building a small village. *What in God's name was a manger?*

As the days passed, they began preparations for whatever they were planning, then one day, right after the sun went down, Flat Jack and Kyle began moving things into the barn. I sat on my haunches in my stall watching and thought they both had lost their minds.

They brought in human-sized wooden cutouts of, well, humans. They were even painted with human faces and then Kyle and Flat Jack dressed them, but not with britches or shirts; they just draped blankets and other cloth over them. I didn't smell any alcohol, so I knew that despite their behavior, they weren't drunk. *What were they doing?*

At least I finally figured out what a manger was when Kyle set what looked like a misshapen crate on the floor in front of the cutouts and then filled it with hay. I still had no idea what it was for until the door opened again, and Flat Jack entered leading a young jenny.

She was just a couple of inches taller than me, but her coat was a shiny black and I thought she was very pretty. But in his arms, Jack held a tiny jack that must have been her son. She kept glancing up at Jack as he held her baby boy, so she never even noticed me.

When they entered, Kyle said that he was glad that Flat Jack had been able to find them and keep them hidden. I didn't know where they had kept her and her son but wondered where her baby's father was.

I was still staring when Flat Jack set the small jack into the manger and then tied his mother's cord to a stake that they'd driven into the floor nearby. I didn't think it was necessary because she wouldn't leave her baby anyway.

Then Kyle called me over and said, "Peanut, this is Hazel. She and her baby will be part of the living creche with you. I need you to stand beside her. We're going to get the rest of the family now and it's important for you to stay there. Okay?"

I appreciated his trust in me to understand and not feel the need to tie me down, so I just nodded as I took my place beside Hazel. It wasn't a great name, but she didn't seem to mind.

We never spoke as we stood side by side, but both of us simply stared quietly at her boy. He was smaller than me, of course, but I imagined that he'd be bigger within a year. Right now, it didn't matter as I stood beside Hazel wondering why the scene was so significant to Kyle and Flat Jack.

It seemed to be hours before the door opened again, but when it did, I looked at the large family group as they entered and saw enormous smiles on their faces. They approached the manger and the children began to talk about Christmas. I had a hard time following their conversation, but I got the gist that we were a representation of the birth of someone from long ago who the family revered, so I was pleased to be a part of it.

As they continued to talk, I heard the children ask about the newcomers' names, and Kyle told them Hazel's, but he didn't have one for her baby yet. They quickly named him Acorn, which struck me as odd, but everyone seemed to like it.

Hazel didn't object as she continued to stare at her son, the newly named Acorn, and as she did, I studied her face.

I suddenly saw in her eyes the same love that I remembered seeing in my mother's eyes when she looked at me. It didn't matter how small or furry I was to my mother, and my obvious lack of courage didn't shame or embarrass her either. My mother would always look at me with love and understanding until the day they took her away. I'd forgotten the look in those eyes over the years that we'd been apart, but when I saw Hazel as she gazed on her son, it was there.

The family didn't stay long because of the cold, but after they'd gone and Kyle untied Hazel, I returned to my stall. I may have gotten over the Lulu rejection, but I wasn't about to go through it again. Hazel had her son and probably missed his father, so I suspected that she'd be leaving soon to return to her own barn.

I was curled up and ready to go to sleep when I heard light hoofbeats and saw Hazel nudging Acorn into the stall. She then nosed him close to me and he snuggled in close before

539

she laid down on his other side. Together we formed a warm cave for her little son.

I couldn't sleep having Hazel so close, but after Acorn slipped into dreamland, she looked at me with those same warm eyes that didn't seem any less visible in the low light.

She told me that the jack that had given her Acorn had been brought to their farm only for that purpose and she'd never seen him again. She was worried that when Acorn was older, they'd take him away from her, but when Flat Jack appeared at their farm, he said that he wanted to keep them together. That had made her happy, even if she didn't know what the future held for them.

When she'd been kept in a different barn for a few days, she didn't understand what was going to happen to them, but now she knew that she and Acorn would be staying here with me.

I should have been happy at that moment, but the whole Lulu experience had opened my eyes to my lack of the qualities that females seemed to appreciate. Not for an instant did I believe that Hazel would see me any differently. At least I'd have company who could converse with me rather than just point and laugh.

When I didn't say anything after she finished telling me her story, she must have sensed my mood because she asked me why I seemed to be so sad on what seemed to be such a happy day for the people.

I didn't want to admit to my shortcomings but told her that I was glad that she and Acorn were here, and it was really a nice home because the large family treated me well.

After I finished, Hazel surprised me when she quietly asked about my own family. I told her about my parents, and then as I talked about my father, I mentioned how disappointed he was in me. I didn't intend to bring it up, it just flowed out of me as part of my tale.

Hazel asked why he was disappointed in me, so I sighed, then asked her how any father could be proud of having a stunted, cowardly son who looked like an odd sheep rather than a well-groomed donkey stud.

She laughed and said that she thought I was cute and that she preferred cute to those strutting males who thought the world revolved around them.

That began a much longer and more fulfilling conversation that lasted until the wee hours of the morning. By the time we joined Acorn in slumber, I felt closer to Hazel than I'd ever been to anyone else, even my mother.

I later learned that the night that Hazel and Acorn were brought to the barn wasn't really Christmas, but the day they called Christmas Eve. So, on the next day when the family exchanged gifts and sang songs, I was given the greatest gift of all. I was presented with my own family and was determined to never let Hazel or Acorn feel any less proud of me than they would if I'd been a tall stallion.

The next Christmas, the family didn't repeat the scene in the barn, but the manger wasn't empty. It was still full of hay and instead of Acorn, it held the newest addition to our family; a handsome young jack they named Chester. We liked the name and thought he was the prettiest baby we'd ever seen.

As I stood with Hazel on my right and Acorn, who was already taller than me, standing on my left, I looked at our newborn son and was immensely content and happy.

They may have called me Peanut because of my size, and many may have thought it was clownish, but as I gazed at my son, none of that mattered anymore.

When Chester was older, he wouldn't call me Peanut.

He'd call me Dad.

1	Rock Creek	12/26/2016
2	North of Denton	01/02/2017
3	Fort Selden	01/07/2017
4	Scotts Bluff	01/14/2017
5	South of Denver	01/22/2017
6	Miles City	01/28/2017
7	Hopewell	02/04/2017
8	Nueva Luz	02/12/2017
9	The Witch of Dakota	02/19/2017
10	Baker City	03/13/2017
11	The Gun Smith	03/21/2017
12	Gus	03/24/2017
13	Wilmore	04/06/2017
14	Mister Thor	04/20/2017
15	Nora	04/26/2017
16	Max	05/09/2017
17	Hunting Pearl	05/14/2017
18	Bessie	05/25/2017
19	The Last Four	05/29/2017
20	Zack	06/12/2017
21	Finding Bucky	06/21/2017
22	The Debt	06/30/2017
23	The Scalawags	07/11/2017
24	The Stampede	07/20/2017
25	The Wake of the Bertrand	07/31/2017
26	Cole	08/09/2017
27	Luke	09/05/2017
28	The Eclipse	09/21/2017
29	A.J. Smith	10/03/2017
30	Slow John	11/05/2017
31	The Second Star	11/15/2017
32	Tate	12/03/2017
33	Virgil's Herd	12/14/2017
34	Marsh's Valley	01/01/2018
35	Alex Paine	01/18/2018
36	Ben Gray	02/05/2018

37	War Adams	03/05/2018
38	Mac's Cabin	03/21/2018
39	Will Scott	04/13/2018
40	Sheriff Joe	04/22/2018
41	Chance	05/17/2018
42	Doc Holt	06/17/2018
43	Ted Shepard	07/13/2018
44	Haven	07/30/2018
45	Sam's County	08/15/2018
46	Matt Dunne	09/10/2018
47	Conn Jackson	10/05/2018
48	Gabe Owens	10/27/2018
49	Abandoned	11/19/2018
50	Retribution	12/21/2018
51	Inevitable	02/04/2019
52	Scandal in Topeka	03/18/2019
53	Return to Hardeman County	04/10/2019
54	Deception	06/02/2019
55	The Silver Widows	06/27/2019
56	Hitch	08/21/2019
57	Dylan's Journey	09/10/2019
58	Bryn's War	11/06/2019
59	Huw's Legacy	11/30/2019
60	Lynn's Search	12/22/2019
61	Bethan's Choice	02/10/2020

Made in the USA
Columbia, SC
18 February 2020